O9-BUC-468

# ELIZABETH PETERS

# GUARDIAN
## OF THE
# HORIZON

AVON BOOKS
*An Imprint of HarperCollinsPublishers*

This is a work of fiction. Names, characters, places and incidents are products of the author's imagination or are used fictitiously and are not to be construed as real. Any resemblance to actual events, locales, organizations, or persons, living or dead, is entirely coincidental.

AVON BOOKS
*An Imprint of* HarperCollins*Publishers*
10 East 53rd Street
New York, New York 10022-5299

Copyright © 2004 by MPM Manor, Inc.
Excerpt from *The Serpent on the Crown* copyright © 2005 by MPM Manor, Inc.
0-06-103246-8
www.avonbooks.com

First Avon Books paperback printing: April 2005
First William Morrow hardcover printing: April 2004

Avon Trademark Reg. U.S. Pat. Off. And in Other Countries, Marca Registrada, Hecho in U.S.A.
HarperCollins® is a registered trademark of HarperCollins Publishers Inc.

Printed in the U.S.A.

10  9  8  7  6  5  4  3

TO CHUCK

aka Charles E. Roberts, owner of several of
the world's greatest bookstores, to whom I
owe many hours of good talk, good gin, and
friendship of the highest order

## Acknowledgments

For many of the details of desert travel I have drawn upon, and am indebted to, *The Lost Oases,* a remarkable book by a remarkable man. Ahmed Mohammed Hassanein Bey, an Egyptian, an Oxford graduate, and a fine athlete, was the first person to cross the Libyan Desert—a journey of three thousand kilometers—by camel caravan, from Siwa to Darfur. He located the "lost oases" of Arkenet and Ouanet and fixed their locations for the first time. Though his epic trip took place fifteen years after the Emersons last visited their "lost oasis," the conditions were pretty much the same. His accomplishments have been to some extent overshadowed by those of later explorers, who used motor vehicles instead of camels, but he was deservedly honored by the Royal Geographical Society with its Explorers Medal.

As always, I want to thank my dedicated prereaders, Dennis Forbes of KMT, Kristen Whitbread of MPM Manor, Erika Schmid, and of course Trish Lande Grader of William Morrow, who have perused the entire interminable manuscript and made suggestions and corrections. Any remaining errors are my responsibility.

## Editor's Note

Just when the Editor believed she was nearing the end of her arduous task of editing the Emerson papers, a new lot of them turned up. They include most of the journals from the so-called missing years, plus miscellaneous letters, newspaper clippings, recipes, lists, receipts, and several unpublished articles. The circumstances under which this discovery was made need not be discussed here. Suffice it to say that Mrs. Emerson's heirs are no longer threatening legal proceedings and have reached a tentative agreement with the Editor that allows her to produce this volume. It is based on Mrs. Emerson's journal for the 1907–08 season, and thus immediately follows the events described in the journal published as *The Ape Who Guards the Balance*. The Editor's reasons for selecting this particular volume are twofold: first, she was dying to know what happened when the Emersons returned to the Lost Oasis; second, up to this time she had only one journal for the years between 1907 and 1914, a period of great importance in the professional, political, and emotional history of various family members. It is hoped that eventually this gap will be filled in; and the Reader may rest assured that astonishing revelations remain to be disclosed.

As before, the Editor has included relevant portions of Manuscript H, written by Ramses Emerson. It seems unlikely that Mrs. Emerson ever read this manuscript, which Ramses seems to have abandoned shortly after the birth of his children (any parent can understand why). One other set of documents provided useful information—the letters herein designated as Letter Collection C. They were found in a separate bundle. Obviously they never reached the persons to whom they were addressed, but were collected by Mrs. Emerson after the events to which they refer, for reasons which should be evident to any intelligent Reader.

# One

When we left Egypt in the spring of 1907, I felt like a defeated general who has retreated to lick his wounds (if I may be permitted a somewhat inelegant but expressive metaphor). Our archaeological season had experienced the usual ups and downs—kidnapping, murderous attacks, and the like—to which I was well accustomed. But that year disasters of an unprecented scope had befallen us.

The worst was the death of our dear old friend Abdullah, who had been foreman of our excavations for many years. He had died as he would have wished, in a glorious gesture of sacrifice, but that was small consolation to those of us who had learned to love him. It was hard to imagine continuing our work without him.

If we continued it. My spouse, Radcliffe Emerson, is without doubt the preeminent Egyptologist of this or any other era. To say that Emerson (who prefers to be addressed by that name) has the most explosive temper of anyone I know might be a slight exaggeration—but only slight. His passions are most often aroused by incompetent excavators and careless scholarship, and during this past season he had—I admit—been sorely provoked.

We had been excavating in the Valley of the Kings at Luxor, my favorite site in all of Egypt. The concession for the Valley was held by an irritating elderly American, Mr.

Theodore Davis, who was more interested in finding treasure than in scholarly research; we were there under suffer-
ance, allowed to work only in the lesser, more boring
tombs. Still, we were there, and we would be there again in
the autumn had it not been for Emerson.

The trouble began when Mr. Davis's crew discovered
one of the strangest, most mysterious tombs ever found in
the Valley. It was a hodgepodge of miscellaneous funerary
equipment, much of it in poor condition, including a
mummy and coffin and pieces of a magnificent golden
shrine; and if it had been properly investigated, new light
would have been shed on a particularly intriguing era of
Egyptian history. In vain did we offer Mr. Davis the services of our staff. Abdullah, who was still with us, was the
most experienced reis in Egypt, our son Ramses was a
skilled linguist and excavator, and his friend David an
equally skilled copyist. Not to mention our foster daughter
Nefret, to whose excavation experience was added medical
training and a thorough acquaintance with mummies. Only
an egotistical idiot would have refused. Davis did refuse.
He regarded excavation as entertainment, not as a tool in
scholarly research, and he was jealous of a better man. He
wanted no one to interfere with his toy.

Watching Davis "rip the tomb apart" (I quote Emerson)
was trying enough. The denouement came on the day when
the mummy fell apart due to careless handling. (It might
not have survived anyhow, but Emerson was in no state of
mind to admit that.) Face handsomely flushed, blue eyes
blazing, impressive form towering over that of the withered
old American, Emerson expressed his sentiments in the
ringing tones and rich vocabulary that have earned him his
sobriquet of Abu Shitaim, Father of Curses. He included in
them M. Maspero, the distinguished head of the Service
des Antiquités. Maspero really had no choice but to accede
to Davis's infuriated demand that we be barred from the
Valley altogether.

There are many other sites in Luxor. Maspero offered

several of them to Emerson. By that time Emerson was in such a state of fury that he rejected them all, and when we sailed from Port Said we had no idea where we would be working the following season.

It was good to be back at our English home in Kent, and I make it a point to look on the bright side, but as spring turned to summer and summer wore on, my attempts to do so failed miserably. It rained incessantly. The roses developed mildew. Rose, our admirable housekeeper, caught a nasty cold that refused to yield to treatment; she went snuffling drearily around the house, and Gargery, our butler, drove me wild with his incessant prying and his pointed hints that he be allowed to come to Egypt with us in the autumn. Emerson, sulking in his study like a gargoyle, refused to discuss our future plans. He knew he had been in the wrong but would not admit it, and his attempts to get back in my good graces had, I confess, not been well received. As a rule I welcome my husband's attentions. His thick black locks and brilliant blue eyes, his magnificent physique, and—how shall I put it?—the expertise with which he fulfills his marital obligations moved me as they always had; but I resented his efforts to get round me by taking advantage of my feelings instead of throwing himself on my mercy and begging forgiveness.

By the end of July, all our tempers had become strained. It continued to rain, Emerson continued to sulk, Rose continued to snuffle, and Gargery's nagging never stopped. "Oh, madam, you need me, you know you do; only see what happened last year when I was not there to look after you—Mr. Ramses and Mr. David kidnapped and you carried off by that Master Criminal chap, and poor Abdullah murdered and—"

"Do be quiet, Gargery!" I shouted. "I asked you to serve tea. I did not invite a lecture."

Gargery stiffened and looked down his snub nose at me. I am one of the few people who is shorter than he, and he takes full advantage. "Tea will be in shortly, madam," he said, and stalked out.

I seldom shout at the servants—in point of fact, Gargery is the only one I do shout at. As a butler he was something of an anomaly, and his unusual talents, such as his skill at wielding a cudgel, had proved helpful to us in the past. However, he was no longer a young man and he certainly could not have prevented any of the disasters that had befallen us. I sighed and rubbed my eyes. It was—need I say?—raining. The drawing room was a chill, shadowy cavern, lit by a single lamp, and my thoughts were as cold and dark. Gargery's words had brought back the memory of that awful day when I held Abdullah clasped in my arms and watched in helpless horror as scarlet drenched the white of his robes. He had taken in his own body the bullets meant for me.

"So, Sitt, am I dying?" he gasped.

I would not have insulted him with a lie. "Yes," I said.

A spark lit in his dimming eyes, and he launched into the familiar complaint. "Emerson. Look after her. She is not careful. She takes foolish chances . . ."

Emerson's face was almost as white as that of his dying friend, but he managed to choke out a promise.

I had not realized how much I cared for Abdullah until I was about to lose him. I had not realized the depth of his affection for me until I heard his final, whispered words— words I had never shared with a living soul. The bitter knowledge that I would never hear that deep voice or see that stern bearded face again was like a void in my heart.

The door opened and my foster daughter's voice remarked, "Goodness, but it is as gloomy as a cell in here. Why are you sitting in the dark, Aunt Amelia?"

"Gargery neglected to switch on the lights," I replied, sniffing. "Curse it, I believe I am catching Rose's cold. Ramses, will you oblige?"

My son pressed the switches and the light illumined the

three forms standing in the doorway—Ramses, David, and Nefret. The children were usually together.

They weren't children, though; I had to keep reminding myself of that. Ramses had just celebrated his twentieth birthday. His height matched Emerson's six feet, and his form, though not as heavily muscled as that of his father, won admiring glances from innumerable young ladies (and a few older ones).

Some persons might (and indeed did) claim that Ramses's upbringing had been quite unsuitable for an English lad of good family. From an early age he had spent half the year with us in Egypt, hobnobbing with archaeologists and Egyptians of all classes. He was essentially self-educated, since his father did not approve of English public schools, and Ramses did not approve of schools at all. He had been an extremely trying child, given to bombastic speeches and a habit of interfering in the business of other persons, which often led to a desire on the part of those persons to mutilate or murder him. Yet somehow—I could not claim all the credit, though heaven knows I had done my best—he had turned into a personable young man, linguistically gifted, well-mannered, and taciturn. Too taciturn, perhaps? I never thought I would see the day when I regretted his abominable loquacity, but he had got into the habit of keeping his thoughts to himself and of concealing his feelings behind a mask Nefret called his "stone-pharaoh face." He had been looking particularly stony of late. I was worried about Ramses.

David, his best friend, closely resembled him, with his bronzed complexion, curly black hair, and long-fringed dark eyes. We were not certain of David's precise age; he was Abdullah's grandson, but his mother and father had been estranged from the old man and David had worked for a notorious forger of antiquities in Luxor until we freed him from virtual slavery. He was, I thought, a year or two older than Ramses.

Nefret, our adopted daughter, was the third member of the youthful triumvirate. Golden fair instead of dark, open and candid instead of secretive, she and her foster brother could not have been more unlike. Her upbringing had been even more extraordinary than his or David's, for she had been raised from birth to the age of thirteen in a remote oasis in the Western Desert, where the old religion of Egypt was still practiced. We had gone there a decade ago, at considerable risk to ourselves, in search of her parents, who had vanished into the desert, and we had no idea she existed until that unforgettable night when she appeared before us in the robes of a high priestess of Isis, her gold-red hair and rose-white complexion unmistakable evidence of her ancestry. I often wondered if she ever thought of those strange days, and of Tarek, prince of the Holy Mountain, who had risked his life and throne to help us get her back to England. She never spoke of him. Perhaps I ought to be worrying about her too.

I knew why David's dark eyes were so sad and his face so somber; he had become engaged this past winter to Emerson's niece Lia and saw less of her than a lover's heart desired. Lia's parents had been won over to the match with some difficulty, for David was a purebred Egyptian, and narrow-minded English society frowned on such alliances. I was thinking seriously of going to Yorkshire for a time, to visit Walter and Evelyn, Lia's parents, and have one of my little talks with them.

Nefret's cat, Horus, did his best to trip Ramses up when they came into the room together, but since Ramses was familiar with the cat's nasty tricks, he was nimble enough to avoid him. Horus detested everybody except Nefret, and everybody except Nefret detested him. It was impossible to discipline the evil-minded beast, however, since Nefret always took his part. After an insolent survey of the room, Horus settled down at her feet.

Emerson was the last to join us. He had been working on his excavation report, as his ink-speckled shirt and stained fingers testified. "Where is tea?" he demanded.

"It will be in shortly. Come and sit down," Nefret said, taking his arm. She was the brightest spot in the room, with the lights shining on her golden head and smiling face. Emerson loved to have her fuss over him (goodness knows he got little fussing from me these days), and his dour face softened as she settled him in a comfortable chair and pulled up a hassock for his feet. Ramses watched the pretty scene with a particularly blank expression; he waited until Nefret had settled onto the arm of Emerson's chair before joining David on the settee, where they sat like matching painted statues. Was it perhaps the uncertainty of our future plans that made my son look as gloomy as his love-struck friend?

I determined to make one more effort to break through Emerson's stubbornness.

"I was in receipt today of a letter from Annie Quibell," I began. "She and James are returning to Cairo shortly to resume their duties at the Museum."

Emerson said, "Hmph," and stirred sugar into his tea.

I continued. "She asked when we are setting out for Egypt, and what are our plans for this season. James wished her to remind you that the most interesting sites will all be taken if you don't make your application soon."

"I never apply in advance," Emerson growled. "You know that. So does Quibell."

"That may have served you in the past," I retorted. "But there are more expeditions in the field every year. Face it, Emerson. You must apologize to M. Maspero if you hope to get—"

"Apologize be damned!" Emerson slammed his cup into the saucer. It was the third cup he had cracked that week. "Maspero was in the wrong. He was the only one with the authority to stop Davis wrecking that bloody tomb, and he bloody well refused to exert it."

Despite the bad language and the sheer volume of his reverberant baritone voice, I thought I detected the faintest tone of wavering. I recognized that tone. Emerson had had second thoughts but was too stubborn to back down. He wanted me to bully him into doing so. I therefore obliged him.

"That may be so, Emerson, but it is water over the dam. Do you intend to sit here in Kent all winter sulking like Achilles in his tent? What about the rest of us? It's all very well for David; I am sure he would prefer to remain in England with his betrothed, but will you condemn Ramses—to say nothing of me and Nefret—to boredom and inactivity?"

Ramses put his cup down and cleared his throat. "Uh—excuse me—"

Emerson cut him short with an impetuous gesture. A benevolent smile wreathed his well-cut lips. "Say no more, my boy. Your mother is right to remind me that I have obligations to others, obligations for which I will sacrifice my own principles. What would be your choice for this season, Ramses? Amarna? Beni Hassan? I will leave it to you to decide."

He took out his pipe, looking very pleased with himself—as well he might. I had given him the excuse for which he yearned. It was what I had intended to do, but a certain degree of exasperation prompted me to reply before Ramses could do so.

"I believe the Germans have applied for Amarna, Emerson. Why cannot we return to Thebes, where we have a comfortable house and many friends?"

"Because I swore never to work there again!" Emerson moderated his voice. "But if it would please you, Ramses... You know your opinion carries a great deal of weight with me."

"Thank you, sir." Ramses's long dark lashes veiled his eyes.

Nefret had brought several of the new kittens. Like Horus, they were descendants of a pair of Egyptian cats we had brought home with us years before. One of Horus's few amiable attributes was his tolerance of kittens, and he endured their pounces and bounces without protesting; but when one of them knocked over the cream pitcher, he was first at the puddle. Emerson, who is fond of cats (except Horus), found this performance highly amusing, and he was wringing out one of the kittens' tails with his napkin when Gargery appeared with a hand-delivered note.

"Well, will you listen to this?" I exclaimed. "The Carringtons have asked us to dinner. Or—such effrontery!—they will be happy to come to us, at our convenience. Ha!"

Emerson growled and Ramses raised his eyebrows. There was no response at all from David, who probably had not even heard me. Nefret was the only one to respond verbally.

"The Carringtons? How odd. We've had nothing to do with them for years."

"Not since Ramses presented Lady Carrington with a moldy bone from the compost heap," I agreed. "It seems they wish us to meet their niece, who is visiting."

Nefret let out a shout of musical laughter. "That explains it! Ramses, do you remember the girl? She was at the reception we attended last week."

"The reception you forced me to attend." Ramses's eyebrows, which are very thick and dark and expressive, took on an alarming angle. "I cannot say that the young woman made a lasting impression on me."

"You obviously made a lasting impression on her," Nefret murmured.

"Don't be ridiculous," Ramses snapped.

Nefret gave me a wink and a conspiratorial grin and I considered my son thoughtfully. His curly black head was bent over the kitten he had picked up, but his high cheekbones were a trifle darker than usual. Another one, I thought. He had pleasing looks and nice manners (thanks to me), but the persistence of the young women who pursued him was unaccountable!

"You must remember her," Nefret persisted. "Dark-haired, rather plain, with a habit of tilting her head to one side and squinting up at you? I had to detach her by force;

she was hanging on to your arm with both hands—"

"May I be excused, Mother?" Ramses put his cup down with exaggerated care and got to his feet. He did not wait for a reply; holding the kitten, he left the room with long strides. After a moment David, who had followed the exchange with furrowed brows, went after him.

"You shouldn't tease him, Nefret," I scolded. "He does nothing to encourage them . . . does he?"

"Not this one." Nefret's laughter bubbled out. "It was funny, Aunt Amelia, she thought she was being soooo adorable, and poor Ramses looked like a hunted fox. He was too polite to shake her off."

"Well, this is one invitation I can decline with pleasure," I declared. "Would that all our difficulties were so easily solved. Emerson—"

"Confound it, Peabody, I am not the one who is making difficulties! It only remains for Ramses to make up his mind."

## From Manuscript H

Ramses sat on the edge of his bed with his head in his hands. Another day had passed without his having got the courage to tell his father the truth.

He looked up at the sound of a tentative knock at the door.

"Come in, damn it," Ramses said.

"Some people might interpret that as less than welcoming," said David, standing in the doorway. "Would you rather be alone?"

"No. I'm sorry. Come in and close the door before Nefret takes it into her head to follow you."

"You can't go on treating her like this, Ramses. You've been avoiding her as if she were a leper and snapping back at her whenever she speaks."

"You know why."

David sat down next to him. "I know that you love her and you won't tell her so. I don't understand why you won't."

"You aren't usually so obtuse, David. How would you feel if a girl you thought of as a dear little sister sidled up to you and told you she was desperately in love with you?"

David smiled his slow, gentle smile. "She did."

"But you were already in love with Lia when she spoke up," Ramses argued. "And her announcement can't have come as a complete surprise; don't tell me there weren't sidelong looks and blushes and—well, you know the sort of thing. Supposing you hadn't returned her feelings—then how would you have felt?"

"Embarrassed," David admitted after a while. "Sorry for her. Guilty. Horribly self-conscious."

"And that is exactly how Nefret would feel. She thinks of me as a rather amusing younger brother. You heard her just now, teasing me about that confounded girl, laughing at me . . ." He propped his chin on his hands. "I've got to get away for a while. Away from her."

"It's that hard?" David asked. "Being with her?"

"It's bad enough seeing her every day," Ramses said despondently. "If only she weren't so damned affectionate! Always patting and hugging and squeezing my arm—"

"She does that to everybody. Including Gargery."

"Exactly. It doesn't mean a damned thing, but I can assure you that it doesn't affect Gargery as it does me."

He couldn't tell David the worst of it—the burning jealousy of every man who talked to Nefret or looked at her—because at one time he had thought she was beginning to care for David. He had dreamed of killing his best friend.

A peremptory pounding on the door brought him to his feet. "It's Nefret," he said. "Nobody else knocks like that."

He opened the door and stood back. "Shouldn't you be changing for dinner?" he asked pointedly.

Nefret flung herself down in an armchair. "Shouldn't you? I'm sorry I teased you about that wretched girl, but really, Ramses, you're losing your sense of humor. What's the matter?"

Ramses began, "I don't know why you should suppose—"

She cut him off with a word she would not have used in his mother's presence. "Don't you dare lie to me, Ramses Emerson. You and David have been eyeing each other like conspirators—Brutus and Cassius, creeping up on Caesar with daggers drawn! You're planning something underhanded, and I insist on knowing what it is. Don't stand there like a graven image! Sit down—you too, David—and confess."

She was enchanting when she was angry, her cheeks flushed and her eyes wide and her slim form rigid with indignation. A lock of hair had come loose; it curled distractingly over her forehead. Ramses clasped his hands tightly together.

Then her eyes fell. "I thought we were friends," she said softly. "We three, all for one and one for all."

We three. Friends. If he had had any doubts about what he meant to do, that speech dispelled them. After all, why not tell her? She wouldn't care. Friendship can endure separation. A friend wants what is best for her friend. Only lovers are selfish.

"I want to go to Germany this year to study with Erman," he said abruptly.

Nefret's jaw dropped. "You mean—not go to Egypt with us this autumn?"

"Obviously I can't be in two places at once."

She put out her tongue at him. "Why?"

"I need some formal grounding in the language, formal recognition. A degree from Berlin would give me that." The speech came glibly; he had practiced it a number of times, preparatory to delivering it to Emerson. "I've learned a lot from Uncle Walter, but Erman is one of the best, and his approach is different. He thinks I can earn a doctorate in a year, given my past work. I enjoy excavating, but I'll never be as good as Father. Philology is my real interest."

"Hmmm." Nefret stroked her rounded chin, in unconscious imitation of Emerson when deep in thought. "Well, my boy, that is a stunner! But I don't understand why you've been so secretive. It's a reasonable ambition."

Ramses hadn't realized until then that he had been hoping against hope she would object. Obviously the idea of a long separation didn't disturb her unduly. Friends want what is best for friends.

"I'm glad you agree," he said stiffly.

She raised candid blue eyes and smiled at him. "If it's what you want, my boy, then you shall have it. You haven't got up nerve enough to tell the Professor, is that it?"

"Yes, well, cowardice is one of my worst failings."

David's elbow dug into his ribs and Nefret's smile faded. "I didn't mean that. You're afraid of hurting him. That's what I meant."

"Sorry," Ramses muttered.

"We all feel that way," Nefret assured him. "Because we love him. But sooner or later he's got to accept the fact that you—and David and I—are individuals with our own ambitions and wants."

"What is it you want?" Ramses asked.

She shrugged and smiled. "Nothing I don't have. Work I love, a family, the best friends in the world . . . I'll help you persuade the Professor. We'll miss you, of course, won't we, David? But it's only for a year."

She got to her feet. "Just leave it to me. I'm going to break it to Aunt Amelia first. Then it will be all of us against the Professor! If worse comes to worst, I'll cry. That always fetches him."

He had risen when she did; they were standing close together, only a foot apart. She put out her hand, as if to give him a friendly pat on the shoulder. He took a step back and said, "Thank you, but I don't need anyone else to do my dirty work for me. I'll tell Father tonight, at dinner."

She let her hand fall, flushed slightly, and left the room.

"Ramses," David began.

"Shut up, David."

"Damned if I will," David said indignantly. "She was offering to help, in her sweet, generous way, and you froze her with that cold stare and speech. What did you expect, that the idea of being parted from you for a year would miraculously arouse latent passions? It doesn't work that way." After a moment he added, "Go ahead and hit me if it will make you feel better."

Ramses uncurled his fists and turned to the desk. He opened a drawer, looking for a cigarette.

"I'm sorry," David said. "But if you don't get over your habit of bottling up your feelings, you're going to explode one day. For God's sake, Ramses, you're barely twenty, and the family wouldn't hear of your marrying anyhow. Give it a little more time."

"Always the optimist. You don't see it, do you? You wouldn't, though; you don't want anything more from her than she is capable of giving you. What I want may not be there at all." He offered the packet to David, who took a cigarette and leaned against the desk.

"Are you still harping on that? Far be it from me to deny that you have to beat women off with a club, but there must have been a few who didn't react. Nefret is one of them—so far. It doesn't mean she's incapable of love."

Ramses felt himself flushing angrily. "Believe it or not, I'm not that egotistical. Maybe you're right. I hope so. But doesn't it seem strange to you that a woman of twenty-three has never been in love, not even once? Lord only knows how many men have been in love with her. She flirts with them, practices her little wiles on them, makes friends with them, and then turns them down flat when they get courage enough to propose to her. All of them! That's not natural, David. And don't tell me I wouldn't have known. Nefret's not the sort to hide her feelings. The signs are unmistakable, especially to the eyes of a jealous lover—which, God help me, I am. After all, we don't know what happened to her during those years before . . ."

He broke off and David gave him a curious look. "The years when she lived with the missionaries in the Sudan? What could have happened, with them looking after her?"

It was the story they had concocted to explain Nefret's background when they brought her back to England. Not even to David had Ramses told the true story—of the Lost Oasis with its strange mixture of ancient Egyptian and Meroitic cultures, and Nefret's role as the priestess of a heathen goddess. Like his parents, he had sworn to keep the very existence of the place secret.

"You're on the wrong track, I tell you." David leaned back, long legs stretched out, face sober. "I believe that in this case I can claim to understand her better than you. I had to make the same transition, from one world to another, practically overnight—from a ragged slave, beaten and filthy and starved, to a proper young English gentleman." He laughed. "There were times when I thought it would kill me."

"You never complained. I didn't realize . . . I ought to have done."

"Why should I complain? I had to wash more often than I liked and give up habits like spitting and speaking gutter Arabic and going about comfortably half-naked, but I was at least familiar with your world, and I still had ties to my own. Can't you imagine how much more difficult it was for Nefret? Growing up in a native village, completely isolated from the modern world . . . It must have been like Mr. Wells's time machine—from primitive Nubia to modern England, in the blink of an eye. Perhaps the only way she could manage it was to suppress her memories of the past."

"I hadn't thought of that," Ramses admitted.

"No, you are obsessed with her—er—sexuality. If I may use that word."

"It's a perfectly good word," Ramses said, amused by

David's embarrassment. "I think you've gone a bit over-board with the English-gentleman role, David. Perhaps you're right, but it doesn't help. Being away from her for a while will let me get my feelings in order."

"Maybe you'll fall in love with someone else," David said cheerfully. "A pretty little fräulein with flaxen braids and a nicely rounded figure and . . . All right, all right, I'm going. Just think about what I've said."

Ramses put down the vase he had raised in mock threat and sat on the edge of the bed, with his chin in his hands, remembering. David's words had brought it all back—the strangest adventure of his life. They didn't speak of it, but he thought about it often. How could he not, with the daily sight of Nefret to remind him of how she had come to them?

They had made plans to work in the Sudan that autumn. The region south of Egypt, from the second cataract to the junction of the Blue and White Niles, had been for ten years ruled by the Mahdi and his successors—religious fanatics and reformers. The Europeans who had not managed to flee were imprisoned or killed, along with a good many of the local inhabitants.

Emerson had wanted for years to investigate the little-known monuments of the ancient civilizations of Nubia—or Cush, to give the region another of its many names. He believed that the Napatan and Meroitic kingdoms had been more powerful and vibrant than most Egyptologists admitted, genuine rivals to the ancient Egyptian monarchy instead of barbarian tribesmen. When the reconquest of the Sudan by Anglo-Egyptian forces began in 1897, he talked his wife into following the troops as far as Napata, the first capital of the kingdom of Cush. Then came the appeal on behalf of Willoughby Forth, a friend of Emerson's, who had vanished with his young wife during the conflagration of the Mahdist revolt. Emerson had scoffed at the message, which purported to be from Forth himself and gave directions to a remote oasis in the Western Desert filled with treasure.

For once Emerson had been wrong. The message was genuine, and the map correct. After Reginald Forthright, Forth's nephew, set off into the desert in search of his uncle, the Emersons followed, accompanied by a mysterious stranger named Kemit, whom they had hired to work for them. It had been a disastrous trip from start to finish—the camels dying one by one, his mother falling ill, all their men except Kemit abandoning them in the desert without water or transport. Ramses had been ill too—sunstroke or heat prostration or dehydration, he supposed. One of his last memories of the journey was the sight of his father, lips cracked and tongue dry, plodding doggedly through the sand with his wife in his arms.

They would never have made it if it hadn't been for Kemit, who went ahead to bring a rescue party. As they learned when they reached the isolated oasis, ringed in by cliffs, Kemit's real name was Tarek, and it was he who had carried the message from Forth to England. It was some time before they found out why.

He would never forget his first sight of Nefret, wearing the white robes of the High Priestess of Isis, with her hair flowing over her shoulders in a river of gold. She had been thirteen, the most beautiful creature he had ever seen. Now that he was older, he was better able to assess the flagrant romanticism of that image and its effect on a ten-year-old boy; but he still thought she was the most beautiful creature he had ever seen, as brave and clever as she was lovely. Tarek had been in love with her, he had as good as said so: "For who could see her and not desire her?" Yet he had kept his word to her dead father, who had wanted her to return to her own people. Realizing he could not get her away without help, Tarek had made the long, perilous journey to England in order to bring the Emersons to the Lost Oasis. In doing so he had risked his life and his throne. He had been a fine-looking young man, chivalrous as a knight of

legend; it wouldn't be surprising if Nefret still cherished
his memory.

Goddamn him, Ramses thought; how can I or anyone
else compete with a hero like that? Tarek had fought like a
hero too, sword in hand, to win his crown. They had repaid
part of their debt to him by helping him in that struggle,
each in his or her own way. Emerson had been at the height
of his powers then—not that he had lost many of them—
and some of his exploits rivaled the achievements of Her-
cules and Horus.

Another hero, thought Emerson's son. And now I've got
to tell him I won't go with him this year.

.
.

So vehement was Emerson's initial reaction to Ramses's
news that his shouts brought Gargery, John the footman,
Rose, and several of the housemaids rushing in to see what
had happened. Our relationships with servants are somewhat unusual, thanks to Emerson's habit of treating them
like human beings and their profound affection for him;
once they learned what had occasioned his wrath, every single one of them felt entitled to join in the conversation, on
one side or the other. Rose, of course, supported Ramses,
and so did Gargery (offering himself as Ramses's replace-
ment, which infuriated Emerson even more). The housemaids were swept off by Rose before they had a chance to
say very much. Still, the consensus was clear, and Emerson
had some justice on his side when he shouted, "You are all
against me!"

Nefret had warned me in strictest secrecy of what Ramses meant to do, so I had had a little time to get used to the
idea. I was somewhat surprised at the strength of my initial
disappointment. I had got used to having Ramses around.
He was a great help to his father.

However, a mother wants what is best for her child, and
at least the news explained why Ramses had been behaving

so oddly. So I had promised Nefret I would help persuade Emerson, and of course my arguments carried the day.

"He'll get himself in trouble all alone over there, you know he will" was Emerson's final attempt to sway me by appealing to my maternal instincts. "He always does."

He always did. However, as I pointed out to Emerson, he did anyhow, even when he was with us.

## From Manuscript H

Now that his decision had been accepted and the time of his departure drew near, Ramses found it easier to deal with Nefret's constant presence. It wouldn't be for long, he told himself. Nevertheless, he spent most of his time in his room, ostensibly working. David had gone off to York-shire, radiant at finally having received an invitation from his beloved's parents. (Ramses suspected his mother had had a hand in that.)

One warm August afternoon he had just finished a tricky translation of a hieratic text when Nefret knocked at his door. She had honored his request that he be left alone—to work—and compunction smote him when he saw her sober face.

"Am I interrupting?" she asked.

"No, not at all. Come in." He stepped back and gestured her to a chair. She sat down, clasping her hands between her trousered knees. Her face was flushed with heat and her loosened hair clung wetly to temples and cheeks. The open neck of her shirt bared her slim throat and offered a distracting suggestion of rounded curves below. Ramses went back to his desk, ten feet away, and leaned against it.

"Rather warm to be riding, isn't it?" he asked.

She made a face at him. "It doesn't take Sherlock Holmes to deduce that that's what I was doing. May I have a cigarette?"

Ramses lit it for her and retreated again. "Something's wrong," he said. "Tell me."

"Are you sure I'm not bothering you? It's nothing, really. I probably imagined the whole thing."

"It would bother me very much if you didn't feel you could come to me with anything that worries you. I'm sorry if I've been—"

"Don't apologize, my boy. I know why you've been hiding in your room."

"You do?"

"You don't want to face the Professor."

"Oh."

"Don't let him upset you. He'll get over it."

"I know. Well?"

"Well. I did go riding, as you deduced. On the way back I stopped at Tabirka's pyramid."

It took Ramses a few seconds to focus on the unexpected subject. Impatiently, she elaborated. "Tabirka—Tarek's brother, who came to England with Tarek. We buried him in the clearing where he died and raised a little pyramid—"

"I know. I was surprised, that's all. I haven't heard you mention him or Tarek for a long time. Do you go there often?"

"Every now and then," Nefret said evasively. (Or was it only his jealous fancy that she sounded evasive?) "It's a peaceful, pretty place. May I have another cigarette?"

Ramses supplied it. She scarcely ever smoked. "What happened?" he asked.

"It was warm and very still," Nefret began. "Not the slightest breeze. All of a sudden the leaves rustled violently, and I heard a voice, distant and hollow, as if it came from deep underground. Ramses—it spoke in the language of the Holy City."

"The Lost Oasis?" Ramses said, stalling for time.

"We called it the City of the Holy Mountain." The words, and the way she pronounced them, warned Ramses that he was on dangerous ground. Her head was bowed and her shoulders stiff, as if in anticipation of laughter or skepticism. Casually he said, "I know. What did the voice say?"

"I didn't understand every word. It was a greeting, I think." She looked up. "You believe me? You don't think I imagined it?"

"I don't believe you heard the ka of poor young Tabirka, calling to you from the next world. Neither do you, you've better sense. Perhaps someone is playing tricks."

"Of course," Nefret said with a sigh of relief. "That's the obvious explanation, isn't it? But you can't imagine how uncanny it was, Ramses. I got away as fast as I could. I—I don't usually run away, you know."

"How well I know."

She returned his smile with a look so bright and grateful, he felt like a mean hound. Had he been behaving so churlishly that she had hesitated to approach him? She had come to him, though, not to his mother or father; that was a hopeful sign, and thank God he had had the sense to say the right thing.

"Let's go and have a look." He held out his hand. "The fellow may still be hanging about. Or he may have left some trace of his presence."

"Thank you, my boy." She took his hand and squeezed it. "For believing me."

Ramses gently freed his hand. "We'll walk, shall we? It isn't far, and we can move more quietly on foot."

Tall elms lined the narrow path through the woods. The leaves hung limp and still in the warm air. As they went on, the shadows darkened. A thunderstorm was brewing; clouds piled up in the eastern sky. The place did have an uncanny atmosphere, especially in stormy weather, for the strange little monument in the glade was a pyramid in the Cushite style, steeper-sided and smaller than those of Egypt. Few people knew of it, and those who did took it to be one of the fake antiquities once popular with English gentry who had an interest in Egypt. On one side was a small enclosure in imitation of an offering chapel. Ramses had himself inscribed on the lintel the hieroglyphs that gave the dead boy's name and titles and a short prayer invoking the goodwill of the gods of the judgment. Tabirka deserved an easy journey to the next world. He had been murdered by Nefret's cousin, who had tried every dirty trick in the book to keep the Emersons from bringing her back to threaten his inheritance.

Ramses really didn't expect to find anything or anyone. She had most probably been daydreaming a little, putting herself in a fanciful mood, and had misinterpreted the sound of an animal or bird. He was caught completely off guard when a hard body crashed into him, knocked him flat, and fell heavily on top of him. Winded and bruised, Ramses stared up into the dark face that hovered over him. It split in a wide, terrifying grin, and hands reached for his throat. Nefret was yelling and raining blows on the fellow's back with a branch. It didn't seem to have much effect.

Ramses found breath enough to yell back. "Get out of the way!" He brought his hands up in time to slam the other man's forearms apart, rammed an elbow under his chin, heaved him up and over onto his back, and scrambled to his feet. Nefret lowered the branch.

"Nicely done, my boy," she said breathlessly.

"Thank you." Ramses stood poised, ready to kick out if his erstwhile opponent showed signs of continuing the fight. The fellow was rubbing his throat, but he was still grinning, and his lean body, clad only in a kiltlike lower garment, was completely relaxed. Ramses stared in mounting disbelief. With his dark skin and bizarre costume he was as out of place in an English woodland as a tiger in a drawing room. There was something familiar about the aquiline features.

"Tarek was right," the stranger remarked. "You have become a man."

⋮

We have entertained a number of unusual guests in our home, but never had I seen one so extraordinary as the young man who was in the drawing room with Ramses and Nefret when I came down to tea. Barefoot and bareheaded, his body uncovered except for a brief skirt or kilt, he might have stepped out of an ancient Egyptian tomb painting. I stopped short; and Ramses said, "Mother, may I present Prince Merasen. He is the brother of Tarek, whom you surely remember."

I am seldom at a loss for words, but on this occasion I was unable to do more than emit a wordless croak of surprise. Nefret hurried to me and took my arm. "Aunt Amelia, are you all right? Sit down, please."

"A nice hot cup of tea," I gurgled, staring. The young man raised his hands to shoulder height and bowed. It was the same gesture shown in innumerable tomb paintings, a gesture of respect to the gods and to superiors. He was far more at ease than I. Well, but he had been prepared for me, and I certainly had not been prepared for him!

"A nice whiskey and soda, instead?" said Ramses. He sounded a trifle sheepish. "I apologize, Mother. I didn't think to warn you."

"Not at all," I replied, taking the glass he handed me. "Will you take a chair, Mr. . . . Er . . . Does he speak English?"

"I speak very good" was the cool reply. "It is why Tarek sent me."

"Tarek sent you?" I repeated stupidly.

"Yes, Sitt Hakim. I am honored to see you. They tell many stories about you in the Holy City. And about the Father of Curses, and the Brother of Demons, and the Lady Nefret."

"Father of Curses" was Emerson's Egyptian sobriquet (and well-deserved, I should add), as Sitt Hakim, "Lady Doctor," was mine. We had been known by those honorifics when we were last in the Holy City. If I remembered correctly, Ramses had not at that time acquired his nickname of "Brother of Demons" (a tribute to his supposedly supernatural talents). Merasen must have heard Ramses referred to by that name during his journey to England, perhaps from Egyptians in London who had given him directions to Amarna House.

I nodded acknowledgment, sipping my whiskey, and trying to collect my scattered wits. The young man bore a certain resemblance to his brother, with his well-cut features and well-made frame—or rather, I told myself, his brother as I remembered him. He must be about eighteen, the same age Tarek had been ten years ago.

"It is good to see you too," I said, politely if somewhat mendaciously—for I suspected his arrival meant trouble. It wasn't likely that Tarek would send an emissary all that long, dangerous way simply to say hello. "Er—Ramses, perhaps you can lend our guest some clothes."

"I have clothes, English clothes." The boy indicated a bundle at his feet. "I will put them on?"

It was a question, not an offer; I rose to the occasion, as any good hostess should when confronted with well-meaning eccentricity. Smiling, I shook my head. "Not if you would rather not. The weather *is* extremely warm."

Nefret, who had exhibited growing signs of impatience, burst out, "Aunt Amelia, perhaps you can persuade Merasen to tell us why he is here. I doubt that he undertook that long, arduous journey simply to make our acquaintance."

"My thought exactly," I agreed. "He has not confided in you and Ramses?"

"No, he was too busy fighting with Ramses," Nefret said caustically.

The boy grinned engagingly. "Tarek said Ramses would now be a man. I wished to see what sort of man."

"You found out," said Ramses curtly.

The overt antagonism and the touch of braggadocio were so unlike him I looked at him in surprise. Merasen only smiled more winningly.

"And she"—a little bow in the direction of Nefret—

"she is even more beautiful than Tarek said. She is not your wife?"

Ramses's countenance became even stonier. Nefret said, "I told you, we are brother and sister, in affection if not by birth."

Realizing, as did I, that the monarchs of the Holy City, like Egyptian pharaohs, often married full or half sisters, Nefret amplified the statement. "I am no man's wife, Merasen, nor about to be."

"Now that we have settled that," I said. "What is the message, Merasen?"

"It is for the Father of Curses."

"Oh, dear," I murmured. "Ramses, will you go and get your father? You needn't mention the identity of our guest," I added.

Ramses smiled and went out of the room, leaving the door open.

"And you, Nefret," I went on, "might just warn Gargery before he brings the tea tray. I don't want any more cups broken."

"He knows," Nefret replied. "We met him in the hall. He was absolutely thrilled."

"He would be," I muttered.

I heard the rattle of the tea cart, which was coming at a great pace. Emerson got there before it. I could tell from his appearance that he had been hard at work, for he had removed as many of his garments as was proper. His shirt was open and the sleeves rolled above the elbow, baring his muscular forearms.

"What is all this?" he demanded. "Ramses said—" His eyes lit upon the prince, who had risen and was making his obeisance. "Ah," said Emerson, without so much as blinking. "A visitor from the Lost Oasis? Sit down, my boy, sit down. I am—"

"Emerson, the Father of Curses," the boy breathed. "Now that I see you, I know the stories are true. That you drove a spear straight through a man's body and killed another with your bare hands, and fought a hundred men with sword in hand to help Tarek to the throne."

Emerson drew himself up to his full height, basking in the admiration that filled the young man's eyes. "At the bottle already, Peabody?" he inquired, smirking at me. I looked accusingly at Ramses. He shook his head. Ramses preferred equivocation to prevarication, so I had to believe he had not mentioned our visitor to his father.

The tea cart rattled in, propelled by Gargery. He was alone; either the maids had been too timid to face the visitor, or, what was more likely, Gargery had seized on an excuse to prolong the service of the genial beverage so that he could listen to our conversation. I had no intention of discussing our visitor's purpose in Gargery's presence, so I dismissed the latter, telling him we would wait on ourselves. He left the door slightly ajar. I slammed it and heard a muffled yelp.

I then turned my accusing gaze on my son. "You told your father."

"No, Mother, honestly."

"Emerson, how dare you pretend you aren't surprised?"

Emerson tried to keep a straight face, but he could not. "I saw him through the study window," he admitted with a grin. "Almost fell off my chair. Well, well. You are welcome in my house . . . What is your name, my friend? You may leave off bowing," he added graciously.

The young man drew himself up. "I am Merasen. I bring a message to the Father of Curses from Tarek, my brother and my king."

Emerson held out his hand.

"I do not have the writing," the boy admitted. "It was lost when the slavers took me. But I know the words. I will speak them. 'Come to me, my friends who once saved me. Danger threatens and only you can help me now.'"

Curse it, I thought. Glancing at Ramses, I saw my sentiments mirrored in his normally inexpressive face. The expression—tightened lips, narrowed eyes—was fleeting.

Emerson—it was just like him!—responded with chivalrous, unquestioning enthusiasm. "Certainly, certainly! How can we do less?"

"Emerson," I said repressively. "You might at least ask what sort of danger Tarek is in before you commit yourself, and us, to what you once referred to as a harebrained adventure."

"I agree," said Ramses.

"That was quite different," Emerson exclaimed. "On that occasion we were following a rumor and a questionable map, and that villainous servant of Reggie Forthright had poisoned our camels. This time—"

"Professor!" Nefret jumped to her feet. "Excuse me. But could we, for once, stick to the point instead of arguing? Aunt Amelia has asked a sensible question. Merasen—what is the danger that threatens Tarek?"

"It is a strange sickness. Not one of our priests can cure it. It comes and goes away, and each time it leaves the sick one weaker. Two times Tarek has fallen ill. He is a strong man and it will take long to kill him, but now the child is sick too. He is Tarek's heir, his only true son. It is for him Tarek sends to you."

"Good Lord," Nefret gasped. "The little boy can't be more than ten years old. We must go, of course."

"Let's hear a little more about this," Ramses said coolly. "How long has it been since you left the Holy Mountain? Surely you did not cross the desert in the heat of summer."

I understood what he was getting at. The journey must have taken weeks, if not months. It might be too late for Tarek and his child. Nefret understood too. Her face paled. "What difference does it make?" she asked passionately. "There is a chance we might be in time, a chance we must—"

"I am not denying your premise." Ramses's voice was like icy sleet on flame. "But we need to learn all we can before we decide what to do. Tell us about your journey, Merasen."

It was a riveting narrative, for the boy spoke with considerable eloquence. He had left the Holy Mountain in the season of Peret—winter—with only six companions. It was a small force to face the peril of the desert, but no more could be spared, for they went in secret, braving the old law of the Holy Mountain that forbade contact with the outside world on pain of death. The others were members of the royal bodyguard, strong men, armed with swords and bows. They had been on their way for several days when they met the caravan—thirty men and as many camels, driving a forlorn line of bound captives.

Slavery had been officially abolished and the trade vigorously suppressed—to the credit of Britain let it be said! But as we all knew, the caravans still crossed the desert with their miserable human cargo, bound for the slave markets of Khartoum and Wadi Halfa and the Egyptian oases. The villains knew that if they were caught it would go hard with them. They had immediately fired upon the small band of strangers.

"The others they killed," the boy said calmly, "but me they took alive."

Yes, I thought sickly, they would. Most of the slaves were women and children and youths of both sexes. He was a handsome boy, and well-made. The older men would not bring so high a price, and they might be dangerous to their captors.

So was Merasen, as they were to learn.

When they searched his camel bags they found the rings of gold Tarek had given him to pay his way to England, and beat him to make him tell where he had gotten them. Though injured and frightened, he had wits enough to invent a convincing lie. He and his companions were treasure hunters, looters of ancient tombs. They had found this cache in a crumbling ruin far to the south, but there was nothing else there, they had taken it all. So the slavers left off beating him for fear of spoiling the youthful good looks that would bring a high price in the market, and ordered one of the women in the caravan to tend his wounds. He pretended weakness and meekness, biding his time until his wounds had healed and he had learned enough of their whereabouts and their destination to make escape feasible. The woman knew a little English and helped him to learn some Arabic. It was she who told him of the soldiers of England who fought the slavers and of the town on the Great River where they were stationed. By one means or another (and I thought I could guess one of those means), he persuaded her to help him get away, promising that if he found the soldiers he would guide them back and win freedom for her and the others. She passed on to him all she could learn from those who knew something of the region; and on a moonless night, when they were less than a day's journey from the Great River, Merasen stole a camel and fled, leaving two men dead.

"I found the soldiers," he said. "So I kept my word to the woman and had my revenge and my reward. They told me I was a brave lad and gave me money. It was not enough. I was on the Great River, but deep in the south, in the country they call Sudan. I worked, yes, and I stole, when it was safe to do it, but it took me many months to make my way here. If I have failed my king, it is on my head."

The narrative had held us spellbound. Emerson had taken out his pipe, but had been too absorbed to light it. Now he cleared his throat. "You have not failed. Few men could have acted with such courage and wisdom."

"Quite right," I said, though it was clear that my commendation meant little as compared with that of Emerson. Hero worship brightened the young man's face. Obviously the stories of Emerson's prowess had become part of the folklore of the Holy Mountain, and I must admit that it would not have been necessary to enlarge them beyond the bare facts.

"Months," Nefret said. "At least five months. And it will be another month before we—"

"We will discuss it later," I said, for dusk was creeping

into the room. "Ramses, will you show our guest to his room—a room—any room—and find him appropriate attire? I don't care what, so long as he is more or less covered at dinner."

"I'll show him," Nefret said, getting to her feet. "David's clothes will fit him better than yours, Ramses, and he can have David's room, at least for the time being. Is that all right, Aunt Amelia?"

"Yes, my dear, thank you for asking," I replied.

She took him by the hand and led him out.

"Father," Ramses began. Emerson held up a peremptory hand.

"Not here. Come to the library."

Leaving Gargery pouting as he cleared away the tea things, we followed Emerson to the designated chamber. He went at once to a cupboard next to the fireplace and took out a heavy steel box, which he unlocked. After rummaging through the papers it contained, he removed a yellowing document and spread it out on the desk.

The three of us studied it in silence. The markings were still clear—numbers and several enigmatic symbols, the picture-writing of ancient Egypt. We had used a copy of this map to reach the Holy Mountain ten years ago. After our return with Nefret I had wanted to destroy it. Emerson had refused. "One never knows," he had said. "The time may come . . ." he had said.

Now I wished we had destroyed it. It was not often I recalled the details of that terrible journey—the heat and blowing sand, the constant thirst, and the treachery of the men we had hired. I had no memory of the final days, since I had fallen ill and was unconscious when Tarek's rescue party found us and took us the rest of the way. Our departure from the Holy Mountain had been made in haste and in darkness, but I retained one very vivid memory. Looking back as we rode away, in constant fear of pursuit, I saw the encircling mountain range rising up against the stars like the ramparts of a medieval castle—a castle ablaze, for fire rose from the central portion like a volcano in eruption. We had left Tarek still fighting for his throne, though he had assured us that most of the opposition had fallen. We had an unspoken agreement not to talk of the place, but I had often wondered how matters came out. Well, at least we knew that Tarek had conquered.

Emerson was the first to speak. "It will take weeks to collect supplies and mount an expedition. In any case we could not possibly start out before September, the desert heat is simply too great. If we decide to go." He looked expectantly at me.

"So you are having second thoughts, are you?" I inquired.

"I am not a complete fool," Emerson retorted. "Of course it would solve the problem of where we mean to work this season."

"Unquestionably," I agreed with a certain degree of irony. "The hazards of the journey and the uncertainty as to what we will find when we get to the Holy Mountain, supposing we do get there, add up to a strong possibility that we will never have to face that particular problem again."

"It wouldn't be as risky this time," Emerson mused. "We were limited as to camels and men, and weren't sure that the map was accurate."

"That is true," I admitted.

"I don't suppose I could persuade you to—"

"Remain behind? Don't be absurd, Emerson."

"I knew you would say that. Well, Ramses? You have been very silent. I will quite understand if you prefer to spend the winter in Germany, as you—"

Ramses interrupted him with an Arabic word that made Emerson's eyes widen. "Good Gad, my boy, where did you learn that one?" he inquired.

"You know I intend to go with you," Ramses said furiously.

"Yes," said Emerson, trying not to smirk.

"You know why I've hesitated."

"Yes." Emerson's smile faded. "I too would prevent her

if I could. But it is impossible. Tarek was a friend, close as a brother. Moreover, she is a trained physician, and this mysterious illness may be one she can diagnose and cure. Short of locking her up, which is illegal as well as impractical, I can think of no way of excluding her. Can you?"

Ramses turned on his heel and walked to the window. He stood with his hands clasped behind his back, looking out into the twilight. Finally his rigid shoulders relaxed, and when he turned he had his face under control.

"No, I can't. She went off with Merasen so she could talk to him about Tarek, you know. He'll fire her up even more, especially if he tells her about the child."

"He is a remarkable young man," Emerson said. "And it was an epic journey. He could not have survived without those same qualities of wit and courage that marked—"

Ramses cut in. "Did you believe his story?"

"Why should we not?" I exclaimed in surprise.

"We have only his word." Ramses began pacing up and down. "There are a number of things about his narrative that bother me. He'd been in Kent for several days before we found him—camping out, near Tabirka's pyramid, waiting for one of us to come to him."

"Perhaps he was shy about approaching the house," I suggested. "But I admit attacking you was a rather odd way of introducing himself."

"Oh, I can understand that," Ramses admitted grudgingly. "I might have done something equally idiotic when I was his age, especially if I had been in strange surroundings, uncertain and a little afraid. Win or lose, you've had the satisfaction of asserting your manhood."

"If you will forgive me for saying so, my dear, you are in no position to criticize," I said. "To judge by his appearance, he is only a year or two younger than you, and you have not entirely conquered your habit of—"

"Hmph," said Emerson loudly. "What makes you doubt his story, Ramses?"

"I simply pointed out that it cannot be substantiated."

"Oh, bah," said Emerson. He began ticking off points on his fingers as he mentioned them. "He resembles his brother. He speaks the language. He knows of our earlier visit, and"—he coughed modestly—"what we did there. In detail. How else could he have learned these things?"

"I don't doubt that he comes from the Holy Mountain, or that he wants us to go there. It is his motive that is unproven. We've nothing in writing, not even Tarek's alleged letter."

"Your point is valid," I admitted. "And there are a number of other points that, in my opinion, require to be explained. We need not make a decision this instant. I assure you, Ramses, that I will bring to bear all my expertise at subtle interrogation."

"Yes, Mother," Ramses said.

"Ha," said Emerson.

"Put the map away, Emerson. It is time to dress for dinner."

"I am dressed," said Emerson, inspecting his ink-speckled shirt. "See here, Peabody, you don't expect me to get myself up in boiled shirt and black tie, do you?"

I took him away. Ramses said he would lock the map in the dispatch case, and we left him brooding over it with a particularly vulturine air. I allowed Emerson to expostulate for a while before informing him that no, I did not expect him to assume formal evening wear, but that he might at least change his shirt and brush his hair. He did so without further argument, humming cheerfully and tunelessly. I supposed the song was one of his favorite vulgar music-hall ditties, but no one could have recognized the melody.

I knew why he was in such a pleasant frame of mind. Emerson enjoys adventure for its own sake, and his archaeological brain was all afire at the prospect of examining again the unique monuments of the Lost Oasis—a culture frozen in time, so to speak, for it had had almost no contact with the outside world since the fourth century A.D., when refugees from the fallen capital of Meroe found their way there, joining earlier immigrants from the late dynasties of ancient Egypt. Furthermore, Merasen's proposal had relieved Emerson of the necessity of settling on an excavation site for the coming year—and it had put an end to Ramses's plan of spending the winter in Germany.

I selected a rather becoming gown of my favorite crimson, for, to be honest, I needed to keep my own spirits up. No matter what precautions we took, the journey would be difficult and dangerous. And what would we find at the end of that journey? A dead child and a dying king—the end of a dynasty, with pretenders crawling round the bodies like flies? Even if we could make our way there without incident, our reception was in doubt. We too had broken the law of the Holy Mountain by the very act of leaving it— and we had stolen their revered High Priestess.

## Two

"What shall we do about David?" Ramses asked.

The leaves outside the windows of his room dripped with water. Pale sunlight had replaced the misty rain of early morning.

It was the first time we had had an opportunity to speak in private since the arrival of our strange visitor. Over the past two days I had become increasingly uneasy about him, and Ramses was the only member of the family who appeared to share my reservations. Nefret's warm heart had been won by the hope of helping her old friend and his child, and Emerson had yearned for years to return to the Holy Mountain.

Now Emerson would get his wish. The expedition was a settled matter. It had never been in doubt, really. No matter how slim the chance of success, the attempt must be made. How could we, as Britons, do less? Noblesse oblige, and the debt we owed Tarek admitted of no other choice.

That debt was visible to us daily: Nefret herself. Had it not been for Tarek's braving the long, perilous journey from the Holy Mountain, we would never have found her, and her own fate would have been dreadful. The women of the Holy Mountain, like those of ancient Egypt and Meroe, married and began bearing children when in their early teens. One of the men who had sought her hand was

Tarek's brother, a thoroughly despicable individual who might well have succeeded in taking Tarek's throne and his life, and Nefret, had we not been present to defend our friend. She would have lived out her life as the unwilling but helpless wife of a cruel despot, instead of brightening ours.

All the same, there were a good many complications that needed to be addressed, and Ramses was obviously the only other one who was capable of thinking sensibly about them.

"David is only one of the many complications that need to be addressed," I said, and looked round for some flat surface on which I might seat myself. Rose had tidied the room that morning, but it was already in the state of utter confusion that prevails when Ramses is its occupant. Apparently he had rummaged through the bureau drawers and the wardrobe in order to find garments he considered comfortable. These consisted of a collarless shirt that had seen better days and a pair of stained trousers I could have sworn I had directed Rose to throw away, since the stains would not come out. (I did not know what chemical substance had caused them and preferred not to ask.) The garments that had not passed muster hung over various articles of furniture. The bed, the chairs, and the desk were covered with books and papers. Two kittens were chasing each other up and down the draperies.

"Oh—sorry," said Ramses, observing my intent. He scooped up the papers from a chair and dumped them on the heaped desk, from which they immediately fell to the floor. "Sit down, Mother. Well?"

"You share my reservations, I know. Let us address them in order."

I took a piece of folded paper from my pocket, and Ramses's grave face relaxed into a smile. "One of your famous lists?"

"Certainly." I unfolded the paper and cleared my throat.

"Do you remember Merasen—from our first visit to the Holy Mountain, I mean?"

The question obviously did not take Ramses by surprise. "No. But he was only a child, the son of a lesser wife of the king, and we didn't meet all the members of the royal family. Thanks to the jolly old custom of polygamy, it was extensive."

"True. The factors your father mentioned the other evening make it probable, if not absolutely certain, that he does come from the Holy Mountain. The next question is—how did he find his way across the desert without a map?"

"He answered that. You remember the oasis that is seven days' journey from the Holy Mountain—the only water along that arid trek? Tarek keeps a garrison there, to watch out for strangers. Once Merasen and his companions had got that far, they had only to head east, toward the rising sun. They were bound to strike the Nile sooner or later. It would have been hard to miss it."

"And he counted on us to guide him back," I mused. "A rather dangerous assumption, that one. Tarek knew we had a copy of the map, but we might have lost or destroyed it."

"It would have been worth taking the chance, if Tarek was desperate enough." Ramses began pacing, his hands clasped behind his back. "The confounded boy's story makes sense, as far as it goes. Anyhow, we haven't any choice but to respond. The question is how to go about it in the safest possible way. The fewer people who know of our plans, the better. That includes David."

"You would prefer he did not accompany us?"

Ramses leaned against the desk and ran his fingers through his hair. It was one of the few signs of perturbation he permitted himself. One infatuated young female had gushed about the "Byronic look" of those tousled black curls; in my opinion, they were simply untidy. I reached up and brushed them back from his forehead. Ramses shook his head impatiently, as if dislodging a fly, and went on.

"I would prefer that no one go except Father and me. You needn't protest, Mother, I am well aware you would never consent to be left behind. Neither would Nefret. But David, so far, knows nothing about this. He'd come, of course, without an instant's hesitation, but he's very much in love and newly engaged; and if Lia knew what he was walking into, she'd be beside herself. God knows our normal excavation seasons are wild enough, but at least we don't go looking for trouble. Well . . . usually we don't."

"You needn't go over the arguments," I said with a sigh. "I have considered them myself—plus the fact that David could not contribute anything to the expedition except his stout heart and strong hands. Does he know about the Lost Oasis?"

"Not from me. Uncle Walter and Aunt Evelyn know."

"That was unavoidable," I said defensively. "Your uncle Walter is a philologist; once he heard Nefret speak in the language of the Holy Mountain he recognized its relationship to ancient Egyptian, and Evelyn's suspicions were aroused by some of Nefret's—er—unusual habits. It seemed safest to tell them the whole story and ask them to take an oath of secrecy, which to the best of my knowledge they have never broken. How do you propose to prevent David from coming out with us, as he has always done?"

"Did you know that Constable, the publisher, approached him in London about doing a series of paintings for a popular book about Egypt?"

"Really? He never mentioned it."

"He didn't mention it to me until just before he left for Yorkshire. He was afraid I'd urge him to accept, and abandon my own plans rather than leave Father without half his staff."

"Emerson would not have taken that well," I agreed. "Hmmm. I believe you have found the answer to this particular dilemma. It would be a wonderful opportunity for David, a chance to build a reputation of his own, without being dependent on us. But it would mean keeping our real purpose a secret."

"We'll have to do that in any case." The kittens were rolling around on the floor in mock battle; one of them let out a squeak of protest and Ramses went to separate them. Holding the victim away from its rougher sibling, he went on, "When we returned in '98, we agreed that the very existence of the place must remain unknown, but although our fiction passed muster with the general public, there were a few people who wondered whether we were telling the whole truth. People who remembered Willy Forth's theory about a lost oasis in the Western Desert; people like your journalist friend O'Connell, who had learned from the officers at the military camp at Sanam Abu Dom about Forth's nephew Reggie setting off in search of him. We should be all right if we can keep such people from making the connection between that last journey and our intention of heading again for the Sudan. The greatest danger is Merasen himself."

He paused for breath, having spoken with unusual quickness and passion. Glancing at my list, I said approvingly, "I commend you, Ramses, on stating the facts almost as logically as I might have done."

"Thank you, Mother. You had, of course, already considered all those points."

I gave him a sharp look, but his face was quite grave—not even a little quiver at the corners of his mouth. "I had, yes. Those and others. I fear your father has not: he is inclined to ignore difficulties once he has set his mind on something. I will have a little chat with him. Will you speak to Nefret?"

Ramses went to the window, where he stood looking out. "Your opinion would carry more weight with her."

"D'you think so?"

"Yes," said Ramses, without turning. "She's out there now, with Merasen. Practicing archery."

They were on the lawn, with half the household watching. When I went onto the terrace the maids scattered in various directions, trying to look as if they had had business in that part of the house, but Gargery stood his ground.

"A proper sport for a young lady," he announced. "If I may say so, madam, it shows off a pretty figure to best advantage."

I did not reprimand him for this familiarity, since a look of almost paternal pride warmed his plain features. She did look very pretty in her neat divided skirt and shirtwaist, her hair clubbed back and bound with ribbons. She loosed the arrow, which flew straight to the target, though not to its center. Merasen said something to her in a low voice; she laughed and looked up at the terrace, where Gargery was clapping his hands enthusiastically.

"Good afternoon, Aunt Amelia. Thank you, Gargery, but Merasen says I need more practice."

"I'd like to see him do better," Gargery declared, scowling at the critic.

Nefret offered the bow to Merasen. He folded his arms and shook his head. "It is a woman's bow."

"Stop for a bit, Nefret," I said. "You look very warm, and I would like to talk to you."

She handed the weapon to Merasen and came up the steps to the terrace, wiping her wet forehead with her sleeve. I got rid of Gargery by asking him to get Nefret something to drink, and went straight to the point, before he could come running back. She looked surprised when I mentioned David's offer from the publisher.

"He didn't tell me either. How nice! It would be just the thing for him. I'm afraid I hadn't given the matter much thought, Aunt Amelia, but you are absolutely right; the fewer people who know our plans, the better. Can we keep them secret, do you think?"

"I am about to consult Emerson on that subject. Once we

have worked out the details we will have a little council of war."

I took it upon myself to beard Emerson in his lair—the library. When I told him what Ramses and I had agreed upon, he gave me an outraged stare.

"I will need David, curse it. Copying the reliefs in the temples and tombs of the Holy Mountain is of paramount importance."

"Emerson, will you try to get it through your head that this is not an archaeological expedition, but a rescue mission? We will be lucky to get there at all, much less get away again. How can you think of risking David's life?"

"We are risking the lives of Ramses and Nefret," Emerson pointed out. He sounded a trifle subdued, though, and his brow was furrowed.

"Only because they were made aware of the situation by Merasen before we could prevent him. David is not aware of it. Given a free choice, he would much rather remain in England this winter with Lia. You must convince him he will not be needed."

"How?" Emerson demanded. "He knows how useful he is to me."

"I doubt that, since you have never paid him a compliment." Emerson looked blank, and I went on in mounting exasperation. "As soon as we announce the date of our departure, all our friends, including Walter and Evelyn, are going to ask where we mean to work this winter and why we are leaving so much earlier than usual. What do you propose to tell them?"

"I do not propose to tell anyone anything," said Emerson haughtily. "I never discuss my plans in advance."

"Not even with Walter?"

"Hmph." Emerson fingered the cleft in his chin, leaving a smear of ink on that admirably modeled member. "I suppose you have a few ideas? You always do."

"Naturally. Everyone knows that you are in a temper

with Maspero; it would be quite in character for you to declare you won't excavate in Egypt this year. Our movements will be observed and commented upon, and we must have a sensible reason for traveling to the Sudan. For instance, a survey of the Meroitic sites, with a view to future excavation."

"That might work," Emerson admitted. "With the dam at Aswan about to be raised, a number of the sites will be underwater all or part of the time." He put down his pen and smiled at me. "As always, Peabody, you are the voice of conscience and common sense. I confess that I hadn't given that aspect of the case much thought."

"You had better," I retorted. The compliment and the smile had softened me, but I felt it advisable to hammer the point home while Emerson was in a chastened mood. "Covering our tracks won't be easy, but it must be done. Otherwise we will have a pack of journalists, archaeologists, and treasure hunters on our trail, not to mention Walter and Evelyn."

Emerson's fingers twitched. He had only agreed with me so that I would go away and let him get back to work. "Confound it, Peabody, your suggestion about excavating in the Sudan makes perfectly good sense, and I am willing to accept it. There is no reason why anyone should doubt the story. Why are you anticipating difficulties that don't exist?"

"Better safe than sorry, Emerson."

"I might have known you would answer with an aphorism," Emerson grumbled. "Oh, the devil, do as you like. I leave it to you to cover our tracks, as you put it."

I had thought he would.

"I have made one of my little lists," I explained, removing the paper from my pocket.

Emerson grinned reluctantly. "I thought you would."

"The first thing is to get Merasen away from here as soon as possible. That we have had such a visitor is known to the servants, but even Gargery, with all his poking and prying, has only the vaguest notion of where he came from or why. Gargery has not enough experience to realize how unusual he is, in appearance, language, and manner, but I assure you, it would not take David long to begin wondering about him."

"That's sensible, I suppose," Emerson admitted. "What do you propose to do with him?"

"Send him on ahead of us to Egypt and to Wadi Halfa."

"On his own?"

"He got here all the way from the Sudan, on his own." Emerson frowned, and I said impatiently, "We will supply him with ample funds and specific directions. The longer he remains, the greater the danger that someone will become curious about his antecedents. What if Kevin O'Connell should drop in without warning, as he is inclined to do? What if Evelyn and Walter should decide to pay us a visit? One word from Merasen in the language of the Holy Mountain, and Walter's linguistic antennae would be quivering."

"Hmph. I must admit," Emerson admitted, "that you have made a point. Very well, I will take the boy to London and make arrangements. What else?"

"You will announce your intentions to the Department of Antiquities— Yes, Emerson, you must. It might be a good idea for you to write to Mr. Breasted—he is back in Chicago, I suppose—and ask him about his survey in Nubia last winter. It must all be open and aboveboard. I propose that we announce we are going directly to Meroe. It is three hundred miles south of Napata, where we were working in '97, and from which we disappeared into the desert, as the journalists so poetically put it. That should put people off the track."

"It will put us off the track, too, by a long distance," Emerson protested.

"We needn't actually go to Meroe," I said impatiently. "So long as people believe we are *not* going to Napata."

Merasen was rather pleased than otherwise to leave us.

We were not very entertaining company for a lively lad whose ideas of amusement were quite different from ours. (I had not seen fit to mention to Emerson that one of the reasons why I wanted him out of the way had to do with the housemaids.) After all, what was there for him to do? We had forbidden him to leave the grounds, and the library was of no interest to him. The men of the Holy Mountain were noted archers, but he had haughtily refused to display his skill, claiming we had no bow worthy of his strength. From time to time Ramses resignedly consented to wrestle with him, but those sessions did not last long, since Ramses was uncommonly rough with him. After one such encounter, which ended (after approximately thirty seconds) with Merasen doubled up like a worm, whooping for breath, Nefret remonstrated. Ramses's only response was a curt "He asked for it." This did not improve relations between Ramses and Nefret, but even she did not object when Emerson took the boy up to London in order to put him on a boat to Port Said. His necessarily extended journey from the Sudan to Cairo, and thence to England, had familiarized him with the country and the language, and he assured us that he had made friends along the way. (I suspected, from his complacent smile, that most of the friends were female.)

"He appears to be taking this delay rather lightly," said Ramses, after we had said farewell to the travelers. "One would have expected him to urge us to press on."

"Why do you constantly find fault with him?" Nefret demanded. "We promised we would follow as soon as is humanly possible, and he knew we would keep our word."

Ramses shrugged and looked particularly enigmatic. Seeing that Nefret was about to pursue the matter, I said, "He has the fatalism of his people—a quality we might be well advised to emulate at this time. What has happened, has happened. We cannot change the past. Nefret, have you any idea what this mysterious illness might be?"

It was Nefret's turn to shrug. "Merasen wasn't much help when it came to describing precise symptoms. It could be something as simple as malaria, or something as deadly as an unknown tropical disease."

"What did you two talk about then?" I asked, for I had wondered before.

"All sorts of things." Her eyes shifted, avoiding mine. "He is immensely curious about England."

"And I," said Ramses, "have been immensely curious about the Holy Mountain. Things must have changed a good deal in ten years, but I wasn't able to get much practical information out of him. Did you have better luck?"

"There haven't been that many changes," Nefret said somewhat defensively.

"I find that hard to believe," said Ramses, raising his expressive eyebrows. "When we took our hasty departure, Tarek had not yet overcome all those who opposed him. His brother Nastasen was dead, but Forthright, your renegade cousin, was still on the loose, and so was the old High Priest of Amon, who had supported Nastasen."

"I also questioned Merasen about them," I said. "He claimed he had never heard of Reggie Forthright."

"What's so surprising about that?" Nefret demanded. "Merasen was only seven or eight years old at the time. Reggie must have been caught by Tarek and executed, as he well deserved. The High Priest of Amon too; he was the ringleader of the rebels."

"There was also a social revolution," Ramses persisted. "Tarek wanted to improve the living conditions of the rekkit, who were no better than slaves. I drew a dead blank when I asked Merasen about that."

"He doesn't strike me as interested in social reform," I remarked. "And it is possible that the changes Tarek hoped to make were frustrated by the dead hand of tradition. If Emerson is correct in believing the rekkit were the original inhabitants of the Holy Mountain, they have been enslaved since the first Egyptians arrived there. What a sad commentary on human nature that the strong do not succor and assist the weak, but rather—"

"How well you put it, Mother," said Ramses.

I took the hint. "Ah, well, we will learn the truth when we get there."

Ramses said under his breath, "If we get there."

Emerson returned from London to announce he had sent Merasen on his way, and that the boy appeared to be looking forward to the journey.

"He doesn't lack self-confidence, I'll say that for him," was Emerson's comment. "Before I got him on board I took him to the Museum and he—"

"For pity's sake, Emerson, why did you do that?" I demanded. "I was under the impression that we wanted to keep him away from people who might suspect his origins."

"Oh," said Emerson self-consciously. "Well, but it's all right, Peabody. The only person we ran into was Budge, and he wouldn't know a Bishari tribesman from a Bedouin."

"That is pure nonsense, Emerson, and you know it. Budge may have attained his position as keeper of Egyptian and Assyrian Antiquities because of his underhanded methods of acquiring artifacts for the Museum, but he has been often in Egypt and the Sudan. Didn't he ask you about Merasen? What the devil did you go there for?"

"I only wanted to show the boy a few objects and get his opinion," Emerson said defensively. "Budge was his usual self, supercilious and insulting. He completely ignored the boy."

"Oh, really? What precisely did Mr. Budge say?"

"Er. You see, as it happened, we were in the section devoted to Meroitic material, and Budge . . . er."

"Asked where you meant to work this year."

Emerson can only be pushed so far. My accusatory tone brought a wicked sparkle to his sapphirine orbs. "Curse it,

Peabody, you told me to be open and aboveboard about our plans."

"Well," I said. "David is due tomorrow, and *we* are overdue for a conference. Shall we meet in the library in half an hour?"

When Emerson got there, now divested of his traveling attire and wearing comfortable rumpled garments, we were waiting for him. Emerson looked at me, settled at his desk with my papers spread out in front of me, and went at once to the table where the decanters were kept.

"Whiskey and soda, Peabody?" he inquired.

"It is too early, Emerson."

"No, it isn't, Peabody. Here. I admit," Emerson went on, settling into a comfortable overstuffed chair near the bust of Socrates, "that perhaps I acted a bit rashly by taking Merasen to the British Museum. I allowed professional curiosity to overcome me."

"I wonder," said Ramses, "if we have fully considered the implications of this venture."

"No doubt you will enlighten us," I remarked.

"Let the boy speak, Peabody," said Emerson, taking out his pipe. "Without, if you please, interrupting him!"

"Thank you, Father. I've been thinking it over, and I have reached the conclusion that this expedition must mark the end of the Holy Mountain's isolation—or at least the beginning of the end. It was bound to happen sooner rather than later. The lure of the lost oases of the Western Desert has never faded, and lately there seems to have been a resurgence of interest. The *Journal of the Royal Geographical Society* had an article only last month about 'The Zerzura Problem.' "

"But the lost city of Zerzura is a legend," I exclaimed. "I remember reading about it in the *Book of Hidden Pearls,* which is nothing more than a medieval collection of fairy tales."

"It is a little more than a legend, Mother, as you are well

aware. The fellows of the Royal Geographical Society are too hardheaded to give credence to legends, but many of them believe there are undiscovered oases in the Libyan Desert. In another few years, if the technology continues to improve as it has done, someone will develop a motorcar that is capable of desert travel, and that will extend the possible range of exploration. As for our trip—I would take certain risks for Tarek, but I will be damned if I will take the risk of mounting any but a large-scale expedition. It is to our advantage to keep our purpose secret beforehand, since we don't want a pack of curiosity seekers and treasure hunters following us, but if we do get there and return, the men who accompany us will spread the word. We can hardly imprison or intimidate all of them." He straightened, hands still in his pockets, and looked challengingly from me to Nefret, who was biting her lip, to his father, who was placidly smoking his pipe. "It's the truth, isn't it?"

"Yes," I admitted.

"But that would be a catastrophe," Nefret exclaimed. "Once the Holy Mountain is known to the world, it will be exploited by treasure hunters and adventurers."

"And archaeologists," said Emerson, scowling. "Men like Budge, who will tear the place apart collecting artifacts for his cursed museum. No doubt you have anticipated this little difficulty, Peabody, and have considered methods of preventing it?"

"I have a few ideas. However," I went on, before Emerson could express his skepticism, "I see no point in discussing them in vacuo, so to speak. At present we have no idea what sort of reception we will receive or what conditions we are likely to encounter. We are agreed, are we not, that until we reach the point of no return—"

"I don't like the sound of that," Emerson muttered.

"The point at which we set out on the final journey—"

"That's not much better, Peabody."

"Oh, Emerson, do be quiet. You know what I mean. Until our expedition is ready to go into the desert, we should be able to keep people in the dark as to our real goal. We have discussed this in general, but we must work out the details—what we must do, what we must say—and to whom it must be said—in order to add verisimilitude to an otherwise—"

"All right, Peabody, all right. Have another whiskey and don't quote Gilbert and Sullivan at me."

By the time David arrived the following afternoon, we had put together a convincing fiction, though it did not really cover all the contingencies and I had an uneasy feeling (I would have called it a premonition if Emerson did not object to my using that word) that we had not anticipated everything.

At first David could talk of nothing but Lia—her grace, her sweetness, her beauty, the interminable years that must pass before he could call her his. She was not yet eighteen, and, as he admitted, he was in no position to support a wife. Not until after dinner, when we retired to the sitting room for coffee, did he ask about our strange visitor, concerning whom he had heard from Gargery.

"Yes, a most interesting young fellow," Emerson said, fussing with his pipe. "His grandfather is an old acquaintance of mine—sheikh of a village in the Sudan, who sent the boy to England to—er—broaden him, and, incidentally, to tell me about some interesting ruins west of Meroe that have never been investigated. I have therefore decided to spend the autumn in a survey of Upper Nubian archaeological sites. I won't be needing you, David, so you may as well accept that offer from Constable."

David looked bewildered, as well he might. Emerson's open, candid nature is not suited to deception. Instead of working up to his conclusion with a wealth of confirmatory detail, he had simply thrown it at David.

"But, sir," he stammered. "That is . . . how did you . . . I don't understand."

"It's very simple," said Emerson, to whom it was; when

he makes a decision, he expects everyone will accept it. "I don't need you, Constable does."

David turned in silent appeal to Ramses, who said easily, "I told Father about the offer from Constable, David. He agreed that it was an opportunity you shouldn't miss."

"But your plans—" David began.

"Have nothing to do with yours," Ramses cut in. "Father means to leave almost at once, and we will finish the most important part of the survey within a few months. I'll go to Germany in January."

Nefret took David's hand and squeezed it. "Lia will be so happy. She was in tears when she spoke of your leaving."

"She was?" The idea of Lia in tears brought moisture to David's soft brown eyes.

"Oh, she'd have sent you off with a brave smile, but," said Nefret, "her heart would be breaking."

I thought she was carrying the pathos a little too far, so I said briskly, "So that is settled. Why don't you ask Gargery to see if he can place a telephone call to Yorkshire, so you can tell Lia the good news?"

"I had better find out whether Constable are still interested," David said slowly.

"They are," I said. David turned to stare at me. Having put my foot in my mouth, I attempted to extract it. "I took the liberty of ringing them up yesterday," I explained. "Mr. Constable was delighted. I—er—wanted to be certain the position was still open before I—we—discussed it with you."

"I see," David said.

"I hope you don't mind, dear."

"Not at all, Aunt Amelia. It was good of you." His eyes moved from me to Ramses. "Come up for a talk?"

I saw Ramses brace himself. He hated to lie to his friend, but I knew he would do it if he had to. And he would have to. David was still hesitating, and no wonder. The story we had concocted was the best we could come up with, but trained copyists would be at a premium on such an expedition and here we were proposing to do without one of the best.

"Do you think we convinced him?" Nefret asked, after the two boys had left the room together.

"Convince be damned," said Emerson. "He will do as he is told. What the devil, one would suppose a young lover would leap at the chance to be with his betrothed, eh, Peabody?"

"What a romantic you are, Emerson."

Whatever Ramses's arguments, they achieved the desired end. David demurred no longer. He went up to London to confer with the publisher and returned bursting with excitement about his assignment—a series of portraits of Egyptian kings and queens, based on statues and, in some cases, actual mummies, but of course "prettified," as David put it, for modern tastes. He and Ramses and Nefret pored over volumes of photographs and engravings, selecting the representations David meant to use. They all appeared to enjoy this; a good deal of laughter and a few rude comments issued from David's room when they were there together.

Perhaps it was the imminence of separation that made them so fond with one another. Even Ramses was less aloof, submitting to Nefret's impulsive sisterly embraces with a smiling grace he had not exhibited for a long time. He had his reclusive moments; from time to time he would go off on long, solitary rambles across the countryside, returning soaked with perspiration and scratched by brambles. I thought he was overdoing it, and said so. He replied that he was trying to get in fit condition for the arduous labors that lay ahead. If by "fit" he meant thin, he certainly achieved that condition. Rose wrung her hands over him and had cook make all his favorite dishes.

By the time we left England, he was as brown and as lean as one of the ancient wooden statues in the Cairo Museum. "You look more and more like Count Hesi-Re," Nefret remarked. She poked him in the chest with a slim forefinger. "Ow. You feel like him too. Solid wood."

"I take that as a compliment," said Ramses. "He's not a bad-looking chap. Shall I grow a mustache to further the resemblance?"

"No, I don't like mustaches. Or beards."

"You may have to put up with them," said Emerson, who had listened to the exchange with interest. He gave me a challenging look and fingered the cleft in his prominent chin. "Can't waste water shaving in the desert."

Emerson is always looking for an excuse to grow a beard. I refused to rise to the challenge. But I made sure his razors were packed.

Once we had announced our departure, Walter and Evelyn came hurrying from Yorkshire to pay us a farewell visit. They brought Lia, naturally, and David said no more about accompanying us. (Love—if I may be permitted a poetic metaphor—settles like a warm blanket on the brain, smothering the critical faculties.)

Walter was not so easily hornswoggled (a most expressive slang word, which I had learned from Cyrus Vandergelt). He managed to corner Emerson and me one afternoon, while Nefret was entertaining Evelyn.

"This is your first visit to the Sudan in a long time," he began.

"Er—yes," said Emerson.

"We wanted then to excavate at Meroe, as you recall," I said, realizing that Emerson was not up to the task of convincing deception. "Since the expeditionary armies had not got that far in '97 and the southern Sudan was still in the hands of the Dervishes, we were forced to settle for Napata. Now we have the opportunity to do a comprehensive survey of the region, and I am told that conditions have improved greatly."

"Yes, I see. So you have no intention of returning to . . . you know the place."

"Walter, you are letting your imagination run away with you," I declared. "Why on earth would we do such a foolish thing? There are a number of nice ruins in Nubia, including pyramids, and they are vanishing at alarming speed. Our primary duty is to preserve and record those specimens of the past. Emerson believes that the remains of the ancient city of Meroe lie under the sands. What a contribution to science its discovery would be!"

"I've never heard such a pack of lies, not even from you, Peabody," said Emerson, after Walter had left us.

"If you think over what I said, Emerson, you will do me the credit of conceding that I did not tell a single falsehood. I never do, unless it is absolutely necessary."

I heard nothing from Kevin O'Connell. Inquiries produced the information that he was in hospital in Switzerland, having fallen off a mountain while following up a ridiculous rumor that the remains of the Ark of the Deluge had been seen there. I was not at all surprised; Kevin specialized in ancient curses and wild invention. After almost dying of exposure, he was making a good recovery, but it would be some time before he could return to work. I sent him a nice box of glacéed apricots from Fortnum and Mason.

One of the advantages of our itinerary (one of the few advantages, I should say) was that we could not possibly take a cat along. One or another of them, starting with Ramses's lost but never-to-be-forgotten Bastet, had usually accompanied us to Egypt, but travel in the Sudan was still inconvenient and complicated—and the very idea of Horus riding a camel through the desert for two weeks boggled the mind. Neither Horus nor Gargery approved of the former's staying at Amarna House, and we left both of them sulking.

On the day of our departure we stood at the rail of the steamer waving farewell to those who had come to see us off. The family had turned out in force, including two of Lia's brothers. Johnny and Willie were as alike as two peas, with their father's refined features and their mother's fair hair, but their temperaments were quite different; Willie was a serious soul and Johnny as ebullient as a schoolboy. He was livelier even than usual that day, playing the clown to keep spirits high; for parting is always painful. He had one arm round David's shoulders and the other round Lia. The twins had been unwavering in their support for the lovers; their influence, as much as my own, had helped to win over their parents. Catching my fond eye, Johnny raised his voice to a bellow. "Don't worry, Aunt Amelia, we'll make sure they behave themselves." He directed a low-voiced comment to David, who blushed.

The ship moved away. David cupped his hands round his mouth and called out to Ramses, "Good luck, my brother!"

"Good luck in what?" Nefret asked.

"Nothing in particular," Ramses replied. Carefully he detached the little hands that clung to his arm. "Excuse me. I must unpack."

If we could have proceeded directly from Port Said to the Sudan, avoiding all our friends and acquaintances, I would have been sorely tempted to do so. I have no moral objection to prevarication when it serves a good end, but—as I had learned from painful experience—it is cursed difficult to avoid slips of the tongue. I was not worried about Ramses, who could look Saint Peter straight in the eye and lie, nor even about Nefret. Emerson was my chief concern. When in a temper, into which he is easily provoked, he is apt to blurt out the most appalling statements.

To have behaved so unusually would only have invited speculation, which we had to avoid at all costs. A few days in Cairo, collecting supplies, a few more days in Luxor with our Egyptian family (Abdullah's kin), telling them the news for which they hungered, and preparing them for our removal to the Sudan, and then we would be on our way. We should arrive at Wadi Halfa by the first week in September. Another fortnight should complete our preparations, and by that time the weather would be, if not comfortable, endurable.

My complacency received its first check when we docked at Port Said and I beheld a too-familiar form amid the throng of porters, customhouse officials, and souvenir sellers who vied for the attention of the arriving passengers. It was impossible to mistake Daoud, Abdullah's nephew and assistant reis; his elaborate turban towered a full head over those of the people around him, and his large, benevolent face bore a smile of welcome. I had to look again before I recognized the slighter man who stood next to him. Selim, Abdullah's youngest son, seemed to have grown several inches since the previous spring, and the beard he had decided to grow in order to give him greater authority as Abdullah's successor had got out of hand. It was neatly trimmed—Selim was a handsome man and something of a dandy—but it stretched clear down to his breastbone.

"The devil," said Emerson. "What are they doing here? I didn't telegraph. Peabody, did you?"

"No." I returned Daoud's salutation.

Slouching against the rail, Ramses said, "The Cairo newspapers print the passenger lists of incoming boats. The word spreads. I assumed you had anticipated that, Mother."

Nefret chuckled. "Just look at Selim's beard."

"Hmph," said Emerson, staring enviously at the appendage.

Daoud was at the foot of the gangplank when we descended. He never pushed or shoved, for he was the gentlest of men (unless provoked); he simply moved forward with ponderous inevitability, clearing a path. Not the slightest shade of reproach marred the sunshine of his smile, but after he had gone off with Ramses to deal with the luggage and the customs people, Selim bent a freezing frown upon me.

"Why did you creep into the country like thieves, without telegraphing us?"

"We wanted to surprise you," Nefret said, taking hold of his arm. "Selim—the beard! Magnificent!"

Selim preened himself, but his grievance was too strong to be so easily overcome. "We heard it from Mohassib, who had been told by Abdul at the Winter Palace, who overheard a guest reading it from the newspaper. For us to get news of you from such people shames us. And why is David not with you? And why have you not told me where we will be working? And what—"

"Don't lecture me, curse it," Emerson shouted. "At least not in public. Good Gad! You sound just like your father."

There was a slight tremor in his manly voice when he pronounced the last words. He cleared his throat. "Hmph. Well, Peabody, what are we going to do with this insubordinate young rascal?"

I had been against taking Selim and our other devoted men into the unknown. None of them, including Abdullah, had gone with us on our first trip to the Sudan; since we had been working in what was technically a war zone, the military authorities refused to give them permission. However, the situation had changed. Emerson and Ramses had pointed out, with depressing logic, that we would have to take some of them at least as far as Meroe in order to support the story about a survey. A point they had not made, which was now apparent, was that Selim would wax even more insubordinate if we attempted to go off without him.

"Tell him our plans," I said with a sigh and a smile. "I hope you don't mind waiting, Selim, until we are on the train. I want to get out of this pestilential place and into the comforts of Shepheard's as soon as is possible."

Selim folded his arms. "The *Amelia* is ready for you, Sitt. Fatima is there now."

"How did you manage that?" I asked with sincere admiration. We had left the dahabeeyah in dry dock; Selim must have bullied, bribed, and threatened at least a dozen people to get it ready so quickly. All signs of pique forgotten, Emerson grinned and slapped the young man approvingly on the shoulder. He hates hotels.

"I am your reis," said Selim. "The best reis in Egypt,

now that my father is no more. Come. I have the tickets for the train."

The train takes six and a half hours from Port Said to Cairo. Emerson and Ramses promptly removed coats, hats, waistcoats, and cravats, and after an apologetic glance at me Nefret unfastened the top buttons of her frock and pushed her sleeves up. As sand sifted into my collar and mixed with perspiration to form a gritty paste, I reflected that this was only a faint foretaste of the discomfort we could expect as we went farther south. We had never been in Egypt so early in the season. I now remembered why.

At first Selim was not enthusiastic about working in the Sudan. However, when I said he and the others need not accompany us, since we could easily find local workers, his beard positively bristled. "Did you hear that, Daoud?" he demanded. "They say we must stay behind."

"No, no," said Daoud placidly. "Where the Father of Curses goes, we go. Where is it he is going?"

Emerson went on at length about the pyramids at Meroe and their ruinous condition and the need to record what was left of them before they fell apart. It was familiar stuff to Selim, and Daoud didn't really care. When Emerson ran down—after quite a long lecture—Selim nodded and stroked his beard.

"So. It should be an interesting adventure. Local workers we can hire, as you say, but you will need trained men to supervise them. How many?"

There was not room for six in a single cab, especially when one of the six was Daoud, so Nefret asked Selim to ride with her. Very little disturbed Daoud's placid temperament, and he had accepted our explanation of David's absence with a nod. "A man must earn money to support a wife. He will work hard and make her happy. When will they be married? They must come to Egypt for that."

I listened with a smile but only half an ear while he proceeded to plan the wedding, interrupting himself occasionally to thrust his head out the cab window and announce Emerson's presence in stentorian tones. Emerson was not at all put out by this, since he likes his presence to be known, and he was constantly hailing old acquaintances, of whom he has a great many in Cairo. After a rather vulgar exchange with one of these, he turned to Ramses. "So much for making an inconspicuous entry," he remarked. "Half the population of Cairo already knows we are here, and the rest will know by evening."

This caught Daoud's attention. "The presence of the Father of Curses is like the sun rising over the desert," he announced. "Even a blind man feels the warmth of his presence."

"Bah," said Emerson.

We went to the docks at Boulaq, where the *Amelia* lay among others of her kind—not as many as in past years, alas, for the private dahabeeyah was no longer the favored method of travel. Cooks' steamers and the railroad had made tourism a popular business. In my opinion the change was not for the better. What had once been a leisurely, educational trip through the most fascinating country in the world had become a whirlwind tour with no time to inspect the sights and very little contact with the local population. Cooks' people went about in flocks like silly sheep, bleating and herded by their guides. They ate English food, lived in rooms furnished in English style, spoke only English, complained constantly, and bargained mercilessly with individuals whose daily income was a few pennies. I must confess I rather enjoyed seeing such a group set upon by the importunate peddlers and vendors and donkey boys.

Fatima was waiting for us. There were rose petals in the washbasins.

After a week in Cairo we had completed most of our necessary business and there had been no word from Merasen.

"Where can the boy have got to?" I demanded, as we

prepared for a little shopping trip. I needed a new parasol, and Emerson another pair of boots. "I hope nothing untoward has befallen him. I told you we ought to have sent him to lodge with one of your acquaintances in Cairo."

"No, you didn't," Emerson snarled. He was not of the opinion that he required another pair of boots. "The fewer contacts with our acquaintances, the better, you said."

He was correct. I had said that.

"You did tell him to leave a message for us here, announcing his safe arrival in Cairo?"

"I told him to leave word at Shepheard's, since I had anticipated we would be staying there. As you know, they informed me there had been no such message and that they would send on any that might arrive."

"Are you sure he understood?" Nefret asked anxiously. She and Ramses were not going with us. She had met a most interesting lady, a Syrian physician, and had hopes of persuading her to participate in a scheme dear to Nefret's tender heart—a clinic which would offer medical services to the miserable prostitutes of Cairo. Gazing into the mirror, she tipped her hat to one side, frowned, and tipped it to the other side.

"We don't really need him." Ramses was sprawled on the sofa. "We have the map. Maps, rather. It was a good idea of yours, Mother, that each of us should carry a copy."

"Good heavens, you aren't proposing we abandon Merasen, are you?" Nefret demanded. "He may be ill—injured—lost."

"He can't find his way back without us," Emerson said, his brow furrowing. "Striking the Nile without a map is one thing; finding a single isolated spot in the middle of the desert . . ."

"He will turn up," I said firmly. "A message might easily have been mislaid. If we do not hear from him by the time we reach Halfa, I will—er—take steps." In fact I was at something of a loss as to how to proceed without involving the police or Emerson's network of Egyptian gossips.

Nefret turned from the mirror. "Ramses, if you are coming with me, kindly assume proper attire. I want to make a good impression."

"You are impressive enough already; you don't need me decked out in a stiff collar and tie," Ramses retorted.

"Please?" She knelt by him and looked up into his face, dimpling and fluttering her lashes.

"Practicing, are you?" Ramses inquired. "Oh, all right. Be back in a minute."

When he returned he was wearing a new tweed suit I had forced him to purchase in England, a collar that reached clear to his chin, and a nice straw boater. "Will this do?" he inquired.

Nefret studied the effect. Her lips twitched. "You look absurd."

"It's the latest thing," Ramses protested.

"I know. It just doesn't suit you, somehow." She removed the hat and ran her hand over his head, smoothing his ruffled black hair. "That's better."

"Thank you. Can I leave off the collar? It's choking me."

Nefret shook her head, laughing. "I appreciate the effort, dear. What you do suffer for me!"

"You haven't the least idea," said Ramses.

## From Manuscript H

"The lady doesn't dwell in a very elegant neighborhood," Ramses remarked, as Nefret led him deeper into the old city.

"She can't afford better," Nefret said. "It's perfectly respectable. I don't see why you and Selim insisted on coming with me."

She glanced over her shoulder at Selim. The lane was too narrow for all three to walk abreast, especially with donkeys and camels contesting the right of way. Ramses had to admit she was right, though. Unlike the infamous Red Blind districts, this part of Cairo was safe enough; it was just poor and overcrowded and dirty. Every foot of ground was built upon, the old buildings rising two or three stories high and nudging one another on both sides. There was no place to bury trash and no one to carry it off, so it was simply left to lie until an occasional rain washed the worst of it away. Piles of donkey and camel dung added their pungent odors to the sour-sweet smell of rotting fruit. Skirts raised, Nefret picked a path through the mess, and since she had declined to take his arm he fell a little behind so he could stare at her—her walk, the tilt of her head, the knot of golden hair at the nape of her neck—without making her self-conscious.

David believed he had changed his mind about avoiding Nefret. Avoidance had been a selfish and cowardly way out of a situation that was no one's fault; he had always known this, so when he told David he had decided to stick it out, cultivate patience, and enjoy the friendship that meant so much without demanding more, he had been partially sincere. The series of noble-sounding cliches had gone over well with David, innocent that he was, and they had succeeded in convincing him that Ramses was not making a sacrifice on his account.

He couldn't have said what warned him—a flash of movement out of the corner of his eye, a fleeting impression of a face. He gave Nefret a hard shove and twisted aside, not quite in time to avoid a stinging slash across the arm he had raised to protect his face. Turning in the same movement, he saw the boy crouched, facing him, white teeth bared. The weapon he held had a wicked shine, and it was considerably longer than a typical Arab knife.

Pedestrians backed off, leaving a clear space for the combatants. Selim forced his way past a donkey loaded with pots and reached Nefret, who had been flung with considerable force against a shop front. She had breath enough left to swear, though.

"Don't get in his way," Selim warned, catching hold of her.

Merasen's smile broadened. "I give you time to take out your knife."

"I don't need a knife," Ramses said in exasperation. A hard kick sent the weapon flying out of Merasen's hand. It squelched onto the muck of the roadway and Ramses slammed his foot down on it.

"What the hell do you think you're doing?" he demanded.

Merasen cradled his bruised fingers tenderly in his left hand and looked up at Ramses with reproachful black eyes. "It was only a game. To see if you are as good with a knife as with your hands. I did not mean to cut you. It was an accident!"

Nefret pushed Selim away. "Are you hurt, Ramses?"

"The greatest damage is to my expensive new coat," Ramses said sourly. "Mother will have a few words to say about that."

Nefret took his word for it; there wasn't much blood visible against the brown tweed of his sleeve. Ramses caught Merasen by the neck of his galabeeyah and hauled him to his feet.

"My finger is broken," Merasen complained, extending a rigid digit.

"Try that again, my fine young friend, and I'll break all ten of them," Ramses said.

"I am sorry," Merasen said earnestly. "It was only a—"

"Game be damned," Nefret snapped. "Let me see your finger . . . It's not broken, only bruised. I want you to go straightaway to the dahabeeyah and report yourself to the Father of Curses. Can I trust you to do that?"

"Oh, yes." Merasen's smile was seraphic.

"Not on your life," Ramses said, tightening his grip. "I will deliver you personally, my lad. Nefret, do you go on with Selim."

Selim had retrieved Merasen's weapon, just in time to prevent a hopeful scavenger from making off with it. It would have fetched a fair price; the blade shone steely gray, and the hilt was decorated with strips of gold.

Merasen made a grab for it. Ramses knocked his arm down.

"Goddamn it," he said. "How long have you been carrying that around with you? If it fell into the wrong hands . . ."

He feared it already had. Selim had wiped the blade clean and was examining it curiously. "I have never seen one like it, Ramses. Too long for a knife, too short for a sword, and too richly decorated. Who is this man and where does he come from?"

"I'll introduce you properly at a later time," Ramses said. "Go with Nefret."

"Perhaps we should help you take Merasen to the dahabeeyah," Nefret said uncertainly.

"Doctor Sophia is expecting you. I assure you, Nefret, I can manage him all by my little self. Merasen, I'll break your arm if you give me any trouble."

Merasen made no attempt to wrench away from Ramses's grip. He was as cheerful and unrepentant as a little boy who has smacked someone with a snowball. Maybe rough-and-tumble wrestling was a custom of the Holy Mountain I missed, Ramses thought. But in most of the cultures with which he was familiar, you didn't attack without warning and with a sharp blade unless you meant to damage the other fellow.

He had directed Selim to take charge of the sword-knife and keep it out of sight, a galabeeyah being more appropriate for such concealment than European trousers. "Be careful you don't slash your leg," he had added, and Nefret had said, laughing, "Or something else. I'll rig up some sort of scabbard for it when we're at Doctor Sophia's, Selim."

She had inspected Merasen's finger but she hadn't even bothered to look at Ramses's arm. What did you expect, Ramses asked himself—that she would rush to you, all aquiver at the sight of your blood? The answer was no—not Nefret—it wasn't the first time—but she might have been a little less nonchalant and a little harder on Merasen.

"Where have you been staying?" he asked, cutting into a vivacious description of Merasen's opinion of Cairo (too big, very dirty, and the women all hiding behind veils). "We may as well collect your luggage before we go on."

Ramses knew the place; it was one of the better-quality lodging houses for "natives." Merasen swaggered off to get his suitcase and the proprietor greeted Ramses obsequiously but without surprise.

"He said you would come—you or the Father of Curses," he explained.

"Did he indeed?"

"He said the Father of Curses would pay."

Merasen came back carrying a heavy case which Emerson must have bought for him in London. His unrepentant smile made Ramses want to shout at him, but this was not the time nor the place to ask what Merasen had done with the generous funds Emerson had given him. Nor was there any use berating him for the damage he had done with his boasts and his extravagance. It was too late now.

⁝

# Three

$\mathbf{E}$merson claimed the boots were too tight. They were certainly tighter than the old pair, which had been battered into shapelessness by several seasons of hard usage. The bootmaker assured him the fit was perfect and I reminded him that new boots are always a trifle stiff, and we had a little discussion.

We then proceeded to the umbrella maker (Emerson limping ostentatiously). I always purchase my parasols at the same shop; the manager has become accustomed to my requirements, which were, I admit, somewhat unusual: a heavy steel shaft and a sharpened tip. For all-round utility, nothing beats a good stout parasol. It serves as a sunshade, a walking stick, and if necessary a weapon. Persons bent on mischief do not expect to be struck by a lady with a parasol. This, as I hardly need point out, gives the lady the advantage of surprise. An additional advantage was the superstitious awe with which some Egyptians regarded the implement. Daoud's tales (a few of them true) had woven an aura of magic about the parasol, and in some quarters it was only necessary for me to brandish it in order to cow an adversary.

That afternoon the parasol served a more conventional purpose, for the sun was hot. Emerson refused its shade and removed himself to a little distance to avoid being prodded by the spokes, so we were forced to converse in shouts to be heard over the bustle of the street. A good deal of the noise was occasioned by animals. There were a few motorcars in Cairo, but most of the traffic was four-footed—horses pulling cabs, donkeys pulling carts, camels heavily laden with everything from sacks of grain to packing cases, and complaining bitterly, as is a camel's wont. Choked by dust, and miserably warm in the proper garments I had assumed, I finally furled the parasol and poked Emerson, who had stopped to chat with one of the dirtiest individuals I had ever beheld and who had slung round his neck a tray of the most dubious scarabs I had ever seen.

"Let us take a cab, Emerson."

"What for?" Emerson demanded. The dirty peddler salaamed and handed me one of the scarabs. It appeared to have been chipped out of a chunk of limestone by a person whose artistic taste was as impaired as his eyesight. I handed it back to him. Emerson, who had removed his coat and lost his hat, studied me more closely. "A bit warm, are you? Why are you wearing those confounded tight-fitting clothes?"

"Because I chose to do so."

"Ah," said Emerson, recognizing a certain tone in my voice. "In that case. . . ."

He handed over a few coins—in exchange for information received, I supposed, since he refused to accept a scarab—bade the peddler an effusive farewell, and hailed a cab.

"What did your unwashed friend have to say that was so interesting?" I asked.

Emerson pushed the parasol out of his way and settled himself on the seat next to me. "He asked why we were going to the Sudan instead of remaining in a civilized country."

"Good Gad, does every beggar in Cairo know?"

"We made no secret of that part of our plan," Emerson reminded me. "Even if we had, the supplies we've been collecting would tell the tale. Especially the money. One doesn't carry that amount of coinage about unless one is going into a remote region." He hesitated for a moment. "However, he also inquired whether we were looking for gold."

"Oh dear," I said in dismay. "I don't like that at all, Emerson. What put such a notion into his head?"

Emerson fingered the cleft in his chin. "People. 'People are saying.' The usual sort of vague speculation. It may not mean anything, Peabody. 'People' have lurid imaginations, especially where we are concerned. Archaeologists have always been suspect, my dear. It is difficult for 'people' to understand why they waste time looking for broken scraps instead of treasure."

Upon reaching the *Amelia* I would have hastened to change had not Mahmud the steward intercepted us and informed us that Ramses requested that we join him in the saloon immediately.

"He's back already, is he?" Emerson inquired. "Is Nur Misur with him?"

("Light of Egypt" was Nefret's beautiful Arabic name.)

"No, Father of Curses." Mahmud rolled his eyes. "But someone else is."

Two others were, in fact. Daoud had dropped by; he had become fond of the English custom of tea and appreciated Fatima's sandwiches and biscuits. In his courteous fashion he was attempting to carry on a conversation with Merasen, while Ramses watched them both in silence. Emerson let out an exclamation of surprise and relief when he saw Merasen. The boy at once got to his feet and began bowing. Ramses was somewhat slower to rise. "Good afternoon, Mother. Good afternoon—"

"Where did you find him?" Emerson demanded.

"He did not find me. I found him," said Merasen complacently.

Ramses's lips tightened infinitesimally. I had observed he was still wearing his coat, which he generally removed as soon as he was in private. The clues were sufficient. "Very well, Ramses," I said. "Take off your coat. I see you have already damaged it. What happened? And where is Nefret?"

"Gone on with Selim to her appointment." Ramses shrugged out of the garment. "We—er—ran into Merasen along the way, and I brought him back with me. Sorry about the coat, Mother. Perhaps it can be mended."

"Not your shirt, though." The left sleeve was stiff with dried blood. "*What happened?*"

"I did it," Merasen admitted. "I did not mean to. It was only a game. He put his arm in the way."

"Careless of me," said Ramses.

Daoud's broad brow wrinkled. "We do not use knives here unless we mean to kill," he said severely. "Be careful, boy, or I will show you how *we* play such games."

"It's all right, Daoud," Ramses said. Merasen gave Daoud a hostile stare.

The cut was shallow. I cleaned and bandaged it while Ramses gave us a brief account of the encounter. Emerson listened in silence, his gaze moving from one young face to the other. Merasen began to squirm under that keen regard.

"It was the wrong thing to do? In the city of the Holy Mountain—"

"We don't do that sort of thing here," said Emerson mildly. "Why are you still in Cairo?"

"I have no more money, Father of Curses. The ticket for the train costs much money." He gave Emerson a broad, innocent smile.

"You had ample funds for the entire journey to Wadi Halfa," said Emerson, in the same quiet voice. "What did you spend it on?"

"I did not spend it! I was robbed. Here, in Cairo. There are many thieves here."

He was certainly right about that. However, this statement was in the same category as others he had made: reasonable, but not susceptible to proof. Under interrogation he said that he had just recently discovered that we were on the *Amelia* and had been about to present himself when he saw Ramses and Nefret leave the boat. He followed them—meaning, as he explained earnestly, to give them a little surprise. While he was explaining, Nefret and Selim came in. She acknowledged Merasen's bows with a rather curt nod and Daoud's greeting with a hug, then took the pins from her hat and tossed it onto a chair.

"I deduce there was no trouble, or Merasen wouldn't be waving his arms so energetically," she said. "I told Mahmud to serve tea. Ramses, are you all right?"

"Flaunting my bandages for the purpose of inspiring sympathy," said Ramses. "It was my fault, for getting my arm in the way."

"Huh," said Selim. Modestly turning his back, he flipped up the skirts of his robe and removed an object which he handed to Emerson. Someone, presumably Nefret, had wound bandages round the blade, but the shape and design of the hilt were familiar to me.

As they were to Emerson. "Why didn't you tell me you had this, Merasen?" he inquired.

"It was not your affair, Father of Curses," said Merasen, repeating a phrase he had probably heard from me (addressed to Gargery).

Emerson ignored this bit of impertinence. "How did it escape the attention of the slavers who robbed you?"

"I stole it back before I escaped. It is sacred to me."

Mahmud came in with the tea tray, which he placed on the table in front of me. He stared curiously at Merasen. I could understand why. On the surface, Merasen could have passed as an Egyptian; Egypt is a country of mixed races, and Cairo has examples of all of them, from fair-skinned Berbers to the darker tribes of the south. The young man was wearing ordinary Egyptian dress and red leather slippers, but there was something about him . . . Perhaps the word was arrogance. He was a prince in his own land, and although he had undoubtedly met with contempt and ill-treatment since he left it, his self-esteem had not been damaged.

He had demonstrated increasing resentment of our questions and implicit criticisms. Rising, he fixed us with a frown. "I will go to my room now," he announced, and stalked out.

"My room, in point of fact," remarked Ramses. "The lad has got a bit above himself, hasn't he?"

"He reminds me of you," I said, pouring tea.

"Good Lord, Mother, I was never that rude!"

"No," I conceded. "But there were times when you looked down your nose at me and curled your lip in precisely that fashion. He is young and a stranger in a strange land, and arrogance is sometimes a way of disguising an underlying sense of insecurity."

"Don't talk psychology, Peabody," Emerson muttered. "Arrogance is one thing; attacking a friend without warning is—"

"A custom of the Holy Mountain," Nefret said. We all looked at her in surprise. She flushed a little. "I'd forgotten. The younger men used to challenge one another, with daggers and short swords. Rather like a duel, to prove their manhood and test their alertness."

"Hmph," said Emerson. "I suppose they also boasted of their scars, like German university students. Damn fools." He stripped off the makeshift sheath and examined the blade. "Steel. They had only iron when we were last there."

"A good many things have changed, I expect," I began, and almost swallowed my tongue when I caught the eye of Selim, who was poised on the edge of his chair, holding his cup like an offensive weapon.

"Where is *there*?" he inquired. "Have you told me the truth, Father of Curses?"

Daoud let out a rumble of protest. "The Father of Curses does not lie."

Emerson might have blustered with Selim but the trusting gaze of Daoud brought a faint blush to his tanned cheeks. "Er," he said. "That is . . . Peabody?"

He did not want to lie to Daoud. He wanted me to do it. The best I could do was resort to the tale Emerson had told David—that Merasen was the son of a sheikh who ruled a remote village in the southern Sudan. It had passed muster with David, but David had never set eyes on Merasen or on that unusual, distinctive sword.

"So it is not to Meroe that you go, but to this . . . village?" Selim persisted. "It must be remote indeed, for never have I seen a weapon like that one. Do all the people of this . . . village attack a friend without warning?"

Emerson felt it incumbent on him to say something, and this question he could answer without being guilty of more than a bit of fudging. "No, no," he said heartily. "The sheikh is an old friend and a man of honor."

"There will be no danger," said Daoud calmly. "We will be with them, Selim."

He and Selim were staying with relatives, since there was no room on the dahabeeyah. After they had taken their leave I reached for a cucumber sandwich, but Daoud had eaten them all.

"Curse it," I remarked. "That wretched boy has already caused trouble. How many other persons, do you suppose, have seen that bl——blooming sword? We had better send him on his way at once, before someone familiar with the remote villages of the Sudan gets a look at him. I presume he will need to be resupplied with clothing and other necessities; Ramses, can you—"

"He doesn't need anything more," Ramses replied. "At my suggestion we stopped by the house where he has been lodging and collected a handsome calfskin suitcase filled with clothes."

"I purchased them for him in London," Emerson muttered. "So it wasn't the people with whom he lodged who robbed him. They would have taken the lot and probably knocked him over the head. What sort of place was this lodging house?"

Ramses glanced at me. "Respectable enough. They wouldn't have dared rob him. He had announced he was a friend of the Father of Curses."

"And that information will spread too," I said with a sigh. "The sooner we get him on his way, the better. I wonder who else knows about the Emersons' interesting protégé?"

### From Manuscript H

Ramses wondered too. Their carefully crafted plot was beginning to leak like a sieve, and Merasen was the one poking holes in it. He had searched Merasen's suitcase, over the latter's furious objections, and had found several items which, according to Merasen, had also been retrieved from the slavers, including the scabbard for Merasen's sword—an object even more remarkable than the sword itself, with inlaid gold foil over thin strips of wood. He didn't doubt the proprietor of the hotel had also searched the boy's luggage, and he hated to think what the fellow had made of that little item, and how many people he had told of it. Ramses wasn't surprised that Merasen should boast of his acquaintance with the famed and feared Father of Curses, despite the fact that Emerson had emphatically ordered him not to do so, except in a dire emergency. But it was the one thing they had hoped to avoid—their connection with a mysterious youth from an unknown place. There had been no emergency, just Merasen being his normal, boastful self.

The fact was that he didn't like Merasen much, and not only because he had got tired of being jumped on. He knew the real reason for his antipathy: Nefret. She and Merasen had spent a lot of time alone together, conversing in the language that she spoke with increasing fluency. Ramses hadn't been invited to join them. From the first, Merasen's behavior toward her had a quality that set Ramses's teeth on edge, though he would have been hard-pressed to define it. Deferential, verging on gallant at times, friendly verging on familiar at others . . . He wondered if he would ever get over being jealous of every man she talked to.

Emerson and he took Merasen (and the suitcase) to the station next day and put him on the train to Aswan with his ticket in his hand and his ears ringing with Emerson's instructions. Emerson was no fool; he too had had his doubts about the purported theft of Merasen's money.

"You have more than enough to get you to Wadi Halfa in comfort," he said sternly. "Go to the house of my friend Sheikh Nur ed Din and await us there. If you fail me in this, Merasen . . ."

"I will not fail you, Father of Curses, I swear!" Merasen had got over his fit of pique and was his smiling, self-confident self. He was wearing European clothes and a tarboosh, and might have been a young clerk or minor official—if one didn't look closely at him. He patted his flat belly. "I have the money belt. If they wish to rob me they will have to take it from my dead hand!"

"Very well, very well," said Emerson. "Maasalemeh. A good journey."

Merasen turned to Ramses and held out his hand. "It is the English custom, yes? To show goodwill. To show you have no . . . what are the words?"

"Hard feelings?" Ramses shook his hand. It would have been rude not to, though his feelings were far from soft. "Good luck, Merasen."

They stood in silence, waiting, until the train left. "Almost teatime," said Emerson, consulting his watch. "Let us go, eh?"

"Go on without me, Father. I have an errand."

"Ah," said Emerson. His heavy brows drew together. "I trust you are not planning anything foolish."

"Not at all, sir. I'll be back in time for dinner."

His "errand" took him to the Gezira Sporting Club. His

father refused to go near the place, since it was an aggressively British institution in the heart of Cairo, complete with golf course, tennis courts, and beautifully landscaped grounds. Ramses maintained his membership at the Gezira and the even more exclusive Turf Club for purely practical reasons; the foreign community, especially the male half of it, frequented both, and they were good places to pick up the sort of gossip his mother probably wouldn't hear from her lady friends. The Gezira admitted some foreigners, including "upper-class" Egyptians, and Ramses knew that when his unquestionably upper-class friend was in Cairo, he generally played golf or tennis at the club before taking tea there—habits he had acquired when he was up at Oxford.

He wasn't on the terrace when Ramses arrived, so Ramses settled himself at a table and surveyed his surroundings. He might have been at an English country house, for the lawn was emerald green and the flower beds were bright with the flowers his mother grew in England—roses and zinnias, petunias and marigolds. A mixed group was playing croquet, the men stripped daringly to shirtsleeves and braces, the ladies in long white dresses and corseted to within an inch of their lives. Ramses wondered idly how they could walk, much less swing a croquet mallet. There was no doubt about it, the female was a lot tougher than the male. Girlish shrieks of laughter arose; apparently some women had to giggle over every stroke, successful or missed. Nefret's laughter was low-pitched and full-throated, and when she missed a stroke or a target, she didn't laugh; she swore.

Finally he saw Feisal coming toward the terrace. Strictly speaking, he was entitled to be called Prince Feisal, since his father was Sheikh Bahsoor, the honored and influential leader of an important Bedouin tribe, and an old friend of Emerson's.

Emerson's "old friends" had become something of a joke in the family; they were scattered up and down the

Nile, from Cairo to Khartoum, and after meeting some of the more disreputable of them Ramses had wondered about the kind of life his father had led during his bachelor years. Emerson didn't talk much about it—at least not to his wife and son.

Feisal was a handsome, hawk-faced young man, and his clothes had obviously come from Bond Street. He carried a tennis racket, and he hailed Ramses with genuine pleasure.

"I heard you were back," he remarked. "How are your distinguished father, and your honored mother, and your beautiful sister?"

They finished the formal exchange of compliments and queries and ordered tea. Ramses wouldn't have minded something stronger, but Feisal was as well known for his piety as for his athletic prowess. He was the unofficial tennis champion of the club and a first-rate shot.

"So it's the Sudan, is it?" Feisal inquired. "Why there? I thought you were all settled at Thebes."

Ramses shrugged. "My father had a falling-out with Maspero."

"And he's punishing the rest of you by dragging you off to Meroe? Or are you looking for Zerzura?"

Ramses managed to conceal his surprise. "It's a myth," he said negligently. "The white city where the king and queen sit sleeping on their thrones, and the key to boundless treasure is in the beak of a carved bird. I thought you'd have abandoned that fantasy by now."

"The fabled city of the little bird is a fairy tale, no doubt." Feisal's long, aristocratic fingers stroked the side of his cup. "But there is an unknown oasis out there, Ramses; Wilkinson mentions it, and Gerhard Rolfe got as far as the edge of the Great Sand Sea before he had to retreat to Siwa, and—" He broke off, smiling. "Did I bore you senseless talking about it last time we met?"

"Idée fixe does come to mind," said Ramses, returning his smile.

"Perhaps. But I'll find it one day, Ramses, wait and see.

If it weren't for my father, I'd start out tomorrow. He'll give me permission one day, so don't you go finding it first."

"Wouldn't dream of it. Whatever gave you the idea we were planning such a thing?"

"Him." Feisal indicated a man sitting alone at a nearby table. He was bareheaded, his hair and beard grizzled, his face brown as a nut and seamed with scars. "Newbold. Calls himself Hunter Newbold. D'you know him?"

"Slightly."

"You don't like him?"

"Not much."

The man's wandering gaze met that of Ramses's. His lips drew back in what was probably intended to be a friendly smile, and he rose and came toward them, limping a little. He was of short stature, but powerfully built, with arms so disproportionately long they looked like a gorilla's.

"Mind if I join you gentlemen?" he asked. He seated himself without waiting for a reply, leaned back in his chair, and hoisted his glass. He wasn't drinking tea. "Good to be back in civilization," he declared.

"How many elephants did you slaughter this time?" Ramses inquired.

Newbold let out a hearty guffaw. "A few. Why not, there are plenty of the brutes and the ladies *will* have their ivory combs and hairbrushes."

Peaceful, herbivorous brutes, who didn't attack unless they or their young were threatened. Unlike human beings. Newbold was the type of Great White Hunter Ramses particularly despised; the man was in demand because he always found impressive game for the parties he led into the interior, but there were a number of unsavory stories about him—rumors that he abandoned his bearers when they became ill or too weak to travel, tales of wounded animals left to die slowly and painfully when pursuit was dangerous—and worse. It was said that not all the ivory he brought back came from beasts he had killed. The previous owners had been handed over to the slavers who still operated in remote regions.

Like everyone else in Cairo, Newbold knew Ramses's views about hunting. His smile was derisive. He drained his glass and snapped his fingers to summon a waiter. "Join me in a whiskey, Mr. Emerson? And you, Your Highness—what will you have? Lemonade?"

Feisal nodded his thanks. "So you didn't find King Solomon's diamond mines? This," he added, glancing at Ramses, "is another man with an idée fixe."

"Africa is full of them," Ramses said.

"Laugh all you want," Newbold grunted. "Africa is also full of unexplored territory, and some of the legends must have a basis in fact. Maybe I've been looking in the wrong area. Been thinking of transferring to the Sudan."

"There are no diamonds there," Ramses said.

"But there's other things." Newbold ordered a third drink—or maybe it was his fourth or fifth. The whiskey had begun to affect him. His eyes glittered and his face was flushed. "When I was in Wadi Halfa I heard an interesting story about a native boy who came out of the Western Desert carrying bars of gold. You wouldn't know anything about that, would you? I hear you and your notorious family are heading for the Sudan."

"We are planning to excavate," Ramses said, trying to hold on to his temper.

Newbold laughed offensively. "Like the last time you were there. Where'd you find the girl, in some rich sheikh's harem? She must have cost you a pretty penny."

Ramses's chair fell over as he rose. Several people turned to stare, and Feisal put a restraining hand on his arm.

"He's drunk, Ramses. Newbold, you damned fool, watch your mouth."

Newbold wasn't that drunk. He studied Ramses with cool calculation. "You wouldn't hit a crippled old hunter who is more than twice your age, would you, boy? Not even when he offends your outdated notions of chivalry toward women? A knight in shining armor, eh?"

Ramses shook off Feisal's hand, and Newbold got unsteadily to his feet. "All right, I apologize. See you in the Sudan."

"Stay out of his way," Feisal advised, as Newbold wove an erratic path toward the door of the clubhouse. The limp was new. Ramses hoped it was an elephant that had gored him.

"Can you imagine telling my father to stay out of the way of a miserable swine like that?"

He had got the information he wanted—or rather, the information he had hoped *not* to get. His notorious father wasn't going to be happy about it, and neither was his equally notorious mother.

⋮

"Dear me," I said. "How disconcerting. I suppose we ought to have anticipated—"

"I certainly did not." Emerson chewed fiercely on the stem of his pipe. We had been enjoying a little preprandial libation in the saloon when Ramses came in. "Didn't you ask the swine from whom he heard about Merasen?"

"Everybody knows he has dealings with slavers," Ramses said. "I assumed . . . You're right, Father, I ought to have pursued the matter. I lost my temper."

"You?" Nefret inquired in exaggerated surprise. "What on earth did he say to bring about that astonishing result?"

"Something about you, perhaps," I said. "You had better tell us, Ramses."

"The point is not his precise words but what they implied," said Ramses. "Merasen and his bloody—excuse me, Mother—his gold, coupled with our declared intention of returning to the Sudan, has reminded people of our last trip to that region and its result. Mother's ingenious story about finding Nefret with a group of kindly missionaries didn't prevent evil-minded persons from gossiping."

"No," I agreed, remembering some of the gossip that

had reached my ears. It had run the gamut of bad taste, from speculation about Nefret's parentage to prurient hints of harems and white slavery. "But at least no one postulated an unknown country of vast treasure."

"That isn't precisely true, Mother," said Ramses, who seemed determined to look on the dark side. "The people who knew Willy Forth had heard of his dream of finding a lost civilization, and before Reggie Forthright set off in search of his missing uncle, he confided in half the officers at Sanam Abu Dom."

"He also babbled to Budge," I said, remembering with dismay a conversation I had had with that gentleman and several of the officers all those years ago.

"I do hope you and young Ramses are not going with the Professor when he sets off in search of the Lost Oasis," Budge had said with a hypocritical look of concern. He had meant it as a joke—a jeer, rather, intended to make Emerson look foolish. But Budge was no fool, however much Emerson might deride his scholarship. Having seen Merasen, was he clever enough to put the pieces together?

A dismal silence ensued. The boat rocked gently at anchor. The sunset colors had died and the stars had come out—though we had to take them on faith, owing to the mixture of mist and smoke that hung over the city like a dark blanket.

"Very well," I said, giving myself a little mental shake—for I had been about to give way to unpleasant forebodings. "Let us consider the worst possible scenario. Who else might harbor suspicions about our real purpose?"

"Aside from Selim?" Ramses inquired. "He saw the damned—excuse me, Mother—the sword. Merasen's landlord probably searched his luggage, which contained several interesting items in addition to the sword. The slavers had seen the gold, and unless they managed to hide it before they were caught, the soldiers saw it too."

Emerson let out a heartfelt swear word. "What about Prince Feisal?"

"He wouldn't interfere with us. But he's in communication with other would-be explorers, and you can be sure our movements are of interest to many of that lot."

"Good Gad," said Nefret in alarm. "Explorers, Egyptologists, slavers, the military . . . Uncle Walter and Aunt Evelyn, of course, and heaven only knows how many random gossips in the antiquities game in Cairo . . . What are we going to do?"

Emerson sucked reflectively on his pipe. It had gone out. He made a face and knocked the ashes out into a receptacle. "Our best hope now is to move fast enough to stay ahead of possible followers. The only alternative would be to squat round the pyramids of Meroe digging innocently and industriously until they give up."

"We can't do that," Nefret exclaimed. "We've lost enough time already."

"I suppose now we will actually have to go to Meroe, in order to throw people off the track," I said with a sigh. "That will mean further delay, transporting ourselves and our gear back north to Napata."

"Don't worry about that," said Emerson. "I have it all worked out."

Ramses's eyebrows shot up. "I hope, Father, you don't intend to strike out into the desert from Meroe? Last time we left from Gebel Barkal, and the route given by the map starts there. Calculating a new route—"

"I have it all worked out," Emerson repeated. "Leave it to me."

"Oh dear," I murmured.

"Your lack of confidence cuts me to the quick, Peabody," said Emerson. "How soon can we be ready to leave Cairo?"

"If the rest of you will condescend to help me supervise the packing, two, possibly three more days."

"Certainly, certainly," said Emerson.

"Ha," I said. "Do we take Selim and Daoud with us? And what about the *Amelia?*"

"We cannot elude Selim," said Ramses. "Any effort to do so would only increase his determination to follow us. Supposing we send him and Daoud off to Luxor tomorrow, with instructions to gather a few of our men and proceed at once to Aswan. We will stick to the story about the interesting ruins west of Meroe until it is no longer possible to conceal our real purpose."

"You mean to go straight through to Aswan, then, without stopping in Luxor?" Emerson asked.

"Are you asking me, sir?" Ramses's dark brows tilted up in surprise.

"You seem to have been more on top of this business than the rest of us," Emerson said.

"Perhaps I have a more suspicious nature than the rest of you." One of Ramses's rare smiles warmed his thin face.

"More suspicious than your mother's? Give her a whiskey, Ramses, she appears to have fallen into a stupor."

"What?" I said with a start. "No, thank you, Ramses, it is time for dinner."

I *had* been in a kind of stupor, induced by sheer consternation. For as we discussed the persons who might know of the Lost Oasis, a name blazoned itself on my brain in letters of fire.

Walter and Evelyn had known—and so had one other individual. I had told him of it myself. To do myself justice, I had not been aware of his true identity at the time, for his masquerade, as one of my old friends, had been perfect. We had first encountered him when he tried to steal the Dahshur treasure out from under our noses, and over the years he had become our most dangerous opponent. He was one of the cleverest men I had ever met, well informed about the antiquities that he specialized in stealing, a master of disguise and a criminal of the deepest dye . . .

Sethos, the Master Criminal.

Rallying, I directed Mahmud to serve dinner. There was no point in mentioning our old nemesis to Emerson, who resented Sethos all the more because of the latter's pro-

fessed attachment to me. No, there was no need. I had
learned how to identify him now, and if he had the audacity
to show his face—one of his many faces—I would know
him and expose him.

We got Selim and Daoud off to Luxor and made arrangements to have the *Amelia* follow at her own pace. It took
longer than I had hoped to gather our supplies, even with
Emerson threatening the merchants. I hadn't had to equip
an expedition of this nature for a long time. Everything
from mosquito netting to tinned biscuits had to be purchased in Cairo, since we could not count on finding them
south of Aswan, and we had to maintain the pretense that
we were bent on archaeological excavation. Cameras and
photographic plates, paper and writing supplies, surveying
instruments, medicines—the list was endless, and I kept
adding to it. Emerson had his own list, and so did Nefret.

The delay was maddening, even though prudence would
have dictated an even longer delay because of the heat. My
sense of urgency had been held at bay hitherto by the im-
possibility of earlier action, but now that we were closer in
space and time to the moment of truth, the more impatient
I became. When there is a dangerous or unpleasant task
ahead, one (I, at any rate) wants to get it over with. I began
to feel as if we were trapped in a web of surmise that
spread daily. The merchants with whom we dealt gossiped
about us, and it proved impossible to avoid all our old
friends, who came round or sent round offering advice.
Emerson's reputation for unreasonableness served us well
with the latter; they had no difficulty in believing he had
settled on the Sudan rather than go hat in hand to M.
Maspero. On the day before our departure we were in receipt of a telegram from Sir Reginald Wingate, the governor general of the Sudan, inviting us, in the most courteous
terms, to call on him in Khartoum.

"The devil," said Emerson. "Does he expect us to go

four hundred miles out of our way to pay him a social visit?"

"He expects us to inform the Sudanese government concerning our plans," Ramses replied. "As other expeditions have done. Wingate has always been interested in Egyptology, and he runs a tight ship."

"Tight, bah," said Emerson. "He let—no, he encouraged!—Budge to rip the pyramids of Meroe apart. Breasted told me some of them had been leveled to the ground and others had huge holes dug through."

He crumpled the telegram in his hand and threw it on the floor.

So much for Sir Reginald, I thought, wondering if we would have his people after us too.

Despite the improvements in transport and communication, travel in the Sudan was still slow and complicated. Between Aswan and Khartoum, the swift flow of the Nile is interrupted by six cataract regions, where navigation is perilous if not actually impossible. From Wadi Halfa, at the foot of the Second Cataract, a railway track ran across the desert to Abu Hamed and thence along the river to Khartoum, but there was still no railway line in the two hundred miles between Aswan and Wadi Halfa. To fill this gap, the government ran a regular service of paddle wheelers from Shellal, the terminus of the Cairo-Aswan line.

It was at Shellal, a few miles south of Aswan, that Emerson had instructed Selim to meet us; and I was not surprised to find him and the others waiting on the platform when the train pulled in. They crowded round, embracing and greeting us, and it was good to see their friendly faces. Selim had selected the best of our men, and the best was very good indeed. There were three of them—Ali, who was in his early twenties, Ibrahim, still strong and stalwart at forty, and Hassan, Selim's cousin. Selim had wanted to bring more, but Emerson had refused. The fewer lives at risk, the better.

The village of Shellal has few amenities, since travelers do not linger there; either they are boarding trains to the north or boats to the south, or they are making an excursion to the temples of Philae—now, alas, under water most of the year. Selim and our fellows had found lodgings which they were very pleased to leave, since they did not measure up to the standards of cleanliness to which they were accustomed.

I had a feeling they would not approve of the boat either.

The government steamers are comfortable and well maintained; but Emerson, being Emerson, rejected them in favor of a dilapidated boat owned by a friend of his. The stern-wheel looked as if it was about to fall off, and the reis, whose name was Farah, was so cross-eyed that both eyes appeared to be staring straight at the end of his nose. When I expostulated, Emerson reminded me that we meant to have as little as possible to do with the government.

"He has you there, Aunt Amelia," said Nefret, as Emerson went off with Farah and Daoud to direct the loading of our baggage. She took off her broad-brimmed hat and fanned away a swarm of gnats. "Don't worry, I brought quantities of insecticides and disinfectants. Shall we go on board?"

"Not until we have to," I said with a slight shudder. "So, Selim, what do you think of Aswan?"

"An ugly place," said Selim promptly. "Not like Luxor."

"That is pure parochialism," I retorted. Selim, who did not know the word, widened his eyes at me. "It is a pretty town, with many points of interest."

"The dam is interesting," Selim conceded. "I talked to one of the engineers, who told me how the sluices work. They are all open now, because the river began to rise in July, but they will be closed, one at a time, until winter."

His cultivated air of superiority had been replaced by the enthusiasm he displayed toward mechanical and engineering subjects, and I knew he would go on and on about the cursed dam unless I stopped him.

"Who was this person?"

"Moncrieff," said Selim. "He was a friend of Emerson's, and he said he hoped he would see you all when you were in Aswan. How long will we stay here?"

"Emerson means to get off at once," I said, mentally adding another group of curious persons to the list. Moncrieff was a pleasant fellow and a dreadful gossip. "We may as well inspect our quarters and start cleaning them. Selim—"

"I must help the men load," said Selim, retreating in haste.

I suppose it is difficult to keep a dock neat and tidy. This one looked as if no one had even tried. Nefret and I picked our way through rusting tools and coils of rope, puddles of oil that shone greasily in the sunlight, and other objects I will not mention, to a shady spot beside one of the loading sheds. There was a good deal of bustle. Not only our men, but porters carrying cargo and several individuals in European clothing who appeared to be passengers. Either they were in too much of a hurry to wait for the government steamer, or they had bargained with Farah for a lower fare.

### From Manuscript H

As he stood watching the loading, Ramses was conscious of what his mother would have called a hideous premonition. He knew what had caused it. There were too many people—the wrong sort of people—preparing to board Farah's wretched vessel.

The scene was familiar to him: porters trotting back and forth with their heavy loads, their half-naked bodies gleaming with sweat. Their complexions ranged in color from pale brown to deep black, and their features showed the mixture of races found in the region—Arab and Bagheera, Dinka and Shilluk. A few women were present, carrying trays of fruit and trinkets they hoped to peddle to the travelers. Some wore the enveloping black burka, but most of them were unveiled, their bodies—more or less—covered with strips of bright fabric. One bare-breasted damsel whose hair was interwoven with gold coins caught his eye and smiled. He knew better than to return the smile. Not with his mother ten feet away.

Normal, all of it. What wasn't normal was the fact that the would-be passengers were not locals. One group of four were talking loudly in German. Another man, obviously English, wore military uniform.

Then the premonition focused onto someone who was pushing through the crowd. He stepped back, stooping a little in the hope that Newbold wouldn't see him, hoping even more that the hunter didn't intend to take the boat. It was a forlorn hope. Newbold started toward the gangplank. He had to stop to let several porters come down, and then Ramses caught sight of the woman who was with him.

She had stopped when he stopped, a little behind him, her head bowed. It was covered by a loose scarf which she had drawn across her face. Newbold held her arm in a grip firm enough to wrinkle the fine linen fabric of the robe that concealed her body from throat to ankles; they were slim, brown ankles circled with heavy gold bands hung with coins. Her wrists and slender fingers were also ringed with gold.

The porters dawdled, in no hurry to pick up additional loads. Newbold cursed their slowness, and the woman let out a little cry of pain and let go her scarf in order to tug at the fingers squeezing her arm.

Not a woman—a girl, surely no older than sixteen. He had expected that, from the delicacy of her bare ankles and the slender curves molded by the hot wind against her linen garment—and by his knowledge of Newbold's tastes. But he hadn't expected a face of such sweetness, her lips gently curved, her dark eyes enhanced by long lashes and winged brows.

He wasn't aware of having moved until he stood beside them. "Let go of her," he said.

Newbold gave an exaggerated start of surprise. "Oh, it's you. Is the rest of the family here?"

"I told you to let her go. You're hurting her."

"Am I? Oh dear. I certainly didn't intend to. Sorry, Daria. This is young Mr. Emerson, the famous Egyptologist."

She looked up at him from under her lashes and smiled. Ramses took off his hat. "Salaam aleikhum, Sitt."

Newbold's grin broadened. "Your mum would be proud of your manners. She speaks English. Answer the gentleman, Daria."

"Good morning, sir," she murmured.

"Pretty creature, isn't she?" Newbold ran a possessive hand over her sleek black hair and played with the end of her veil. "I bought her in Khartoum."

Ramses knew the man was goading him, but he didn't entirely succeed in hiding his disgust. Newbold howled with laughter. "Just a joke," he sputtered. "Slavery is against the law. You don't suppose I'd break the law, do you? Her dad and I came to an agreement—with her consent, of course. Isn't that right, Daria? You wanted to be with me."

Face calm as that of a lady saint in a painted icon, she nodded, and responded, unresisting, to the pressure of Newbold's hand as he guided her up the gangplank.

Newbold's complacent grin filled Ramses with impotent fury. Slavery was against the law, but there was no interfering with the old tribal customs, which included arranged marriages and the sale of women by the men who owned them. The girl took this for granted, he reminded himself; perhaps she had gone uncomplaining to the effendi who had loaded her with ornaments.

And perhaps the compliant father had been one of Newbold's fabrications. Her origins might have been less innocent. There was something about the way she moved, hips swaying and little feet stepping daintily . . . And she certainly knew how to use those wide dark eyes.

⁚

It took the rest of the day to load our boxes, so we were not able to get off until the following morning. By that time Nefret and I and two of the crewmen whom I had commandeered had cleaned out the worst of the dirt in the three minuscule cabins that had been assigned to us. Our fellows would have to sleep on deck with the crewmen, but Selim assured me they did not mind.

That evening we dined on board, in what Farah proudly referred to as the saloon. It was spacious enough, though the windows had obviously not been washed for months. I got out the serviettes I had brought, since I assumed (correctly) that Farah would not think of supplying them.

Most of our fellow passengers were present. One was a youngish fellow in uniform, who was not, for a change, an old friend of Emerson's. He knew us, though, and after he had introduced himself as Captain Moroney, returning to his post at Berber after a few weeks' leave in Cairo, he reminded me that we had met once before.

"No reason why you should remember me, ma'am," he said modestly. "I was assistant to the veterinary surgeon at Sanam Abu Dom, back in '98. You were good enough to advise him about treating the camels. Quite a coincidence that we should meet again in the Sudan."

"Isn't it," I said, and left him to Emerson.

Four of the others, two married couples, were tourists, though they would have disdained that description. Male and female alike, they were amusingly similar in their looks: the ladies had shoulders almost as massive as those of their husbands', and all four faces were wrinkled and brown from frequent exposure to the sun. Frau Bergenstein merrily informed me that they called themselves the wild birds, for they "flew" to the farther reaches of the world. They had climbed Mount Kenya, crossed the Negev by camel, paddled dugout canoes down the Niger to the Atlantic, and searched for the tomb of the Queen of Sheba in Ethiopia. I fully expected she would mention Zerzura, but she did not, so I left her to Ramses, at whom she had been rolling her rather protuberant eyes.

We were about to settle down to the meal when another passenger entered. He had a neatly trimmed grizzled beard and a frame almost as muscular as Emerson's, though he was not so tall. Emerson let out an oath at the sight of him, and Ramses turned rudely away from Frau Bergenstein.

He came straight to me and bowed. "I have not had the privilege of meeting you, Mrs. Emerson, but I am acquainted with your husband and son. Newbold is my name."

"I have heard of you, sir," I said stiffly.

"I don't doubt you have." He smiled, the lines at the corners of his eyes multiplying. "But I hope you will not be prejudiced against me by anything your son may have told you. Mr. Emerson, I am happy to have this opportunity to express my regrets for my ill-chosen words at our meeting in Cairo. I had—I am ashamed to admit it—I had taken too much to drink. Intoxication is not usual with me; in my profession, it is a danger one cannot afford; but when I return to civilization after months of privation, I occasionally celebrate too well. Accept my profound apologies."

"That depends on what the devil you are doing here," said Emerson. It was the same thing I had wondered about, but Emerson does not always have the sense to keep his thoughts to himself. The statement was, in my opinion, unnecessarily provocative, and I attempted to mitigate its effect.

"He is on his way back to central Africa, I presume. Is that not the case, Mr. Newbold? Another safari to arrange?"

"Precisely, Mrs. Emerson. It is still early in the year, but I am expecting a group of gentlemen from England in two months' time. I have some . . . personal business to carry out before I meet them in Cairo."

Ramses's tight lips parted. "Isn't the young lady dining?"

"As a proper young Moslem lady, she prefers to dine in our cabin," Newbold said smoothly. "Naturally I respect her wishes."

Ramses did not reply; after a moment Newbold went to take a seat at the far end of the table.

"Curse it," said Emerson. "Has the bastard got a woman with him? What's she like, Ramses?"

"Young," was the curt reply.

"Pretty?" Nefret asked.

"Yes."

"Shameful," I declared. "Perhaps if I were to have a word with her—"

"Leave it alone, Mother," said Ramses. "She's no helpless innocent."

"How do you know that?" Nefret demanded. Color rushed into her cheeks. "Have you met her before? Surely you didn't—"

"Encounter her during one of my frequent visits to the Cairo brothels?" Ramses snapped, his face as flushed as hers. "No. And I didn't try to seduce her either, if that's what you meant."

"For pity's sake, Ramses, lower your voice," I exclaimed. "You too, Nefret. I cannot understand why you are both getting so worked up. Nefret, your implied accusation was unjust, as you must be aware. Ramses, you ought not have let it upset you. You know she didn't mean it. Apologize, both of you."

As usual, Nefret was the first to respond. She was quick to lose her temper and just as quick to repent—whereas the reverse was true of Ramses. He sat with his head bowed, refusing to meet Nefret's eyes. She put her hand on his.

"I do apologize, Ramses," she said sweetly. "It's just that I get so angry about the filthy game of prostitution and the poor women who are forced to practice it. I was lashing out at random—not at you, my boy."

"I beg your pardon for being unable to tell the difference," said Ramses.

"Ramses," I said warningly.

"It's all right, Aunt Amelia, it was my fault," Nefret declared. She gave his taut, unresponsive hand a little squeeze. I couldn't help wondering what the girl had done to crack that impenetrable self-control of his.

## From Manuscript H

After dinner his mother convened an emergency council of war. Ramses had thought he was the only one to question the presence of so many unusual passengers, but he might have known his mother would be equally suspicious.

"Any or all of them could be following us," she declared. "It looks as if we must go on to Meroe after all."

"There's no doubt in my mind about Newbold's intentions," said Emerson, chewing on the stem of his pipe. "He's after us, all right. What precisely did he say to you that day at the club, Ramses?"

Ramses had no choice but to repeat the conversation in its entirety. His hearers reacted precisely as he had expected, but once Emerson had got over his outrage at Newbold's implications about Nefret ("You didn't punch him in the face? Why the devil not?"), he was able to bring his keen intelligence to bear on the more dangerous implications.

"Between what he picked up at Wadi Halfa and what he undoubtedly learned in Cairo, he's got enough—by his filthy standards—to justify following us. He won't get far," Emerson added smugly. "I have a plan—"

"I trust," said his wife, giving him a baleful stare, "that it does not involve putting Mr. Newbold in hospital. You could get yourself in serious—"

"Kindly refrain from interrupting me, Peabody," Emerson growled. "If worse comes to worst I would have no

compunction about—er—temporarily immobilizing the
fellow. But I do not believe it will prove necessary."

"What about the girl?" Nefret asked. Her only reaction
to Newbold's insult about her had been a shrug. "Why
would he bring her along?"

"To satisfy his own filthy appetites," said Emerson, with
a snap of his teeth.

He was only partly right.

Ramses was reading in bed later that night, or trying to;
the lamp flame swayed distractingly with the movement of
the boat. The soft creak of a hinge made him look up; and
he saw the door of his cabin open, just enough to allow a
slim, dark form to slip through. He jumped up, dropping
the book.

"What are you doing here?"

"What do you suppose?" She closed the door and came
toward him. She wore only a simple shift, sleeveless and
low cut, and she had left off her bangles and head scarf.
Her hair fell in jetty waves over her bare shoulders.

Ramses snatched up the shirt he had tossed over a chair
and put his arms through the sleeves. "If he learns you have
come here, he'll kill you."

"He sent me." She stopped a few feet away.

A flood of fury and disgust choked him for a few seconds. "I see."

"Let me stay—for an hour—or two. Then I can go back
and tell him I did my best, but failed."

He tried to control his anger. It wasn't her fault, but at
that moment he was almost as furious with her as with
Newbold. "Let me get this straight," he said softly. "He
told you to offer yourself to me in exchange for information about our plans. And you agreed?"

The contempt in his voice brought a dark flush to her
face. "I had no choice. I have told you the truth, instead of
the story he ordered me to tell—that I fled from him because he was drinking and would have hurt me. I was sup-

posed to plead for your protection, and embrace you, and . . ."

She looked very young and helpless and desirable with the warm lamplight stroking her slim curves. Newbold had selected precisely the right woman to appeal to his protective instincts—and to the others that might have succeeded them if he had taken that slender, trembling body into his arms.

Because he was fighting those instincts, he spoke harshly. "What makes you suppose I won't accept the offer and give nothing in return? I don't babble to the women I take to bed."

The color in her face deepened. "You may believe me or not. I have told you the truth."

"Wait," Ramses said, as she turned toward the door. Curiosity and a shamed consciousness of his cruelty had replaced anger. "I'm sorry. Sit down—over there, in that chair. You didn't have to tell me. Why did you? Sit down, please. I won't touch you, I promise."

He perched on the edge of the bed, as far from her as he could get. She studied him thoughtfully and then a curious little smile curved her lips and she did as he had asked.

"You don't have to stay with him," Ramses said. "My parents will help you."

"To find a respectable husband, or become a servant?" The pretty mouth hardened. She looked, suddenly, a good many years older. "I have my own reasons for staying with Newbold. He is not unkind. When he twisted my arm today it was to get your attention."

"I had already deduced that," Ramses muttered.

She went on in the same detached voice. "I told you the truth because you would not have believed the lie. You are already suspicious of him—as you should be."

"Who are you?" Ramses demanded. "You're no village maiden. Where did he find you?"

She rose, tossing the black locks back from her face in a movement as graceful as it was practiced.

"It has been long enough," she said. "He won't doubt that you refused me. He said you might take me because you are young and—how did he put it . . ."

"Never mind," Ramses said, feeling his face heat up.

"But he considers you weak and a naive romantic, as he expressed it. So he will believe me. Will you tell your parents?"

"What?" The question caught him unawares. So Newbold considered him a weakling, did he? "Yes, I shall. Don't go yet. You haven't answered my questions."

She moved with quick grace, reaching the door before he could rise. She looked back at him over her shoulder, frowning a little. "You wanted me, I could tell. Why did you refuse? Were you afraid of your mother finding out?"

"That's right," Ramses said wearily. His other reasons would have made less sense to her.

She was out the door before he could stop her. Just as well, he thought wryly. Newbold hadn't been so far wrong, damn the man. He had to tell his parents, but the very idea made him cringe; for it would mean admitting that his first, unthinking assumption had been based on a contemptible combination of male ego and physical desire. Nefret would certainly spot that, even if his parents didn't. He felt his face burning and picked up his book, but it failed to distract him. Her English was excellent and her appearance extraordinary. Where had she come from? There was European blood in her veins—or Persian, or Circassian. And was the "true story" only a subtler lie?

⋮

# Four

The government steamers take two days to cover the stretch between Shellal and Wadi Halfa. It took us four. However, the region through which we passed was fraught with interest, and the prevailing north wind was pleasantly cool under a shaded awning. Without entering into details which the majority of my readers would find tedious as well as extraneous, I should explain that the area had been called by a number of different names over the centuries: the Land of the Bow, Cush, Nubia, the Sudan, to mention only a few. The Meroitic civilization flourished in southern Nubia after the fall of the earlier Cushite kingdom at Napata. Ruins of all periods abounded, for the conquering pharaohs of ancient Egypt had been succeeded by kings of Napata and queens of Meroe, and by Greek and Roman invaders; Christianity had raised its churches and Islam its mosques. Sitting on deck, we studied them through field glasses and Emerson mumbled discontentedly. "There'll be nothing left of them in another century, Peabody. Those villains at Aswan keep raising the water level."

Additional entertainment was provided by bits of the boat falling off. Obviously this was not an unusual occurrence, for the crewmen remained unperturbed as they retrieved (most of) the bits and tied them back on. On one occasion we came to a dead halt in the middle of the river and it required some brisk steering by Farah to keep us from going aground while the engines were being repaired. Selim, who could not keep away from machinery of any kind, assisted in the repairs. He came back to us shaking his head in mingled horror and admiration. "I do not know how this boat has stayed afloat," he declared. "The engine is held together with wire and rust."

Even this somewhat alarming encounter did not bring two of our fellow passengers on deck. According to our captain, they were missionaries, on their way to the southern Sudan. Wingate, the governor, had wisely restricted the ardor of these individuals in the Moslem areas, for Islam does not take kindly to proselytizers. Denizens of the "pagan" areas farther south were fair game, however, and it was thither our fellow passengers were bound. We did not set eyes on them until the last day, when we were only a few hours from Wadi Halfa. They had, as Captain Farah solemnly explained, bad stomachs.

Alimentary disorder had not prevented them from exhibiting their religious zeal. The partitions between cabins were flimsy affairs; every evening, prayers and hymns echoed through the walls and went on so long that Emerson was eventually inspired to shout demands for silence. He could shout much more loudly than they could sing, so that put an end to the performances.

Yet so uneasy had I become that I could not help wondering whether these persons were what they claimed to be. Sethos had a strange sense of humor, and it would be like him to disguise himself as a man of the cloth. When they finally appeared in the saloon on the morning of the day we were to dock, I stared unabashedly.

They were not a married couple, but brother and sister— the Reverend and Miss Campbell. The lady was tall and slim and in my opinion rather too beautiful for a missionary. She was plainly dressed and her face was bare of cosmetics, but this only emphasized the delicate modeling of her cheekbones and the white brow framed by masses of auburn hair. Her voice was low, her accent well-bred, her manner frank and open, her smile engaging.

She was certainly not Sethos.

Nor was her brother, I decided. He was as ugly as she was beautiful, with scanty light brows and a pathetic wisp of a beard. The eyebrows might have been plucked and bleached and the lumpy nose a result of putty and greasepaint, but the shallow jaw, only partially veiled by the beard, and the narrow shoulders were not those of the man I had known. I judged him to be a good many years her senior. His voice was almost as high as hers, and as I had discovered, neither could carry a tune.

At first I could not understand why he should take such a girl, to whom he was clearly devoted, into such a remote and perilous region. Then psychology offered a clue. When she addressed a few courteous words to Ramses, her brother immediately interrupted.

"You are traveling with us as far as Khartoum, I believe. What can you tell us about conditions in that region? Will we find the authorities receptive to our labors for the Lord?"

Emerson had taken a dislike to Mr. Campbell even before he met him, over and above his general dislike of missionaries. With characteristic bluntness he replied, "The authorities, yes. Other conditions are not so receptive. I wonder, sir, why you would risk your sister's health, possibly her life, in such an insalubrious region."

"Her life belongs to God, sir. She was called to this mission of rescue, as was I."

"Rescue, bah," said Emerson. "How do you know it was God who called you?"

"The heathen walk in darkness but must be brought to the light." The Reverend Mr. Campbell's eyes, magnified by the lenses of his eyeglasses, took on a fiery glow. "They are believers in black magic and fetishism. I have heard of practices of immorality that shocked me to the depths of my soul. Concubines! Orgies!"

"Nakedness," Emerson said helpfully. "The women go about bare to the waist, and some of them are quite—"

"Emerson," I exclaimed.

"We must get our gear together," Nefret intervened tactfully. She had been looking at the other girl with sympathetic interest. "Is there anything I can do for you, Miss Campbell, in the way of medical assistance? Farah said you had been ill. I have a well-equipped medicine chest and some training."

The young lady replied with proper expressions of gratitude, saying she was almost recovered. Mr. Campbell did not appear to be listening. His eyes were half closed and his lips moved as if in silent prayer. The man was a religious maniac. In his eyes his sister was as much a prisoner as any Moslem woman, belonging not to him or any other man, but to God. He had not complete faith in God as a chaperon, however; he would risk the health, even the life, of his sister, rather than take the chance of her meeting a young man whose attentions might weaken her zeal.

As we chatted, there was a hail from on deck.

"Did he say crocodile?" Miss Campbell asked eagerly. "I've never seen one."

"Here's your chance, then," replied Emerson, who was looking for an excuse to end the encounter. "Shall we go up and have a look?"

Everyone wanted to have a look. Crocodiles had almost vanished from Egypt itself, and they were becoming rare in this area. Passengers and crew crowded round the rail. The landscape had opened up and the river was broad. Behind the floodplain with its green fields and groves of palm trees the desert rose in a series of terraces, pale yellow in the morning light. Here and there, wadis had cut their way through the soft sandstone. The river had begun to subside, leaving long sandbars strewn with flood debris—reeds and pieces of wood and fallen logs. The German quartet aimed cameras, and Newbold pushed one of the sailors out of his way. His companion was not present; I had not set eyes on her the entire trip.

"I don't see," Miss Campbell began.

"There," said Ramses, pointing. She let out a gasp of delighted horror and leaned forward as one of the logs opened its jaws and slid from the bank into the water. Two others followed. Ramses, who happened to be standing next to the girl, put his arm round her waist. "Be careful."

Campbell, on her other side, let out an exclamation of protest and snatched her away from Ramses, who immediately stepped back. Watching them, I failed to see what happened. I only heard a scream and a splash, and an outcry from the watchers. Selim's voice rose above the others. "Hassan! Help him, Father of Curses!"

"Stop the engines!" Emerson called. He caught Selim in an iron grip and pushed him back. "No, Selim! Leave it to . . . Curse it—Ramses—!"

Ramses climbed onto the rail and dived. He began swimming toward the flailing arms and distorted face of poor Hassan. The boat shuddered to a stop, but the pair were already some distance astern—and beyond them the surface of the water was broken by a triangular wake, with a long ugly head at its apex.

"Throw them a rope!" I shrieked, though to be sure I feared it would not do much good. The crocodile and Ramses were converging on Hassan, or rather on the spot where he had been. There was no sign of him now. Ramses went down after him. And so did the crocodile. Blood stained the muddy surface of the water. Miss Campbell screamed and fainted gracefully into the arms of her brother, who stood staring in paralyzed horror.

Then I realized Emerson was gone.

Not into the water, surely; I would have seen him jump. I was about to call his name when he came running, thrust the watchers aside, including me, and stood with his feet braced and his arms extended. He was holding a heavy pistol.

The water boiled and bubbled, and all three heads reappeared. Ramses appeared to be supporting Hassan, who appeared to be unconscious; the crocodile appeared to be in some distress. It rose half out of the water, jaws snapping. Emerson fired. There was a hideous bellow from the wounded animal. Ramses was swimming, strongly but too slowly, burdened as he was with Hassan. Emerson took careful aim and fired a second and third time. How he managed to hit the thrashing target I cannot imagine, but the third shot finished the creature. It sank like a stone amid a spreading crimson stain.

"Get a rope to them, Peabody," said Emerson, moving neither his eyes nor the pistol. "I will just make sure the other beasts don't take a hand. Or should I say a 'jaw'?"

"How can you jest, sir?" Campbell demanded in a shaken voice. "You should be praising God for his infinite mercy."

"Well, you see, I don't know yet how merciful he has been," said Emerson coolly. "Peabody . . ."

"Yes, my dear. At once."

We got them on board. Hassan was a dead weight, unconscious and bleeding heavily. After a quick look at him, Nefret whipped off her belt and fashioned it into a tourniquet. Hassan's left leg ended in a bloody stump.

"Oh, my God," I gasped. "The crocodile had him by the foot!"

"Yes." Ramses dropped to a sitting position, knees raised and head bowed. He was streaming with water and gasping for breath. "How is he?"

"Daoud, Selim, get him to my cabin and put him on the bed," Nefret ordered. "I'll operate there. Hurry!"

"He's lucky to be alive," Emerson said grimly. "Once a crocodile gets hold, he rolls and drags his victim down. Ramses, how did you persuade the creature to let go?"

"Knife," said Ramses briefly. He was still short of breath. "Lost it."

"We will get you another, a better, the best that can be found," said Selim, his voice unsteady. Hassan was his first cousin. "You saved his life."

"Not me," said Ramses. "All I could do was . . . distract the brute." He pushed the wet hair back from his face. "Never believed those white-hunter stories . . . Hassan and I would both be crocodile food but for Father."

"I was too damn slow," muttered Emerson. "Should have carried the damned pistol instead of leaving it in my suitcase. But who would have supposed . . . You aren't hurt, my boy?"

"No, sir. Thank you for asking," he added.

"Praise God from whom all blessings flow!" exclaimed the Reverend Campbell.

I took Emerson away.

At Wadi Halfa we had to go through the laborious business of unloading and transporting our baggage a second time. The steamers lie too close to the railroad station, but thanks to Emerson's preference for a semi-derelict vessel, we had missed the Saturday train. There was not another until Thursday.

"All to the good," declared Emerson, unquenchably optimistic. "It will take a while to make arrangements for Hassan's care. We cannot simply walk off and leave him."

"Obviously not," I replied. "There is a hospital here, I believe? What is it like?"

"I leave it to your imagination, my dear."

"I would rather trust the evidence of my own eyes, Emerson," I retorted, mopping my brow. There had been a nice breeze on the river, but now that we were standing still, the heat was really horrid.

"The market at Halfa is one of the best in the Sudan," Emerson said. "You will want to do some shopping, Peabody."

"Will I?"

"You always do, my dear. Remember, this is the last good-sized town we will encounter. Kalabsha, the stop for Meroe, hasn't much beyond a railroad station and a rest house."

"What about Berber?" Ramses asked.

"Oh. Well, we won't be getting off the train at Berber, will we? No sense in wasting two or three days there. Straight on to Meroe, that's the plan."

"What are you shouting for, Emerson?" I inquired.

"Was I? No, I wasn't." He tried the door of the station house and found it locked. A crowd had gathered, drawn by the arrival of the steamer and the hope of earning a few piastres. They were talking excitedly among themselves; then one of them advanced and bowed. "Welcome, Father of Curses. Is it indeed you?"

"Aywa," Emerson replied. "Myself and no other. Salaam aleikhum, Yusuf Sawar. Send someone to fetch the station master, will you?"

It was not long before this individual came hastening up. He was, of course, an old friend. While Emerson exchanged greetings and gave instructions to him, I felt a touch on my arm and looked round to see Mr. Newbold. His hat was in his hand and behind him stood a veiled female figure.

"May I beg a favor, Mrs. Emerson?" Newbold asked. "I must make arrangements for the transfer of our luggage, and I don't like to leave my daughter unattended in such a crush of men."

"Your what?" I exclaimed, staring in open curiosity at the slender, silent figure. "Ramses said—"

"Oh dear," Newbold murmured. "I'm afraid I yielded to the temptation to tease your son just a bit. Daria is my child, whom I have only lately found again. It is a sad story, which I will tell you one day. Would you look after her, only for a few minutes? Your presence will deter anyone from approaching her rudely."

He moved away before I could answer, but of course only one answer was possible. Curiosity as well as compassion demanded acceptance.

"It is kind of you," said a soft voice from behind the fabric she had drawn across her face.

"You speak English?" An unnecessary question, since she obviously did. "Let us step aside," I went on. "Out of the way of all these people."

There were a number of questions I wanted to ask her. Why was she a practicing Moslem when her father was Christian? (Not that he was much of a Christian, if the rumors I had heard were true.) What was the "sad story"? Why, if modesty of attire were her aim, was she wearing garments that set off rather than concealed a nicely rounded figure and comely features? It was costly attire, linen as fine as the fabric worn by queens and pharaohs in ancient times, a thin silken scarf covering her head and the lower part of her face—and she was absolutely clanking with jewelry. Courtesy prevailed, however, and as we withdrew, I contented myself with saying only, "You are on your way to Khartoum, I presume. It is a long, arduous journey. Is there anything that I can do to make it easier for you?"

She lowered the fold of silk that had concealed her nose and mouth and looked at me in surprise. Ramses had understated the case. "Pretty" did not do the delicate features and tinted lips justice. Her skin was as fair as that of a southern European. The wide dark eyes were skillfully outlined with kohl.

"Why should you offer to do that?" she asked.

"Good," I said, pleased. "You are direct. I like that. Why, because you are a woman, and young, and a fellow human being. No matter how thoughtful your—er—father may be, he is a man, and men do not always understand the needs of women."

My brief hesitation before the word "father" passed without comment. I felt certain Newbold had lied to me about the relationship and that the story he had told Ramses was the true one. Even he would not have had the temerity to introduce me to his concubine. Most ladies would have refused in withering terms. In that he did me an injustice, of course.

"You are kind," she said again. "But I need nothing. Your son was kind to me too. Did he tell you that I came to him in his cabin?"

"Yes, he did," I replied. The big dark eyes widened; I believe she expected the question would come as a shock, which it certainly would have done had Ramses not told us what had happened. It hadn't been easy for him. I understood why, of course, and now that I had seen the girl, I understood even better. He had been attracted, and tempted. Quite natural, in my opinion, and all the more credit to him for resisting. Unfortunately Nefret had not seen it that way, and I had to insist she apologize.

"He said he intended to, but I wondered if he would have the courage."

"No one could accuse my son of lacking in courage," I replied somewhat acerbically. "Nor in the instincts of a gentleman. Do you wish to be free of that man? I assure you that my husband and my son, to say nothing of myself, are capable of ensuring that, if you wish it."

"Mother," said a voice behind me. Ramses walks like a cat, and I had been too interested in the conversation to notice him approaching. "Please come with me. Father is ready to leave."

"I can't just yet," I explained, turning to meet a scowl almost as dark as one of his father's. "Mr. Newbold asked me to stay with—er—the young lady until he comes back."

Ramses looked round. It was certainly a rather rough crowd, and a noisy one, as would-be porters shoved and shouted, vying for the attention of the passengers. Torn between his chivalrous concern for females—instilled in him by me—and his obvious dislike of the young woman, he hesitated.

The girl had not replaced her veil. "There are your friends, come looking for you," she said with unmistakable mockery. "Another . . . young lady."

The young lady was Miss Campbell, accompanied, of course, by her brother. Miss Campbell was buttoned up to the chin, her prim white collar and cuffs wilted by the heat, and her hair concealed by a broad-brimmed hat. She looked miserably hot compared with Daria, in her loose garments and light head scarf—and her conspicuous respectability made the other girl look even less respectable. They eyed each other and then, as if a signal had passed between them, both turned and stared at Ramses.

Mr. Campbell noisily cleared his throat. "I beg your pardon, Mrs. Emerson, but would you be good enough to come and talk to those porters? I can't seem to make them understand me."

"I'll come, sir," said Ramses, with relief. "Mother?"

Daria murmured, "There is my . . . father coming. Thank you, Mrs. Emerson, for protecting me, though it was unnecessary."

"You are welcome," I said. "Good-bye and good luck."

Miss Campbell took out a limp white handkerchief and wiped her perspiring face. "Is she really . . . Oh dear. I feel rather . . ."

"Come out of the sun," I said, putting an arm round her swaying form. "Your attire is quite unsuitable for this climate, you know."

"It is suitable for her position," said Mr. Campbell, and let out a bleat of alarm as she sagged heavily against me.

I could do no more than keep the girl from falling, for she was a dead weight. "Ramses," I gasped.

After a wary glance at Mr. Campbell, who was wringing his hands ineffectually, Ramses lifted the young woman, who had gone quite limp. "Now what shall I do with her?" Ramses demanded. "There's no place to put her down."

"Sit on that packing case and continue to hold her," I instructed. "Mr. Campbell, if you wish to be useful, open my parasol and hold it over her. Over her head, you silly man!" As I spoke, I unfastened Miss Campbell's collar, took the pins from her hat, removed that article of clothing, and began fanning her with it.

Ramses had laid her as flat as possible, across his knees,

one arm under her shoulders. Her head had fallen back and she looked quite pretty and pathetic with her loosened hair framing her face and her lips half parted. I fully expected Campbell to protest, not only the loosening of the girl's clothing but the intimate proximity of a young man; however, he obeyed my orders without comment, his face anxious. Perhaps, I thought, it has finally dawned on the idiot that he is risking her health, even her life.

She was showing signs of returning consciousness when Nefret came hurrying toward us. "What on earth . . ." she began.

"It is just the heat, I think," I said, as, with an exclamation of concern, she bent over the young woman. "Get some water."

The application of this substance to face and throat soon brought Miss Campbell round. When she became aware of her position, a deep blush warmed the pallor of her face and she tried feebly to stand.

"Mary . . . Mary, dear," her brother cried, attempting to support her. "Lord, we are in your hands. Help us, guide us!"

"You would be better advised to ask *me* for help," I said irritably. "I presume you have made no arrangements for lodgings here? No, I didn't suppose you had. Take your sister to the government rest house, get her out of those hot clothes, and apply copious amounts of water internally and externally. Ramses will carry her if she cannot walk."

"Daoud," Ramses said shortly.

"Oh," I said. "Yes, that would be better."

We got them off with their luggage, such as it was—two suitcases and a small valise. Daoud carried the girl as easily as if she had been a kitten, his large friendly face wearing a reassuring smile. When he came back to announce they had settled in, Emerson—who had completely ignored the little drama—was ready to proceed. Our packing cases had been stored, except for our bags, which our own fellows had taken in charge.

"Peabody, my dear, I expect you are anxious to—er—change your clothing and bathe."

"I bathed this morning," I retorted. "Not much of a bath, in muddy water in a basin, but I doubt the government rest house here offers more elegant facilities."

"Who said anything about the rest house?" Emerson offered me his arm.

"Oh, no, Emerson," I said firmly. "Not your dear old friend Mahmud—what was his name?"

"El Araba," said Emerson. "I don't know why you should protest, my dear. He was most hospitable. However, the poor old fellow is dead these many years."

"Well, wherever we are going, let us go," Nefret said impatiently. "I want to make Hassan comfortable, and I refuse to deliver him to the hospital until I have seen what it's like."

Wadi Halfa marks the border between Egypt and the Anglo-Egyptian Sudan; once a bustling military depot, it was now a pleasant, placid little town, capital of the mudiria (province) of the same name. We left the German tourists arguing with the station master and proceeded on foot toward the center of town, which boasted a hospital and several government buildings. Over one of them, a low structure of whitewashed mud brick shaded by trees, flew the British and Egyptian flags. My spirits rose at the sight.

"Is the mudir an old friend, Emerson?" I inquired hopefully.

"Good Gad, no," said Emerson, as shocked as if I had implied he was well acquainted with Satan. "The mudirs are all British officials. The local ma'mur is Nur ed Din, splendid fellow, met him while he was running guns to Kordofan. His place is down this way."

We were expected and were greeted with flattering enthusiasm by the ma'mur himself. The Nubians are a very clean people; the only exceptions I have known happened to be friends of Emerson's, which says more about my husband's notions of sanitation than about his friends. The ma'mur's house was spacious and tidy enough to suit even me, with thick walls of mud brick, some of which were adorned with elegant painted designs. His servants led us to a pleasant little suite of rooms reserved for guests, which included an actual bath chamber and several sleeping chambers. We got Hassan settled in one of them; he was full of morphine and only vaguely aware of his surroundings.

"There," said Emerson. "Isn't this better than the cursed government house? Plenty of privacy, you see." He gave me a meaningful smile. "And no cursed missionaries singing hymns."

Ramses had picked up his suitcases and gone off to find a room for himself. He was back almost at once, sans luggage. "You'll never guess who I found," he said.

"That's not difficult," retorted Emerson. "I told Merasen to meet us here and asked the ma'mur to look after him. Where is he?"

"He was asleep. Bare and innocent as a baby. I took the liberty of waking him and announcing our arrival. He'll be along as soon as he puts on some clothes."

Merasen professed himself as delighted to see us, and indeed his broad smile and deep bows confirmed it. He had arrived in Halfa only two days before us. When Emerson inquired why it had taken him so long, he replied with wide-eyed candor that he had stayed over for a few days in Aswan, "to see the sights." Observing, from Emerson's expression, that this was not well received, he reached into the breast of his galabeeyah and produced a handful of coins.

"Here is the rest of the money you gave me, Father of Curses."

"Your expenses were heavy," said Emerson dryly.

"I bought gifts." Again he dipped into a pocket. "For Nefret and the Sitt."

Strings of beads, very pretty and very cheap.

Nefret and I went off to inspect the hospital. It consisted

of two widely separated buildings, the smaller of which was the native hospital. I daresay the doctor was doing his best, but we declined his kind offer to add another bed to the overcrowded ward. The flies were as thick as raindrops in a brisk shower, and the temperature was in the high nineties.

When we returned I summoned the others, including Selim and Daoud, to a council of war. "The first thing is to make arrangements for Hassan," I said, as Emerson dispensed whiskey. (He had assured me our host had no objection to our indulging in this deplorable practice so long as we did it in private.) "The hospital is impossible. He must be sent home as soon as he is able to travel, and one of us must stay with him. I wouldn't trust a stranger, however well intentioned, to look after him properly."

"I can't," Nefret said wretchedly. "You know I can't, Aunt Amelia."

"But you can tell Ibrahim what to do," said Selim. "And give him medicines."

Among the medicines, I felt sure, would be the green ointment made by Daoud's wife Kadija from a secret recipe passed down by the women of her Sudanese family. Hassan would have demanded it even if Nefret had not come to believe in its efficacy. So it was agreed. After Selim and Daoud had gone off to discuss the matter with the others, I said soberly, "We will now be without two of our men. Was it an accident?"

Nefret looked up. "Hassan said someone pushed him. He couldn't tell who. He may have been mistaken."

Ramses was stretched out on the soft cushions of the divan. He was as agile as an eel underwater. Only that, and the fact that the crocodile had been busy with Hassan, had saved him from serious injury, but I suspected he had not come out of the encounter entirely unscathed. He had refused to allow me or Nefret to examine him. However, he had accepted a pot of the green ointment before he went to his room to change his wet clothing.

"There was a great deal of pushing and shoving," he said without raising his head. "It is an odd coincidence, though."

"And too cursed many suspects," Emerson muttered. "Ramses mentioned several groups of people who might be aware of our ultimate goal, and by Gad, two such persons have already turned up. The Great White Hunter and the military, in the person of that fellow who, by another strange coincidence, was at the camp when Reggie Forthright was confiding in all and sundry. The only ones we haven't encountered are representatives of the Egyptological community and the slavers!"

"You could hardly expect the latter to show themselves," I said.

"My dear, a number of highly respectable persons deal on the sly with slave traders."

"You aren't suggesting that those stout German tourists are among them, are you?"

"I don't like their looks," Emerson grumbled. "They are too stereotypical to be genuine. As for the missionaries—"

"You always suspect missionaries."

"That is because religious persons always use God as an excuse for unprincipled acts," Emerson retorted.

We dined with the ma'mur that evening and, as courtesy demanded, stuffed ourselves with lamb and rice and couscous, dates, and heaven knows what else. Repletion did not prevent Emerson from taking full advantage of our newfound privacy.

The following day we sallied forth to visit the market. These markets are fascinating, and very enjoyable once one gets over European squeamishness about bloody carcasses of butchered animals swarming with flies, and streets littered with a variety of refuse. Our purchases were limited by practicality; any perishable item, such as fruit and vegetables, would have rotted before we reached Meroe. Nefret indulged herself in a few strips of bright fabric, declaring that as soon as we were away from civilization she intended to return to native costume.

While we were drinking tea in a café, at the invitation of the Greek proprietor (an old friend of Emerson's), a procession went by, heading for the mosque. The personage of chief importance was riding a handsome black stallion and was escorted by several guards wearing gaudy uniforms and carrying long lances with gold-and-green pennants fluttering from their tips. Unlike the guards, who were upstanding, sturdy men, he was fat and puffy around the face, which was marred by deep lines of overindulgence and temper. Next to him rode a younger man, dressed as richly in silk and brocade.

Emerson said, "Hell and damnation!"

Emerson's normal speaking tones are quite loud, and he did not bother to lower his voice. The older man turned his head. I had the feeling that he had been aware all along of our presence; his expression did not alter nor did he stop, but the younger dignitary examined us curiously, turning his head and continuing to stare as he went past.

"Now there," said Emerson, saluting him with an ironic flip of his hand, "is a fellow you should avoid if you can."

"Another old friend of yours?" I asked.

"That would be stretching it a bit. The last time I ran into him we . . . er . . . had a slight difference of opinion about—er—well, I was forced to incapacitate him and make a hasty departure from Darfur, where—"

"It was about a woman, I suppose," I said.

"You make me sound like some sort of philanderer," Emerson protested. "She was only a girl, who had been stolen from her young husband and her family. When she appealed to me, I had no choice but to help her."

"I know, my dear," I said affectionately. Emerson's soft heart and chivalrous nature are immediately apparent to any female. So are certain other attributes of his, but I had sworn never to reproach him for anything he had done before we met.

"Who is he?" Nefret asked.

"Mahmud Dinar, the sultan of Darfur. The fellow next to him is his eldest son. He's the only independent governor in the Sudan—a reward for his remaining loyal during the Dervish revolt. He pays a sizable tribute, though."

"He looks as if he can afford it," Nefret remarked.

"The slave trade pays well," said Emerson dryly. "He turns a blind eye and collects his cut. Well, well. The only ones we're missing are a journalist and an Egyptologist."

When we returned to the ma'mur's house we found a message from the mudir, a Captain Barkdoll, inviting us to tea.

"Shan't go," said Emerson, removing his hat and unfastening the remaining buttons of his shirt.

"Oh, yes, we shall. I had intended to call on him. All open and aboveboard, remember? You may be sure that if we don't turn up he will come looking for us."

Captain Barkdoll was young and very conscious of his authority. His mouse-brown hair looked as if it had been parted by a razor, and his mustache was so perfect it might have been painted on. Since he had no hostess, he asked me to pour, which of course I did.

"You did not notify the Sudan agent in Cairo of your intentions, Professor Emerson," he began.

"Why should I?" Emerson stirred sugar into his tea. "I don't need his permission to excavate at Meroe, and I certainly don't require assistance from fellows like you."

Standing stiff as a poker, his cup in one hand and the other behind his back, Barkdoll pressed on. "I must ask you for a list of the supplies you brought and for your papers."

Ramses, who was also standing, looked from his father to the young officer and allowed a faint smile to curve his mouth. He knew what was coming.

"Papers be damned," said Emerson amiably. "You know who I am. Everybody knows who I am."

"Are you aware, sir, that the importation of rifles and

ammunition of .303 caliber is absolutely forbidden and that you require a license to hunt with other weapons?"

Emerson rolled his eyes heavenward. "License A," he retorted with an audible sneer, "entitles the holder to shoot elephant, hippopotami, rhinoceros, giraffe, antelope, and any other unfortunate animal that passes by. We, sir, do not hunt."

Barkdoll was, as I have said, quite young, and no match for Emerson's tactics. "Then what have you got in those damned long wooden cases?" he shouted.

"I believe, sir," said Emerson in freezing tones, "that you have forgotten there are ladies present."

The young man glanced at Nefret, who was trying to look shocked. At my insistence she had attired herself in a proper frock and flower-trimmed hat, and she looked like what she was not—an innocent, well-bred young English lady. "I—I beg your pardon. I didn't mean—"

"How does it happen that you are familiar with the contents of our baggage?" Emerson demanded. "We are British citizens, sir, and are not accustomed to being spied upon by our own people."

"No! I was told—"

"Go down to the station, then, and rip the cursed boxes apart," Emerson shouted. "I will hold you personally accountable for any missing item or for any damage to our cameras and surveying equipment."

"Really," I said, rising. "I had expected more courteous treatment from a British officer and a gentleman. Pray excuse us."

Barkdoll wilted. "Naturally, Professor Emerson, if I have your word—"

"My word," said Emerson grandly, "is my bond. Come, Peabody."

Once we had left the house, "What is in those cases, Emerson?" I inquired.

"Rifles and ammunition of .303 caliber, of course," said Emerson, stamping along with his hands in his pockets.

* * *

The ma'mur was more than happy to offer his hospitality to Hassan and Ibrahim for as long as they liked. Ibrahim was a quiet, easygoing older man, very much like his second cousin Daoud, and he listened intently and intelligently to Nefret's directions. We left him amply supplied with funds for the journey to Luxor, which would take place as soon as Hassan was able to travel. Thanks to Nefret's quick and vigorous intervention, the wound was healing without any sign of infection, and Selim had already begun designing an artificial foot for Hassan.

On Thursday we bade them farewell and betook ourselves to the railway station, where we found our goods undisturbed. All the passengers from the boat were there. There was nothing surprising or suspicious about that, since they were all on their way to places farther south. I exchanged a few pleasant words with Captain Moroney before he took his place in the train. Newbold nodded and tipped his hat, but did not approach us. He hurried his companion into one of the cars. Her face was veiled and her form completely concealed by her garments.

The train was described as deluxe, with supposedly dust-proof dining and sleeping cars. Compared with my earlier travels by train in the Sudan, it was deluxe. There were actually windows in the carriages and reasonably good food to be had in the dining car. After luncheon we went back to our compartment, taking Merasen with us. I didn't want him swaggering up and down the train smirking at the women and inspiring the interest of people like Newbold.

On the east ran a chain of bare, violet-colored hills and an endless stretch of stony desert, quivering with heat. The view was not inspiring and the cars were not, in fact, entirely dust-proof; I put my head on Emerson's shoulder and closed my eyes. I was just drifting off when Emerson got to his feet.

"Sorry, Peabody," he said, as I tipped over sideways. "I

did not realize you were asleep. We're almost there, so get your gear together."

I sat up and stared out the window. There was nothing to be seen but sand, rock, and a few spindly palm trees. "What do you mean, we are almost there? Almost where? Not Meroe, it is at least—"

"Abu Hamed," said Emerson. "Or, to be more precise, Station Number Ten, just outside Abu Hamed, where we connect with the branch line to Kareima."

"Kareima," I muttered, being still somewhat befuddled by drowsiness. "What? Why?"

Nefret handed me a dampened napkin. Though somewhat rumpled and glowing with perspiration, she was as bright-eyed as . . . as I was not. "Wipe your face, Aunt Amelia. So we are going straight to Napata and Gebel Barkal instead of on to Meroe? Very clever, Professor!"

"Well, I thought so," said Emerson modestly. "Throw any pursuers off the track, you see. They will be expecting us in Meroe, and by the time they realize we aren't there, we will be on our way. And if any of our fellow travelers get off here, we will know them for what they are."

The dampened napkin was most refreshing. I looked from Emerson, who was smirking in a particularly annoying fashion, to Ramses, whose thin brown face, for once, betrayed his feelings. They were not those of surprise. Amusement, rather. As a rule I like seeing Ramses's imperturbable countenance soften. Not on this occasion, however.

"You took Ramses into your confidence," I cried accusingly. "But not me. How could you, Emerson?"

"No, Mother," Ramses protested. "Honestly. Father said nothing to me. It was, however, a predictable and logical course of action—er—as you no doubt—um. I'll go and alert Selim and Daoud and the other fellows, shall I?"

The train was slowing. I looked longingly at the seat, which opened into a nice comfortable bed, a bed which I was destined not to enjoy, and put on my hat. "Give

Merasen a poke, will you, Nefret? Goodness, I believe that boy could sleep through a sandstorm."

Since the railway to Abu Hamed cut across the arid desert, miles from the river, a series of wells had been sunk to supply needed water. Station Number Ten marked one of these. It merited no worthier name. There was nothing there except the station itself, a gray wooden building from which any paint had long since been scoured away by sand and sun. The train to Kareima was certainly not a train deluxe—in addition to the aged engine, there were only half a dozen carriages and a baggage car—but at least it was there, waiting for passengers, when we drew to a stop. The inevitable small merchants hawked fruit and water and sand-sprinkled bread. At my suggestion Ramses bought a supply of food and Nefret persuaded the dining-car steward to fill our water bottles with cold tea.

The transfer of our by now mountainous heap of baggage took some time. A few of the other passengers took advantage of the delay to get off and stretch their limbs. Among them were the Germans, who strode up and down, swinging their arms as if they were running a footrace. Several men in native garb bargained with the food sellers. They were the only ones who boarded the Kareima train.

While we waited, I saw a horse and rider, motionless atop a low dune some distance away. They were the most interesting objects in that dismal scene, and well worth looking at—figures of pure romance, the noble steed poised as if ready to break into a gallop, the rider straight in the saddle. He was too far away for me to make out his features, but the sun, now past the zenith, shone on his long robes and the folds of the white khafiya that covered his head. In one hand he carried a long lance. As I stared, raising my hands to shield my eyes from the glare of the sun, the man raised the lance and shook it in greeting or—which seemed more likely—menace.

"Emerson," I said, tugging at his sleeve. "Look there."

"Not now, Peabody, not now. Quickly, my lads, get those

boxes aboard. Be careful with that one, Selim, it has the camera and plates. Well, Peabody, what is it?"

The horseman had gone. "Nothing, Emerson."

We took our places in the train. I have seen worse, though some of the windows would not open and others would not close. There were only two classes—first and worst. Except for our party, the train was almost empty, so we were able to spread out. Merasen announced he was going to find an unoccupied compartment and have a little sleep. "You may wake me when we arrive," he informed Selim, who curled his lip but refrained from retort.

"How long?" I asked Emerson wearily.

"Only ten hours or so."

"You may wake me when we arrive," I informed him.

I thought sleep would be impossible, because of the jolting and the insufferable heat. It did not seem to me that I slept; but suddenly, between one heartbeat and the next, I was in another place, a place I knew well. A cool breeze touched my face, and the sky was the pale, translucent blue that precedes the rising of the sun. That rising was behind me, for I faced west—the western cliffs of Thebes, with the stately ruins of Deir el Bahri to my left, and straight ahead the winding path that led to the top of the plateau and onward to the Valley of the Kings. I began to climb, as I had done so many times before. It is a steep climb and I was breathing quickly when I reached the top. And there, coming toward me with long strides, was a man, tall and straight, black-bearded, his turban snowy white, the long skirts of his galabeeyah wafting round him.

"Turn, Sitt, and see the sun rise," he said.

I pressed my hand to my heart. It was beating hard, and not with the effort of the climb. "Abdullah. Is it really you? You look so young!"

He stopped a few feet away and smiled, his teeth white against the unmarked black of his beard. "There is no time here, Sitt. It is a dream. Did you not know?"

"The happiest dream I have had for many a month," I

replied, and it was the truth. Joy filled me like water over-flowing a cup, leaving no room for grief or surprise or doubt. I laughed aloud and held out my hands to him. Still smiling, he shook his head, and something told me I must not move closer, or touch him.

"Turn, Sitt," he repeated. "And we will watch the sunrise again together."

Of all the memories I had of Abdullah, this was the strongest, for as the years went on and his beard whitened, he found the climb harder. Being Abdullah, he would never have admitted it, so I had got into the habit of pretending I needed to stop and catch my breath before following the others to the Valley where we were working. To see the molten orb of the sun lift above the eastern cliffs across the river and watch the light spread across green fields and rippling water, ruined temples and modern villages was a glorious experience. I had sometimes thought that if I were allowed to return to the world of the living, this was the place I would choose. (After, of course, making sure Emerson was where I wanted him to be and the children were doing well.)

I turned obediently and felt his presence close behind me. He whispered something that sounded like an invocation and I said, "Are you a sun worshipper, Abdullah? I always suspected you were something of a pagan."

"Then so are you, Sitt Hakim. But let us not talk religion, which is a waste of breath. What in the name of God (whichever name it may be) has taken you on the road you now follow? Turn back before it is too late."

"So you have returned to warn me, have you?"

"I have. Though that too is a waste of breath," said Abdullah grumpily. "You do not heed warnings. You take foolish chances."

"It wasn't my idea," I retorted, and laughed again, his scolding and my defense were so wonderfully, realistically familiar. Impulsively I turned to face him. He moved back a few steps.

"Why do you laugh like a silly girl, instead of listening to me?" he demanded, scowling.

"Because I am so glad to see you. I have missed you, Abdullah."

"Ah. Hmmm." He stroked his beard and tried not to smile. "The time allotted me is almost over, Sitt. If you will not turn back, at least take care. Trust no one, not even the innocent. You are followed by enemies, more than you know."

Hot air replaced the cool breeze of a Luxor morning. I felt Emerson's arm round me and the wet cotton of his shirt under my cheek. So wonderful had been that vision that I was loath to see it vanish. Vision or dream—or something more?—it had taken away some of the pain of Abdullah's death. I smiled to myself, remembering his complaints.

"She's smiling," said Nefret's voice.

"Don't wake her." Emerson's grumble was his best attempt at a whisper.

"The heat seems to bother her quite a lot," Ramses said, his even voice softened by concern. "Father, can't you persuade her to remain at Gebel Barkal instead of—"

"Certainly not," I said, and sat up. "What time is it?"

A single lamp, with a cracked shade, smoked redly, casting gruesome shadows across the faces of my companions.

"Time for a bite to eat," said Emerson, avoiding the question of how much longer the jolting journey would take. "We have waited for you, my dear. It was clever of you to think of purchasing food."

"I knew you wouldn't think of it," I retorted. "Have Selim and the others been supplied?"

Ramses assured me they had, and we tucked into the food with good appetite. "You look much better, Aunt Amelia," Nefret remarked. "You were smiling in your sleep. Did you dream of something pleasant?"

"Quite pleasant, my dear. I saw—"

My voice cracked, and Ramses at once handed me a cup

of tea. Sipping it, I reconsidered what I had been about to
say. There was no way I could convey the potency of that
dream and its effect. They would think me silly and sentimental if I spoke of Abdullah. Emerson might pat me on
the head. He means it to be comforting, but he pats too
hard and musses my hair.

"I dreamed about Luxor," I explained. "The cliff above
Deir el Bahri. The air was beautifully clear and cool and
the sun was rising."

Emerson cleared his throat noisily. "It won't be long before we are there again, Peabody, my dear. I promise."

He patted me on the head. "Ouch," I said.

The interminable trip dragged on. I dozed fitfully in the
circle of Emerson's strong arm. Nefret had also suc-
cumbed, curled up on the seat with her head on Ramses's
lap. He was reading, or trying to, by the dim light, but he
seldom turned a page.

At last the first faint blush of dawn lessened the darkness. "There it is!" Emerson shouted in my ear. "Gebel
Barkal!"

In fact it was not. The great mountain temple of the ancient Cushites was still several miles away. However, the
train was slowing, and I was willing to make allowances for
Emerson's imagination.

Ramses closed his book and put his hand lightly on Nefret's shoulder. She murmured sleepily and turned her
head, her face rosy with sleep.

"Wake up," Ramses said. "We are arriving. Mother, how
are you feeling?"

"Perfectly fit," I assured him. "What now, Emerson?"

"Everything is quite in order," said Emerson proudly.
"You remember my old friend—"

"Not Mustapha, Emerson! I hoped he was dead!"

"Peabody!" said Emerson in shocked surprise.

"I meant—that is to say—I thought he must be dead."

Ramses had turned away, his hand raised to hide his

mouth. He remembered Mustapha and my blistering comments on that gentleman's ideas of a comfortable dwelling. A tent in the desert—a cave in the cliffs—would have seemed like Shepheard's compared with the house Mustapha had furnished us.

"Oh," said Emerson. "Well, he's not. And there he is, right on time. Admirable chap!"

The years had left no mark on Mustapha, possibly because he had already been as wrinkled and cadaverous as he was likely to become—and as dirty. As before, he was so *very* glad to see us, it was difficult to resent the old fellow. There were real tears in his eyes when he embraced Emerson and saluted me. He praised Nefret's beauty and grace, looked wonderingly at Ramses, who had been a boy of ten at their last meeting, and burst into a litany of praise with which I was becoming only too familiar. "Just like your honored father! Tall and handsome and strong, pleasing the women with your—"

"Quite," said Emerson, with a little cough. "Well, Mustapha, I see you have a number of stout fellows ready to help us. This is our reis, Selim, and his cousin Daoud, and his cousin Ali."

Kareima was the end of the line. I watched the train empty. Apparently Emerson's ruse had succeeded, for I saw no European travelers. The other passengers were locals.

During the train ride I had tried several times to make Emerson tell me how he planned to proceed once we reached Napata. He had simply smiled with insufferable smugness. "You said you would leave it to me, Peabody."

I really regretted having done so, though to be fair I do not suppose I could have improved on Emerson's arrangements. The route we had followed was not the one we had taken ten years earlier, when we arrived by steamer from Kerma—in other words, from the opposite direction. This part of the extensive region known as Napata was new to me and I cannot say I liked the looks of it. Except for the depot, there was nothing at Kareima except a collection of the round huts known as tukhuls. The palm branches of which they are woven offer hospitality to a variety of insect and rodent life. The inhabitants are very generous, and most would willingly turn out of their own houses in order to lend (hire out, I should say) them to visitors; but intrepid travelers who visit this region are well advised to bring their own supplies, including tents.

We had brought tents. It was a cheering thought.

"We will set up our first camp at Gebel Barkal," said Emerson, stroking his chin. "It is only a few miles farther on. Unless, Peabody, you would like to rest for a while. Mustapha has offered his—"

"No!" I exclaimed. "That is—it is good of Mustapha, but I would rather go on. By what means of transportation, may I ask?"

Mustapha proudly indicated a variety of means. I declined to ride in the carts, which were already being laden with our belongings, and rejected a camel in favor of a gloomy-looking donkey. Mustapha had also provided two horses, which kept prancing and rolling their eyes in a menacing manner. I had the feeling Mustapha expected some entertainment from watching us attempt to ride the creatures. His face fell when Ramses, who can ride anything on four legs, sprang into the saddle and brought the balky beast under control with knees and hands. Emerson took the other horse. He had no trouble either. Even an obstreperous horse knows better than to argue with Emerson.

Leaving the men to finish loading the carts, we proceeded on our way through the village. Before long, the Holy Mountain came into sight. It was an impressive natural feature, a flat-topped mountain of sandstone rising up over two hundred feet from the plain. At its base were the ruins of temples that had stood on that spot for over a thousand years, raised to the glory of the god Amon-Re and numerous other deities. As we drew nearer, I saw that there was movement among the tumbled stones.

"What is going on?" I asked Mustapha.

"They are digging, Sitt Hakim." He added, in a tone of mild disgust, "Digging for broken stones and empty pots, like you. They have found no gold."

Emerson and Ramses were some distance ahead, but I heard Emerson's "Hell and damnation!" clearly. I believe Ramses attempted to restrain him, but he was in such a passion he paid no attention. He set the horse to a gallop. It was not a sensible thing to do, considering the broken ground. We went after him as fast as we could, but before we caught him up the horse stumbled and Emerson flew over its head, landing with a thump at the feet of a man who had appeared from behind one of the broken walls. He was wearing European clothing and a pith helmet. With an exclamation of concern he assisted Emerson to rise.

Our worst forebodings had been fulfilled. The tally was now almost complete. The man was a confounded Egyptologist!

## Five

"You aren't going to wash the damned camels, are you?" Emerson inquired, in the tone of one who hopes for a negative answer but does not really expect it.

"Certainly I am. Have you ever known me to shirk my duty to man or beast?"

"These camels look extremely clean," said Emerson, in a last-ditch effort to stop me.

"Without wishing to be rude about a friend of yours, Emerson, I refuse to take on faith any object, animate or not, brought to us by Mustapha."

"Curse it," Emerson muttered. "Well, don't expect me to help you. Bloody nonsense!"

It was only a token protest. Emerson would never mistreat an animal or allow it to be mistreated. Besides, he knew I would go ahead anyhow. On my first visit to Egypt I had discovered that most of the little donkeys bestrode by tourists suffered from sores and mistreatment, and I had made it a point ever since to wash and doctor all the animals we employed. I had to give Emerson credit; he had refrained from mentioning the dismal fate of the last batch of camels I had doctored. I have to give myself credit; it was not my fault that someone had put poison in my camel medicine.

"It won't take long, Emerson. I believe I have the hang of it now."

This proved to be a somewhat optimistic assessment. I have reached the conclusion that it is impossible for anyone to wash a camel quickly and easily. Camels have perfectly vile tempers and, I could almost believe, more joints than a normal quadruped. Ropes around the camel's legs and around its neck were held by our men, two to each rope, but this did not prevent the creature from protesting in its mournful howl and kicking for all it was worth. I stood on a little mound with a bucket of soapy water and my brush, and scrubbed whatever part of the camel came within reach. Ramses and Nefret helped by rinsing the beast off while trying to avoid its flailing feet. They were both good with animals, but as Ramses remarked once the job was done, even Saint Francis would have come a cropper with a camel. It was a rather vulgar way of putting it, in my opinion, but since he was wet to the waist and rubbing his shin, I allowed him a little leeway.

We had been at our present camp, at the pyramid field of Nuri, for two days. It was across the river and several miles downstream from Gebel Barkal. Emerson had insisted we move on as soon as he identified the "confounded Egyptologist" (he had employed a more emphatic adjective). Fortunately he had been somewhat winded by his tumble off the horse, so I was able to get to him before he burst into a denunciation of the unfortunate man, who, I felt certain, was guilty of nothing more than being where Emerson did not want him to be. I stuck to that opinion even after Mr. MacFerguson, shaking hands all round and smiling broadly, mentioned that he had worked this past summer at the British Museum.

"Budge," growled Emerson, this being the first word he had breath enough to utter.

"No, sir, MacFerguson," said that gentleman in surprise. "May I say, sir, what an honor it is to meet you—and Mrs.

Emerson—and young Mr. Emerson—and Miss Forth—"

"Selim and Daoud," I said, indicating those two stalwarts. "Our reis and his able assistant."

Mr. MacFerguson shook everybody's hands again. He was a comical-looking man, with a round blob of a nose and a long chin, and ears that had spread out to remarkable dimensions as soon as he removed his pith helmet. "Dear me, this is an unexpected pleasure!" said he, in a prim little voice like that of someone's maiden aunt. "I had heard you planned to work at Meroe."

"Had you, indeed?" said Emerson, who had been in receipt of several sharp pokes from my parasol.

"Yes, yes, word of your plans gets about, even to such a remote spot as this. I received a communication from Mr. Reisner only last week."

"Ah," I said. "So you are connected with Mr. Reisner's Nubian Survey, not with the British Museum."

"No, no. That is—yes, yes, the Nubian Survey, under Mr. Reisner. But how rude I am to keep you standing here in the sun! Allow me to offer you a glass of tea while you tell me how I may assist you. This is a huge site, and I would be absolutely delighted to share it with individuals of such distinction."

Emerson shook his head irritably. Then a new idea seemed to occur to him. His eyes moved from Mr. MacFerguson's preposterous nose to his equally remarkable ears.

"Hmmm," he said. "That is—thank you. Most kind."

While MacFerguson bustled about, finding seats for us in the shade of his tent and directing his servants to make tea, I whispered to Emerson, "I know what you are thinking, Emerson. You are mistaken."

"How do you know what I am thinking? How do you know I am mistaken? That nose is too good to be true."

"Be that as it may, Emerson, and be MacFerguson who he may, he is not Sethos. For one thing, Sethos is almost as tall as you, and MacFerguson is several inches under your height. For another, his eyes are dark brown. For a third thing, he has short stubby fingers and broad palms. It is impossible to change the shape of one's hands. Sethos's hands are narrower and more flexible, with long slender fingers."

Emerson's glare informed me that I ought to have omitted this last criterion. I said hastily, "And his shoulders are much narrower than yours, my dear. So please don't pull his nose."

"Bah," said Emerson, convinced against his will but still aggravated. "All the same, he may have been sent here by Budge."

"Nonsense, Emerson. His being here is pure coincidence. Be nonchalant, my dear. Be agreeable. Smile. Do not arouse suspicions which are, in my opinion, as yet unaroused."

"Ermph," said Emerson, thereby acknowledging the justice of my remarks.

I cannot say that his attempt at a smile was particularly convincing, though it did show quite a number of teeth. He declined Mr. MacFerguson's eager offer to share the site, however.

"We mean to have another go at the pyramids of Nuri," he explained. "Finish the job we started ten years ago. Better be on our way, eh, Peabody?"

MacFerguson's face fell. "At least let me show you round the site, Professor. There has been a great deal done since you were last here."

"Another time," said Emerson, with a longing glance at the looming bulk of Mount Barkal and the ruins that stretched out around its base. They had never been properly excavated, and it was Emerson's contention that they were the remains of temples of various periods, stretching back in time to the sixteenth century B.C. or even earlier. Emerson loves temple ruins, the more complicated, the better. I gave him an affectionate pat on the arm.

The resourceful Mustapha summoned up a small flotilla

of boats and we got ourselves and our baggage across the river. My attempts to persuade Emerson to postpone this activity until the following day fell on deaf ears. "May as well get it over, Peabody. I want to be on our way within forty-eight hours, before that fellow MacFerguson can report we are here."

"I cannot believe he is one of the vultures, Emerson. Our change of plans was so sudden, no one could have anticipated we would head for Napata, and he had been there for almost a week."

"So he claims," Emerson muttered. "I have never heard of the fellow. Have you?"

"No, but perhaps he is new to the field."

"Hmph," said Emerson.

We left the animals behind. There would be, Mustapha assured us, other donkeys and camels awaiting us. I sincerely hoped so. The pyramids were on the plateau, a mile and a half from the river, and the sun was hot. However, Emerson was in the right; the crossing had to be made sooner or later, and unpacking and repacking our goods would be an unnecessary waste of time.

It was late afternoon before my donkey ambled up the slope and I saw the pyramids ahead, black against the blazing reds and purples of the sunset. An even more welcome sight were the flatter pyramid shapes of tents. The men had gone on ahead, with the baggage camels and what appeared to be half the local population, and many willing hands had made light work of preparing camp.

A quick look round told me that Budge, or someone of his ilk, had been at Nuri since we worked there in '98. The poor pyramids were even more dilapidated than they had been then.

"There's Mother," called Ramses, as I and my escort approached. "All right, are you, Mother?"

"She'll be fine as soon as she gets her whiskey," said Emerson, assisting me to dismount. "See to it, will you, Ramses? This way, Peabody, my dear."

### From Letter Collection C

*(These letters and the ones that follow, from Nefret Forth, were not found among the papers of the persons addressed, but in a separate bundle once in the possession of Mrs. Emerson.)*

My dear Evelyn,

In my opinion it is highly unlikely that you will ever receive this letter. When we return from our projected expedition, you will hear of our adventures from our own lips. However, a sensible individual takes even remote possibilities into account.

We are returning to the Lost Oasis. An unexpected visitor brought us a plea for help from our friend Tarek, of whom you have heard me speak. I need not explain to you why we felt obliged to respond.

I will leave this sealed packet with my excellent solicitor, Mr. Fletcher, with instructions to deliver it when and if he deems it appropriate. (Gargery would most likely steam it open.) It contains this brief account and a copy of the map of which you have heard so much. Emerson strictly forbade me to enclose the map, remarking in his bluff fashion that Walter might be fool enough to dash off to the Sudan looking for us, and die of thirst in the desert. I have more confidence in Walter. Should he decide to act, it will be with all due deliberation and caution—and the choice, in my opinion, should be his.

You will, I expect, take David into your confidence. Persuade him if you can that our failure to include him was due to our great affection for him. Do not assume if we fail to return within a reasonable time that we are no more. It sometimes takes us a little longer than we expect to carry out our plans.

:

## From Letter Collection C

Dearest Lia,

I don't know whether you will ever receive this letter. It seems unlikely, but I felt the need to write it. There is a chance we may not return, and I would hate to vanish without a word of love to someone who means so much to me.

Aunt Amelia has written your parents. If you don't already know about my life before I came to England, and the epic journey that brought the Professor and Aunt Amelia—and Ramses—I mustn't forget Ramses—to the Holy Mountain, your parents will tell you when they deem it advisable to do so.

We have always been confidantes, Lia dear, but on this one subject I have been mute. I had promised I would not speak of it, but that wasn't the only reason for my silence. As the months and years went on, the memories faded until they seemed as unreal as a strange dream. Aunt Amelia would probably claim I didn't want to remember. It may be so.

We are about to set out on the same journey. There are still great gaps in my memory, Lia, I don't know why. But I remember Tarek, who was my foster brother, kind and gentle and brave. I loved him very much. Yet I had forgotten what he looked like until his young brother, Merasen, arrived at Amarna House with an appeal for help from Tarek. Tarek and his son, his only heir, are suffering from a strange illness which none of his people can cure—not too surprising, when one considers that their notions of medicine are derived from the mixture of magic and unscientific theory that characterized ancient Egyptian medicine. I've read everything I could find on tropical diseases and I hope and pray I can be of assistance. In any case, we had to make the attempt. I owe Tarek my very life, for I doubt I would have survived long in the City of the Holy Mountain.

I had wondered, now and then, what happened after we fled, leaving Tarek still fighting for his throne. What was the fate of my despicable cousin Reggie Forthright, who had done his best to prevent me from returning to England to claim the inheritance he hoped to get? Was Tarek able to alleviate the suffering of the common people, the enslaved and downtrodden rekkit? Did he marry and have children? For all I knew, the City of the Holy Mountain itself might have fallen into ruin, overrun by enemy tribesmen or destroyed by some unforeseen natural catastrophe.

I know the answers to some of those questions, and soon (inshallah) I will find out the other answers. The journey will be difficult and hazardous, and yet I look forward to its culmination with an eagerness you may find hard to understand. Whatever happens, I will be glad I attempted it. Remember that, dear Lia, if the worst should befall us. I don't for a moment believe it will, though. Aunt Amelia would never allow such a thing.

⁝

"The die is cast," said Emerson in reverberant tones. "The time has come."

We were seated round a campfire, which had been kindled for comfort rather than warmth, though the sun had set and the air was already cooler. The moon had not yet risen, and the outlines of the tents glimmered palely in the darkness.

"What die?" I demanded irritably. "What time? We will not be ready to leave for several more days. You sound like the oracle of Amon Re."

"How do you know what it—"

Ramses broke into his father's complaint. "What Father means is that the time has come to tell Daoud and Selim the truth. Up until now they have heard only the story we told the hired drivers—that we are looking for ruins west of here."

"And a cursed unconvincing story it is too," I declared. "The number of camels and drivers we have hired is far too great for such a short trip. The men are already speculating."

"Let them speculate to their hearts' content," said Emerson. "They don't know anything. Good Gad, Peabody, you are in an excessively critical mood this evening. Get her another whiskey, Ramses."

I accepted the offering in the spirit in which it was meant.

"You are both right," I admitted, after a cheering sip or two. "Ramses, will you ask Selim and Daoud to join us? You might see if you can locate Merasen too. He has rather avoided us lately."

"He's been making friends with our men," Nefret said, as Ramses went off toward the little camp our fellows had set up. "I told him his autocratic manner wouldn't serve him well with them—or us—and he seems to have taken my lecture to heart. He and young Ali have become chums."

I couldn't help laughing a little, the word "chum" sounded so incongruous in connection with Merasen.

Ramses was back almost at once, with our two stalwarts. "I couldn't find Merasen," he explained.

Selim scowled. "He and Ali have gone off together. You must speak to the boy, Emerson; he is too interested in the women of the village, and Ali is young and a fool."

"We won't have to worry about the women of the village any longer," said Emerson. "This is our last night here. Er—our last for some time to come. Selim—Daoud—my friends—the journey on which we embark tomorrow is longer and more hazardous than I have led you to believe. I am about to tell you of our true purpose, so that you may decide whether or not to accompany us. The choice will be yours."

Placid and unmoving as a monumental statue, Daoud said, "There is no choice. Where the Father of Curses goes, we follow, even into the fires of Gehenna."

Emerson cleared his throat noisily. "Hmph. Thank you, my friend. But you have not yet heard the facts."

"There is no need," said Selim. The moon had risen; its cold light outlined his sharp handsome features with shadows. "Daoud has spoken the truth. Your words come as no surprise, Emerson. The boy is no villager, and the weapon he carries is no Arab sword."

Without further ado, Emerson launched into the story of the Lost Oasis. Daoud listened with interest but without surprise; he had an almost childlike sense of wonder about the world, which meant that nothing surprised him—or that everything did. Selim's mobile features expressed a variety of emotions, but the predominant one was delight.

"It will be a great adventure," he exclaimed.

"Think well, Selim," said Emerson, in sepulchral tones. "At the end, our bones may lie whitening in the sand."

Daoud's deep voice replied, "Or they may not. It is in the hands of God."

Emerson had been speaking his fluent and somewhat florid Arabic. I now said, in English, "We have a proverb: God helps those who help themselves."

Selim threw his head back and laughed aloud. "And so we will, Sitt Hakim. How can we fail, with you and the Father of Curses to lead us?"

I could think of a number of ways, but there was no sense in raising doubts. It is a well-known fact that courage is based to some extent on the failure to recognize danger (stupidity, in other words) and also on self-confidence.

After swearing Selim and Daoud to secrecy, we went early to bed. Emerson dropped off to sleep at once, but I could not. Forebodings seldom trouble my husband; he does not believe in them, or so he says. They troubled me

that night. Small wonder, considering what the morrow
would bring. At last I gave up the attempt to woo slumber;
rising quietly, I put on my dressing gown and slipped out
of the tent. The moon was nearing the full. Its silvery rays
were bright enough to illumine a familiar form standing
still as a statue some distance away. His back was toward
me; he looked toward the west. He must have heard the
rustle of my skirts as I approached, but he did not turn.

"Is something the matter, Ramses?" I asked.

His voice was as soft as mine when he replied; the stillness forbade loud speech. "I was remembering a certain
night ten years ago, when you found me outside my tent,
and I told you I had heard a voice summoning me. A voice
I took to be yours. It was on this very spot."

"Or near it," I agreed cautiously, for he sounded very
strange. "Please don't tell me it has happened again. That
imagined voice was the result of a post-hypnotic suggestion planted in your mind by Tarek in order to—"

"I know why." His face looked like stone, his eyes sunk
in pits of shadow, his high cheekbones and firm mouth
sharply outlined. In a sudden panic I caught hold of his arm
and was ridiculously relieved to feel warm, hard human
muscle. He shivered. The air was cold. Then he looked
down at me and said lightly, "No, Mother, nothing has happened, not even a ghostly voice from the past. I couldn't
sleep and stepped out for a breath of air. I hope I didn't
waken you."

"I couldn't sleep either."

"It will be all right, Mother."

"I know."

"Good night."

"Good night."

I was drinking my tea when Selim came striding toward me.

"Ali has not come back," he said, too worried to give the
conventional greeting. "The boy is not in camp either, unless he is with you."

I turned in silent inquiry to Ramses, whose tent Merasen shared. He shook his head. "He didn't come in last night."

"Send someone to the village to look for them." Emerson's teeth snapped together. "If they are sleeping off a night of—er, well, if that proves to be the case, I will make them run behind the camels for a day or so."

They were not in the village. Daoud returned to report that they had been there, but had left shortly before midnight. "The boy (he had adopted Selim's contemptuous name for Merasen) drank much beer and boasted to the girls. Ali drank too."

Selim sprang to his feet with a furious exclamation. "Never has he done such a thing. He knows the Law. When he returns I will—"

"I don't think we should wait for him to return," Ramses said in a curiously flat voice. "I'll go back to the village and start from there. Perhaps someone saw which way they went."

This seemed the most sensible procedure, so we all accompanied him. We got little information from the locals; the virtuous among them had been asleep and the habitues of the illicit tavern too drunk to be observant. We spread out, searching behind every outcropping and hillock. It was Ramses and I who found Ali, in a little gully only ten feet from the path. One look was enough. The pool of blood in which poor Ali's body lay had already dried. Ramses made me look away when he turned the body over, and I did not protest. Ali's throat had been cut. There was no trace of Merasen.

"That takes care of coincidence," said Ramses, after we returned to camp. Selim and Daoud were preparing Ali's body for burial, which must be done before sunset. The villagers had offered all possible assistance, including a grave in the cemetery near the small mosque. The poor souls were afraid they would be blamed, and horrified by the brutality of the murder.

"It wasn't one of the villagers," Ramses went on. "They

had everything to lose and nothing to gain by such an act. And Ali is the third of our men to be taken from us."

"Yes, yes, Ramses, we all understand that," Emerson grunted. He was smoking furiously, which would have been a sure sign of distress and anger even if his scowling countenance had not made his feelings clear. "When I get my hands on that boy—"

"Merasen?" Nefret stiffened. "Why do you assume he is guilty? He may have been carried off by the people who killed Ali."

"It is possible," Ramses said.

Nefret's pale cheeks regained some of their color. "You're against him. You always have been."

"That will be quite enough, Nefret," I said firmly. She had been badly shaken by the death of Ali, a merry, laughing lad whom we all liked. "The situation is too grave for recriminations," I went on. "We now have proof that someone is working actively against us. Who that person may be, we do not yet know. There is one strong point in Merasen's favor: he was not on the boat when Hassan fell, or was pushed, overboard."

"That's right," Nefret said eagerly.

"However," I said, "I suggest that we look through our baggage and that of Merasen. I would like to know whether anything is missing—money, personal possessions, papers of any kind."

"Well done, Mother," said Ramses.

"How good of you to say so, my dear."

At first glance Merasen's precious suitcase and other bundles appeared to have been undisturbed. But when we opened the former we found that most of the clothing was gone, along with the sword and its scabbard. Ramses so forgot himself as to use bad language.

"Goddamn it! I thought I was being so clever when I insisted on his sharing my quarters, but I obviously wasn't clever enough. He must have squirreled his things away earlier, I'd have waked up if he had come crawling in last night."

"You did suspect him," Nefret said.

"A pity no one else did," said Emerson, in the cool, quiet voice that was more ominous than his bellows. "Not your fault, my boy. Let's see what else he has taken."

Emerson had already dispensed part of the money, in return for the hire of the camels and their drivers, and a considerable baksheesh to the obliging Mustapha. The rest, according to his count, was intact, which did not surprise me, since he had kept it close to his person throughout. Our next concern was for the weapons. The heavy boxes, which had been in Selim's charge, appeared to be untouched; but Emerson wrenched them open.

"All here," he said. "I meant to hand them round before we left, but I may as well do it now." He lifted one of the rifles, a great heavy thing longer than my arm, and handed it to Ramses. "Load it. Now."

"Yes, sir."

Ramses refused to hunt and preferred not to carry firearms, but after an incident a few years earlier he had taken up target shooting, explaining in his cool fashion, "There are circumstances under which proficiency in this particular skill might come in useful."

I reached for another of the weapons. Emerson slapped my hand away. "It's too heavy for you. The recoil would probably break your shoulder, even if you could hold it steady. You too, Nefret."

Nefret was watching Ramses, who had taken shells from another box and was expertly loading the weapon. "I don't want it," she said in a choked voice.

"What about the pistols?" I inquired hopefully. There were seven of them, large, efficient-looking weapons.

"You are the world's worst shot, Peabody," said my husband without rancor. "You have never even managed to hit anything with that little pistol of yours—anything you aimed at, that is."

"I could learn, Emerson."

"Not with this," said Emerson.

There were enough weapons to arm all of the men, with several extra. We left Ramses to mount guard over them and went to carry out the next stage of our search. I had a horrible foreboding of what we would find—or rather, not find.

It was Nefret's copy of the map that had disappeared. At first she refused to accept this, tossing papers all over the floor of the tent in a frantic search.

"Face facts, my dear," I said, putting a sympathetic hand on her shoulder. "He had ample opportunity to take it."

"So did others," Nefret muttered, as she knelt, head bowed, among the scattered papers.

"We are wasting time," said Emerson. "The sooner we get off, the better. Masud is watering the camels. I will hurry him up and tell him to start loading. Nefret, get your gear together. Peabody, find Selim and tell him we are leaving immediately after the funeral."

"You mean to go on, then?" I asked.

"Have we any other choice?"

In fact, we did not. It would have been unthinkable to abandon Tarek if there was the slightest chance that we might be of service to him. As Ramses had been the first to point out, Merasen had carried no written message, and his behavior since had given us good cause to question his veracity. Yet I had known men to be proved innocent with even stronger evidence against them.

The evidence against another, unknown party was mounting. Merasen could not have been responsible for Hassan's injury; Ali's brutal murder and the theft of the map from Nefret must be part of the same deadly plot. The map in itself would be of no use to Merasen; he could not read the compass bearings; yet, as we had realized, he could not find his way to the Holy City, or guide another there, without such an aid. Whoever this "other" might be, his intentions could not be honorable or harmless, toward us or toward Tarek. We knew only two things about him.

He could use a compass and follow a map; and he had been on the boat to Wadi Halfa.

The missionaries, the Great White Hunter, the garrulous German tourists, the agreeable Captain Moroney? Or someone else, cleverly disguised as one of the crewmen?

The sun sank slowly in the west. (Or, to put it in scientific terms, the turning globe on which we stood revolved slowly in the opposite direction.) Like most sunsets in sandy regions, this one set the horizon ablaze with streaks of brilliant color, and the last rays of the solar orb cast a theatrical effect of light and shadow over the forms of man and beast.

It was a scene to capture the imagination of the most romantic—the line of heavily loaded camels, their long shadows even more grotesque than the beasts themselves, and the men attired in long robes and a variety of exotic headgear. Except for the incessant grumbles of the camels, an eerie silence reigned. We were to travel at night, avoiding the daytime heat, while the moon was at the full.

It was the evening of the day following our discovery of Merasen's treachery. Emerson's intention of leaving that same night had been overly optimistic. Camels cannot be hurried when they are being readied for a long expedition; they must be allowed to drink their fill and rest afterwards. Proper loading also requires time and deliberation. Zerwali had politely pointed out these facts to Emerson.

He was the leader of the Bedouins we had hired to accompany us. Most of our men were Nubians, but the Bedouin know the desert well and were valuable additions to our crew. Zerwali was a slight, wiry fellow who had—of course—known Emerson before. When he joined us that evening, he was wearing the usual Bedouin garb of shirt and long calico drawers, with the voluminous woolen jerd wrapped round him to ward off the chill of the night air. He was accompanied by Masud, the Nubian, who was to accompany us, and from whom we had hired the majority of the camels.

We had just returned from seeing poor Ali laid to rest, as was his due. When the brief service was concluded, Selim had been the first to turn away. Daoud's eyes were red-rimmed, but there was no sign of grief on Selim's face, only a fierce determination. It bore the same expression as he sat listening to the exchange of compliments between Emerson and Zerwali and Masud. Finally the latter got to the point.

"It is said, Father of Curses, that our destination is farther distant than we believed."

"I contracted with you for thirty marhalas (days' travel)," Emerson replied. "I did not inform you of our destination."

Masud accepted this snub with a shrug, but persisted. "Is it to the southwest we go?"

"Yes."

"Wallahi, it is a dangerous route," Masud muttered. "And many a caravan has been eaten up by the wild men of the hills along the way. They do not fear God. They are like birds; they live on the tops of mountains . . ."

"We made an agreement," Emerson replied, monumentally calm. "If you are afraid to keep it . . ."

Zerwali let out a derisive laugh. "Yes, let the cowards depart. We are with you, Father of Curses."

Masud turned on him with a snarl, and Emerson said, "There are no cowards here, and I will not allow quarreling among you. Go now. We will load the camels tomorrow, after they have rested."

There was no further dissension, but I saw trouble ahead. When I mentioned this to Emerson he made a rude remark about forebodings and then went on, "Sufficient unto the day is the evil thereof, as you are so fond of saying, Peabody. We will deal with difficulties as they arise."

The camels were brought in about midday and the loading was about to begin when Daoud spoke to Emerson. "We must bless the baggage, Emerson."

"What? Oh, curse it," said Emerson. "But, Daoud, there is no holy man—"

"I have brought him," said Daoud. The wrinkled old man who had conducted Ali's funeral service stepped forward, his fingers on the amber beads of a rosary. With a polite nod at Emerson, the old gentleman went from pile to pile of baggage, saying little prayers over each. Then he turned to the men who had gathered round him and raised his hands, palms up. "May God guide your steps. Allah yesadded khatak. May he give success to your undertaking."

"It was a good thought, Daoud," said Ramses, who, like myself, had seen the faces of the travelers brighten.

"Hmph, yes," Emerson muttered. "Thank you, Daoud." He rewarded the imam extravagantly and then ordered the loading to begin, courteously asking the advice of both Masud and Zerwali. When the loads had been carefully arranged and balanced, he rode back along the long line for a final check. He had hired a pair of riding camels which we were to use in turn, and several of the pack camels' loads had been lightened to accommodate other riders. The men would walk most of the time, mounting a camel periodically in order to rest. A camel's pace, of approximately two and a half miles per hour, is not hard to match.

Emerson came back, followed by Daoud.

"Ready, my dear?" inquired my spouse.

"As ready as I will ever be," I replied, shifting position slightly. The new position was not much of an improvement. In my opinion there is no comfortable position on a camel. "But first, Emerson—I know you do not share my belief in Divine Providence, but—"

"Oh, good Gad, haven't we had enough praying?" Emerson demanded. "Very well. Make it short."

I bowed my head and murmured a few words, then turned to Daoud. "Will you say a blessing, Daoud?"

"I have already asked for His mercy, Sitt," said Daoud calmly. "But one can never pray too much, is it not so?" His reverberant voice rose up over the grumbles of the camels (and, I am sorry to say, those of Emerson). "Praise be to God, the Master of the Universe, the Compassionate . . ."

Other voices joined his in the recitation of the Fatah. Ramses's was among them, and I am not ashamed to admit that mine was also. It made a good impression on the men, but that was not why I did it.

It was a long night. The sun had been up for several hours before Emerson let out an exclamation and pointed. "There it is—the rock outcropping where we stopped last time after the first day's journey. We'll make camp there."

I didn't know how he could be so certain it was the same place. There were a number of outcroppings, for this was not the Great Sand Sea or the Sahara with their great rolling dunes, but a region of red and black hills interspersed with stretches of sand like pools of gold. However, I was more than ready to get off the cursed camel. Pride forbade I should admit weakness; I waved Ramses away when he offered me his hand to help me dismount—and waited until he had turned his back before I slid stiffly to the ground.

The men made haste to erect the tents, for there was not much shade, and that little would shrink as the sun rose higher. Selim started a small fire to boil water for tea, and we gathered round it to eat bread and extremely warm oranges and soft goat cheese that would be rancid before the day was over. From now on we would subsist on the basic supplies of desert travelers: rice and flour, baked into unleavened bread, sugar and tea, with a handful of dates now and then. The dates were not the sweet, soft fruit to which we were accustomed; the camels lived on them when there was no fresh fodder available, and we ate them only for nourishment. I had packed some tinned food—tomatoes and bully beef and fruit—but the weight of such items prohibited excess.

Physical fatigue sent me quickly to sleep, but I woke gasping for breath after what seemed only a brief nap. It was later than I had thought; the sun had sunk down the

west, brightening one side of the tent. Emerson sat cross-
legged nearby, writing in his notebook. Perspiration trick-
led down his cheeks and dripped onto the paper, but he
went on with his scribbling as placidly as if he had been in
his study at Amarna House. Whereas I felt like Saint
Lawrence on his griddle, toasted on front, back, and both
sides.

"Ah, awake, are you?" he inquired when I stirred. "Did
you have a good sleep? Dear me, you appear a trifle warm.
Would you like a drink?"

"I would like a cold bath," I croaked. "But I will settle
for a sip of water and a damp cloth."

Emerson supplied these luxuries, and after I had wiped
my face and throat I felt quite myself again. I looked out
the open flap of the tent and saw that the others were stirring. The red rays of the declining sun turned the baked
ground into a fair imitation of the infernal regions. A hot
wind blew hair into my eyes.

"Did you sleep at all?" I asked, removing the pins and
shaking out my heavy locks.

"It was too hot."

"Oh, really?"

Emerson looked up. Seeing what I was doing, he came
to my side and lifted my hair, spreading it across his big
hands.

"Not now, Emerson," I mumbled through a mouthful of
pins.

"Just helping to dry it, my dear. The sun will be down
soon, and then the air will be delightfully cool. A perfect
night for a ride in the moonlight."

"What a poet you are, Emerson."

Emerson grinned. "Don't swallow your hairpins,
Peabody."

After a supper of tinned peas, tinned beef, and bread
baked on hot stones, we reloaded the camels and were
ready to ride when the moon rose. The effect is quite magical; in the clear, dry air of the desert, the light of the lunar

orb is so bright one can see almost as clearly as by day, and
the stars blazed with diamond fire. The ground that had
been a sullen red was now silver. I felt quite refreshed, but
Emerson was not inclined toward conversation, so for a
while we rode side by side in silence and I contented myself with admiring the strong outline of his profile and the
glimmer of moonlight in his black hair. We stopped once to
stretch our stiff limbs and have a sip of water, and then we
went on . . . and on . . . and . . .

A hard hand closed over my upper arm. "Here now,
Peabody," said Emerson, in some alarm. "If you fall asleep
you will topple off the damned camel. I'll take you up with
me, shall I?"

"No, thank you," I said, my energy restored by the suggestion. If there is anything more uncomfortable than riding a camel, it is riding in front of someone who is riding a
camel. "I am wide awake now. Quite a refreshing little nap.
Thank you, for looking out for me, my dear."

"I was about to indicate a point of interest. Over there."

They shone as if luminescent, bleached to a pearly white
by moonlight—a pile of tumbled bones. We had seen the remains of a few small animals, gazelle and hare and antelope,
but these were not those of a small animal. They had been
stripped bare by predators of some kind. Reflected moonlight twinkled in the empty sockets of the skull as we passed.

"A camel?"

"Not just any camel," said Emerson. "One of ours. Formerly one of ours, I should say. The first of the lot to die."

"Not a good omen, Emerson," I said, remembering how
the cursed beasts had perished one by one, leaving us
stranded.

"You and your omens! It is a good sign. We are on the
right track."

Leaving the desolate heap of bones behind, we went on
until the stars faded and the sky began to lighten. We were
making good time, better than we had on our first trip, but
Emerson gave no indication of halting. The sun rose be-

hind us, sending our shadows leaping forward across the ground. One elongated outline grew more rapidly and I saw that Ramses had come up beside us.

"Father. Look there."

At first it was only a little puff of pale yellow, but it soon expanded, like a moving cloud.

"It is a sandstorm?" I asked apprehensively.

"Worse," said Ramses.

"Can you tell how many?" Emerson asked.

"No. They're still too far away."

"Hmph," said Emerson. He yanked violently on the head rope of his camel, turning it. "You know what to do."

"Yes, sir." Ramses set his beast to a trot and rode toward the end of the caravan.

I do not approve of cruelty to animals, but the only way to get the attention of a camel is to whack it. The men needed no such inducement; they too had seen the approaching cloud and knew what it portended. With blows and shouts they formed the recalcitrant beasts into a rough circle and forced them to kneel.

"Quite like the Old West, is it not?" I said to Nefret. "Camels instead of wagons, but it is the same principle, and—"

"Get down, Peabody," Emerson said, reinforcing the suggestion with a push that made my knees buckle. "And pay attention."

"Let me have one of those guns," I demanded. It was possible now to see moving forms in the dust, the forms of mounted men.

"Not on your life," said Emerson. "Selim, Daoud, here, on my right. Ready, Ramses?"

The armed men knelt behind their camels, their weapons aimed. Most of them had rifles, and some of the Bedouin prided themselves on their marksmanship. However, according to Emerson, they were inclined to exaggerate their skill, and many of the guns were old, verging on antique. We appeared to be outnumbered by at least ten to one. I crept closer to Emerson and took out my little pistol.

"Don't fire until I give the word," said Emerson coolly. He repeated the order in Arabic. "That includes you, Peabody. Aim high, over their heads. On second thought, Peabody, don't fire at all. Ready? Now."

A somewhat ragged volley shook the clear air. "Again," Emerson said.

The second volley slowed them, but the leader came on. He was brandishing a weapon—not a rifle, a huge sword. So it was to be hand-to-hand fighting! I heard Nefret gasp and saw her grip the hilt of her knife. I wondered if Emerson would have the decency to shoot me after all hope had failed. I wondered if I could bring myself to shoot Nefret rather than let her endure the hideous alternative—capture and slavery in a Turkish harem. They might not bother taking me prisoner, since by their standards I was a trifle elderly, but Nefret was a prize worthy of a pasha.

To my horror, Emerson suddenly bounded to his feet. Exposed from the waist up, he raised both arms and shouted something in Arabic. The leader was now so close I could make out his face—hawk-nosed and bearded, decaying teeth bared in a ferocious fighting grin. The blade of the sword flashed as he whirled it over his head. Emerson dropped the rifle, folded his arms, and stood motionless.

"Shoot," I shrieked. "Ramses, shoot the bas—— the man immediately, do you hear me?"

His finger was on the trigger and the gun was aimed at the rider's breast. Then it shifted, just a little, and he fired. The bullet struck the raised sword blade with a ring like that of a gong, and the weapon flew out of the rider's hand. With a howl of pain and surprise, he jerked at the camel's head rope and the beast veered off, followed by the rest of the attackers. They swept past in a cloud of sand.

"Well done," said Emerson, giving his son a clap on the back. "Thank you, my boy, for ignoring your mother's hysterical order."

"Yes, sir," Ramses said. He lowered the rifle and sat down rather suddenly.

"It was a wonderful shot," Selim said. "Now what do we do?"

"Wait," said Emerson, still upright. "Here, Peabody, what's the matter? You aren't going to faint, I trust."

"No, I am going to kill you. How dare you, Emerson? How dare you frighten me so?"

"I am beginning to suspect," said Ramses, wiping his wet forehead with his sleeve, "that my flamboyant gesture was unnecessary."

"No, no, it was a nice added touch," Emerson said soothingly. "Well, let's make camp, shall we? Stand down, all of you," he added in resounding Arabic. "The Father of Curses will protect you."

A short time later Selim, who had appointed himself sentry, let out a hail. "A rider approaches, Emerson."

"Ah," said Emerson. "One man, Selim?"

"Yes, Father of Curses. He stops. He holds up a white flag. Does that mean I cannot shoot him?"

"I'm afraid so," said Emerson. "Keep him covered, though."

"Aren't you going to invite him to join us for breakfast?" I inquired with, I believe, a pardonable touch of sarcasm.

"Presently. I want my tea first. Is it ready?"

I handed round the cups and went to join Selim. The envoy was the leader himself. He had a rifle slung over his shoulder and a sword stuck through his sash, but his hands were empty except for the makeshift flag of truce. Emerson continued to sip his tea. He was delaying for two reasons: first, to annoy me, and second, to assert his superiority over the envoy. Finally he stood up and stretched.

"I am going with you," I said.

"No, you are bloody well not. Good Gad, Peabody, how would it look to have a woman trailing at my heels?"

"Ramses, then."

Ramses, who had not risen, said evenly, "There is a kind

of etiquette in these matters, Mother. He'll have to go
alone. Not on foot, but unarmed."

"Quite right," said Emerson. He mounted one of the
kneeling camels and induced it to stand up.

We crowded round Selim, watching Emerson ride
slowly toward the waiting man. "I do not approve of this,"
I announced. "Who are these people, anyhow?"

"Tebu, I think." Ramses did not take his eyes off his father. "Of the Guraan tribe."

Emerson reined up beside the other man. I couldn't hear
what they said, but after a brief exchange the raider burst
into a peal of laughter and the two rode back toward us,
side by side.

Ramses said softly, "Mother and Nefret, go into one of
the tents and stay out of sight."

"Why?" Nefret demanded. "I have never behaved like a
proper Moslem lady and I won't do it now!"

"The majority of the Tebu are peaceable enough, but the
renegades among them are the most dangerous raiders in
the Western Desert. They still take slaves," Ramses said
through tight lips. "This fellow may be another of Father's
old friends, but I see no sense in waving a tempting morsel
like you in front of him. Get inside."

"But—"

"Mother, make her go, or I will."

"You are right," I said. "Come, Nefret. We can peek
through a crack."

We beat a hasty retreat and just made it inside the tent
before Emerson and his "guest" entered the camp. At the
sight of the latter, Nefret's resentful scowl faded. Of
medium height, dark-skinned as a Nubian, and lean as a
feral dog, he was not an impressive figure physically, but
there was a certain look about him—the look of a man who
acts as he chooses with no inconvenient interference from
his conscience.

He seemed to be in quite a jovial frame of mind, his
bearded lips parted in a smile; but as he settled himself on

the rug and accepted a glass of tea, his eyes moved around the camp, as if taking stock of our numbers and our gear. Then they fixed on Ramses, who was sitting cross-legged next to him.

"Your father tells me it was you who shot the sword out of my hand. A lucky shot."

"I hit what I mean to hit," Ramses said, looking down his nose at the other man. "I could have put the bullet through your head if I had wished to. You were wise to turn aside when you did."

It wasn't like him to boast, but, as he knew, modesty is wasted on Arabs. The man, whom Emerson had introduced as Kemal, acknowledged the retort with a nod and a grin.

"It was the sight of your father that turned me aside, boy. They did not tell me this was his caravan."

They were all speaking Arabic, except for an occasional aside in English from Emerson to Ramses, or vice versa. "Who hired you?" Emerson demanded.

"A man of honor does not betray his employer" was the smooth reply. "Secrecy was part of the agreement."

"It seems an unnecessary part," said Emerson, equally bland. "If your aim is to leave none alive to tell the tale."

"But no, Father of Curses, that was never our aim." He widened his eyes and shook his head. "We were told you had money—many camels—weapons . . . Other treasures."

He looked toward the tents—the only places of concealment. Ramses stiffened, and Emerson said in English, "Don't look round." To Kemal, he said, "So you were to have these . . . treasures as your reward for—what? For massacring the lot of us?"

"But I said it, Father of Curses—I did not know it was you." He grinned. "If I had known, I would have asked for payment in advance."

"And now?"

Holding his glass as delicately as a lady might hold her cup, Kemal finished his tea before he replied.

"We would overwhelm you in the end, but you would kill

many of us first." He pursed his lips and looked thoughtful. "I ask myself whether the cost would be too high."

"This is becoming tiresome," said Emerson to Ramses. "And time is passing. Have you any suggestions?"

"He wants a bribe."

"Naturally. The question is, will he stay bribed?"

He turned back to his guest and shook his head. "My son is young and hot-tempered. He tells me that if your men attack, you will be the first to die. In the name of our old friendship, I would regret that."

"So would I," said Kemal, with admirable candor. His eyes shifted sideways, toward Ramses, who stared stonily back at him. "Hmmm. Perhaps we can come to an agreement."

After some discussion, a barbaric little ceremony ensued. At Emerson's request, Ramses handed over his knife. Emerson drew the blade across his palm and handed the knife to Kemal, who did the same. They clasped each other's hand and maintained the grasp for several long seconds, while their mingled blood dripped down onto the sand. Then Kemal offered the knife to Ramses. It was clear that he was not simply returning the weapon, but proposing a similar ceremony. Eyebrows raised, Ramses looked at his father. Emerson, who was (confound the man) wiping his bleeding hand on his trousers, nodded and watched benignly while Ramses and the bandit also became blood brothers. The look of barely concealed distaste on my son's face would have been amusing if the situation had been less grave.

"In the name of God the Great," said the marauder piously. He made another leisurely survey of the camp. I could almost hear him counting to himself. A dozen armed men—and Daoud, who had not taken his eyes off Kemal and who looked willing and able to murder him with his bare hands. "So," he said. "It only remains to seal our friendship with an exchange of gifts."

After further discussion and the presentation of a heavy

leather bag, Emerson escorted his dear old friend to his camel, and Nefret and I emerged from our hiding place.

"Is it safe to come out now?" I inquired—somewhat belatedly, since we were already out.

"He's riding off," said Ramses, who had been watching them. "But you might have waited until I told you it was all right."

"Bah," said Nefret, brushing sand off her front.

Emerson came back, looking somewhat pensive.

"Well?" I demanded. "I didn't understand everything that was said, you were both talking so rapidly toward the end, but I saw you hand over what appeared to be most of our remaining money. How are you going to pay the drivers? Shouldn't we move on at once instead of waiting for nightfall? Why didn't you insist he tell you who hired him? How do you know you can trust him to stay bribed?"

Emerson sat down, his back against the nearest camel, and took out his pipe. "I beg you will keep quiet for a while, Peabody, while I explain the subtler nuances of our encounter."

"I saw nothing subtle about it. His meaning was clear; he had been told to intercept and rob us, if nothing worse; his reward would have been money, modern weapons, camels—and Nefret."

"And you," said Emerson. "He said 'treasures.' Plural."

"Oh, bah," I exclaimed. "Don't tease, Emerson, I really cannot endure your idea of humor just now. He couldn't get much of a price for a—er—mature lady like myself."

"Now there you are mistaken, my dear. There is one individual who would pay any price, including his fortune, his life, and his sacred honor."

In the intense warmth of those keen blue orbs my vexation melted. I could even forgive him the florid rhetoric. One gets into a certain verbal pattern after speaking a formal language like Arabic. And I knew he meant every florid word.

"More than one," said Ramses matter-of-factly. "Kemal's primary purpose was robbery and abduction, though he would not have balked at killing a few people. We would have been taken prisoner and held for ransom. The drivers—those who survived—would have been left here without transport or water. Some of them might have made it back to the river."

"Might," Nefret repeated. "The man is completely without conscience!"

"Not at all," said Emerson, smoking placidly. "His moral principles are different from ours, but he will not break them, always supposing one can pin him down in such a way that he cannot squirm out of a promise. I believe I have done that. Anyhow," he added, smiling at Ramses, "that flamboyant gesture of yours wasn't wasted. He has a very healthy regard for his own skin, and a very healthy respect for your marksmanship. It was quite a compliment for him to offer blood brotherhood."

"It was a lucky shot," Ramses said flatly. "But next time, if there is a next time, I am reasonably certain I can put the bullet into his body."

"That's horrible," Nefret exclaimed.

"Not nearly as horrible as what might happen to you if you fell into his hands," Ramses retorted. "You aren't in jolly old England, Nefret, nor in Egypt, where your person is sacrosanct."

"Now, now, don't quarrel," said Emerson. "There won't be a next time. He was honor-bound not to betray the name of the man who sent him, but he dropped a few hints. It was Mahmud Dinar, the governor of Darfur. We would have been handed over to him, and he wouldn't run the risk of taking English persons prisoner for the sake of a paltry ransom—or even for Nefret, though I expect he would regard her as a pleasant bit of lagniappe. He must be after Merasen's gold, or rather the location of the place from which it came."

"He would have questioned us," Nefret murmured. "Torture?"

"Oh, yes," said Emerson placidly. "And we would have told him." His eyes moved from Nefret's white face to Ramses, who sat with head bowed, staring at his clasped hands. "You owe Ramses an apology, Nefret; he was not being vindictive, he was being practical."

After I had cleaned and bandaged the cuts on their palms, Emerson ordered us all to our tents. Though he had expressed confidence in the honor of his bandit friend, he took the precaution of arranging for sentries. He took the first watch himself. Nefret, who had spoken very little, went off without further comment, and as I watched her drooping little figure vanish into her tent, I decided I would have to have a word with her if she did not snap out of it. We could not afford girlish qualms or sulks. It was so unlike her! I supposed she was still upset about Merasen— unwilling to accept the evidence of his treachery and resentful of the rest of us for suspecting him. Especially, and unfairly, of Ramses. He had been quite right to scold her.

Sleep did not come easily, but stern self-discipline prevailed. I did not even hear Emerson return. When I woke, later in the afternoon, he was snoring placidly beside me. I crawled over him and went out, to find most of the men in the same state of somnolence, and Ramses standing guard behind a convenient camel.

"All quiet?" I inquired.

"I assure you, Mother, that if it had not been, you would have been made aware." His eyes, squinted against the glare of light, continued to sweep the horizon.

"Do you share your father's belief that we can trust in that scoundrel's word?"

Ramses lowered the rifle and turned, leaning against the camel. "You didn't hear what he said just before he left?"

"I heard, but I did not understand all of it."

"It was a warning. The word has spread among the Bedouin that a group of Inglizi are heading west with a rich caravan. Some of them consider infidels fair game."

"That is very comforting, I must say."

"You would not accept a comforting lie."

"No." I cleared my throat. "Er—I have a little favor to ask."

"Of course, Mother." He spoke absently, without looking at me.

"If we are attacked and overrun, and all hope is lost, will you be obliging enough to shoot me?"

That got his full attention. He whirled round, the orbs that were usually half veiled by lowered lids and long lashes wide with consternation. "For the love of God, Mother!"

"Don't tell me the possibility of some such contingency arising had not occurred to you. I saw how you looked at Nefret this morning. Nefret too, of course," I added.

"Nefret too," Ramses muttered. He passed his hand over his mouth. "Do you mind which I do first?"

"I know it is asking a great deal of you, my dear," I said, undeceived by his attempt at insouciance. "But I cannot depend on your father to do it. He is such a confounded optimist that he might wait too long. I feel sure I can count on you to assess the situation accurately. Premature action would be equally ill advised."

"That is certainly one way of putting it." Ramses rubbed his bristly chin. He had neglected to shave that morning. I reminded myself to keep closer tabs on him and his father. Emerson would certainly grow his confounded beard again if I let him.

"You realize, don't you," Ramses said, "that if I miscalculated with—with you and Nefret—and escaped death at the hands of the bandits, I would have to turn the gun on myself? Assuming Father didn't shoot me." His voice was uneven, and his mouth was twitching.

"Ramses, are you laughing?"

"No! Well . . ." He got his mouth under control. "It was such an appalling suggestion that I couldn't . . . I couldn't take it seriously."

"Laughter can be a defense mechanism," I explained. "I was quite serious, of course, but perhaps I was asking too much. Never mind, I will just do it myself."

"I'll try, Mother." If I had not known better, I would have said there was a trace of moisture in his black eyes. "I can't promise more. But it won't come to that."

"I don't suppose for a moment that it will. It is only that I believe in planning for all contingencies."

"Yes, I know." His hand rested on my shoulder in a grip as hard as it was brief. "There's Father."

"Say nothing of this to him."

Emerson came striding toward us. The sun was sinking westward. After a comprehensive survey of the terrain, he nodded with satisfaction. "You can relax now, Ramses. Come along, Peabody, don't stand here chatting, we must be on our way as soon as the moon rises."

Our rather nasty meal of tinned tomatoes and rice was enlivened by a discussion with Masud. He was so terrified of Emerson that his voice kept breaking into falsetto, but he persisted in his complaints, which were, I was bound to admit, legitimate. He and his men had seen Emerson hand over a bag of money—their money. How were they to be paid? They deserved more than they had been promised. They had agreed to drive camels, not fight raiders.

"Well, you didn't have to fight, did you?" Emerson demanded. "The power of the Father of Curses saved you, as it will continue to do. You knew and accepted the dangers of desert travel. You will get your money—more than you were promised, if you are faithful. And if you should fall, I will be a husband to your widows and a father to your children."

"I'm not sure that was the right thing to say, Emerson," I murmured.

Daoud cleared his throat, like a small rumble of thunder. "The word of the Father of Curses has never been broken."

"Aywa," the wretched man mumbled. "Yes."

"And," said Daoud, "the curse of the Father of Curses will follow a man to his death."

"That's a good one," Ramses said appreciatively. "New, is it?"

Daoud beamed and Masud backed off, wringing his hands and nodding energetically. Whether it was the promise or the implicit threat, he had been cowed, and although the rest of the men did not look happy, I did not believe they would rebel, as our former crew had done.

Emerson agreed. "These fellows are loyal; they are only a bit timid. Ah well, tomorrow will tell the tale. By morning we will be halfway between the river and the first oasis. If we can get them past that point, they will have to come on with us or risk getting lost and running out of water. Let us hope there are no more untoward incidents tonight."

"Untoward incidents, indeed," I said sarcastically. "Another attack, you mean."

"The Tebu do not attack at night," said Emerson, with a certainty I wished I shared.

As it turned out, they did not. Morning dawned clear and bright and the first rays of the sun illumined the landmark we sought: a tumble of black stone, marked by a pair of columnar shapes. As Emerson had discovered on our first trip, it was the ruin of a small building, most probably a shrine, dating from Meroitic times. The desert had been less arid when the noble families of that vanished civilization traveled westward. There may have been water here two thousand years ago, though there was certainly no evidence of it now, nor of any life.

The fact that the night had passed without "untoward incident" had restored the confidence of our drivers. I had thought they might entertain superstitious fears of the ancient ruin—which, as all men knew, were haunted by ghosts and afrits—but as I overheard one of them remark, "The Father of Curses and the Sitt Hakim know how to drive off demons, and if evil men come, we can hide behind the stones."

It was a very sensible way of looking at the matter.

So there was relieved laughter and even a snatch of song as the men set up the tents and tended to the camels. As I had expected he would, Emerson immediately discarded his coat and began crawling round the tumbled stones, emitting little yelps of excitement like a dog nosing out rabbit burrows. Ramses paced restlessly back and forth, while Selim and I boiled water for tea. I did hope Ramses was not still brooding about my request. It did not seem likely. My son was not one to let his imagination run away with him.

"Father," he said suddenly. "Have a look, will you?"

"What is it?" I exclaimed, rising to my feet. "Oh dear, not the Tebu again!"

"No, it's all right," Ramses said. "But something's coming this way. I can't make it out, the sun is in my eyes. Father?"

Emerson's eyes followed the direction of his pointing finger. "An animal of some sort."

"Yes, sir," Ramses said patiently.

"Well, curse it, your eyes are better than mine. If you can't tell what sort of animal, how do you expect me to? It's not moving very fast. A gazelle?"

"Out here?"

In my opinion this was no time for idle speculation, however much they appeared to enjoy it. "Use the binoculars," I said, somewhat sharply.

"What? Oh," said Emerson. "Where are they?"

"Where you left them, I suppose. Never mind, I will get them."

I went back to the tent and located Emerson's binoculars, under his coat and hat, which he had thrown on the ground. When I returned to the group, the men, including Selim, were still arguing. They had agreed that the animal must be a camel, but could not identify the nature of its rider.

"It is a strange shape," Selim said somewhat nervously.

"Not like a man. Does it have—does it have two heads?"

Honestly, I thought. Men. Raising the binoculars to my eyes, I adjusted the focus. The animal was a camel. There were two heads, which was not surprising, since there were two people. I recognized one of them immediately—Mr. Newbold, the Great White Hunter, who did not look very great at that moment. In one arm he held the other individual, who lay limp in his grasp. The features were hidden, but I felt sure I knew who it was.

## Six

**R**amses couldn't get the image out of his mind: Nefret, sprawled on the sand at his feet, her shirt crimsoned by her heart's blood . . . not dead but dying, slowly and in agony, because his hand hadn't been steady enough to do the job right. The surer alternative was a bullet through the head, but he doubted he could bring himself to do it. He had seen men die that way. It was not a pretty sight.

Shooting his mother wouldn't be much fun either.

If worse came to worst, a quick death was preferable to slavery, especially for a woman . . . Wasn't it? Or was that one of those hoary old sayings that people recited but never really thought about? Like "England expects every man to do his duty" and "Better death than dishonor." Did women really believe that, or was it something men wanted them to believe?

At least he was no longer in doubt as to how his mother felt. Hearing that brisk, matter-of-fact voice propose the unthinkable had shaken him. But he oughtn't have been surprised; that was his mother for you. She could look a fact in the face without flinching, no matter how unpalatable it was.

Which was more than he could do. He closed his eyes,

as if that could shut out the image of Nefret; and then it wasn't Nefret, but the girl Daria, her blood soaking into the sand and her wide, dead eyes staring emptily, and he knew he had killed her . . . And he started out of a half-doze to see dawn pale in the eastern sky, and close ahead the twin black columns that had been their first landmark.

Knowing his father would want him to spend most of the day investigating the miserable ruin, he walked back and forth, stretching his legs and trying not to look at Nefret. Emerson had apparently decided his old acquaintance had "stayed bribed," but Ramses wasn't so confident. His eyes kept straying toward the east, hoping not to see an ominous cloud of sand. What he did see eventually was not so much ominous as strange. The beast could only be a camel, but what was a single camel doing here?

His mother's surprised identification of the camel's rider brought them all to attention. "He appears to be in distress," she added, raising her voice to be heard over Emerson's curses. "And he is holding someone before him on the saddle. Someone who is unconscious or . . . Oh dear."

She started impetuously forward. So did Nefret. Emerson threw out his arms and barred their path. "Stay back, both of you. What the devil did I do with my . . . Give me that, Selim, and keep the women back!" He snatched Selim's rifle and stalked off to meet the approaching riders.

Ramses followed more slowly. Unlike his father, who had divested himself of binoculars, weapon, and extraneous clothing, he was armed, but he didn't draw the pistol. Newbold was not fool enough to start trouble with an enraged Emerson. He had both arms round the girl. She was a limp white bundle, wrapped in dusty garments, except for her head, which had fallen back against his shoulder.

"What the devil are you doing here?" Emerson demanded.

"Following you, what do you suppose?" Newbold's haggard face twitched as if he were trying to smile. "Ran into trouble, though. Barely got away. No water. Please . . ."

Emerson nodded at his son, and Ramses caught the girl

as she slipped through Newbold's failing hold. She was as light as a bird. Her eyes opened, and a dreadful ripple of déjà vu ran through him. It was the face he had seen in his dream, pale and empty-eyed. Then her eyelids fell and she turned her face against his breast.

"Take her to your mother, Ramses," Emerson ordered. He held the heavy rifle in one hand, as easily as he would have held a pistol. "Come ahead, Newbold. You can stick on for another twenty feet, I presume."

Nefret broke away from Selim and came running to meet Ramses. "Is she hurt? Poor little thing, that brute had no business forcing her to come with him on a trek like this. Put her in my tent, Ramses."

Ramses left her crooning reassurances as she divested Daria of her muffling garments. The girl hadn't spoken, but she was awake and aware; the wide dark eyes followed him as he went out of the tent.

His mother was ministering to Newbold—in her own fashion. She prodded the bruise on his face with sufficient force to wring a grunt of protest from him and then snatched the cup of water from his hand. "Your injury is superficial. Not too much water; you ought to know better."

"This isn't my kind of country," Newbold said. "Thank you, Mrs. Emerson. Now may I lie down and get some sleep? I've been on that camel for almost twenty-four hours."

Ramses had to admire the man's nerve; he was behaving as if he were an invited guest. His nonchalance had no effect on Selim and Daoud, who stood over him like prison guards. Emerson's scowl grew even darker.

"So was the—er—young lady, I presume. How is she, Ramses?"

"Just tired and thirsty, I think. Nefret is looking after her."

"Very well, Newbold, start talking," Emerson said. "You can rest after you've told us what you are doing here. It will probably be a pack of lies, but I believe I can winnow the truth out of it."

"There's no point in trying to lie about why I'm here," Newbold said coolly. "I've been on your trail ever since Cairo, where I heard a number of things that made me believe you were after something more lucrative than a wrecked archaeological site. Your sudden departure from the train at Abu Hamed caught me unawares—but it also confirmed my suspicions. You wouldn't have lied about your destination if your purpose had been what you claimed." His voice had grown hoarse. "Mrs. Emerson, may I trouble you for another sip of water?"

Face grim, she provided it. "Go on, Mr. Newbold."

"We left the train at Berber and hired camels and drivers. You had left Nuri by the time we arrived there, but the obliging villagers told me which way you'd gone, and it wasn't difficult to follow your trail, since you were only a few hours ahead. Then we ran into the trouble I mentioned—a band of raiders. They killed my men—shot some of them in cold blood after they had surrendered. Their camp is a day's ride to the southwest—there's a well, which they keep cleared."

Again his voice failed. He took another sip of water. "They intended to hold me and Daria for ransom, or so they said. I thought it wiser not to take that for granted. Early yesterday morning, several hours before dawn, most of the men rode away, and I saw my chance. Stole back one of my camels and Daria, and made my escape."

"Daring escape, don't you mean?" Emerson inquired. "Why didn't you head back to the river instead of trying to locate us—a needle in a haystack, so to speak?"

Newbold looked back at him without expression. "Followed the raiders' trail, I suppose," said Emerson. "Lucky you were able to elude them when they were on their way back, eh? Oh, the devil with it. Find him a blanket and a bit of shade, Daoud, and stand guard over him until I relieve you."

Already the sun was high enough to make the ground shimmer. Ramses heard his mother humming to herself.

The melody was one of her favorite Gilbert and Sullivan songs: "Here's a state of things—here's a pretty mess."

"You've got that right, Mother," he said. "What shall we do with the bastard?"

"Tie him up and leave him here," Selim said promptly. "We can make the knots so he can free himself after we have gone, and we will leave one of the camels and enough water for him to reach the Nile."

"The girl too?" Ramses inquired.

His mother gave him a look of mild surprise, and he realized she had been about to ask the same question. She hadn't expected him to make it first. Neither had he. To cover his confusion he took out a cigarette. It was an indulgence he seldom permitted himself, since his supply was limited, and smoking dried the throat.

"I fear that idea is not feasible, Selim," Emerson said, filling his pipe. "In addition to the objection Ramses has raised, supposing he wasn't able to free himself? He would die horribly and slowly of dehydration. Much as I despise the fellow, I don't want his death on my hands. And if he were able to free himself soon enough, he would be right back on our trail." He shook his head regretfully. "I can only think of two alternatives. Either we take them along or we send them back with enough of our men to make sure they do go back. Well, Peabody, what is your opinion? I feel certain you have one."

"I am not certain I do, Emerson." Her husband gave an exaggerated start of surprise, and she went on, with less than her usual assurance. "Neither alternative is ideal. Showing him the way to the Holy Mountain is precisely what we wanted to prevent and what he hoped to achieve. On the other hand, providing an adequate escort would mean divesting ourselves of at least half a dozen men and camels. That would leave us dangerously short-handed."

"There is a third alternative," said Emerson, puffing thoughtfully.

"Not alternative, Emerson. There can only be two. The derivation of the word—"

"Never mind the confounded grammar lesson, Peabody. We could take them as far as the first oasis and leave them there, along with the slowest and most timid of our drivers."

After a moment Ramses said, "I think you've hit on the only possible solution, Father. From the oasis we will be escorted by Tarek's men."

And, he added to himself, we'll have fewer deaths on our conscience if something goes wrong. If only they could persuade his mother and Nefret to stay too.

"Are we agreed, then?" Emerson asked. "Good. Get some rest, Peabody."

"You too, Emerson."

"Shortly, shortly. Ramses and I want to do a bit of excavating, isn't that right, my boy? You too, Selim."

"Yes, sir," said Ramses.

"Yes, Father of Curses," said Selim resignedly.

⋮

From that point on, Emerson changed the routine of our march. The bitter cold of the night and the steaming heat of midday were equally unbearable, so he broke the trek into two parts, the first from around midnight until nine or ten A.M., the second from late afternoon until men and camels both gave out, which usually happened around eight.

As we went on, day after steaming day and night after starry night, there were fewer bones and other evidences of life along the trail. The men were tired. More and more frequently they dropped out of line to snatch half an hour's sleep before running to catch us up. We were delayed for several hours when one of them failed to return; he had "walked to his fate," as the desert men put it, losing his head and his sense of direction after unremitting hours of sand and heat. Emerson finally located him, wandering aimlessly at right angles to the trail, and brought him back.

Emerson kept riding back, looking for signs of pursuit. He returned from one such foray with a furrowed brow, and I inquired apprehensively, "Did you see anything suspicious?"

Emerson shook his head, and Ramses, who was walking with me, said, "That's good."

"I'm not so sure," Emerson replied. "We've had encounters with the slavers and Newbold. We have yet to hear from the military and the Egyptological community."

"Surely not now," I protested. "We are too far from the river."

"I'm not so sure," Emerson repeated. "And what about Merasen and his confederates, whoever they may be?"

"They have the map," Ramses said. "They wouldn't have to keep close on our trail."

Newbold plodded along in sullen silence. Nefret had kept Daria with her, and Emerson had refused Newbold's demand that she be returned to him with such eloquence that the request was not repeated. The girl now shrank from Newbold, hurrying to whichever one of them was closest to her when he approached. I wondered what the fellow had done to her. She had claimed she wasn't afraid of him.

Forth's second landmark, the dead tree, had fallen at last. Its bleached white branches looked like the skeleton of a mythical monster. As we sat round the campfire that night, Emerson said, "Only three more days to the oasis. I wonder what we will find there."

"Water, I trust," I said. "The stopper came out of one of the fatasses today and several gallons were lost before anyone noticed."

"There is plenty of water," Emerson replied. "I was wondering whether Tarek has sent an escort to meet us."

"He surely will," Nefret said eagerly. "He must be as anxious to see us as we are to see him."

Ramses, who had been tracing abstract designs in the sand with a stick, looked up. "He may have given us up by now. It took Merasen—" He stopped, with a snap of teeth, at a warning gesture from Emerson. Newbold was not a part of the group—he never was, since we had made it plain his company was not wanted—but he was sitting a little distance away, listening. We had told him nothing about our final destination or the circumstances that had prompted our journey, only that we proposed to leave him in safety and relative comfort within a few days. He had not given up trying to learn more, however. After his attempts to ingratiate himself with Selim and Daoud had failed miserably, he took to chatting with the drivers. This too was a failure; they knew even less than he did, and his attempts at bonhomie were not convincing, since he considered "natives" beneath him.

The terrain began to change, becoming rougher and more broken. Walking was difficult, and the men complained of sore feet. Their heel-less slippers were not suitable for country like this. Even the hardy Bedouin were showing signs of uneasiness. One morning, while the men were unloading the camels, Zerwali the Bedouin approached Emerson. After the formal greetings, he asked how much farther Emerson meant to go.

"I hired you for thirty marhalas," Emerson reminded him. "We have only been seven days on the march."

"But you did not tell us where we were going. This is new country to me. We do not come this way."

"We have only encountered one group of raiders," Emerson pointed out. "And as you saw, they surrendered as soon as they recognized me."

"It is not ordinary raiders that keep us from this path." He hesitated, reluctant to admit fear, and then went on, "Years ago, some of the young men among our people heard of a rich oasis to the west and set out to find it. They did not come back. Others went forth. None came back. And there are legends . . ."

"Ah yes, the customary legends," said Emerson to me. "Told by those who never saw the fearsome sights they describe." He went on in Arabic, "What sort of legends, Zerwali?"

"Of burning mountains and fiery rain, O Father of Curses. Of men—if they are men and not afrits—eight feet tall whose arrows never miss their mark and who can out-run the fastest stallion."

"Hmmm," said Emerson, stroking his by-now horrible beard. "Well, Zerwali, you have my word—the word of the Father of Curses—that we will meet no such dangers as you have described. Don't tell me you are afraid—you, who jeered at the Nubians for cowardice?"

Zerwali gave him an evil look but left without further comment.

We had been amazingly lucky, in fact. We had not lost a man or a camel, and despite the slight accident to the fatasse our water supply was holding up, even if it did taste vile.

Late on the following day we passed a grotesque jumble of dried skin and white bones. "Could that have been our last camel?" I asked Emerson, who was walking with me. "I have been keeping track of the time, and it seems to me that we have just about reached the point where it collapsed."

"It's possible," Emerson said indifferently. "Not that . . . Here, Peabody, where the devil are you going?"

He followed me, of course. I stood by the miserable heap, remembering that terrible day, when the demise of our last camel had left us stranded miles from water, with little hope of reaching it before dehydration and exhaustion overcame us. Yet my strongest memories were of courage and loyalty—Tarek, who had never deserted us and who was to save us in the end; Ramses, only ten years of age, plodding doggedly through the sand without a whimper of complaint; Emerson, the bravest of men . . .

"Are you going to say a prayer over it?" inquired the bravest of men disagreeably.

I forgave him his little joke. If it was a joke.

"I only wondered if the things we had to leave behind were still here."

"Hmmm," said Emerson, his interest revived by the prospect of digging.

We found nothing, though we excavated all round the

cadaver. "No great loss," said Emerson. "Changes of clothing and a few books—that was about all we abandoned,
wasn't it?"

"Do you suppose Tarek came back and retrieved them?
He was a great reader."

Emerson gave me a long look. "Peabody, don't tell me
you loaded us down with a supply of trashy novels for
Tarek."

"Naturally I brought gifts," I replied composedly. "Mr.
Rider Haggard has written several other novels in the in-
terim, and I also thought Tarek might like *The Prisoner of
Zenda* and *The Scarlet Pimpernel*."

"I don't doubt he would," Emerson muttered. "He had a
weakness for romantic twaddle! It is getting dark. We had
better catch the rest of them up."

He persuaded me to ride for a while, so I mounted his
camel and he walked beside me, his long strides easily
matching the pace of the beast. I had been about to ask him
how much farther we had to go, but he kept mumbling to
himself—the word "twaddle" was oft repeated—so I decided to work it out for myself. We had been approximately
one marhala from the first oasis when the last camel perished, but our pace from then on had been slowed by my
feverish malady and Ramses's short legs, to say nothing of
a deficiency of water. When we stopped that night, Emerson had predicted it would take us two more days to reach
the oasis, and Kemit had replied—how well I remembered!—"Half a day for a running man." We had waked
next morning to find him gone. Though of course we went
on, we hadn't got very far before even Emerson's giant
strength at last failed, and I was unconscious when the rescue party Kemit led back along the trail arrived in the nick
of time to save us.

So then . . . with a strange little thrill I realized we were
within a few hours of our destination. I could not recall
much about the place; on our initial journey I had been in a
coma, which lasted until after we reached the Holy Moun-

tain, and on the return trip—which might more accurately be called a "flight"—we had stayed only long enough to rest for a few hours and acquire fresh camels. It had been a pleasant spot, with flourishing palm trees and rich grass. One could easily understand why the desert men fought over such places, their emerald grass more precious than emerald gems in the midst of the wilderness. Would we reach it by the end of this night's march? Now that we were so close, my impatience could hardly be contained. I yearned for greenery and shade, for cold, pure water instead of the foul-tasting liquid in the fatasses—and, of course, for word of our friend. When Emerson called a halt shortly after midnight I protested.

"Surely we can reach the oasis by morning if we go on, Emerson. I yearn for greenery and shade, for cold, pure—"

"Yes, yes," said Emerson. "Come now, Peabody, you ought to know better than suggest we ride blithely up to the place in the dark. Tarek keeps a garrison there, and its purpose is to intercept curious travelers—by one means or another."

"Oh. You are in the right, Emerson," I admitted generously. "It is just that I yearn—"

"So does Nefret," said Emerson, as the men began barrakking and unloading the camels. "I had to speak firmly to her. Try to talk some sense into the girl, will you? And get into your blankets, the cold is bitter. As soon as it is light Ramses and I will go on ahead and reconnoiter."

By now the men had become adept at efficient unloading, so it was not long before the tents were set up and our personal baggage placed in them. Excitement filled me with energy, and I wanted a cup of tea before I retired, so I joined Selim by the fire he had started. He had already begun brewing—or stewing—the tea. The Arab method of making tea is to boil the leaves until the liquid is dark brown.

"This is almost the last of the firewood, Sitt," he said.

"It does not matter, Selim. Tomorrow we will be with friends, who will supply us with everything we need."

At least I hoped so. We had been proceeding on the assumption that though Tarek's messenger might be untrustworthy, Tarek's need of us was genuine. For our friend's sake we dared not assume otherwise. Tarek knew we would come if we could, but he had no way of knowing when.

"Ah," said Selim. "And we will be rid of him, is it not so?"

He nodded at Newbold, who was edging up to the fire. He had let himself go rather badly. None of us was fit for polite society, since bathing was impossible, but we had made the best use of the small amounts of water we allowed ourselves for washing, and Ramses had shaved every day, without having to be reminded more than three times. I had also reminded Emerson, who chose to take my remarks as suggestions which he felt free to disregard. His beard was now luxuriant, but at least he kept it clean and trimmed, which Newbold did not.

"Am I to be allowed a cup of tea?" the hunter asked. "Or am I still persona non grata?"

"You have had the same comforts we have had, so don't whine," I replied, handing him a cup.

I had planned to have a little chat with Nefret, but she had retired with Daria into their tent, and when I approached it I saw the flap was closed. I understood how she must be feeling; all these long weeks she had worried about the little boy, Tarek's heir, and whether or not she would be in time to help him and his father. In a few hours she would find out, and the suspense was terrible. It was obvious that she preferred to be alone, so I did not force my company upon her.

The moon was on the wane and the air was icy cold. Shivering, I retreated to my tent. I knew I would not sleep a wink . . .

I was rudely awakened by a loud shout. Removing Emerson's arm from my person, I snatched up my parasol, crawled over him to the flap of the tent, and emerged into the chilly predawn light.

The camp was ringed round by motionless forms, black against the paling sky. They were taller than any human could possibly be, their heads were oddly deformed, and each carried a long lance.

"Friends?" said Selim to me. He had waked early in order to start a fire, and his shout had aroused the sleepers. I could hardly blame him for crying out in alarm, though as the light strengthened I realized that the seemingly abnormal height of the newcomers was caused by the fact that they were mounted on camels and that their heads were covered by helmetlike caps crowned with feathers. The spears were very long, and the quivers slung over their shoulders bristled with arrows.

Emerson was among the last to appear, rubbing his eyes and cursing, but the sight brought him awake in a hurry. "Friends, yes," he said.

"They do not look friendly," said Selim dubiously.

Emerson turned in a circle, examining the riders. None of them had moved. "They are unquestionably from the Holy Mountain," he said, stroking his beard. "The headgear is unfamiliar—Tarek must have changed his guards' uniforms—but the shields are the same, and the bows."

"If they are friends," said Daoud, who had been thinking it over, "why do they not greet you?"

"Hmmm, well, I'm not sure," Emerson admitted. "Hold your fire, you damned fools," he added. "Ramses, will you—"

A loud explosion interrupted him. Zerwali and the other Bedouin had crowded round, their weapons in their hands. It was Zerwali who had fired. Before the echoes of the shot died, he screamed and fell, clutching at his throat. An arrow had gone straight through it.

"They are the demons of whom we told you," one of the Bedouin cried.

"Are you men or children?" Emerson demanded. "Put

down your weapons. They are human beings, like your-selves, and Zerwali was a fool who deserved his fate. Is he dead, Nefret?"

"Yes." A single look had been enough. Nefret straight-ened. "Let me talk to them."

Emerson frowned at her. "Go inside the tent and dress yourself," he said. "Ramses, come with me."

He seldom used such a brusque tone with her. When he did she knew better than to disobey, but her face was mutinous.

"My dear, it is a man's world," I said with somewhat forced cheerfulness. The immobile forms were beginning to get on my nerves. "Leave it to Emerson and Ramses. Ramses's Meroitic is not as good as yours, but it should be adequate."

With his customary (when he is fully awake) acuity, Emerson had identified the leader of the troop. The man had more feathers on his hat and a medallion or pectoral depending from a cord round his neck. It shone like gold, as did the heavy armlet on his right arm. Like all the oth-ers, he was young and strongly built, with a thin, keen face and piercing dark eyes. Emerson and Ramses walked slowly toward him. The men had gathered round me, like nervous chicks around a mother hen. Emerson's orders, or, more likely, Zerwali's fate, had had a distinctly sobering effect.

"So I was right," Newbold said, his eyes glittering with greed. "Even a lowly soldier wears a fortune in gold."

"You don't know how lowly he is," I retorted. "Do be quiet."

Ramses and Emerson were only a few feet away when the captain suddenly called out, "It is he. It is the Father of Curses. The Great Ones have returned!"

All the camels knelt, with remarkable precision for a group of camels, and the riders raised their spears in salute. The captain dismounted and dropped to his knees before Emerson.

I had not realized I was holding my breath until it left my lungs in an explosive sigh.

## From Manuscript H

Emerson's Meroitic vocabulary was limited, but as Ramses pointed out to him, he wasn't required to do anything but look lordly. It had not been necessary for Ramses to translate the captain's announcement; his action had spoken louder than words, and most of the words had been familiar to Emerson. Emerson drew himself up and accepted the homage with a gracious wave of his hand, remarking in English, "Quite an impressive performance, eh? It was meant to honor us."

"Zerwali didn't get that impression," Ramses said. "Poor devil."

"Damn fool," Emerson corrected. He had little patience with stupidity or with insubordination. "He might have brought a rain of arrows down on us."

"I think the leader is waiting for you to address him, Father."

"You do the talking, my boy. Introduce yourself, ask his name, tell him how delighted we are to see him, and that sort of thing."

Ramses couldn't help being somewhat flattered at the captain's reaction when he mentioned his name. The fellow had risen when Emerson indicated he might do so; he promptly knelt again. The "great lady of the house"—and her parasol—were acknowledged with equal respect, but when the captain—whose name was Har—saw Nefret, he bowed so low the feathers in his headdress dragged in the dust.

"Since I am not allowed to speak," said Nefret in cutting tones, "ask him about the little boy."

At first Har didn't seem to understand what Ramses meant. When Ramses elaborated—the child, the prince, who had been ill—he repeated, "The prince. Yes. He is well. Now will you come with us, you and your servants?"

The men were obviously not keen on the idea. In daylight the true nature of their would-be escort was apparent, but the warlike aspect of the troop was hardly reassuring. However, there was really no alternative, as Ramses pointed out to one of the waverers. "Would you prefer to stay here? The camels are weary and so are your men, and the water is running low."

It was a rhetorical question; they wouldn't have been allowed to stay behind, even if they had been foolish enough to choose that alternative. Masud went off, muttering, to join the burial party.

Emerson allowed them time for prayer and a few glasses of tea before urging them to load up.

"There is fresh water and fresh meat ahead, and shade where you may rest. They are preparing a feast for us!"

Ramses couldn't remember hearing Har mention a feast, but it went over well. Even the camels appeared to sense that they were nearing water. They moved faster than they had for days. Emerson promptly urged his riding camel to the head of the procession, slightly in front of Har, and Ramses grinned to himself. No one had to teach his father new tricks.

He walked alongside the camel on which Nefret and Daria were riding and tried to make conversation. "Not far now," he said encouragingly. Nefret only nodded, but Daria turned and looked down at him, her eyes wide.

"Who are these people? They do not ride like tribesmen, but like soldiers the British have trained."

"I can assure you the British had no hand in their training," Ramses said. "They live far away and have no contact with the outside world. You'll be all right, Daria, I promise."

She withdrew rather quickly. Ramses saw that Newbold was close behind him. The hunter's gaze was fixed on the nearest soldier, one of the youngest of the troop, who sported a thin golden armlet. Ramses felt as if he could read Newbold's mind. There was the gold he sought, worn by a common soldier. He'll try something, Ramses thought. But what can he do?

If he hadn't known the oasis was near, he would have taken the vision of palms and verdure for a mirage. The men saw it too; a low chorus of amazement and relief arose.

"So the Father of Curses spoke truth," exclaimed Masud, his bloodshot eyes narrowing.

"The Father of Curses does not lie," said Daoud.

The place was larger in extent than Ramses remembered—acres of lush grass, with several small pools and trees of various species. They rode for a quarter of an hour into the green heart of the place before the escort halted in a clearing. In the shade of the date palms was a cluster of huts, constructed like the Nubian tukhuls of branches and mud brick.

Ramses hurried to his father, who appeared to be having some difficulty understanding the officer's remarks. As soon as Har saw Ramses he made his camel kneel and dismounted, bowing and raising his hands.

"These have been made ready for the Great Ones," he said, indicating the huts. "All that you need and wish will be brought to you."

"I wonder if Selim and Daoud rank as Great Ones," said Ramses, watching the troop lead the rest of the caravan away. "And Daria." He addressed the officer in Meroitic. "Where are they taking our people?"

"To a place where they can camp. It is not fitting that they should be close to the Great Ones. Now, will you go within? Rest well tonight, for tomorrow we will go on. Servants will come to you."

"Tell him we want Selim and Daoud with us," Emerson ordered.

"What about Newbold?"

"Him too," said Emerson ungrammatically but forcibly.

"I want to keep my eye on the bastard. There are enough huts to go round."

"You aren't going to let him take Daria—"

"No," said Emerson, in a voice like a large boulder slamming onto stone.

He helped his wife dismount and led her to the largest of the huts. She gave it a quick inspection. "Excellent," she said happily. "One of them must have ridden on ahead to warn of our arrival. There are even basins of water for bathing!"

Emerson proceeded to allocate houses, directing Newbold to one on the edge of the group. Nefret and Daria shared another, next to the elder Emersons, and Daoud and Selim a third. Half a dozen servants turned up while Ramses was selecting his abode. They wore kilts and a few strings of beads, and they were carrying a miscellaneous lot of luggage. Bent over from the waist in a token of deep respect, one of them murmured something which Ramses translated. "He says if we give them our clothes, they will wash them."

"Splendid," said Emerson. "That should make you happy, Peabody. Come in and freshen up a bit, eh?" He lifted the curtain over the door invitingly.

"Everything appears to be quite satisfactory," his wife conceded.

Except for one little detail, Ramses thought, watching his parents vanish into comparative privacy. All the servants were men. He hadn't set eyes on a single woman. This was a military encampment, after all; no doubt the garrison was changed at regular intervals, and the men were expected to get along without distracting female companionship while on this duty. How could they leave Daria here, alone with Newbold and several dozen soldiers?

⁚

After a refreshing if limited bath, I assumed the least grubby of my garments and settled onto a stool with my journal. I had fallen rather behind with it and there was certainly a great deal to write about. We had been served a light repast—dates, so sweet and fresh they might have been an entirely different fruit than the hardened objects we had eaten along the way, fresh-baked unleavened bread, and wine. The servants assured us better and more ample food was being prepared.

Emerson went to the door and raised the curtain. "Would you care to take a little stroll, Peabody, or do you want to rest for a while?"

"As you can see, I am not in need of rest, my dear. But I suppose my journal can wait a bit longer."

When we emerged we found Ramses deep in conversation with Selim. There was no need to ask about Daoud; reverberant snores issued from the hut he shared with Selim. The girls must be resting too, for the piece of matting over the door of their house was lowered. We decided not to disturb them, but Ramses and Selim were pleased to join us. We walked more or less at random, through a grove of date palms and past a stream of clear water that flowed into a large stone basin, enjoying the shade and the cool air. In the distance I heard the bleating of goats and the quacking of ducks.

"It is as large as Siwa and Kharga," Selim exclaimed. "How is it that this place is unknown?"

"Not so large," replied Emerson. "But sizable enough to support herds and raise crops. They have quite an effective irrigation system," he added, as we passed several small plots of vegetables. "It is unknown because the people who control it take pains to make sure it remains unknown."

The trees had thinned out and fingers of sand intruded onto the green grass. "We had better go back," I said. "Nefret will wonder what has become of us."

We followed another route on the way back, along a well-trodden path that led from the fields to what seemed to be the servants' village. It was a bustle of activity—meat turning on spits and pots boiling. Our unexpected appearance threw the cooks into complete disarray. One of them dropped a roasting fowl into the ashes, and the others exhibited such consternation that we went on without stopping.

Nefret was pacing up and down in the little clearing when we reached it. "Where have you been?" she demanded. "That bastard Newbold has gone wandering off too. I wanted to follow him, but I was afraid to leave Daria alone."

"I doubt he can get into mischief here," said Emerson, though he frowned a little.

"We only saw the domestic quarters," I explained with a smile. "I fear dinner may be late; we disturbed the cooks."

However, it was not long before a procession arrived bearing food and drink, low tables, and mats on which to sit. Looking quite refreshed after his nap, Daoud tucked into the food with good appetite, and Daria was persuaded to venture out of the hut. I suggested we ask the captain to join us, but was voted down.

"One musn't be polite to inferiors," said Emerson with a grin. "Leave it to him to sue for an audience."

"Newbold hasn't come back," said Ramses. "Where do you suppose he's gone?"

"I don't give a curse where he's gone," said Emerson. "I have his weapons, and if he thinks he can corrupt Har's lot, he will get a rude surprise."

Some of us—I must include myself—ate more than we ought to have done; the roast fowl and fresh bread were so tasty after our sparse diet. The sun had sunk below the tops of the trees before we finished, and the servants began clearing away the remains of the food. Emerson leaned back with a sigh of repletion and began filling his pipe.

"Perhaps I ought to locate our men," he said lazily. "Make certain they are comfortable, and have a little chat with Masud on the subject of afrits."

"It can wait," I said, stifling a yawn. "We won't be able to go on for a few more days. I won't mind resting awhile. This is such a pleasant place."

Nefret opened her mouth and snapped it shut again. I knew what she had intended to say. She wanted to go on as quickly as possible. The captain's reassurance about the sick child had not entirely convinced her.

Ramses glanced at her and then said, "Far be it from me to spoil your plans, Mother, but I'm not sure we will be allowed to linger. Har means to press on tomorrow."

"But the camels," I exclaimed. "They will need to be watered and fed."

"Our camels, yes," said Ramses. "Theirs are rested and ready. Do you suppose Har will allow any of our men to go on to the Holy Mountain? He's here to prevent that very thing."

Emerson let out an exclamation. "By Gad, you may be right. It's high time we had a talk with Har. Here, you—" He caught one of the unfortunate servants by the arm. I feared for a moment that the fellow was going to faint, but he rallied long enough to listen to Emerson's order. Emerson had enough Meroitic to say, "Fetch Har to me." He was particularly familiar with the imperative form of verbs.

When Har appeared he was not alone. Two of his men were with him; struggling in their grip, teeth bared, was Newbold.

"We found him hiding behind one of the houses, listening to you speak," said Har, without so much as a preliminary bow. "If he is a friend, why was he not with you?"

"He is no friend," Nefret exclaimed indignantly. Har glanced obliquely at her and averted his eyes. It occurred to me then that he had never looked directly at her. The women of the Holy Mountain were not required to seclude themselves, or go about veiled—except for certain priestesses, the handmaidens of the goddess Isis, who were swaddled from head to foot when they appeared in public. Har's attitude toward Nefret must be a token of respect.

"Hold on a minute, Nefret," said Ramses. He proceeded to translate what Har had said. He didn't have to translate Nefret's response. Emerson gave her a stern look.

"Contain yourself, Nefret. Ramses, tell them to release him. He is no friend, but he is our responsibility. If there is such a concept in Meroitic," he added. "Newbold, what the devil were you doing?"

Newbold shook himself free. He had not bothered to freshen up, and he looked like a wild man with his unkempt beard and long dirty hair. "Sparing you my unwelcome company," he said with a sneer. "I wanted to see what this place is like, since you intend to leave us here at the mercy of these savages."

Daria, who was, as usual, close to Nefret, murmured something to her, and Nefret burst out again. "Professor, you can't mean to—"

"You can trust me, I believe," said Emerson, "to do what is right without advice from you. Let me remind you—all of you—that we have a certain dignity to maintain. Squabbling and disagreement do not help."

Nefret's eyes fell. "I'm sorry, sir."

"Hmph," said Emerson. "Newbold, sit down over there and keep your mouth closed. Ramses, ask Har to share his thoughts with us."

It was as Ramses had surmised. We were to move on at once, under military escort, for the king's heart ached to see us.

"We" being our four selves only.

"That won't do," said Emerson, who had lit his pipe—a procedure that made the imperturbable captain stare in wonder. "I suppose it makes a certain amount of sense to leave our fellows here; they will be comfortable, and we will be amply escorted. We intended to leave Newbold behind anyhow. But Selim and Daoud must come with us. And, of course, Daria."

"See here," Newbold exclaimed. "You can't—"

"I fail to see how you can prevent me," said Emerson with excessive politeness. "Good Gad, man, there are no women here. At least I haven't seen any. Do you claim you could keep Daria safe from these savages, as you have been pleased to call them? Even if she wanted to stay?"

"May I speak, sir?" Nefret inquired with equally excessive sweetness. "Daria has already told me—"

"Let her speak for herself," said Emerson. "Well, Daria?"

"Please don't leave me here." Her expressive dark eyes moved from Emerson to Ramses, and, after a long moment, to me. "Please."

"Certainly not," I said.

"That settles that," said Emerson. "Ramses, you may inform Har of our decision. Don't ask him," he added. "Tell him."

"Using the imperative form of the verb?" Ramses inquired.

"As often as possible," said Emerson, returning his smile.

The people of the Holy Mountain are a courteous lot. Har had listened to the discussion in silence, with no sign of impatience and without attempting to break into it— which would have been a waste of time, since he had not the least idea what we were talking about. He listened with equally attentive silence to Ramses's speech, and then nodded. "It shall be as the Father of Curses says. With his permission, we leave tomorrow at dawn."

"That was easier than I expected," I remarked, after Ramses had translated. "We had better get some rest if we are to leave so early."

"Not just yet," said Emerson. "Ramses, tell him I must talk with our men first. I want his word, the word of an officer and—er—a devout follower of the gods—that no harm will come to them while we are away."

"I am fair game, I suppose," Newbold said with an ugly twist of his lips.

"Him too," said Emerson regretfully.

He got the oath he had demanded. I recognized the word "Aminreh" and knew the officer had sworn by the chief god of the Holy Mountain, the most binding of promises.

By the time we had everything settled, darkness was complete and the moon had risen—a waning moon, which gave little light. Selim, indignantly refusing the assistance of the servants, started a nice little bonfire and began stewing tea—a commodity which was not included in the cuisine of the oasis. Emerson returned from his visit to our men, escorted by soldiers carrying torches. He had refused Ramses's offer to come with him, remarking that he was beginning to pick up some of the language and that he knew the words for "protect," "safe," and "swear," along with the essential pronouns.

"I made him swear again," he announced, looking quite pleased with himself. "And say he would protect them and that they would be safe."

Emerson does have a way of making himself understood, even in a language he speaks poorly.

"How did the men take it?" Ramses asked.

"Masud wasn't well pleased," Emerson admitted. He accepted a cup of tea from Selim and sipped it appreciatively. "I had to point out the obvious: that even though he and his men had rifles, it wouldn't do them a particle of good to overpower the garrison, even supposing they could. They don't know the way back. The others were less resistant. They had just gorged themselves on the first meat they have had for days, and some of them were washing their clothes. I assured them they would be paid for the days they spend here, and that seemed to satisfy them."

"You seem pretty cheerful yourself," I said. (Self-satisfied would have been closer to the mark.) "Emerson, are you sure we are doing the right thing?"

"What do you mean?" Emerson asked in surprise.

I lowered my voice and glanced over my shoulder, at the hut to which Daria had retired, pleading weariness. "Taking her with us."

I was the recipient of three outraged stares—no, only two. Ramses's fixed gaze was less condemnatory than speculative. "You don't mean it, Aunt Amelia," Nefret cried. Emerson shouted her down. "For God's sake, Peabody, we cannot leave a defenseless young woman at the mercy of—"

I shouted him down. "Don't bellow!"

Emerson subsided, simmering, and Ramses anticipated Nefret's protest. "Mother meant nothing of the kind. We must take her with us, there is no question of doing otherwise. She was simply expressing doubts—doubts I share—as to Daria's real motives."

A peremptory gesture from me reminded Nefret that Newbold was nearby. Her voice was not loud, but it was acid-sharp.

"You've always been against her. I never thought I would find you so puritanical."

Ramses made no attempt to defend himself against that unjust charge. "May I remind you," he said patiently, "of what she said the night she came to my room. She said she had her own reasons for staying with Newbold. She rejected my offer of help."

"She has changed her mind," Nefret said. "Women are prone to that weakness, you know. Perhaps it was your charm that influenced her to change it."

"That will be quite enough, Nefret," I said. "I cannot think of any way in which she could constitute a danger to us, but I am in full agreement with Ramses that we must be on our guard. Trust no one, not even the innocent. That was what Abdullah—what Abdullah always said."

"I don't recall his ever saying that," remarked Emerson.

"He said it to me."

I spoke the literal truth. I never prevaricate unless it is absolutely necessary.

· ·

# Seven

· ·

**N**ewbold did not come out of his hut to bid us farewell. No one expressed disappointment. Escorted by a few of the servants carrying our hand luggage, we were led to the place at the edge of the oasis where the caravan awaited. The camels had been loaded, and as the stars paled and the rim of the sun peeped over the horizon, I saw that the men of our escort had exchanged their uniforms for long, hooded robes woven of camel hair. They were practical garments for desert travel, and in the dim light the tall shrouded forms were eerie enough to strike terror into the heart of the superstitious. Then I observed a strange, balloonlike structure on the back of one of the camels. It rather resembled the bassourab used by Bedouin women when they are on the march with their men.

"Curse it," I exclaimed. "Are we expected to ride in that contraption?"

Har indicated that we were. I gave in for the moment, since the captain was obviously impatient to be off, but I had no intention of occupying it for the entire time, and I knew Nefret would feel the same. It was comfortable enough, though extremely cramped for three; rugs and cushions formed a soft surface on which to sit, and the curtains could be adjusted to admit air. When Emerson announced his intention of checking the loads, to make sure nothing had been left behind, Daoud nudged Selim, and the latter said somewhat apologetically, "It is the time for prayer, Emerson."

"Curse it," said Emerson. "Get on with it, then. Ramses, come with me."

I apologized to Selim, who replied with a grin that there was no need.

I calculated that approximately half of the original escort was now with us, the rest presumably having been left to guard the oasis. Emerson confirmed this when he returned, and went on to say, "Everything seems to be in order. Here, Peabody, let me hoist you up."

I will not test the Reader's patience by describing the last part of our journey in detail. In fact, there was nothing much to see once we had left the palms and greenery of the oasis behind—sand and stony ground, rock outcroppings, and an occasional vulture swinging through the empty sky. One event broke the monotony: a sandstorm which went on from midmorning until shortly before sunset. There was no thought of stopping; a stationary object would soon be buried. The camels knew this. At times, when the force of the wind and sand was at its fiercest, they moved at a snail's pace, but they never stopped. As the interminable hours wore on, one came to think of the sand not as a natural force but as millions of tiny, malevolent beings, attacking the bent heads of men and camels, driving through the drawn curtains of the bassourab and penetrating even the cloth we had wrapped round our heads and faces. When the wind finally died, as suddenly as if someone had pressed a switch, our camel came to a halt.

Naturally I immediately parted the curtains and put my head out. The first sight my anxious eyes beheld was the face of Emerson. He had assumed one of the hooded robes, which had protected him to some extent from the driving sand, but his face was red and raw. "All right, are you, Peabody?" he inquired hoarsely.

"Yes, my dear. What about the others?"

"Still with us and still on their feet. Brace yourself, I believe your camel is about to kneel. Can't blame the poor brute."

Har came plodding back along the line of camels. He inquired solicitously after the well-being of Nefret and me and announced we would stop for a while. For once I was in full agreement with the camels, some of whom had already knelt.

We gathered round the little campfire Selim had started. The sullen crimson of the sun was dulled by fine falling dust.

"Are we still on the right path?" I asked. "I cannot imagine how he could see where we were going, and the storm has obliterated any landmarks."

"There haven't been any signs of life for several days," said Ramses. "No bones, no tracks, not even a pile of camel dung. I wouldn't be surprised if these patrols are ordered to obliterate such signs. They probably have their own private landmarks."

As soon as the dust had settled, Emerson checked the compass, but when he approached Har with the information that we were off course, he was politely but firmly brushed aside. "I know that, Father of Curses. We will return to the right path tomorrow."

As usual, Har and his men left us to ourselves, settling down in their blankets a little distance away. This vexed Daoud, who was a sociable soul and wanted to make friends. "They are strange people," he announced.

"They are people like us, Daoud," Ramses said. "They speak a different language and their customs are not like ours, but they are good men."

"They do not pray," said Daoud, who had punctiliously observed the times of fatah when it was practicable.

"They pray to their own gods," Nefret explained.

"They are not gods, but false idols," declared Daoud.

"No doubt that is true, Daoud," said Emerson. "But do not say so to these men."

"That would be discourteous," said Daoud. "If Allah wishes to show them the right path, he will do so in his own way."

"The world would be a better place if everyone thought as you do, Daoud," I said, patting his arm. "Now what about a language lesson?"

At my insistence we had tried to do this every evening, and I had beguiled some of the long hours of riding by speaking Meroitic with Nefret. I should add that although I have used the word for convenience, strictly speaking, the language of the Holy City was neither Egyptian nor Meroitic, though it contained elements of both. It had once been Nefret's native tongue, but I confess I was surprised at how quickly she had regained her former fluency. Ramses's gift for languages stood him in good stead; I realized he must have begun studying Meroitic even before we left England, and he became even more proficient as the days passed. His father did not. However, as I have said, Emerson generally gets his point across in one way or another.

Next day we passed through a region of heavy sand dunes. It was hard going for men and camels, and very boring. Squatting uncomfortably in the bassourab, I had fallen into a half-doze when an outcry from Emerson awoke me. I put my head out.

"You must see this, Peabody," he exclaimed. "Let me help you down."

We were nearing the top of one of the higher dunes. The sun was setting. At first I saw nothing except more cursed sand, but as we plodded onward and upward, a fantastic vision seemed to rise up out of the ground ahead: towers and battlements, black against the crimson sunset, like the ramparts of a medieval castle.

"There it is," said Emerson. "The Holy Mountain."

We stood staring in fascinated silence until we were joined by Ramses and Selim. The sight was magical, and a trifle ominous. Daoud, slightly behind the others, gave voice to my feelings. "Surely it is the castle of the King of the Afrits. We are going there?"

"Yes," said Emerson.

"Ah," said Daoud. And down he went, onto his knees to rub face and hands with sand in lieu of water. It was the proper time for prayer, but I suspected he would have done it anyhow. After a sidelong glance at Emerson, Selim joined him. We waited in silence, while the patient camels plodded past; and when our friends had finished their prayers Emerson said, "We had better catch them up now. Take my arm, Peabody, it's all downhill from here."

Though the mountains had appeared so close, we were still a full day's journey away, and I began to suspect that Har was in no hurry to get there. He camped at the foot of the last large dune and allowed everyone a full night's sleep. His men were in a more cheerful mood now that home was in sight; there was laughter and even some song round their fire that evening. Our own assemblage was not so merry, despite Daoud's efforts to cheer us up. With full confidence in Allah and, if I may say so, in us, he had decided afrits presented no threat and related several stories about how evil demons had been routed by devout and clever people. Nefret was quiet and thoughtful, and Daria stayed close to her. Ramses avoided both of them. He appeared to be brooding about something, but when I asked he denied that there was anything on his mind.

We went on next day through the foothills of the massif that loomed ahead. Early in the afternoon, eyes weary of stony ground were cheered by the first sight of greenery—a few patches of grass and a single tree, of a species unknown to me. We were by then at the foot of the massif. It was an impressive sight, over five hundred meters in height, fringed with fallen boulders about its base. Only the most intrepid climber would have tackled those cliffs. There was only one way through them, and it took us another two hours to reach it: a long, slow ride round the southwest corner of the mountain mass. The entrance was barely wide enough to admit one camel at a time, and as my beast passed through, the framework of the bassourab scraped the rocky walls, which were of masonry, crudely but solidly built. That was the last I saw for some time, for dusky darkness closed in as we went on. The path twisted and turned. High above, the slit of twilit sky darkened and stars shone out. Torches flared along the length of the caravan; the camels quickened their pace. They sensed they were close to the journey's end, to food and water and rest. Then I heard a grating rumble, like the voice of a great beast. I knew what it was, but I did not blame Daria from seizing my hand and crying out.

"What is this place? What is happening?"

"Don't be afraid." Nefret's voice was remote, eerily distorted by echoes. "This entrance is secret and well guarded, but we are with friends."

The sound had been that of the great rocks that barred the inner entrance being rolled aside. We rode through into a place I remembered well—a cleft open to the sky, which had been widened to serve as an animal corral and storage place. It was brightly lighted by torches and crowded with people. Daria kept tight hold of my hand, and Nefret said impatiently, "There is nothing to be afraid of. Come, Aunt Amelia, let's get out of this horrible contrivance. Goodness, but I'm stiff."

"Hang on a moment, my dear. I suspect the cursed camel is about to—"

It did. Stiff as Nefret, I rolled out into the arms of Emerson, who gave me a quick squeeze before he lowered me to my feet. Ramses was there to lift Nefret down. He left Daria to Emerson.

"Good to be back, eh, Peabody?" said Emerson, smiling broadly.

"Hmmm," I said. "In my opinion, Emerson, that statement is a trifle premature. Many things may have changed since we were last here, and not all for the better."

"One thing at least has not changed," Ramses said. He

indicated several carrying chairs. The bearers stood beside them: short, heavily muscled men, dark of skin and bare of clothing except for a loincloth. Heads bowed, they waited passively for their orders like beasts of burden—which was what they were. Ramses went on, "The rekkit are still enslaved."

We were now handed over to the civilian branch, in the form of a portly individual wearing the elegant pleated garment and rich ornaments of a high official. After he had exchanged a few words with Har, the latter gave us a generalized bow and went off. I had the distinct impression that he was relieved to get us off his hands; though perfectly courteous, he had avoided my attempts to strike up a conversation, and he had been no more forthcoming with Ramses. Nefret he had not addressed at all, except for brief, formal inquiries as to her well-being.

The official approached us, bowing and smiling, and launched into what I took to be a speech of greeting. He spoke very rapidly, and my intellectual faculties were dulled by fatigue, so I asked Nefret to translate.

"He said, 'Welcome to the Holy City, O Great Ones. The king and your loyal people await you.' "

"How nice," I said, nodding graciously at the gentleman. "Tell him we—"

"Ask him what he means by bringing those poor devils here," Emerson broke in, frowning at the litter bearers. "I will not be carried on the shoulders of slaves. And furthermore—"

"Father, if I may?" Ramses did not wait for a response but went on quickly, "I suggest we postpone questions and complaints until we are with Tarek. I have a feeling the situation is more complicated than it appears."

"Hmph. Well, I won't ride in one of those damned litters. It is a matter of principle," Emerson added loftily.

The official, whose name is irrelevant to this narrative, had to accept this, since wrestling Emerson into one of the litters presented obvious difficulties, but I thought he would burst into tears when Nefret also declared her intention of walking.

"Forget your confounded principles for the time being," said Ramses, who appeared to be in a state of mounting exasperation. "Let's just get to where we are going. Mother is tired, and Daria is about to drop in her tracks."

I was a trifle surprised that Tarek had not come himself to greet us, but Ramses had the right of it. So we proceeded, we three women and the official in the carrying chairs, and the men walking behind and beside us. The winding passages through which we passed were rock-cut and narrow. The ramparts of the Holy Mountain were honeycombed with such passages, leading under and into and through the cliffs, excavated over the millennia by thousands of hands. Impossible to tell whether we had traversed this particular part of the maze before; the walls all looked the same.

I expected we would emerge into the open air, with the city spread out before us, framed and hidden from the outside world by the heights all around. Instead, the rock-cut passage changed into a wider corridor, which debouched into a series of antechambers and at last into a large pillared room where the bearers stopped and lowered the litters to the floor.

A single glance told me that this was not the same house in which we had dwelled on our first visit. Even after ten years I could recall every detail of that place; I had spent many weary hours in its confines. This room was airy and cool and prettily furnished with chests and tables and low bed frames piled high with embroidered cushions. Carved pillars supported the roof, and there were several curtained doorways along the walls. The litter bearers took up their burdens and went out through the doorway by which we had come. The official was about to follow them when Emerson interposed his person.

"Take us to Tarek," he demanded in his primitive Meroitic.

Visibly intimidated by the large form towering over him, the official began flapping his hands and talking very fast. "The king will send for us tomorrow," Ramses translated. "Tonight we are to rest and refresh ourselves after our long journey."

"That makes sense, Emerson," I said. "We are travel-stained and weary, and Tarek has courteously allowed us time to rest before he greets us."

Emerson abandoned his aggressive stance and came at once to me. "Are you tired, Peabody?"

"Tired, hungry, thirsty, and filthy, Emerson."

"Oh." Emerson rubbed his chin in mild perplexity. He hadn't shaved for days, and his beard was at its worst, thick and bristly. I meant to see to that later, but at the moment all I could think of was water—cool, clean water, quantities of it, running over my entire body. I had fond memories of the baths of the Holy Mountain—one of my few fond memories, I should add.

"Let us settle in and make ourselves comfortable," I urged. "Where are the servants, do you suppose?"

"Perhaps they are waiting to be summoned," said Nefret. She clapped her hands.

"I refuse to deal with those swaddled handmaidens of the goddess," Emerson grumbled. "If one of them turns up I will send her away."

The women who sidled in were not swathed in veils, nor were they the little dark-skinned rekkit who had waited on us before. We had had attendants like these too: women of what one might loosely term the middle class, wives and daughters of minor officials. Their ornaments were of copper, not gold, and their garments were of coarser linen than those worn by the nobility. An equal number of male attendants followed them, eyeing us warily. Nefret issued orders in Meroitic, and I saw that Ramses was watching her with that hooded look of his. She spoke with fluent authority; her tone and manner had changed in a way I could not quite define.

The servants scattered, and Nefret said to us, "I have told them to bring our luggage and prepare food. Do you want to bathe before we eat, Aunt Amelia?"

"I believe we all should," I replied.

"Go ahead, Father," said Ramses. "I believe the men-servants are indicating that our quarters are through that door. I will join you shortly."

"Going to have a look round, are you?" Emerson inquired. "Hmmm. Don't do anything I wouldn't do, my boy."

"Don't do anything he might do," I corrected. "Are we to go this way, Nefret?"

"There are several suites of rooms here," Nefret said with the same unnerving assurance. "Come with me, Daria."

Our suite consisted of several small bedrooms and a bath chamber. Daria pleaded to enter the bath with Nefret; she had scarcely spoken a word since we arrived and shrank away from the servants. Nefret, who did not suffer from false modesty, readily agreed. I, who did suffer from it, took my turn after they had finished. Pure physical pleasure drowned all thought as I allowed the women to minister to me with the skill I remembered, washing and drying my hair, rubbing oil into my dry skin after weeks of perspiration and dust had been removed, wrapping me at last in towels of linen. When I joined Daria and Nefret, I found them examining the clothing that had been laid out for us: robes of sheer pleated linen held in place by colorful sashes. "Dear me," I said. "This won't do. We will have to wear clean undergarments beneath them."

"I haven't any clean undergarments," Nefret said with a grin. "And I doubt you do, Aunt Amelia."

The bags containing our clothing and other personal necessities had been brought to the bedchamber. I didn't have to open them to know Nefret was unfortunately correct. "Well, you cannot appear before persons of the male gender in that transparent garment. The men are joining us for dinner, I presume? Yes. Hmmm. Let me think . . ."

It took a while to convince the servants that I meant what I said, but they finally brought us robes like their own. We put the pleated linen on over these, and after I had inspected Nefret and Daria, I decided it would do.

"You have been very silent, Daria," I remarked.

"I am in wonderment" was her low-voiced response. "I had heard . . . I had heard tales of such places, but believed they were only stories."

I patted her shoulder. "You are adapting admirably to these new experiences. Continue to do so. Now let us see what there is for supper. I do look forward to a proper meal."

As I had expected, the men were already in the sitting room, if I may so term it. Emerson's beard was as ebullient as ever, but Ramses was clean-shaven and Selim had trimmed his beard. A thrill passed through me at seeing my spouse once again attired in the costume that became his stalwart form so well: a knee-length kilt of white linen fastened at the waist by a jeweled belt. Ramses and Selim wore similar garments, but Daoud, modest man that he was, had wrapped himself in a large piece of linen—probably a bedsheet.

Nefret clapped her hands again, and the servants began to carry in small tables and stools, two to each table, and dishes of food. Daoud sniffed appreciatively.

"But I cannot sit on one of those," he protested, indicating the little stools.

"Sit on the floor, then," I suggested. "The tables are low enough. Do sit down, all of you, you needn't be so formal."

"There is nothing formal about this costume," Emerson grumbled. "They wouldn't give me a shirt." The fixed regard of Daria—fixed, to be precise, on the magnificent musculature of his bare chest—seemed to disconcert him. He turned red and subsided onto one of the stools.

"My dear, you look splendid," I said, carefully not looking at his bare legs, which were of a considerably paler shade than the rest of him. "So do you all."

"Yes," Daria murmured. She had transferred her interested stare to Ramses. In the becoming but barbaric costume he bore an uncanny resemblance to the ancient Egyptians shown in statues and reliefs, broad of shoulder and slim of waist, his skin the same shade of reddish brown. The moisture of the bath chamber had caused his thick black hair to cluster into curls, and the result was strikingly like one of the short Nubian wigs worn by noblemen of the New Kingdom.

At first we were too hungry to converse. Roast goose and fresh vegetables, bread still warm from the oven were a welcome change after days of short rations. Even the thin, rather sour wine was refreshing. Daoud refused to touch it until I explained that the local water was probably not safe to drink. "Does not the law admit exceptions in cases of necessity?" I asked.

Daoud allowed that perhaps it did, and after a time we all became very cheerful. Selim, who had spent most of his life working in the tombs and temples of ancient Egypt, was intelligently fascinated by everything around us. He kept jumping up to peer closely at a row of hieroglyphs or a painted bird, and bombarded Emerson with questions, which the latter was of course delighted to answer. While the others were laughing over one of Daoud's stories (which would probably not have been quite so funny without the wine), Ramses got up and began prowling round the room. I joined him.

"Is something troubling you?" I asked.

"A good many things trouble me." He glanced at his father and lowered his voice. "There is something wrong here. Can't you feel it?"

"You intended to do a little exploring, I believe. Did you find anything to make you uneasy?"

He drew me behind one of the columns and leaned against it. "I didn't have time to explore the whole place. It's even larger than the other palace we stayed in, with a confusing maze of rock-cut chambers at the back. I suspect there is a back entrance, as was the case in the other house, but it is well hidden, and when I started prodding at the walls, I was politely but decidedly urged to leave." He hesitated for a moment and then said, "The front entrance through which we came is now closed by a heavy door. It is locked or bolted on the other side."

"That could be for our protection."

"Against what? Oh, I agree it means nothing in itself, but . . ."

I patted his arm. "Perhaps such uneasiness is solely the result of fatigue. We have been welcomed as honored guests—they didn't even blindfold us when we passed through the tunnels."

"Yes." His face softened. It was not quite a smile, but close to it. "I didn't mean to cause you uneasiness, Mother. You must be very tired. Why don't you go to bed?"

"All that food and wine has made me uncommonly drowsy," I confessed. "We should all retire, I believe. I do not doubt that all our uncertainties will be resolved in the morning."

Emerson gave me a reproachful look when I sent him off with the other men, but he was too shy about such things to announce his preference publicly, or to take me by the hand and lead me into my bedchamber with everyone looking on. As for me, I had no intention of going to bed with that beard.

The two girls took one of the sleeping chambers and I another. The room was cool and dim, lit by a single lamp. The bed had springs of woven leather with pads of folded linen atop; after the surfaces on which I had reclined of late, it felt as soft as a feather bed. Weary as I was, I had no trouble in falling asleep, but my slumber was not sound. Fragments of dreams slipped in and out of my sleeping mind. Once I thought I saw Abdullah's face, but he did not linger or speak. Another image was that of Nefret, clad as I had first beheld her in the white robes of the High Priestess of Isis, with her loosened hair falling over her shoulders.

There were birds too—the jewel-bright birds of the fabled city of Zerzura, fluttering and swooping and uttering high-pitched cries, more like human voices than birdsong.

I woke quite refreshed, however, to find rays of sunlight piercing the shadows through the high clerestory windows. The first creak of the leather springs brought one of the serving women, who helped me into a loose robe and bowed me into the next room, where breakfast was being brought in. It was not long before Emerson joined me, similarly attired and rubbing his eyes.

"What I wouldn't give for a cup of coffee," he mumbled. "I dreamed I could smell it."

"So did I," I said, and so strong was the power of imagination, I fancied I still could. "I have some tea and sugar left, though, and as soon as I have sorted out our baggage I will instruct the servants how to brew it. Where are the others?"

"Coming." One of the servants offered him a bowl of fruit, and another presented a platter of little cakes, sticky with honey. "Urgh," said Emerson. "I swear to you, Peabody, I can still smell—" He broke off, his eyes widening, as with great empressement another servant poured a dark, fragrant liquid into our handleless earthenware cups. Emerson snatched his up and drank.

"Good Gad," I exclaimed, after sampling mine. "It *is* coffee. Where do you suppose they got it?"

"I don't give a curse where they got it," said Emerson, motioning the servant to refill his cup.

Ramses came in, followed by Selim and Daoud. "Good morning, Mother. Good morning, Father. My olfactory sense must be out of order; I thought I smelled—"

"You did," Emerson exclaimed, beaming. "A delicate attention on the part of Tarek, I expect. He must have gone to considerable trouble to obtain it for us."

Ramses's expressive black brows tilted, but he accepted the cup the servant handed him without comment.

"It is good," said Daoud, unsurprised. "But not strong enough. Or sweet enough."

"They use honey as a sweetener here," I explained. "However, I have some sugar left. I will get it, and waken Nefret and Daria."

"They must have been very tired to sleep through this racket," said Emerson, whose voice had been the loudest. He went on sipping his coffee with a look of utter bliss. Ramses put his cup down.

"Mother. Did you look in on them this morning?"

"Why, no. I thought it best not to disturb—"

He moved so quickly I had to trot in order to catch him up. He parted the curtains with a single sweep of his arms.

Nefret and Daria had vanished, along with the bags and bundles that contained their personal belongings. The tumbled coverings on the two beds were the only sign that anyone had been there.


"One of them must have called out in the night," I exclaimed. "I took it for the cry of a bird."

We had searched the entire house, including the dark rock-cut storage chambers at the back, looking for some indication of how the girls had been carried off. Their disappearance could not have been voluntary; Nefret would never play such a trick, leaving us to wonder and worry. There was no doubt in my mind that the wine had contained a sleeping potion of some sort.

If there was a back door, we did not find it. The servants were nowhere to be seen. Emerson's fury and frustration rose to such a pitch that he kept flinging himself against the wooden door in the sitting room. He succeeded only in bruising his shoulder. He was finally distracted by Selim, who dragged out two of the menservants whom he had found trying to hide under the low bed in his room. Daoud took one of them by the shoulder and began shaking him, while Emerson shouted at them both in a mixture of English and Arabic.

"There is no use going on with this, Father," said Ramses, who had managed to interpose a few questions in

Meroitic. "They dare not admit knowledge even if they possess it. Selim, sheathe your knife. Daoud, stop shaking that poor fellow, you will snap his neck."

"Yes, we must keep our wits about us," I cried.

"Quite right, Mother." Outwardly he was the coolest of us all. Only a keen observer like myself would have noticed the unnatural calm of his voice. "May I suggest you leave off brandishing that jug before you hit yourself on the head? I don't believe the girls are in imminent danger, and until we learn what and who are behind their abduction we cannot take the proper action. The only person who can help us is Tarek himself."

With a wordless snarl Emerson rushed back to the door and began beating on it with his fists. The result was instantaneous and so unexpected that Emerson stumbled forward through the opening straight into the individual who had flung the portal wide. He and Emerson both fell to the floor. Beyond them I saw three other men attired like the first, in military uniform—brown linen kilts and wide belts to which were attached long daggers or short swords. They carried spears, and on the left arm of each was a long oval shield covered with animal hide.

Ramses pounced on his father, and by main strength managed to drag him off his victim, whom he had by the throat. "Father, stop it," he gasped. "Mother, can you make him—" He let out a whoop and doubled up as Emerson's elbow drove into his ribs.

My intervention was not necessary. His son's cry of pain had struck through the red mists of anger into the strong core of paternal affection.

"Good Gad," Emerson exclaimed. "My dear boy, accept my profound apologies. I didn't realize it was you. Not hurt, I hope?"

Ramses shook his head dumbly. Taking advantage of his temporary inability to speak, I remarked, "Pull yourself together, Emerson. I believe we are about to receive a delegation. At least we were, until you knocked one of them down. I am sure I do not know how they are going to re-spond to—"

"It was his own fault," Emerson said sullenly. "Coming at me like that."

Ramses had got his breath back. "If you remember, Fa-ther, this procedure is the one followed before, when we were visited by an emissary. Distinguished persons were always preceded by an armed escort. We were told the king would see us this morning; I expect this gentleman has come to take us to him."

He slipped past his father and addressed several sen-tences to the person whose white-clad form I could see be-hind the guards—several yards behind them. The man was an official or a priest, to judge by his pleated garment and beaded collar. He replied in a high-pitched voice but kept his distance.

"Gentleman be damned," said Emerson. "I want to know what they have done with Nefret."

"Then, sir, may I respectfully suggest the sooner we are ready to go, the sooner we will be able to ask that question?"

"Shall we take the guns?" I asked.

"You aren't taking anything of the sort," Emerson snarled.

"It would be advisable to leave them here, I think," Ramses said. "We don't want to give Tarek a false impres-sion of bellicosity."

"I am feeling quite bellicose at the moment," said Emerson. "But I suppose you are right. Tell the fellow we will be with him shortly. Peabody, why aren't you getting dressed?"

The servants had taken our clothes away and returned them, laundered and neatly folded. After I had assumed proper attire I considered whether I should take my parasol. I did not consider for long. It was a weapon, but it didn't look like one. I then hastened back to the sitting room, where I found Ramses in conversation with our visitor.

He was a man who had obviously lived well; his cheeks

were pink and plump, and a roll of fat circled his neck above the broad collar of gold and gemstones; as he bowed and raised both hands in salute, the pleated sleeves of his robe fell back to display broad armlets of gleaming gold.

"Mother, may I present Count Amenislo, overseer of the royal storehouses and Second Prophet of Aminreh."

"How nice," I said, acknowledging his bow. The round pink face was vaguely familiar. "Haven't we met before?"

"Yes, yes," said the count, bowing again. "I speak some of the English to you. In welcome."

"He was one of Forth's students and Tarek's brother," Ramses said. "Only a youth when we last met."

"Enough of these empty courtesies," exclaimed Emerson, to the obvious bewilderment of Count Amenislo. He understood the next sentence, however. "Take us to Tarek."

"Yes, yes. We go. To the king."

The four soldiers stood at attention, two on either side of the door. I was relieved to see that Emerson's victim appeared unhurt, if somewhat disheveled. With ironic courtesy, Emerson gestured to the count to precede him.

"What about Selim and Daoud?" I asked. "Are they included in the invitation?"

"No," Ramses said. "Apparently they are considered to be servants. We'll have to set Tarek straight on that, but not this time."

The escort fell in behind us as we passed along a corridor whose walls were prettily painted with geometric patterns in bright colors of orange-red and blue, green and yellow. I expected it would lead eventually to a terrace looking out over the valley; instead, after several abrupt turns, we found ourselves in a similar passageway lighted by hanging lamps. Here were scenes of feasting and entertainment—slender girl dancers and acrobats, musicians, tables piled high with food—scenes familiar in their subject matter from many such in Egyptian palaces and Cushite tombs. Emerson, who would normally have lingered, examining each detail, gave them not a glance, but walked so close on Amenislo's heels that the count was forced to break into an undignified trot.

As I began to suspect—a suspicion which was later confirmed—we had been housed in apartments usually inhabited by princesses or queens, connected directly to the king's apartments so he could visit the ladies without the inconvenience of going out-of-doors. We met only a few people—servants, by their dress—who flattened themselves against the wall and averted their gaze as we passed.

A square of sunlight ahead, where the corridor ended in a room open to the outer air, indicated that we had almost reached our goal. Amenislo stopped.

"No need to announce us," said Emerson. "Here, Peabody, take my arm. Let us make a dignified entrance."

Another group of soldiers, wearing uniforms like our four, fell back as we entered the throne room—not the imposing state throne room that we had seen before, but a smaller, brighter, less formal chamber. Painted papyriform columns supported the clerestory roof, and sunlight streamed in through the narrow openings above. At the far end, opposite the door through which we had come, was a raised dais, with several heavy curtains behind it. On the dais stood the throne, a chair with feet carved like lions' paws and arms supported by carved scarabs and sun disks. It was entirely covered with gold leaf. Arranged in a semicircle before the dais were three smaller chairs of plain wood. The man who occupied the throne wore over his heavy black wig a diadem with the twin uraeus serpents of Cushite kingship. To one side, and slightly behind the throne, stood a younger man. I recognized him at once, though he was now richly dressed in the garments and ornaments of a prince. The man was Merasen.

The other man—the king—was not Tarek.

Though I was momentarily struck dumb by this discovery, I realized I ought to have been prepared for it. Tarek would have been the first to greet us had he been able. He must

have lost his throne, through death or usurpation, and
Merasen had deliberately deceived us. Even if Tarek had
passed on after Merasen's departure from the Holy City,
there could be no innocent explanation for the theft of the
map and the death of poor Ali.

As the truth dawned on my companions, I feared for a
moment I would have to restrain two infuriated male persons instead of only Emerson. Ramses had never concealed his dislike of Merasen, but the emotion that
darkened his features was a good deal stronger than dislike. I caught hold of his arm in a grip he could not break
without hurting me and said urgently, "Ramses, no! Contain yourself."

"He's taken Nefret," Ramses said. "That is why he
brought us here, he wanted—"

"That may be so, but attacking a royal prince when the
odds are heavily against you is not a sensible procedure."

"Quite right," said Emerson, in a voice like stone grating
on stone. "I am surprised at you, Ramses. Let us hear what
they have to say. Will you do the talking, my boy, and
translate for us? I don't want to miss a word."

Ramses settled back on his heels, breathing hard. I was
relieved to see that Emerson had risen to the occasion. He
prefers not to control his temper, since shouting and shaking people relieve his mind, but when calm and cunning
are required, he displays them. Usually.

Merasen stepped forward. Not a shadow of guilt clouded
his smooth young brow and his smile was as guileless as
ever. "I will talk for the king my father in your language, so
that you will all understand. He welcomes you and bids
you sit yourselves. He is the Horus Mankhabale, Son of Re
Zekare, Lord of the Two Lands—"

"Yes, yes, never mind the rest of it," said Emerson with
a dismissive gesture.

The king nodded benignly. He was a fine-looking man,
with a broad brow and the lean, hard body of a soldier. I
would have put him in his late thirties.

"What has happened to Tarek?" I demanded. "Did he die, then, of the strange sickness, and the child too?"

Merasen laughed and Ramses, who was watching him like a cat with a bird, said, "The strange illness was a lie, wasn't it, Merasen? A lie designed to bring us here. Is Tarek dead—of another cause, such as assassination?"

Merasen translated this speech and the ones that followed; and very odd it was to hear the older man's deep baritone followed by the boy's higher voice, like a piping echo.

"He is not dead" was the royal reply, accompanied by a contemptuous sneer. "He ran away, like the coward he is, with those few who were loyal to him. One day when I have nothing better to do I will crush them like beetles."

None of us had accepted the king's invitation to "sit ourselves." Emerson stood with arms folded, looking down on the king. It was a deliberate act of rudeness, for persons of lower rank are required to kneel or sit so that their heads are not higher than those of their superiors. The king appeared more amused than offended. If I had not known him to be a usurper, and his son a cheat and a liar, I would have thought him quite a pleasant fellow.

"Be damned to that," said Emerson. "I want to know what you have done with Nefret. It must have been you, or those acting by your orders, who took her and her friend away, coming like thieves in the night, violating the honor of your house and the hospitality owed to strangers."

It was quite an eloquent speech, in my opinion, and Merasen must have translated it accurately, for the king's jaw tightened. Without waiting for a reply, Merasen said smugly, "The priestess is safe again in her house with her handmaidens. The shrine of the goddess is no longer empty."

"And the other girl?" Ramses demanded.

"The servant of the priestess is with her. The goddess has accepted her."

I said, "Do I understand you correctly, Merasen? Nefret

has been brought here to resume her former role of High Priestess of Isis?"

"She has always been High Priestess, lady," Merasen said. "For she never chose a successor. When she was taken from us, the goddess abandoned her shrine and the prayers of the faithful were not answered. Now the goddess too will return."

"My goodness," I said, finding myself at something of a loss for words, and distracted by seeing a slight movement of one of the curtains behind the dais. They must cover doorways or niches. There had been a similar arrangement in the great throne room—and one of the curtained niches had been occupied by the highest of high priestesses, the God's Wife of Amon, whose power was even greater than that of the king. As we discovered later, to our horror and dismay, she was Nefret's mother, who had lost her mind and forgotten her true identity. My attempt to save her had been in vain; she had perished of pure rage and an excess of spleen. Was her successor lurking therein? I decided there was no harm in asking.

"Is the Heneshem present?" I inquired, interrupting a loud speech from Emerson, who was demanding to see Nefret.

He stopped shouting and stared at me. "Good Gad, Peabody, the woman is dead. She—"

"Must have been succeeded in the position by another woman. Someone is there," I said. "Behind the curtain. I saw it move."

Merasen stared too. "Why do you ask about the Heneshem? She is not there, she is in her own place. She has no power here. It is my father who—"

"I insist upon seeing Nefret," Emerson shouted. "How do I know she is unharmed?"

"You will see her soon. After she has resumed her duties. Who would harm her? She is the most honored of women, beloved of the goddess."

Ramses put a heavy hand on his father's shoulder—in

the nick of time, since Emerson's intense concern about his daughter had been exacerbated by the references to religion, of which he does not approve. He subsided (I could hear his teeth grinding, however), and Ramses said quickly and softly, "Mother is right, as always. Violence would only end in our being injured and confined. We must retire and discuss this."

"But we have not yet ascertained all the facts," I protested. "I have a good many more questions to ask His Majesty."

"I feel certain you do, Peabody," said Emerson, forcing himself to calmness. "But if I have to listen to any more rubbish about goddesses from that treacherous little puppy, I may do something rash."

Merasen's lower lip protruded like that of a sulky child. We had used a number of words he did not know and his amour propre was damaged. The king had shown signs of increasing impatience as the conversation went on and Merasen did not translate. Now he rose to his feet. "Come," he said in Meroitic, with an expansive gesture that would have made his meaning clear even if it had not been one of the words we all knew. We followed as he strode toward an open archway. Beyond was an anteroom, pillared and handsomely decorated, and beyond that a series of arches that opened onto a terrace with statues of divinities.

The sun was well up, and the long valley of the Holy Mountain stretched out to the right and left below the high balcony on which we stood—fields and small villages on the floor of the valley, fine mansions and temples on the slopes. A broad staircase lined with sphinxes led down to the roadway that followed the curve of the cliffs, leading from the quarter of the nobles past the palace to the Great Temple of Amon Re, or, as he was called here, Aminreh. Gold-tipped obelisks glittered in the sunlight, and the painted reliefs on the pyloned gateway shone with brilliant color. On the left, the mighty figure of a king or god grasped a kneeling enemy by the hair while the other arm raised a long spear. Behind the king stood a smaller, female figure who also brandished a weapon. I was familiar with such scenes, which were common in Egyptian temples, but here the colors were fresh and bright: the black hair of the king, the brownish red of his body, and the woman's paler yellow skin. Her hair was also black. I squinted, trying to make out details, for there was something unusual about the figures, especially that of the woman. She was slimmer than a conventional Cushite queen, those ladies being notorious for their extreme corpulence; and what weapon was it she held?

"That pylon is new," Emerson muttered. "At least the reliefs are. I wonder who the female figure represents. A goddess? Not Isis, she hasn't the right sort of headdress, or Maat, or—"

Ramses let out a strangled sound. "It's Mother," he gasped. "You and Mother. Don't you see the parasol?"

## From Letter Collection C

Dear Lia,

Chances are you will never see this letter. But I don't like journals, they seem so impersonal, and I don't know what has happened to the others, and I must keep track of what is going on, and I'm all alone—except for Daria. Have I told you about her? No, of course I haven't. I keep forgetting things. She's a strange girl, very young, very pretty—the companion of a horrible man named Newbold, a hunter and treasure seeker. She pleaded for my protection, so we brought her on with us to the Holy Mountain. The trip itself went well enough, as such things go, and we were welcomed as honored guests. I went to bed that night tired but comfortable and happy at the prospect of seeing Tarek next day. I awoke next morning . . .

How can I explain it? I went to bed as Nefret Forth. I awoke next morning as High Priestess of Isis. The rooms were the ones I had occupied ten years ago; every ornament, every piece of furniture was the same, including the low bed with its linen sheets and draperies, where I lay. The women who surrounded the bed were robed in white, their face veils thrown back—the handmaidens of the goddess.

Lia, it was the most awful feeling! For a horrible moment I thought I had never left the Holy Mountain—that the intervening years had been only a dream. You, the Professor, Aunt Amelia, Ramses, all the others—only a dream. I started crying. I'm so ashamed. But you can't imagine the dreadful sense of loss, the loss of everyone I loved.

One of the maidens bent over me, opened my loose robe, and placed her hand over my heart. The handmaidens are physicians here, and they know about "the voice of the heart." She smiled and nodded, and another girl approached with a cup containing a liquid of some kind.

Like the switch of a torch bringing light, I was suddenly in control of myself again. Can you guess what did it? It was the sight of my own body, Lia—a woman's body, not that of a thirteen-year-old whose breasts have just begun to grow.

I sat up and pushed the cup away. "No. How did I come here? Where are my friends?"

The handmaidens clustered round. I didn't recognize any of their faces. Another sign, if I had needed one, that time had passed. All the ones I had known—Mentarit, Amenit—had grown to maturity and left the service of the goddess. The girl who held the cup—she had a round-cheeked face with full, pouting lips—thrust it at me again. I pushed it so hard, some of the liquid spilled onto her pristine robes. I enjoyed doing it.

First things first, as Aunt Amelia would say. I was terribly thirsty, but I was afraid there might be some drug in the liquid—wine, from its appearance. "You drink first," I ordered, pointing at the cupbearer. She scowled as she obeyed, but my imperious manner impressed the others. One of them, a sweet-faced girl of about thirteen, ventured, "Does the priestess wish her servant to be brought to her?"

They meant Daria. My heart lifted at the sight of her—someone from my own world, another verification of reality. She was clad in the night robe she had worn when she went to bed and her hair hung down over her shoulders. I jumped up, pushed through my hovering attendants, and went to her.

"Are you all right?"

She was a little pale, but quite composed. "They have treated me well."

"Do you remember what happened?"

"Men took us away, in the night. You were sleeping soundly. I woke and tried to call out, but one of them covered my mouth and carried me away. What will they do with us?"

I was beginning to get a pretty good idea of what they meant to do with me. After we had been served food and drink, I submitted without protest to the all-too-familiar rituals—being bathed in several waters, anointed with oil of lotus, dressed in sheer linen and the ornaments of the High Priestess—the broad, beaded collar, the brightly embroidered sash, armlets and anklets, and the curious little cap of golden feathers. The process took the entire morning. The only answer I got to my incessant questions about the others was a repeated promise: "The High Priest will come soon."

"He damned well better," I said to Daria. One of the handmaidens—the scowly one—had tried to send her away, remarking that I didn't need lowborn servants, but I insisted on keeping her with me, and in that matter at least my word was law.

"They treat you with great reverence," she said, watching one of the girls clasp a bracelet round my wrist.

"I seem to have been conscripted for my old position," I said, trying to smile. "I am desperately worried about the others, though. If it was only me they wanted . . ."

"But you have power. They obey you. You can speak for your family."

"I hope so."

The heavy ornaments settled into place. I remembered only too well the helpless feeling the sheer weight of them brought: the collar pressing down onto my shoulders, the bracelets weighing my arms. The last step was familiar too: long translucent veils of white draped around me and over my head and face. Stiff-limbed as a doll, I was led into an adjoining room and guided to a thronelike chair. No one tried to stop Daria when she followed and took up a position behind the chair. I felt a thrill of gratitude for her presence and her astonishing composure. I certainly wouldn't have blamed her for losing her head.

I could see through the face veil, though not distinctly. The man who entered the room was only a blur at first; when he came nearer, I made out the form of a man bowed with age, leaning on a staff. I hauled myself to my feet, to the consternation of the handmaidens, lined up in two rows before my chair.

"Murtek! Can it be you?"

I had spoken English. The answer was in Meroitic. "The High Priest Murtek, the worthy, went to the gods long ago, lady. I am Amase, High Priest of Isis, First Prophet of Osiris."

I ought to have anticipated that. Murtek had been an old man when I knew him. I felt lonelier than ever.

"Then I order you to tell me why I was taken away from my friends. Where are they? What has happened to them?"

"The Great Ones? They dwell in the house where you were before your servants brought you to your own place. They are content, they are honored, they rejoice."

I let out a squeak of hysterical laughter. I could picture the "rejoicing" once they realized I was gone: the Professor shaking his fists and cursing, Aunt Amelia brandishing her parasol, and Ramses . . . He wouldn't show emotion, not Ramses; he would be thinking and planning.

"Have they been told where I am?"

"They are with the king now, lady."

"I want to be with them. I want to see the king. Take me to him at once."

I hadn't expected those orders would be obeyed, nor were they. The old gentleman made a long speech, full of circumlocutions and ambiguities; but I got the idea. The goddess must be brought back to her empty shrine—by me and no other. He would help prepare me for the ceremony. It must be faultless. There could be no mistake in movement or word.

He didn't say what would happen if I did make a mistake—divine retribution, by Isis in one of her less pleasant attributes? I sat in silence, my mind racing, while he backed away, bowing. I was perfectly willing to go through with the performance, supposing I could remember it; but why hadn't Tarek simply asked me to do it? Why hadn't he come to me, his little sister, his friend?

"Wait!" I said sharply. The old gentleman jerked to a stop and I went on, "The Horus Tarekenidal is my brother. I will bring the goddess back to her shrine after I have seen him and spoken with him."

Amase threw up his hands. "Do not say that name again! It is forbidden, it does not exist. The Horus is Mankhabale Zekare."

"What has happened to Tarek?"

The old man put his hands over his ears—in order to avoid hearing the forbidden name, or because I was screaming at the top of my lungs. He limped out. I took the nearest handmaiden by the shoulders and shook her till the veils flapped. "What has happened to him? Is he dead? Answer me!"

"Not dead, no," she panted. "Gone."

"Where?"

"Far from here. Lady, please—you hurt my neck—"

I let her go and sank back into the chair. "It is bad news he has given me, Daria," I said. "Many things are now clear."

She edged forward. "I don't understand, Nefret. Did you speak to me?"

I had spoken Meroitic. I caught hold of her hand. "Please stay with me, Daria. Talk to me—in English. Remind me of who I am."

⁘

It was something of an anticlimax to observe, on the right-hand side of the pylon, a smaller male figure presenting an ankh—the symbol of life—to the nose of a seated king. The smaller person had the braided side lock that indicated youth, and its nose was considerably larger than that of the king.

Zekare appeared quite pleased at the effect of his little surprise. When he indicated that the audience was over, we went unresisting. Emerson kept muttering, "Good Gad! Good Gad!"

After we had gone a little way down the entrance corridor I said thoughtfully, "I wonder that the new king would leave that relief. Surely it must be the one Tarek promised he would commission in order to honor us, and therefore the royal image must be his."

Ramses had been somewhat disconcerted by his own image—the nose was really a bit much—but he had the answer to my question. He usually does.

"The cartouche has been changed, Mother. That was standard procedure in Egypt, if you recall, whenever a monarch usurped the representation of a predecessor. The name in itself conferred identity; it wasn't even necessary to remodel the features."

"Hmmm, yes," said Emerson. "I am beginning to get an idea—"

"Let's not discuss it now, Father," Ramses cut in. He gestured at Amenislo, who was trotting along ahead of us. Emerson glared. "Quite right, my boy, we don't want to be overheard. He has obviously turned his coat. Against his own brother!"

"All the members of the upper classes are closely related," I said. "I expect the new king is a first or second or third cousin of Tarek's. He must have had some connection with the royal family in order to claim a right to the throne."

None of us spoke again until we had reached our own quarters. "Ramses, fetch Daoud and Selim," Emerson said. "You"—he pointed at Amenislo, who was bowing and smiling—"get out. Go. Leave us."

"Well!" I exclaimed. "We are in a pretty fix."

"Get rid of them too," grunted Emerson, indicating the servants.

"They don't understand English," I replied. "Unlike Amenislo. I will tell them to serve luncheon. I expect Daoud is hungry, and I am a bit peckish myself."

"How can you think of food at a time like this?" Emerson demanded.

"It is necessary to keep up one's strength," I replied. "At least we know the girls are in no danger."

Daoud settled down to eat with his usual placidity, but Selim was in a considerable state of agitation. "Ramses says they have taken Nur Misur to be a priestess of their false god," he exclaimed. "What are we to do?"

"The Sitt Hakim will make a plan," Daoud said.

"Yes, of course," I said with a little cough. "But we must think very carefully about how to proceed. These people take their religion quite seriously, and—"

"Don't be a credulous fool, Peabody," growled Emerson, who never takes religion seriously. "In this society, as in all the others with which I am familiar, religion among the ruling classes is only a cloak for politics. If the new king were powerful enough, he could install his own High Priestess, and be damned to tradition."

"As he has apparently done with the position of God's Wife, who is known here as the Heneshem," Ramses said. "You recall how it was done in Egypt—when a new king took the throne, he had his daughter adopted by the reigning God's Wife as her successor. Nefret's mother was an aberration and, unlike Nefret, she died in office. She may have already had an adopted 'daughter,' who took her place, but has not her power, and if the usurper forced his daughter on the new Heneshem—"

"Yes, yes," Emerson said impatiently. "All very interesting, my boy, but off the point."

Selim let out an exclamation. "Nur Misur's mother? Do you mean she was the God's Wife here? I thought she died when Nur Misur was born."

"That is what Nefret believes," I said. "And you must never, ever, tell her differently, Selim. Her mother went mad, denied her husband and her child, and forgot her true identity. She is dead, and there is no need for Nefret to know the truth, which would make her very unhappy."

"Yes," Selim murmured, stroking his beard. "For a mother to deny her child . . ."

"God had taken her mind away," said Daoud. "She was not to blame. Would it make Nur Misur unhappy to know that?"

"Yes," I said with an affectionate smile. "Very unhappy."

"Then I will be silent," said Daoud. "Forever."

"Yes," Selim agreed. "Forever."

"Now that we've settled that," said Emerson, "can we return to the point? Zekare may be powerful enough to control the position of God's Wife, but he obviously needs us and Nefret to prop up his throne."

"I cannot imagine that our influence is that great, or his position so weak," I protested.

Emerson had been hoarding his store of tobacco. Now he took out his pipe and pouch. He claims the nasty weed aids in ratiocination. I sincerely hoped so, for never had we been in direr need of clear thinking.

"Such must be the case," said Emerson, "or we wouldn't be here. Never mind pointing out that I have just committed some horrible flaw in logic, Peabody, only consider the probabilities. We are obviously persons of some importance, or that pylon would not still display our images. Tarek was a popular ruler, especially among the lower classes, but a military coup could have overthrown him, especially if it were supported by the more reactionary of the nobles and by the priesthood. Those sanctimonious bastards are always poking their noses into affairs of state."

This was grossly unfair, and an example of Emerson's prejudice against religious persons, but I let it pass, for in this case his accusation might have a basis in fact. The priesthood of Aminreh, chief god of the Holy Mountain, had supported Tarek's brother for the kingship, and the High Priest had been one of his bitterest enemies.

Daoud swallowed a mouthful of bread and looked at me. "Have you made a plan yet, Sitt?"

"By God, Daoud is right," Ramses burst out. "We should be planning what we mean to do, not engaging in idle speculation on the basis of insufficient information."

"What do you propose?" I inquired, resisting the temptation to point out that he was as prone to that error as I.

"The most important thing is to find a way of communicating with Tarek. There must be people who are still loyal to him—an opposition party. No doubt it has gone underground, but we've got to find some of its members and offer our support, in return for theirs. We have firearms, but not enough of them. We can't get the girls away without outside help."

"That makes sense," said Emerson, puffing away. "It may be significant that our servants this time do not include any of the common people—the rekkit. The majority of them probably support Tarek, but they are powerless and it won't be easy to reach them. You remember how much trouble we had last time getting permission to visit their village."

"That's the next step," Ramses said. "Or the first, really. We must be free to move about. That means convincing the new regime that we are on their side. Father, can you bring yourself to be ingratiating to the king and Merasen?"

"More easily than you, I fancy," said Emerson, giving him a sharp look.

"That shouldn't be too difficult," I mused. "People who love power are extremely susceptible to flattery."

"I will leave the flattery to you," said Emerson. "What I'll propose is a practical quid pro quo: our loyalty, publicly demonstrated, if necessary, in exchange for permission to record the reliefs in the temples and explore the tombs."

"No man who knows the Father of Curses will believe he would be disloyal to a friend, or let his daughter be taken from him," said Selim, who had followed the discussion with furrowed brow.

"He doesn't know me," said Emerson, trying to look sly.

"He knows you well enough, by reputation, at least, to know you would never consent to remain here indefinitely," I retorted. "You must ask when we will be allowed to leave. He will lie, of course. He can't afford to let us go, with or without Nefret."

A united outcry from the others arose. "Of course we won't leave without her," I said impatiently. "But since we cannot enforce our will, we must, for the moment, pretend to believe any lies the usurper chooses to tell—especially about Nefret. The High Priestess does not serve for life. Once she has chosen a successor—"

"Do you know what happens to the High Priestess after she gives up her position?" Ramses asked quietly.

"I can guess. That isn't the point, Ramses. I will ask the king if we may take her with us after she has appointed another in her place, and he will say yes, we may, and he will be lying, and we will pretend—do you hear me?—we will pretend to believe it. I am only trying to gain time—time enough to locate Tarek and figure out how to overthrow the usurper."

"Where is this friend, this Tarek?" Selim asked.

"That's a good question," Ramses said. "He must be holed up in a place which is defensible and/or well hidden, or the king would have crushed him and his followers already. One doesn't leave a pocket of rebellion to fester if one can easily clean it out. The difficulty is that we learned very little about the city and the surrounding area; we were closely guarded prisoners most of the time."

"Do you suppose Tarek knows we are here?" I asked.

"If he doesn't, he soon will. The usurper can't make use of our prestige without announcing our presence. I wouldn't count on Tarek's being able to reach us, though. He'd be a fool to venture into the city when there's a price on his head."

"We need more information," I declared. "Let us send word to the king requesting another audience. We will present him with a list of our demands. First and foremost, we will insist on seeing Nefret."

"I share your anxiety, Peabody," said Emerson. "But I think we ought not make the first move. It is poor diplomacy, especially in a society like this one." He sauntered toward the right-hand wall and began examining the painted reliefs.

"Emerson," I said, "if you begin copying inscriptions or taking notes I will—I will—"

"You had better do the same," said Emerson, without turning. "We must convince old Zekare that our fascination with the culture of the Holy Mountain is great enough to win us over to his side, at least for the time being."

"You are right," I acknowledged. "Very good, Emerson."

"So what is the plan?" Daoud inquired. "Is there time for me to finish eating? Is there more food?"

"Take all the time you like," I said, indicating to the servants that they should replenish the bowls. "We can do nothing until . . . Tomorrow, Emerson? I cannot contain myself much longer than that."

"Dear me, Peabody, I had not expected to find you so lacking in patience. Why don't you make one of your famous lists? Selim, would you be good enough to find our notebooks and writing implements? I don't know where they stowed the rest of our luggage, but I expect one of these pleasant young women will show you if you ask nicely."

He winked in a vulgar fashion, and Selim's lips relaxed into a knowing smile. "Yes, Emerson. I will ask very nicely—with gestures, since I do not know the words."

"I expect gestures will work quite well," said Emerson. "Now then, Peabody, feel free to speculate to your heart's content, since that is all we can do at present. Perhaps a brief incisive summary of the situation to begin with?"

"Don't patronize me, Emerson!"

"I wouldn't dream of it, my dear."

"Well . . ." I said. "To sum up, then: Merasen was sent not by Tarek but by the new king, whose position is less secure than he wants us to believe. Merasen was promised higher rank, possibly even the position of Royal Heir, if he succeeded. It does seem a trifle callous of the king, though, to risk his son on such a trip."

"Unless he has so many of them he can spare a few," said Ramses cynically. "It may not have been as great a risk as Merasen implied. I don't doubt his escort was greater than he admitted. And it may be that the king doesn't entirely trust him. I sure as hell wouldn't. Don't you realize he must have been brought up in Tarek's household, where he was taught English—and other things?"

"You may be right," I said. "The boy seems to have no moral sensibilities whatever. He has now allied himself with someone from the outside world—someone who could use a compass and get a caravan together. Does the king know about this, or is Merasen playing a double game with him too?"

Selim came running back into the room. "The guns," he exclaimed. "The guns are gone!"

## · ·
## Eight
## · ·

"It's my fault," Ramses said, eyes downcast and jaw set. "I advised against carrying weapons into the presence of the king."

"No, it is mine," Selim cried. "I should have stood guard over them."

"I should have put a curse on them," Emerson bellowed, waving his fists.

They were all pacing up and down the room, wringing their hands and beating their breasts (figuratively speaking), except for Daoud, who sat waiting patiently for someone to say something sensible. Daoud was a great comfort to me.

"There is no use crying over spilled milk," I announced. "Are they all gone?"

"Yes," said Emerson, so overwrought that he did not even complain about my voicing an aphorism. "We left our rifles and pistols in our rooms with the rest of our personal belongings. They must have been taken last night. The remaining weapons and most of the ammunition were in a single packing case. I made certain it was loaded onto one of the camels when we left the oasis. It isn't here now, though all our other luggage is—cameras, notebooks, surveying equipment."

"Are you speaking of the guns?" Daoud inquired. It was the first chance he had had to get a word in.

"Yes," Selim groaned. "All of them. Rifles, pistols, ammunition—"

"Not all," said Daoud. Reaching into the breast of his robe, he took out a pistol. "The rifle is in my bed."

I have seldom seen three men look more foolish—especially those three. Ramses was the first to get his voice back. "Daoud, you are—you are a wonder. Er—in your bed?"

"Yes," said Daoud in surprise. "It is what they tell the soldiers. I heard an officer say so. 'This is your gun. Eat with it, sleep with it.' The rifle got in my way when I was eating, but I ate with the pistol and slept with both."

Emerson's mouth was hanging open. "Good Gad! Well done, Daoud. Though a single pistol and rifle—"

"May come in useful," I interrupted. "In circumstances which are as yet unknown. Very well done, Daoud! The loss of the other weapons is unfortunate, but as Ramses pointed out earlier, we couldn't have relied on them to get us out of here. We must endeavor to demonstrate the stiff upper lip for which we are famous. I include you and Daoud, of course, Selim. Get out the cameras and notebooks, please. We will continue on the course Emerson so wisely suggested."

Emerson perked up a bit. "Where shall we start?" he asked.

"With a general plan of this palace," I replied, giving him a wink and a nod. "Including, of course, the storage and servants' areas."

We spent the rest of the afternoon at this pursuit, making copious notes and taking occasional photographs of nothing in particular. The servants, who had incontinently fled when Emerson began raging about the missing weapons, ventured cautiously out, and curious eyes watched our every move. I made it a point to smile and speak pleasantly at them, and urged my companions to do the same. One of the young women became so emboldened that she followed us from room to room, though of course at a respectful distance.

Our survey was superficial in the extreme, since none of the servants was in a position to judge its effectiveness and our primary purpose was not scholarly. The rock-cut chambers were, some of them, mere cubicles, less than six feet square and six feet high—empty of everything except dust, and extremely hot. Others served as kitchens and temporary sleeping quarters for servants. Though ventilated by an ingenious system of air shafts, and decorated, rather pathetically, with a few woven mats and baskets containing cosmetics and extra clothing, they were scarcely more comfortable than the storage chambers.

We returned to the sitting room dusty and crumpled and dripping with perspiration.

"Well, well," said Emerson, rubbing his hands together. "Several points of interest, weren't there? Ramses, will you begin on that plan?"

"I will ask for something to drink," Selim announced. And he did so, directing his gestures at the young woman who had been our most assiduous follower. She appeared to have no difficulty in understanding.

I said, "If you will all excuse me, I am going to sponge off some of this dust."

"Don't be long," said Emerson. "I have a little surprise for you, Peabody."

I accepted the assistance of one of the serving girls, humming a cheerful tune as she helped me into a clean robe and tied a bright red-and-blue scarf round my waist. (I added several safety pins along the opening.) When I returned to the sitting room, Emerson had his hands behind his back. "You look very charming, Peabody. Guess what I have for you."

I wished I could say the same about him. He had at least washed his hands, which was all to the good if my guess about his "surprise" was correct. I had not the heart to spoil it by guessing correctly, however. The smile he had forced himself to keep in place all afternoon was beginning to show altogether too many teeth.

"Why, Emerson, what can it be?" I asked. I let out a cry of girlish delight and clapped my hands as Emerson produced . . . a bottle of whiskey.

"I have been hoarding it," he explained. "And I think we deserve it tonight. Ramses?"

"Yes, sir, thank you."

Selim and Daoud were drinking tea. Selim must have shown the servants how to prepare it and how to set out something that bore a rather amusing resemblance to a tea tray. The cups were without handles and the pot was just that—a brown, elegantly shaped earthenware jug with a pierced clay strainer atop. We settled ourselves comfortably and Emerson raised his cup. "To a successful end to our quest," he announced. "May I stop smiling now, Peabody? I feel as if my face is paralyzed."

"Just try to look affable, my dear. You have done very well. We have all done well, in my opinion. Our performance this afternoon must convince the king that we have accepted the situation."

"Grrrr," said Emerson, forgetting himself for a moment. "Ramses, have you anything to report? You were quite a long time in one of those back rooms."

"This one," said Ramses, producing a rough sketch. "There is a raised stone bench along one wall, reminiscent of a similar structure in one of the rooms of the palace we formerly inhabited."

"Aha!" exclaimed Emerson. "The bench whose top lifted to give access to the subterranean passages?"

"Yes, sir. Unfortunately, although there was a corresponding depression under the lip of this slab, my attempts to release the catch were in vain."

I recognized, with some regret, a return to the youthful pedantic speech patterns which Ramses had almost overcome. He must be even more worried than I had realized. My own spirits had lifted a trifle. We were acting—making plans—taking steps! Or it might have been the whiskey.

"Drink your whiskey," I said to him.

"Yes, Mother," he said absently.

He ate very little at dinner. I had had an idea that I thought might cheer him up, so I proposed it. "When we see the king I am going to ask if I may pay Nefret a visit. The priestesses are secluded, but I might be allowed when a man would not be. If the king agrees—and I will be very insistent—I can report back to you, not only on her health and state of mind, but where she is."

"That is a good idea, Mother," Ramses said, looking, if not cheerful, a trifle less gloomy. "It is important that we be able to communicate directly with her. If I know Nefret, she won't take this lying down. Persuade her to appear submissive and tell her we are putting on a show of acquiescence in order to—"

"Yes, my dear, that was precisely what I had in mind."

Ramses went back to his plan and Emerson and I took a little stroll in the garden. It was a pleasant place in the twilight, with vines covering the walls and a pool lined with blue tiles. The lotus blooms had closed into tight buds, but the velvety green leaves waved in a gentle breeze, spilling crystalline drops as perfectly formed as beads of mercury. Emerson is not unmoved by natural beauty, but on that occasion he spent most of his time inspecting the walls. He had to climb on a low stone bench to look over them, for they were eight feet tall.

"Well?" I asked. "Are there guards?"

"No need for guards. There's a sheer drop, into a ravine thirty feet down. We could probably descend safely if we had ropes or some substitute for them."

"Not much point in that unless we had some idea of how to get up the other side, and where to go once we were up."

"Quite," said Emerson. "Let us get rid of these damned servants, eh?"

He did so, with peremptory gestures, and then suggested somewhat pointedly that the others retire as well.

"Emerson," I said, as he advanced toward me. "I hope you won't take this in the wrong way, but I really am not in a proper frame of mind for—er—that. Not this evening. And not with that beard."

"My dear Peabody." He gave me a reproachful look. "That was not what I had in mind. Well—to be honest, I always have it in mind, but for once it was not my primary reason for wanting to be alone with you. We have lost Nefret; I will not let the bastards carry you off too."

I took his outstretched hands. "My dear Emerson. I beg your pardon."

"Granted. Er—did you mean it about the beard?"

I made it clear that I did.

Emerson's presence was a great comfort in every way, but sleep did not come easily to me, perhaps because I was trying too hard. I wanted to dream of Abdullah, not only in the hope that he might have a useful suggestion, but because I was beginning to fear that that wonderful vision would never be repeated—that the comfort it had given was the sole reason why it had been vouchsafed to me.

I was in that state of drowsy discontent that can be more tiring than full wakefulness when a faint sound broke the stillness. There was always at least one lamp left burning, to save the laborious business of making a new fire, which was done in the old way. The lamp on a stand near the bed illumined only a small part of the chamber and bred shadows that huddled in distant corners. The sound had come from the doorway. I lay on my side, facing in that direction, but the large bulk of Emerson—lying flat on his back, arms folded across his breast like a pharaoh of old—blocked my view of the lower part of the curtain. The sound came again . . . No, I thought, not the same sound—the first might have been a soft footfall, the second was that of expelled breath. It might be Ramses, on the lookout for intruders. Or—it might be the intruder himself! My heart beat faster with excitement. I lay motionless, waiting for him to creep into the chamber. If they expected to find me alone, they might not have sent more than one abductor. I would have to climb over Emerson and locate my parasol, but I felt confident I could deal with one man. If there were more than one, I would have to fight them off until Emerson came fully awake, which always takes a while.

The fighting blood of the Peabodys was up, but I reminded myself that I must not be hasty. It was possible—not likely, but possible—that Tarek had heard of our being there and was attempting to communicate with us as he had done once before, secretly and by night.

Whoever he was—or they were—they—or he—was in no hurry. The seconds ticked by. The curtain moved slowly and cautiously away from the right-hand wall and a pale oval appeared in the gap, visible only because it was not so dark as the darkness behind it. A face! Surely it was a face, though I could not make out the features. I felt eyes upon me—eyes that burned with the intensity of their regard—heard another exhalation of breath, louder than the first . . .

Emerson let out a shout. "Peabody!" His hand groped wildly, trying to find me. It was the wrong hand. I was on his other side.

The face vanished, the curtain fell into place. I cried, "Curse it! Emerson, wake up!" Eluding his flailing arms, I got out of bed and ran for the doorway. I was too late. Nothing moved in the moonlit room.

"Burning eyes, indeed," growled Emerson. "You admitted you could not make out the fellow's features."

"I felt the eyes, Emerson. Ramses, may I have a drop more of that whiskey?"

Aroused by Emerson's cries and mine, the others had rushed out of their rooms to find us embracing in the sitting room. The embrace was not friendly. Convinced I was suffering from nightmare, Emerson was attempting to keep me from pounding on the door. It was, as he proceeded to demonstrate, immovable.

Ramses fetched the whiskey and we sat down to discuss this latest development.

"You were dreaming," Emerson insisted. "The door is still bolted. How could anyone get out that way?"

"By bolting it again after he had gone out the way he came in," I snapped. "I resent the implication, Emerson. If you think I cannot tell the difference between a dream and reality . . . Hmmm."

No one took notice of my momentary confusion. Ramses ran his fingers through his tangled curls and said tactfully, "Go over it again, Mother. Every detail."

So I did. I thought it better to omit the adjective to which Emerson had objected, but stuck to the eyes. "We all know the feeling—that of being the object of a prolonged, intense stare. What I saw was a real face, and a real hand drew the curtain aside. If Emerson had not frightened him off and interfered with my pursuit of the fellow, I might have caught him!"

"Just as well I did, then," said Emerson. "Do you suppose you could have stopped him if he were intent on getting away? You didn't even have your parasol!"

"There wasn't time to find it."

"Oh, bah," said Emerson. "They wouldn't have sent a single man."

"They would have done if 'they' was not the current regime but Tarek." My generally excellent syntax was suffering from annoyance at Emerson's skepticism. They all knew what I meant, though.

"Tarek and his supporters are in hiding, Peabody. This purported visitor purportedly left by the front door, which is guarded by Zekare's men."

"Purportedly guarded, do you mean?" We glared at each other.

"It was not a dream," Selim said. He had been crawling

on hands and knees, inspecting the floor outside my chamber. Now he rose and held out his hand.

White against his brown palm was a small circular object. A button.

When we gathered round the breakfast tables, Emerson drank his coffee with less pleasure than he had the day before. "This proves they have some contacts with the outside world," he declared. "Not only through places farther west, but with traders who deal in imports from the east."

"We have better evidence than that," I said. "Evidence of direct contact. They do not use buttons here, and that one came from a man's shirt. I have sewn enough of yours back on to know."

"Are you absolutely sure it isn't one of mine?" Emerson asked.

"You know perfectly well that none are missing from your shirts, or those of Ramses's. You watched me inspect them. Anyhow, the one Selim found is slightly larger than the normal sort. I believe it to be of French or German manufacture."

Emerson and Ramses exchanged doubtful looks.

"I don't know why you are so reluctant to accept the truth," I said in exasperation. "We agreed, did we not, that Merasen must have had a confederate who was responsible for the attacks on our men and who guided him here. He is still here. The logic is inescapable."

"Logic, bah," said Emerson, glowering. "It need not be the same man. Whoever the devil he is."

"The most likely suspect," I began, but was interrupted by Ramses.

"Excuse me, Mother, but I can't see the point in speculating about that. Shouldn't we be ready in case the king sends for us?"

"Yes, quite," said Emerson. "But we must appear surprised, even reluctant, when that occurs. Let's get back to work."

As the morning wore on without a summons, I began to wonder if we had exaggerated our importance to the new regime. "Unlikely," said Emerson, when I expressed my sentiments. "He's playing the same game we are, and the first to approach the other will lose prestige. Hand me that piece of drafting paper, will you, please?"

We had divided forces, sending Ramses off by himself to continue his exploration of the back rooms and hoping that our busy activities in the sitting room would keep the servants interested. By midday we had collected quite an audience, and I was about to suggest we stop for luncheon when there was a disturbance at what we had decided to call the front door. It was flung open, and in dashed Count Amenislo, in such a rush he pushed past two guards. His wig was askew. He ran to Emerson and began plucking at his sleeve.

"Hurry! Hurry! Come, come!"

Emerson turned, with awful dignity. Amenislo's fat hands fell as if they had been burned.

"We do not go or come at the orders of underlings," said Emerson. "We are busy with our work."

Amenislo dropped to his knees and raised his hands. "The king sends for you. Come, hurry!" His brow furrowed, as if he were trying to remember a word he seldom used. "Pliss?"

"I believe he is attempting to say 'please,'" said Emerson to me. "That is much better. But shall we linger awhile? I do enjoy seeing him get so worked up."

Amenislo groaned. "I will be punished . . ."

"I would enjoy seeing that even more," remarked Emerson. "Oh, very well." He let out a shout that made the count jump. "Ramses!"

Ramses came running. "It's all right, my boy," said Emerson. "I didn't mean to alarm you. We have been invited to call on His Majesty."

Ramses looked in wonder at Amenislo, who was bouncing round the room trying to push at us without actually touching us. "What's wrong with him?" Ramses asked.

"He keeps telling us to hurry," said Emerson, motionless as a column.

"Yes, yes, hurry, come!" His eyes moved from the impassive face of Emerson to the equally inexpressive countenance of Emerson's son, and in desperation he tried the magic word again. "Pliss? Pliss!"

Emerson condescended to take one step toward the open door. "Don't forget your parasol, Peabody," he said.

I took the parasol, and the arm Ramses offered, and we followed Emerson and the count. Emerson moved like a mourner at a funeral, with slow, dragging steps. The count twittered and gabbled.

"Something is up," said Ramses.

"So it seems," I said uneasily. Badgering Amenislo had been entertaining, but I had begun to think of all the things that might have gone wrong—wrong for us, that is. The capture of Tarek? Something to do with Nefret?

"Could you please pick up the pace a bit, Emerson?" I said.

The small throne room was deserted—not even guards. Amenislo hurried across the room, waving us on. As we proceeded through a series of antechambers and short corridors, I began to hear a strange sound—a murmur like the magnified buzzing of a nest of wasps. It grew louder as we went on, rising to its highest pitch when we entered the chamber where the king awaited us.

He was not alone. Merasen was there, and others who wore the regalia of high rank, including several dressed in the snowy pleated mantles of priests. Zekare was standing at a wide aperture, like an open window with a waist-high sill. Instead of formal robes, he was garbed in a long-sleeved shirt and short kilt, both of them bright with colored embroidery. A sword was slung in a scabbard across his back.

Amenislo flopped down on his face. The king ignored him as if he had been a beetle. With a peremptory gesture he beckoned us to come forward.

The aperture reminded me of the Window of Appearance found in Egyptian palaces, where the king appeared to his adoring subjects and rewarded the worthy with collars of gold. Zekare stepped aside as we approached.

Below the window was a stone-paved court or plaza, opening off the main highway. Plaza and highway, as far as the eye could see, were teeming with people—people of all sorts, men, women and children, including a group of the small, dark-skinned rekkit. Hands brandished stones and sharpened sticks, voices were raised. The words were indistinguishable, but the tone was indubitably hostile. The crowd swayed back and forth, but did not advance, for a very good reason: the spears and arrows of a troop of soldiers drawn up in solid ranks below the window.

At the sight of us the wordless clamor died. A sea of faces stared up at us. (A trite metaphor, I admit, but descriptive.) In the silence the king's deep baritone rolled out.

"They have come, the Great Ones, as I promised. Now go to your homes."

No one moved. The king bit his lip in vexation. "Speak to them," he ordered. "Tell them you are with me in friendship. Tell them to . . ."

"Disperse," said Ramses, before I could ask what the word meant.

"Damned if I will," exclaimed Emerson. "By Gad, the news of our presence has already spread."

"Father, we must do as he says," Ramses said urgently. "Or be responsible for a bloody massacre. There are women and children in that crowd."

"Oh, curse it," said Emerson, somewhat abashed. "You are correct, of course, my boy. You talk to them. I would choke on the words—even if I knew what words to use."

Ramses leaned over the wide rim of the window and raised his hands. There was no need to ask for attention;

every eye was fixed on him. It was as if no one in that vast assemblage breathed.

I did not understand everything he said, but the gist of it was clear. He was the Brother of Demons—he gestured at the extraordinary figure on the pylon, and the heads swiveled as one, toward the pylon, and back to him. He had returned with the other Great Ones to bring peace and prosperity. "Go quietly to your homes now, and no one will be hurt," he concluded. "We will speak to you again."

"Nicely done," I remarked to Emerson. "He carefully avoided expressing loyalty to the king."

"Indeed? I didn't understand much of it."

"You really must apply yourself to the language," I said severely. "Ramses, they are not dispersing. What seems to be the difficulty?"

"I detect a certain level of skepticism," said Ramses dryly. "One can hardly blame them; I don't much resemble that caricature on the pylon. Let them have a closer look at you. You needn't speak, just give them the royal wave and gracious smile."

His point was well taken. Even those who were old enough to remember the ten-year-old "hero" might have found some difficulty in recognizing the grown man. For all they knew, he could be one of their own people, an impostor presented by the king. But when Emerson moved forward into the glare of sunlight, all doubts were dispelled. It would have been impossible to imitate that stalwart form and those sapphirine eyes (accurately rendered on the pylon). The collectively pent breath was released in a great shout, and when I leaned over the sill and waved my parasol, another cheer arose.

"Go home," I shouted. "Go with our—er—what is the word for 'blessing,' Ramses?"

Slowly, reluctantly, the crowd dispersed. Most of them continued to look up at the window. Some of them were weeping.

"Now," said Emerson, with a broad, evil grin, "we are in an excellent position for negotiations."

**From Manuscript H**

The negotiations took place in the small throne room. Zekare had dragged out all the big guns, secular and religious—the high priests of Aminreh and Isis, the commander of the household troops, the vizier, and Uncle Tom Cobley and all, as his mother remarked later. And Merasen. Two of the officials were other sons of the king, tall, soldierly men who appeared to be older than Merasen. They were all decked out in their best attire, the priests in snowy pleated robes, the commander in a helmet sprouting feathers like a rooster's tail, and everybody clanking with gold ornaments and broad collars of semiprecious stones.

If the purpose was to impress them with the solidarity of his support, it didn't do the job. The two priests kept exchanging sullen glances—those priesthoods had always been rivals—and the commander hardly took his eyes off Emerson. Merasen strutted round the room bragging of his exploit in bringing the Great Ones back, and the two older princes watched him like vultures.

Ramses had considered offering to act as translator, if only for the pleasure of taking Merasen down a peg, but had decided not to emphasize his command of the language. People are inclined to speak more freely when they believe they cannot be understood, and he wanted to find out how accurately Merasen reported their comments, and the king's replies.

Emerson began by making a little speech. They, the Great Ones, were graciously pleased to accept the homage that was their due. The petty quarrels of small kingdoms did not concern them; they were seekers of knowledge and had come to the Holy Mountain primarily in order to make drawings and take photographs. Merasen had to stop and explain that word, but otherwise his translation was reasonably accurate. He didn't have to translate the king's response, which consisted of a vigorous nod and a broad smile.

If the fellow thought he was going to get off that easily, he was mistaken. Emerson got down to business. "When we have finished our work we will return to our own place. You will provide camels and drivers for us."

The nod was less emphatic and the smile less broad this time. Merasen added a few words on his own account. "The king hopes you will remain for a long time."

"May I ask a few questions, Father?" Ramses inquired.

It took a while. Merasen's translations of the king's replies became increasingly inaccurate, and the king became increasingly restless. None of the others took an active part, though there was a certain amount of scowling and muttering.

The discussion came to an abrupt end when the king rose. "We will speak again of these matters. You may go now."

He stalked out through one of the curtained doorways behind the dais. "I take it we are dismissed," remarked Emerson. "What did he say that Merasen didn't bother to translate?"

"You have an evil, suspicious mind, Father," Ramses said. "I'll tell you as soon as we are in private."

Merasen had followed his father out of the room, and the others began to leave, one or two at a time. The commander of the guard lingered, lining his men up in proper order. As if struck by a sudden thought (which was probably not the case), Emerson strolled up to him.

"Good, your men," he said. "Good leader, you."

Instead of bowing, the fellow stiffened and stood at attention, like a subaltern who has been addressed by a general. "I know the stories," he stammered. "The spear . . . straight through the body till it stood out a handsbreadth behind his back. Harsetef told me . . ."

Emerson, who had only understood a few words, brightened at the familiar name. "Harsetef, yes. My friend. He was there."

"My friend," the captain repeated. "You saved his life, the lives of his wife and child."

Ramses took the liberty of translating this. Emerson waved a negligent hand. "The least I could do. How is the old chap?"

While Ramses was trying to think of a reasonable translation for these idiomatic remarks, one of the princes came back into the room. He barked out an order. The captain saluted and started to turn away.

"Your name, my friend?" Emerson inquired with magnificent condescension.

"Alare, O Great One." He saluted Emerson as he had done the prince, with raised hands and bowed head.

Ramses had followed the proceedings with a feeling almost of awe. His father was famous for his violent temper and physical strength; he hadn't fully realized that Emerson was capable of twisting a man's mind as efficiently as his body.

"Well done, Father," he murmured, as they started back toward their rooms.

"Divide and rule, my boy. I detected at least four different factions in that single room; if we can't play them off against each other we deserve to be stuck here. I'll concentrate on the military, since"—Emerson coughed modestly—"I seem to have some prestige in that quarter. Peabody—"

"The High Priest of Isis" was the prompt reply. "He seems a timid little man, and Nefret is in his charge."

"What about me?" Ramses inquired.

"I leave it to you, my boy. Merasen's older brothers are obviously green with envy. Only a suggestion," he added.

"Yes, sir."

This time Emerson didn't dawdle. Daoud and Selim were eating when they entered their sitting room. Selim jumped up. "What happened? Is Nur Misur—"

"Nothing to do with her," Ramses said, smiling at him. "It's good news, in fact. Mother will be allowed to see her tonight."

"I thought that was what he said," remarked that lady.

"But I got the distinct impression that Merasen did not report everything accurately."

The servants brought more food—Daoud had finished the first course—and Ramses told Selim and Daoud what had happened.

"We are to be allowed a limited amount of freedom—with a guard of honor, naturally."

"You didn't ask about the rekkit's villages," Emerson said.

"I thought it would be better if we simply barged straight ahead until somebody stopped us." Ramses paused long enough to swallow a spoonful of soup, and then went on. "Your speech was well received, Father. I think Zekare will buy it, because disinterested loyalty is a quality he doesn't believe in or expect."

"That is a not uncommon characteristic of tyrants," remarked his mother sententiously. "They fail to understand that a man whose loyalty can be bought is open to a higher bid." She caught Emerson's eye and went on smoothly, "The high priests of Aminreh and Isis have always been at odds. We may hope to insinuate a wedge."

"As Father did with the commander of the guard," Ramses said. "The man is obviously in awe of him. If he is faced with a choice of obeying his king or the great and powerful Father of Curses, he might waver."

"He won't waver when I'm through with him," said Emerson complacently. "But we still have a way to go. What do you say we take a little stroll? Show ourselves to our admiring public and incidentally get a better idea of the terrain."

"What else did they say?" Selim asked. "Will they give Nur Misur back to us?"

"We didn't get round to that," Ramses said. "There are still a number of ambiguities. We stopped a riot this morning, but there is obviously a great deal of discontent among the populace at large. He wants us to make a formal com-

mitment—a great public festival, with ceremonies and sac-
rifices and God knows what else."

"Yes, I understood that," Emerson said. "When?"

"He didn't say."

"All the more reason to get out and about," Emerson declared. "I am willing to be accommodating up to a point,
but I draw the line at crowning the bastard."

The front door yielded at once to Emerson's hard shove.
The soldiers on guard in the corridor stepped back to let
them pass and then fell in behind them. Another foursome
awaited them in the antechamber. Led by Emerson, the
procession, which included Daoud and Selim, emerged
into a larger room open on one side, like the mandarah of
Moslem houses. A blaze of sunlight dazzled their eyes.

At his father's suggestion Ramses had brought a sketch
pad and pencils. Leaning over the balustrade, he began a
rough plan of the surrounding area—not an easy task,
since the City of the Holy Mountain was in part perpendicular. The stony flanks of the interior mountains had
been cut back on different levels to allow for the building
of temples and houses. It had been a monumental undertaking, which must have taken centuries—almost thirty
of them, since the first emigrés had come during the
breakdown of Egyptian society in the tenth century B.C.
Paths and staircases crossed the slopes, many of them
leading down to the great roadway that circled this end of
the valley—an engineering feat of no small magnitude,
cut into the solid rock of the cliffs and bridging the
smaller ravines. They were across the valley from where
they had stayed before; Ramses thought he made out a familiar roofline. If he could get into that house he knew a
way into the subterranean passages that honeycombed the
cliffs. The visible city was like the top of an iceberg,
much of it underground.

"I thought so," Emerson said in a satisfied voice. "This

section is only part of the area enclosed by the mountain heights. The valley stretches farther to the north. Can you make out anything, Ramses?"

"Not much, the sun is too bright." Ramses shaded his eyes with his hand. "The cliffs close in, and then—yes, they open out again. It's too far away to make out details; there is open water, and a stretch of green beyond the pass, and what appear to be side valleys or wide ravines. No signs of dwellings that I can see."

"They are clustered at this end, I think," said Emerson. "Around the royal palace and the temple. Do you suppose Tarek could be holed up somewhere in that area? A rhetorical question," he added, before Ramses could reply. "We'll have to have a closer look with binoculars. Should have brought them with us."

Selim offered to go back and get the binoculars. At Emerson's suggestion he gave one pair to Ramses, who announced his intention of going farther along the road before using them.

Wide, rather steep steps led down to the road. Four of the guardsmen scrambled to get ahead of Emerson; the other four followed the party. When they reached the bottom of the staircase, Emerson inquired, "Well, Peabody, which way? Right or left? Or shall we see if we will be allowed to descend into the village?"

"Left" was the immediate reply. "We have never been north of the Great Temple, and," she added with a smile, "Selim will enjoy seeing it."

It was the warmest part of the day, the time when sensible people in hot climates rest in the shade. Only a few people were abroad. A gang of the little dark-skinned rekkit were at work patching the section of roadway to the right of the steps. No rest for them in the heat of the day, Ramses thought. The road surface must be constantly in need of maintenance; it wouldn't do for a litter bearer to trip and shake up his master or mistress.

Emerson stopped short. "Beaded collars!" he shouted.

Ramses fought an unholy desire to laugh. "Father, I think you mean meri—friends—not meni."

"It got their attention," said Emerson, unabashed. The workers had dropped mallets and chisels. When he saw their expressions as they looked up at Emerson, Ramses no longer wanted to laugh. They bowed their heads and a soft murmur arose.

Realizing that his father was about to make a speech, Ramses said urgently, "We had better move on, Father. I don't like the way the guards are handling those spears."

"I thought I just might say a few more words," said Emerson. "And perhaps ask a question or two about—"

"We don't want to stir up trouble, sir. Not yet." He knew that truculent scowl, and appealed to the ultimate authority. "Don't you agree, Mother?"

His mother patted her forehead and cheeks with a square of linen. "Quite. Come along, Emerson. The king cannot object to us showing ourselves to the workers, but a prolonged conversation would probably result in punishment to them and confinement for us."

She took his arm and they went on. The soft murmur followed them. It was a single phrase, repeated over and over. "The friends. The friends."

The royal palace sprawled along and up and around the hillside, a huge, disorganized pile of buildings which had been added on to over thousands of years. It was impossible to get an idea of the internal plan from outside, since the apartments extended far back into the cliff. Their quarters were at the south end. The central facade, reached by a flight of stairs lined with sphinxes, was heavily guarded. All the local ducks and geese must have been divested of their tail feathers to uniform this lot. The more feathers, the higher the rank, one must assume.

The Window of Appearance and the plaza below it were on the north side, facing the Great Temple. Selim, who was walking with Ramses, stopped dead at the sight of its obelisks and gold-tipped flagstaffs and the gigantic painted figures on the pylons. "It is like Thebes in the great days of the pharaohs," he breathed.

"Not really," said Ramses. "This city is only a faint imitation of Thebes in its glory. Take a closer look at the paintings."

After an eye-popping interval Selim laughed so hard he had to sit down on the pavement. "I don't see what's so amusing," said Emerson, who had been studying his image with a complacent smile.

"Ramses," Selim gasped. "It is Ramses, yes? The nose—the name—"

The name was there, all right, in an inscription behind the unflattering little figure. "Ramses the Great One, who speaks for the god, gives the breath of life to His Majesty." Close up, the changes in the royal cartouches were obvious. They had been done hastily and without skill.

"You're too clever by half, Selim," Ramses remarked. He proceeded to translate the inscriptions identifying his father. " 'The Great One, the Father of Curses, smites the enemies of Maat.' They've transliterated 'Emerson' alphabetically—*m* bird, *r,* the horizontal *s,* chick, water sign. You get the determinative of nobility, Father."

"So I see," said Emerson, pleased. The determinative, that of a striding man carrying a long staff, was a foot high. Like the larger image, it had blue eyes.

"Hmmm," said his wife, who had been trying to read her own inscription. "Curse it, the hieroglyphs are quite different from those of Egypt, aren't they? Ramses, can you make them out?"

"Not as well as Uncle Walter, but I remember a bit. You are the embodiment of Sekhmet, raging for the king with her—"

"Oh, good Gad," exclaimed Emerson. "Don't tell me . . ."

"I'm not sure, but it looks as if they have tried to spell the English word as it sounded to them, like your name." He added with a grin, "The determinative is unquestionably a sunshade."

"We must have photographs," Selim exclaimed, jumping up. "And drawings. Wallahi, but we miss David."

"We'll do the best we can, Selim," Ramses said. Even if they could never display the drawings and photographs, they would make a wonderful addition to the family archives. "But not now. Father, why don't we divide up? You and Mother go on, to the end of the roadway if it isn't too long a walk. We've none of us ever been past the temple. I'll go back the other way."

"For a sentimental look at our former home?" his father inquired. "Excellent idea, my boy. We can cover more ground that way. Don't do anything impetuous."

"Ha," said Ramses's mother pointedly. "Selim, you go with Ramses. We will meet back at our house in . . . shall we say an hour?"

The little people were gone when Ramses and Selim passed the place where they had been working. Followed by half the original escort—the other four had accompanied his parents and Daoud—they walked on around the southern curve of the cliffs. A good deal of new construction was underway: temples and shrines, by the look of them. Workmen swarmed over the face of a half-built pylon and others dragged cut blocks of stone from a quarry below the road. The whips of the overseers rose and fell.

A spacious villa high above them was the one Tarek had occupied as crown prince. Someone else was living there now; a pair of guards lounged by the steps. Their former dwelling, a little farther on, had obviously been abandoned. Ramses recognized it by the statues along the terrace, though Bastet had lost her head and Sobek had fallen over. The potted plants were dead.

He climbed the broken stairs, with Selim beside him and the guards close on his heels. The entrance gaped open. Blown sand and withered palm leaves littered the floor of the antechamber and a curtain hung in tatters from the doorway beyond.

He turned and addressed the nearest guard. "No one lives here now?"

"No, Great One. As you see."

"It is not guarded."

"What need to guard an empty house?"

Ramses gave him a closer look. The insolent tone reminded him of Merasen. There was a physical resemblance too. That didn't necessarily mean they were close kin; the upper classes were so interbred, it was a wonder they could still reproduce, and to judge by the capful of feathers and the width of his gold armband, this fellow was a high-ranking officer. Nothing but the best for us, Ramses thought. Aloud he said harshly, "When I ask a question you will answer only yes or no."

The man's faint smile faded. "I . . . Yes, Great One."

"Will we go in?" Selim asked. "There is no light, and I did not bring a torch."

"Neither did I. It isn't necessary."

They continued along the road for another mile or so. There were fewer houses on this stretch, all unoccupied, and the road surface began to deteriorate. They were heading almost due west now as the road curved and descended. The men preceding them slowed and then came to a stop— and so did the road. It ended abruptly in a ragged break.

They had reached the pass. Straight ahead, across a gap of forty feet, was the other end of the road. Selim let out an exclamation. "Once the road stretched straight across, Ramses, do you see? Below are the ruins of buttresses that supported a great arch of stone. What engineers they were! But no longer. The break is not fresh and they have not repaired it."

"I doubt they have the manpower or the initiative." Ramses got out the binoculars. "You're right, Selim, as usual. Most of the pass is filled with enormous cut stones, the ruins of the bridge and the buttresses." He scanned the rubble, awed by the size of the blocks of stone. At one time the workmen of the Lost Oasis had almost equaled the pyramid builders. "There's a break—barely ten feet wide—which has been filled in with rougher, smaller boulders. If Tarek is there, it's no wonder the usurper hasn't been able to get at him."

"But he cannot get out," said Selim shrewdly. "There are soldiers below. Many soldiers."

And a guardhouse, solidly built, that stretched a secondary wall across the inner part of the pass. Selim was right. Neither side could roll the blocking boulders away without coming under fire from their opponents. The natural rocky walls on either side were sheer, and the men of the Holy Mountain were skilled bowmen.

They started back. The sun was sinking and there were more people abroad, some on foot, several in curtained litters carried by the muscular rekkit.

"The friend" was what the rekkit had called Tarek when he worked in secret as their deliverer before he claimed the throne. He had intended to better their lot, improve their living conditions, grant them a certain degree of liberty. Ramses didn't doubt that he had tried. Tarek was a man of his word, and—God help him—an idealist.

A taste of freedom gives a man an appetite for more. That incipient riot had been an encouraging sign. The rekkit had never had the courage to rebel before, and they were not the only ones who resented the new regime; the crowd had included people from other walks of life, craftsmen and scribes. But without weapons and leadership they were powerless. Was it possible . . . Don't be an idiot, he told himself. You're no rabble-rouser, you haven't the skill.

His father, on the other hand . . .

⁝

## . .
## Nine
## . .

That afternoon's explorations brought home to me how limited our knowledge of the topography of the Holy Mountain had been. We had not been allowed to explore on our earlier visit, and our departure had been hasty and unexpected. What an astonishing place it was, and what mighty works the men of old had created! The natural grandeur of the rugged heights framed the remnants of a rich and sophisticated civilization—handsome villas and lush gardens, towering temples, and the great road itself, an engineering feat of no small magnitude, for it had been carved out of the vertical face of the cliff and swept grandly across the smaller ravines on bridges whose supports rested on massive blocks of cut stone.

It was, I reminded myself, a civilization built on slavery. How many lives had been expended to make the great road safe and smooth for the sandaled feet of the ruling class?

The signs of decay were visible, however. Many of the handsome houses were unoccupied. As we tramped on, graciously acknowledging the respectful greetings of those we met, the road curved, following the curve of the cliffs, and began to descend until it was only thirty or forty feet above the valley floor. Emerson's steps slowed. "Well, well," he remarked. "I thought we would encounter something like this."

"This" was a troop of soldiers drawn up in military order across the road. With Emerson in the lead, we marched straight up to them, halting only when we were nose to nose with the front rank. Emerson hailed them jovially.

"Greetings. Move aside"—he gestured. "The Great Ones go on."

A certain amount of agitation ensued. Some of the men bowed, some exchanged worried glances, a few uncertainly lifted their spears. Finally one of them stepped forward.

"The Great Ones cannot go on," he said slowly. "The road does not go on."

No one objected when Emerson indicated we would see for ourselves. A rough barricade had been built at the end of the roadway, and a good thing too, since the drop was sheer. Emerson leaned perilously over the barricade and looked down. "Tarek?" he asked, pointing to the narrow pass, which was filled ten feet high with stones. The soldier looked askance and did not reply. To judge by the width of his gold armlet, he was a lower-ranking officer, the equivalent of a junior lieutenant. We had put him in a difficult position, and he was taking no chances on saying the wrong thing.

"Must be," said Emerson to me. He took out the binoculars and made a long, leisurely survey of the pass and its surroundings. A murmur of curiosity and alarm arose from the watching soldiers, and the officer dared to address Emerson.

"What is that? What are you doing?"

With an ingratiating smile Emerson offered the binoculars to the officer. The fellow shied back. "It is magic," said Emerson. "Our magic. You are—you have . . . Curse this cursed language. Peabody, tell him the magic will be safe for him since I can turn it on and off at will."

The young man was no coward. It was clear that he believed he was taking his life as well as the binoculars in his hands, but once he had got them in place, fascination overcame fear. "It is for seeing far away," he exclaimed. "How far can it see?"

"Many miles," I replied. "To the heavens and the world beyond. But only for those who know all the magic. It would not be safe for you to see so far."

We lingered for a while, chatting and answering the questions of the bolder souls. They had abandoned discipline to crowd around Emerson, who basked in their respectful admiration. Somehow I was not surprised when one of them raised the story of the mighty throw that had pierced a strong man's body. Emerson grinned and held out his hand. The fellows jostled one another in their eagerness to give him a spear.

"Emerson," I said in alarm. "You wouldn't—"

"What do you take me for, my dear? I doubt I could repeat the feat anyhow," Emerson admitted. "I was extremely angry at the time."

He drew his arm back, braced his feet and shoulders, took a breath so deep two buttons popped off his shirt, and hurled the spear. It flew straight across the gap and clattered onto the other end of the road.

For several seconds there was not a sound, not even that of a drawn breath. Then everybody yelled.

"Oof," said Emerson.

"I hope you haven't put your shoulder out again," I remarked. "Emerson, I know you are having a splendid time, but we must go back. I don't want to give Zekare an excuse to keep me from seeing Nefret."

"I did not do that to show off, Peabody," said Emerson reproachfully, after we had bid our new friends a fond farewell.

"I know, my dear," I said, and patted his shoulder.

We found the others waiting for us at the house, and we immediately began comparing notes. "The only way down to the valley floor and the barracks on this side of the pass is a stairway on the west side," said Emerson. "Very narrow, very steep. Easy to defend."

"There are other stairways up to the palace and the Great Road," Ramses pointed out. "Near the village."

"Same problem," said Emerson, frowning at the sheet of paper on which he had sketched a plan. "An attack in force at any one point is impossible."

"Tarek must know that." Ramses pushed the paper away. "Sorry, I can't concentrate on strategy. You are supposed to see Nefret tonight, Mother. Why the devil haven't they come for you?"

"They didn't specify a time. Now, dear boy, don't worry. We have no reason to suppose the king will not keep his promise. There—I think I hear the escort coming now."

### From Manuscript H

"Yes, I saw her." His mother had been gone less than an hour. She put her parasol down with exaggerated care. "Emerson, perhaps just a drop of whiskey . . ."

Emerson stood frozen. "For the love of heaven, Amelia, she isn't—she can't be—"

"No, Emerson, no. I didn't mean to frighten you. Thank you, Ramses." She took a restorative sip of whiskey. "It could be worse. A great deal worse. Let me tell a connected narrative, if you please. I need to get my own thoughts in order; I am still struggling to assimilate what I saw."

"Stop struggling and get on with it," Emerson demanded, relieved and reassured. So far as he was concerned, the only foe he could not defeat was death itself, and if Emerson wasn't ready to go, the Grim Reaper would have a fight on his hands. Ramses wished he could be so confident. He had seldom seen his imperturbable mother so perturbed.

"Take your time, Mother," he said.

She leaned back against the cushions. "As you know, I expected I would be escorted to the dwelling of the High Priestess. Instead they took me to a smallish temple above and south of the palace. Not the Great Temple. The goddess has a shrine there, as you remember; this was another

shrine, dedicated solely to her. The ritual we saw before
was the same, however; the handmaidens whirling in their
dance and the High Priestess, her robes glittering with gold
thread, joining in the dance and performing the invocation.
She made offerings of fruit and flowers before the statue—
a very beautiful statue it is too—and then fluttered out, escorted by the handmaidens. I tried to go after her, but the
two females who took me there held me back, politely but
quite firmly. They were both rather stoutly built and I realized the futility of resistance. They led me away and made
me get back in the litter and brought me here."

She took another sip of whiskey and Ramses said quietly, "Go back a little. The shrine is near the palace? What
was it like? Where were you? Sitting, standing, at what distance from the statue?"

She gave him a rueful smile. "Dear me, I was not as coherent as I had hoped, was I? Well. The statue was at one
end of the room, which was relatively small: fifteen feet by
twenty, at a guess. I was at the other end, behind a row of
columns—lotus columns. They had placed a chair for me.
There were lamps near the statue, but none where I was sitting. It was a pretty little place, almost homey compared
with the Great Temple; the statue shone in the lamplight. It
was pale gold—a good deal of silver mixed in, from the
look of it. The goddess was standing, hands at her sides."

"Well done," Ramses said.

"How kind of you to say so" was the response, in her
normal brisk voice. His mother did not appreciate kindly
condescension, especially from him.

"Go on," Emerson urged.

"Certainly. There were curtained doorways, one on either
side of the statue; I was somewhat puzzled by the ambience,
but I still expected Nefret would emerge from one of the
doorways and come to me. Instead, the handmaidens
popped out, clacking their rattles and sistra, whirling and
chanting. Nefret was the last to appear. It seemed rude to interrupt the ceremony, but when she left, without so much as

a glance at me, I am ashamed to admit that I—er—I rather lost my head."

"How do you know it was Nefret?" Ramses asked. "I assume the girls were all veiled, including the Priestess."

"You are correct. But my dear, I couldn't mistake her. I know the way she moves, and those little hands, so much paler than those of the other girls, and the glimpses of golden hair . . ." Her voice faltered.

"Yes, all right," Ramses said quickly. "It must have been distressing to see her and not be able to speak to her, or receive even a glance of acknowledgment; but she may not have known you were there."

"That isn't what concerns me. She . . . Oh, dear. It is difficult to explain. She didn't falter once during that complex invocation. Every step was confident, every word correct. It was as if something or someone else were controlling her."

"Good Gad," Emerson exclaimed. "Peabody, what are you suggesting?"

"An afrit, perhaps," said Daoud helpfully. He was the only one who hadn't displayed signs of shock at that horribly evocative description. "You will cast it out, Father of Curses, when we have her back."

"Yes, yes, certainly," Emerson muttered.

"Stop it!" Ramses said angrily. "All of you. Mother, think. How do you know she performed the ceremony correctly? It's been years since you saw her do it. For all you know, she may have been improvising."

"It is difficult to improvise in such a complex dance," his mother retorted, practical as always. "Nobody ran into anybody. However—you are right to remind me that we must not yield to superstition."

"What about Daria?" Ramses asked. "Was she present?"

"Why, no, now that you mention it. Unless she was one of the dancers."

"Most unlikely. The handmaidens are selected from the highest-born girls in the land, and they go through a rigorous training period," Ramses said. "I expect they took Daria only because she was with Nefret, and they didn't want to leave a witness. We can't simply dismiss the girl, Mother. We brought her here, we are responsible for her."

His father was pacing up and down the room. "No one has any intention of abandoning her, Ramses. We must see the king again and demand to speak with Nefret."

"We can try," Ramses said. "But he's a wily devil; he said Mother could see Nefret, and see her she did. He'll stall and equivocate and delay. With all respect to you, Daoud, I don't believe in afrits, but I don't like the sound of this. We must talk to Nefret as soon as is possible."

Emerson stopped pacing and gave him a piercing stare. "How?"

"I have an idea."

\:

I had several ideas of my own, and I did not at all like the one Ramses proposed. He was the only one of us who stood a chance of passing as a native of the Lost Oasis, and the clothing with which we had been provided was appropriate for the role he hoped to assume. But . . .

"How do you plan to get out of here unobserved?" I demanded.

"You'll have to distract the guards while I slip past them," Ramses said coolly.

"I expect I could do that," said Emerson, flexing his hands. "Then what?"

"Then I'll find the temple Mother described. There's a good chance the High Priestess's living quarters are connected with it. If I can't find a way in, there's another possibility—the subterranean passages behind the house we occupied before. I can get into the house with no trouble, it's been deserted, and I remember where the entrance is located. If I can find the underground chamber where Nefret first met us, there's got to be a way into her rooms from there."

"Too many ifs," I exclaimed. "Good Gad, Ramses, your scheme is foolhardy in the extreme. Nefret's rooms are certainly closely guarded, you will be caught or killed if you try to reach them by way of the temple. As for going down into the subterranean passages, I strictly forbid it. You could lose your way in that endless maze! And how do you plan to get back into this house?"

"I don't mean to come back." He saw my stricken face; kneeling beside me, he took my hands in his. "Mother, you are a realist, or so you claim. Face the facts. One of us must be on the loose. Cooped up like this, our every movement watched, we cannot count on seeing Nefret or communicating with Tarek. And what about your mysterious visitor, who is now missing a shirt button? We need to know who he is and what role he is playing. I may be able to track him down."

Emerson cleared his throat noisily. "Don't argue with him, Peabody. He is in the right. It will require some careful planning, however."

"Yes." Ramses squeezed my limp hands and rose. "We'll aim for tomorrow night. Mother, don't look at me like that. This isn't as foolhardy as it sounds. The worst that can happen is that I'll be caught in the act—some act or other—and locked up. The king won't be well pleased with you four either, but if he wants our cooperation he won't do anything violent."

"Inshallah," I said.

"Yes, it is in his hands," remarked Daoud. "I will go with you when you go, Ramses, wherever you go."

"And I," said Selim.

It required some argument to convince them that their presence would only constitute a greater danger to Ramses. Daoud was slightly consoled by Emerson's promise that he could help "distract" the guards. Ashamed at my brief relapse, I put on a brave face and began one of my little lists. After all, I told myself, it might prove unnecessary. Tomorrow was another day. Something might yet turn up.

It was Merasen who turned up, bright and early next morning.

We were finishing breakfast and making plans for another excursion when he strolled in, looking as much at home as he had when he visited us in Kent, and garbed with extravagant elegance, from his diadem to his gold-inlaid sandals. Exclaiming with pleasure, he shook hands with Ramses and Emerson—who allowed the liberty, but with the look of a man who had taken hold of a rotten fish.

"So, are you pleased with your rooms?" he inquired solicitously. "Is there anything you require?"

"Yes, there is," said Ramses, before his father could voice a ruder response. "Some straight talk, Merasen. Do you know that expression?"

"Yes, I heard it often in England," said Merasen, grinning. He selected a date from the plate of fruit.

"It obviously didn't make much of an impression," Emerson muttered. "We received you as an honored guest, and you lied to us and deceived us. You also betrayed Tarek. Wasn't it from him that you learned English?"

"I was one of the children of the palace, taught with the royal children," Merasen admitted. "Tarek himself favored me because I was clever and quick to learn. Others were not. My brothers . . ." He laughed and shrugged. "You have seen them. Worthy and brave, but not clever. He told us stories about you, like the stories of the gods—about the beauty of the High Priestess, and the strength of the Father of Curses, and about the Sitt Hakim, who could fight like a man and smile like a woman. How could I say no when there came the chance to see you for myself?"

The sheer brazenness of the excuse left all of us without words for a moment. Then Emerson said, "What of your loyalty to Tarek?"

"I am loyal to my father. I could not be loyal to both."

"Outflanked again," Emerson muttered.

"I have done nothing wrong," Merasen insisted. "You wanted to come back to the Holy Mountain. For years you wanted to come back, I heard you say so. And now that you are here you are honored, and my father will reward you with rich gifts."

Emerson waved his hand in front of his face, as if brushing away a persistent fly. "Now see here," he began.

"Let me ask a few questions, Father," Ramses cut in.

"Go ahead, my boy. I don't seem to be getting anywhere."

"You say you have done nothing wrong," Ramses addressed Merasen. "What's your excuse for murdering Ali?"

"Ali dead? My friend Ali?" Merasen's eyes opened wide. "How? I grieve for him."

"It wasn't you who cut his throat?" Ramses persisted.

"He was alive when I left him. But very drunk." Merasen's grief had been short-lived. He gave Ramses a man-to-man smile.

"You stole the map from Nefret."

"No, that was not I. Why do you speak of the past? It is finished. Let us speak of the future, and what I can do for you and you can do for me."

"You know what you can do for us," Ramses said through tight lips. Even his controlled temper was beginning to fray. "Make it possible for us to leave the Holy Mountain, with Nefret. What do you want in return?"

"Guns," said Merasen promptly and unexpectedly.

"You stole ours," Ramses said, visibly taken aback.

"Not enough." Merasen reached for the last date, but Daoud got it first. Merasen scowled. "Send these servants away so we may talk in private."

"They are not servants, but friends," Emerson said. "We have no secrets from them. Say what you have to say."

As Emerson later remarked, the ensuing conversation was illuminating.

"My father still believes in the old ways, the edge of the sword and the skill of the archer," said Merasen. "But I saw the guns when the soldiers attacked the slavers, and I knew that fifty men with guns could conquer a kingdom such as this. I could not carry so many back with me, even if I had

had gold enough to buy them. So . . ." He shrugged and smiled his engaging smile.

"So you lured us here with the lie about Tarek," I said. "But your original purpose was not to acquire weapons, was it? That was an afterthought."

"A good thought," Merasen said complacently. "I was sent to bring the High Priestess back to the Temple of Isis. The people are restless. When they see her take her rightful place, in the temple and in the palace, they will submit." He shrugged again. "So my father believes. As for me, I believe in guns. Fifty at least."

"It will take months for us to go and return," Emerson said. "By that time Tarek may have reconquered the city."

A flash of some quickly overcome emotion brightened the boy's dark eyes. He waved a negligent hand. "It is what you call stalemate. Tarek has enough men to hold his own territory, but he is a weakling, he will not risk their lives to retake the city."

"And your father has not enough men to force the pass and conquer Tarek?" I asked. "Is that it?"

Merasen shrugged, and Ramses said, "Your brothers— your older brothers—are strong, able men. Why is it that you, the youngest, have been raised over them?"

This was apparently not a tactful question. Merasen jumped to his feet. "We have talked enough. What is your decision?"

"We will think it over," Ramses said. "You'll have to give us additional guarantees, Merasen. I wouldn't trust your word if you swore on every god in the Holy City."

"We will meet again soon," Merasen said, no longer smiling. "And perhaps—another wrestling match?"

"Any time," Ramses said.

"Well, well," said Emerson, after the door had closed behind our visitor. "I now know what Merasen's title is, or should be: Chief Liar of the King. He can't even stick to a single story. I felt as if I were trying to nail down a gust of wind."

"I wonder if we are doing him an injustice," Ramses said slowly. "We are judging him by the standards of our own culture, which is not his. He may honestly believe he has not acted against his own moral code."

"Oh, come," Emerson exclaimed. "There is no culture with which I am familiar, including that of ancient Egypt, that does not condemn murder."

"We can't prove he killed Ali," Ramses argued.

His father gave him a critical look. "You are leaning over backward to be fair because you dislike the fellow so much. It is an admirable quality for a clergyman, but it is damned impractical.

"At any rate," Emerson continued, "he confirmed our theory about Tarek's whereabouts. He is holding out in the northern part of the valley, and as we saw, neither side can force the pass without considerable losses. Guns in the hands of Zekare—"

"He doesn't want weapons for his father," Ramses said flatly. "I think he has his eye on the throne. He might be able to pull it off if he had our enthusiastic cooperation, and enough modern weapons—and Nefret."

"What?" I cried.

"He didn't say so in so many words, but it was implicit in his reference to her place in the temple and in the palace. The High Priestess does not serve for life; like the hand-maidens, she is married off after a certain time. And she would remain here, as hostage, while we returned to the Sudan to get the damned weapons. Would you care to speculate on what would happen to her while we were away?"

"No," said Emerson through his teeth. "I would not. What the devil, Ramses, one minute you are trying to make out a case for Merasen and the next minute—"

"I was simply considering all the possibilities."

"Well, don't," snapped Emerson. "We aren't leaving Nefret here, no matter who promises what."

"There's a chance for us in that scheme, though," I said hopefully. "If we are allowed to get a caravan together, we can snatch Nefret away at the last minute and make a run for it."

"Hotly pursued by soldiers, some of them armed with our rifles?" Ramses inquired caustically. "And what about Tarek? And the rekkit? Sorry, Mother, but it's back to my original plan. We may have to start—and win—a civil war before we can get away with Nefret. Are you ready to go out? A bit more reconnoitering would seem to be in order."

Emerson followed me into my room. "Peabody, my dear," he began.

"Emerson, he is only a boy—barely twenty. You must forbid him to do this!"

"He is the only one of us who can do it," said Emerson, taking me into his arms. "He may be young in years, but he's proved himself more than once. There is a great deal at stake, my love. Don't cry. It will be all right."

"I am not crying. I am simply annoyed with Ramses for taking so much on himself."

We made our way directly to the temple area, and I pointed out the small shrine where I had been the previous night. It was a miniature version—a condensed version, one might say—of the larger temples, with a single columned courtyard, an antechamber, and the inner room where the ceremony had taken place. In Egyptian temples the innermost shrine was usually small, just large enough to contain the divine statue. Such was not the case here, as we had observed.

"Why don't we just march up there and ask to see the High Priestess?" I suggested.

"Barge straight ahead? I like the idea," said Emerson, fingering the cleft in his chin.

Ramses was already halfway up the steep causeway, with two of the guards in agitated pursuit. They had to run like fury to get ahead of him. He stopped when they blocked his path, and as we joined him I heard him expostulating. Had not the king given us permission to go where we liked? We intended to pay our respects to the goddess and her priestess, who was his sister and the daughter of the Father of Curses. How dare they interfere with the Great Ones?

"Reminds me of the time we insisted on visiting the cemetery, and the captain of the guard was torn between violating his orders and interfering with us," remarked Emerson, listening with interest to the debate between Ramses and the officer in charge of the detachment. "I wonder what has become of Harsetef? I gave him one of my pipes as a memento."

"Yes, my dear, I remember. Ah, Ramses. Have you won your point?"

"I bullied him into letting us go up to the facade," Ramses replied. "It would be all his life is worth to let us enter."

"A happy thought," said Emerson. "I don't care for this fellow's tone. Harsetef, now—"

"This fellow and the others are Merasen's personal guard, Father. He's won them over by bribes or promises of promotion, and it would be a waste of breath to argue with them. Let's take what advantage we can."

We inspected the front and two sides of the temple. There were paved walkways on either side, which ended abruptly in solid walls of stone.

"Curse it," I said, as we returned to the facade. "I was afraid of that. The inner apartments are rock-cut into the cliffs. You haven't a chance of getting in there, Ramses."

"Not necessarily true, Mother. Look up. No, don't stare! Just a casual glance."

The cliff face over and behind the roof of the temple had been cut back and smoothed. There were several openings, black against the golden glow of the rock—squared-off openings, obviously man-made. I hadn't seen them the night before. I looked from them—twenty feet or more above the roof—to the intent face of my son, and my heart sank.

"You don't know for sure that they are the windows of the apartments of the High Priestess," I muttered.

"They must be. One couldn't keep a woman immured for years without access to air and light. There's something up there, anyhow."

He nudged his father, who had ignored his admonition, and was staring fixedly. "The cliff face is as smooth as glass," said Emerson in a flat voice.

"Not really, Father. Come, let's go on. Our escort isn't liking this."

"Where now?" I asked.

"The village. They aren't going to like that, either."

Several flights of steep stairs led down from the roadway to the floor of the valley, where the rekkit village was located. We took the nearest. Emerson, who obviously enjoyed tormenting our guards, gave them no chance to stop us; he pushed past the foursome who were in advance and started down. The steps were so narrow and Emerson is so large that once he was on them no one could get past, and he ignored the officer's impassioned demands that he stop. We all followed, single file, with Ramses behind me holding me firmly by the coattail and Daoud bringing up the rear and the officer shouting loudly and ineffectually.

Like most villages, this one had grown more or less at random, with winding paths leading off from the wider street that ended in a central space with a stone-rimmed well and a few spindly trees. Some of the houses were built of mud brick, some of reeds and sticks like the Nubian tukhuls. The air was humid and hot; the sun reached these sunken depths only at midday, and deep springs moistened the air.

The place had changed, though, since our last visit. Drainage ditches and low embankments controlled the water that had formerly turned the paths into mud. They were relatively clear of rotting vegetation and human trash. One could not say that the air was pure and odor-free, not with so many people living in so confined a space, but the improvement was impressive.

There was another difference. Few people had the

temerity to show themselves when we had been there before. Now faces appeared at window apertures; some persons lifted the mats that hung over the doorways and fixed wondering eyes upon us. By the time we reached the village square, a small group of the bolder spirits had gathered, keeping a safe distance from our escort. They were all women and children, except for a few aged men.

Emerson inspected them with a pleased smile and cleared his throat.

"Emerson, no. Don't make a speech," I begged.

"But, Peabody, don't you understand what an astonishing thing this is?" His sapphirine orbs blazed with excitement. "Tarek didn't simply give these people better living conditions, he gave them the will and the ambition to live better! He has been out of power for months, yet the streets are still clean and the drainage ditches maintained. They are doing it themselves! They have gained the courage to defy their oppressors, to venture forth in order to . . . Here, now, none of that!"

Turning with pantherlike quickness, he snatched the spear from one of the guards. The others lowered their weapons and backed off, staring at Emerson.

"Time for a little subversion," said Emerson. His arm went back, balancing the spear. It was aimed at the captain, whose face had gone as white as the shade of his complexion allowed.

"Emerson," I murmured. "You wouldn't . . . Would you?"

"They've all heard the stories," said Emerson. "Look at them. Ramses, translate if you please."

It was one of Emerson's more eloquent speeches, and Ramses did it justice, pitching his voice into a fair imitation of Emerson's basso.

"The Father of Curses has returned! The curse of the gods will fall on any who do not obey him. He could drive this weapon through your body, but he spares your life because he is merciful as well as all-powerful. On your knees before him!"

A positive drumbeat of knees hit the ground.

Ramses let out his breath. "Congratulations, Father. May I suggest that we leave, before one of them has time to think it over."

"Have you any objection to my smiling and waving?" Emerson inquired.

"Not at all, sir. Smile and wave all you like—as we walk away, slowly and with dignity."

Most of the audience had fled into nearby houses and shops when the scuffle broke out, the women pulling their children with them, the old gentlemen tottering as fast as they could. One woman had retreated only as far as the doorway of her house, where she stood holding the matting aside. She was a little person, like most of the rekkit, dark-skinned and thin. Her black hair was liberally streaked with gray and her coarse brown garment barely covered limbs that showed the swollen joints of rheumatism. Her arms were folded across her breast. Her black eyes moved from me to Ramses, and then to Emerson; he directed one of his broadest smiles at her, and she dropped to her knees, raising her hands in salute. "We serve the king," she cried. "The king who is our friend."

She had, by chance or intent, used simple words. Emerson's eyes flashed. "We too serve him," he said loudly. "Ahem. Ramses, tell her—"

"Not now, Father, please. Let us go."

Emerson allowed himself to be led away. Looking back over my shoulder, I saw the woman was still on her knees, watching us.

"Did you learn what you hoped to learn?" I inquired of my son.

"It was a useful encounter." He took my arm to help me up the stairs. "There is one more piece of information I would like to verify, but I'm pretty sure I already know the answer."

"What is that?" I inquired.

We had reached the top of the stairs. Ramses turned and

looked down into the village. "There are paths leading
north from the village, into the fields and beyond. The
rekkit once had free access to the northern valley and their
kin in villages there. As we saw, the pass is now blocked
and guarded. I suspect the paths are guarded too, with the
equivalent of roadblocks at strategic intervals. Shall we go
back to our rooms now? We've a lot of planning to do."

"Do you still mean to leave tonight?" I asked, refraining
with some difficulty from trying to dissuade him.

"Yes. I have a strange foreboding," said Ramses, smiling
at me, "that from now on your movements are going to be
even more circumscribed."

I noted the pronoun.

His foreboding, which I shared, was correct. We were at
dinner—roast goose, bread, and onions—when we had a
visitor. Poor chubby Count Amenislo entered with dragging steps and the expression of one who wished himself
anywhere but there. He got his message out in a rush of
words. We were summoned to the king next morning. In
the meantime we were forbidden to leave our rooms.

His attempt to beat a hasty retreat was forestalled by
Emerson, for no reason that I could see except my husband's delight in tormenting the fellow. Lifting Amenislo
onto tiptoe, he began shouting indignantly. We were as anxious to see the king as he was to see us. He had deceived us,
whereas we had done only what we had been told we might
do. We would go now, this instant, to complain.

"Not now," Amenislo gurgled. "The king rests. The king
is with his women. The king dines. The king—"

"Oh, bah," said Emerson, tiring of the game. "Go away,
you miserable little traitor."

He gave him a shove that sent him staggering out the
door.

"Apparently you were right," I said to Ramses. "I wonder
precisely what it was we did today that annoyed His
Majesty."

It took us several hours to make our arrangements, such

as they were. We went through our baggage looking for anything that might be useful to Ramses. It made a pitifully small bundle. As I was beginning to expect of him, Daoud contributed the most useful items—one of the hooded cloaks worn by the camel riders and a coil of rope. He tried to make Ramses take the weapons, but was refused.

"I have my knife," Ramses said, clapping him on the back. "And you may need them more than I. Thank you, Daoud. The rope is a godsend. Whatever made you think of bringing it?"

"The Sitt Hakim carries rope, to tie up prisoners," Daoud explained. "I thought on such a long, dangerous journey we might have to tie up many prisoners."

The hour was late, the lamps burning low by the time we had finished discussing contingency plans. Obviously we could not anticipate everything, but we had at least arranged for a possible means of communication. Ramses had inspected the gully below the garden wall and thought he detected a way of descending into it from the far side. The vines that covered the wall and hung down on either side were not strong enough to bear his weight, but he might be able to leave a message.

When Ramses came out of his room, wearing only a knee-length kilt and buckling a knife belt around his narrow waist, my breath caught. At least he looked the part; I had trimmed his hair into a fair imitation of the short curled wig, and in the shadows he bore an unnerving—and reassuring—resemblance to the men of the Holy Mountain. He came straight to me and, after a moment of hesitation, gave me a quick, awkward hug. "Don't worry, Mother. It's all right, you know."

Selim and Daoud embraced him in the Arab style, and then he turned to his father and held out his hand. "Good-bye, Father."

"Not good-bye," said Emerson hoarsely. "À bientôt. Good luck, my boy."

Ramses strapped his bundle onto his back and put on the

long robe, pulling the hood over his head. "Ready," he said. "Go ahead, Father."

Emerson nodded brusquely and went to the door. As we had already ascertained, it was barred from the outside.

We had rehearsed our movements in advance, and Ramses had coached Emerson in what he was to say. He proceeded to say it, at the top of his lungs, as he pounded on the portal. "Help! Help! Murder! Thieves! Attack! Hurry! Murder!"

We heard the bar being lifted and cries of alarm. Daoud, Selim, and I began running back and forth, shouting. The door was flung back, and a half dozen men rushed into the room. We converged upon them, waving our arms in seeming agitation (and, in Daoud's case, in calculated assault). Out of the corner of my eye I saw a lithe, dark form slip from behind the hanging into the corridor beyond.

### From Manuscript H

As Ramses moved noiselessly along the passageway, his father's furious voice, amplified by echoes, followed him. "My daughter and now my son! Anubis take you; what have you done with my son?"

It had been his mother's idea to pretend he had gone missing, as mysteriously as Nefret. She was a great believer in taking the offensive. Ramses stepped into a niche beside a statue of the lion-headed god Apomatek as several more soldiers ran toward the disturbance, which had not abated. When the uncertain light of the torches they carried had faded, he went on his way. Yes, it had been one of his mother's better schemes. The king might even believe the fabrication if Tarek's people had managed to pull off a few acts of sabotage in the city. He didn't doubt Tarek had sympathizers everywhere—and now he was pretty sure he knew where to find one of them.

Keeping to the shadows, he moved through the antechambers onto the terrace, observing with satisfaction that the family had got the entire group of guards out of his way. He could still hear his father, and he grinned as piercing soprano shrieks blended with Emerson's bass bellowing. The night air was cool, the stars were bright, and he felt an enormous sense of relief at being on his own, able to act without interference from the king's men and—to be honest—from his parents.

The moon was a slender crescent. He knew what he had to do, but it was hard to turn away from the little shrine of Isis, glimmering like mother-of-pearl in the starlight. Anxiety about Nefret gnawed at his mind. However, common sense—and his mother's forceful arguments—had told him that his initial plan of scaling the wall to what might or might not be her window was as impractical as a fairy tale, for the time being, at any rate. His parents had a better chance of communicating with her, and he had other things to do.

He hitched up the long skirts of his robe, tucking them into his belt, and felt his way down the steep stairs to the village. The darkness was opaque. If he hadn't counted the steps earlier he would not have known when he was nearing the bottom. He stopped before he reached it and strained his eyes and ears. Hearing rather than sight told him that the guard he had expected was there, huddled on the ground to the right of the stairs, sound asleep and snoring. Obviously the fellow didn't expect trouble—or a visit from an officer. He stirred, muttering, when Ramses ran light fingers along an outflung arm, up to his exposed neck. Leaving him in an even sounder sleep, Ramses went on along the narrow street.

He felt his way with bare feet, following the mental map he had memorized, not daring to use his torch or light a candle. The houses were dark and silent. Then he went round a sharp curve in the street and saw ahead the sign he had hardly dared hope for—only a narrow strip of light along the edge of a curtained window—but it was long past the hour when a poor villager would have extinguished a lamp, and the house was the one he had noted. He scratched lightly at the window frame, ready to turn and run for it if he had been mistaken. The ragged curtain was drawn aside, exposing a single apprehensive eye and a tangle of gray-streaked black hair.

Ramses pushed the hood back from his face. "Friend," he whispered.

She extinguished the lamp before she let him in the house and made sure the cloth over the window fit tightly before she lighted it again. It was a single room, with a few pots and a few mats on the bare floor and in one dim corner a pile of what appeared to be rags or decayed matting. There were three other people present—a boy who might have been ten or eleven, a pregnant girl, and a man who rose from the mat on which he was lying. As he limped toward Ramses, supporting himself with a crude crutch, Ramses saw that his face was horribly scarred and that one foot was missing.

"Friend," he said, and his ruined face twisted into a travesty of a smile. "You came."

He tried awkwardly to kneel, as the others were doing. Ramses caught him by his shoulders. "Friends do not kneel to friends. Sit, rest. What happened to you?"

"I lifted a weapon against the usurper. It should have been my hand they took off, but I am a skillful potter."

"Dear God," Ramses murmured. "You kept the lamp burning. What if I hadn't come tonight?"

"She said you would come."

The object he had taken to be a pile of rags stirred. A face protruded—a brown, dry face, carved into a thousand wrinkles. In spite of himself Ramses took a step back. In the dim, shifting light the effect was that of a mummy rising up out of its wrappings.

Ramses hastened to offer the support of his arm. A clawed hand closed over it and a pair of clouded eyes stared up at him. He didn't need to ask who, or rather what, she was: the village wise woman. There were always such women, healers and seers, intermediaries with the supernatural for people too humble to approach the great gods directly. In medieval Europe they had been called witches.

"Sit here, Mother," he said, hoping the title was acceptable. "You foresaw my coming?"

Her cackle of laughter was like the scrape of rusty metal, but her voice was stronger than he had expected, with an unmistakable ring of authority. "You do not believe. It does not matter. Believe this, then. I am trusted by Tarek, his representative in this village. Will the other Great Ones come?"

Ramses resisted the temptation to point out that she shouldn't have had to ask. "They can't. Not yet. But I promise you, we will not leave the Holy Mountain until the rekkit are free and Tarek is on his throne again."

"Will you stay here tonight?" the father of the family asked. "Will you eat?"

"He must not stay," the wisewoman said. "They will look for him in the village. In the morning they will come."

It didn't require clairvoyance to figure that one out, Ramses thought. He nodded agreement. "All I want is information. Where is Tarek? How can I reach him?"

"The boy will take you," the woman of the house said.

"Your son?" The quick desperate look she gave the boy confirmed it. "No. It would be too dangerous for him."

"I am not afraid," the boy said, squaring his shoulders.

"I can see you are brave," Ramses said, putting his hand on the boy's bony shoulder. "But you are the only son, is it not so? Stay here. Tell me where to go."

"He will take you part of the way," the wise woman said. "Past the guards and into the hills. There you will find another guide, one of the men of Tarek who keep watch."

"The king knows you are here," the father said. "We sent word, and he sent word back to us, by the paths known only to us. Steep, dangerous little paths, suitable for rats."

His mouth twisted as he repeated the word the contemptuous nobles had used for their slaves.

"Then they will suit me," Ramses said.

The mother had put together a little bundle containing food and a water jar. The boy slung it over his shoulder. His eyes shone with excitement and pride.

Ramses was burning with curiosity about a number of things—how long Tarek had been out of power, the circumstances surrounding his fall, the extent and effectiveness of the network that worked for his return—but time was passing and they must be in concealment by morning. He tried to think of something to say. There was no word for luck in the language of the Holy Mountain.

The old wisewoman had withdrawn into her wrappings. Only her eyes showed. "The gods be with you," she mumbled.

"And with you."

"Tell the king we will be ready when he sends word."

"Ready," Ramses repeated. "Ready for what?"

But he knew what she meant. Revolution, an armed uprising. Armed with sticks and stones.

"The king will know," she said. "Go now, the hour is late."

The following hours dealt Ramses's self-esteem quite a blow. He prided himself on his skill at rock-climbing, but the terrain was unfamiliar and the night was dark. Meekly he let the boy guide his feet and hands from one hold to another as, avoiding the stairs, they ascended the rocky wall to the level of the road. When he peered over the low parapet he saw that they had crossed the valley and were on the eastern side, below the abandoned villa he and his parents had occupied before. None too soon, either. Looking back, he saw the lights of torches spreading out across the floor of the valley. Most of them were clustered in the village.

"Your family. Will they be all right?" he whispered.

"Yes. Come. Hurry."

There were more moving lights near the Great Temple and the palace, but the road above them was dark and unguarded.

Then followed another humiliating period when he had to depend on the frail arms and small hands of a boy half his age. After they crossed the road at a scuttling run they began to climb again. Ramses soon lost his sense of direction as they wound back and forth across the cliff face; it required every ounce of concentration to find the hand- and footholds. He was short of breath and perspiring, despite the chill of the night air, when his guide reached a narrow ledge.

"We stop here. The boat of the god will soon arise."

Ramses was glad to lower himself onto the first horizontal stretch of land he had encountered all night. The ledge went back under an overhang, forming a shallow cave. It would help conceal them from sight and provide a little shade during the noonday heat—though probably not enough.

"You do not travel these paths by daylight?" he asked, unfastening his pack and offering the boy the dates and bread his mother had provided.

"Not unless we must." Pale light washed over the ledge. The sun had risen over the eastern heights above them. As the light strengthened, Ramses got his first good look at his companion. He was a typical member of the rekkit, small and thin, dark-skinned and black-haired. "What is your name?" Ramses asked.

"Khat."

"Mine is Ramses."

The boy looked up, his eyes widening.

"No, lord. You are the Great One, the friend, who speaks to the gods."

"Not all who speak to the gods are answered." Good Lord, Ramses thought, I'm beginning to talk like Mother. He decided to change the subject before, of all things, he found himself in a theological discussion. A pity his father wasn't with them.

On second thought, perhaps it was just as well he wasn't.

"Do we wait here until nightfall, then?" he asked.

"Yes. One will come then to take you onward."

He curled up at the back of the recess, his head on his own little pack, and promptly dropped off to sleep. Ramses was too keyed up to follow his example. He removed the binoculars from his pack.

The ledge was approximately halfway up the cliff, a hundred feet above the road, and at its far northern end. It offered an excellent vantage point, but he was too far from the temples and palaces of the southern cliffs to distinguish details. He turned his gaze northward. There was certainly a considerable area of land there, but mist veiled the valley floor. He would have to wait until the sun was higher. Philosophically, he retreated into the recess and lay down.

It was late afternoon before he woke, to find Khat sitting cross-legged beside him, unblinking black eyes fixed on his face. As soon as Ramses stirred, the boy whipped out his water bottle and offered it. The sun was a fiery blaze in the western sky; the light struck straight into the niche, and now Ramses made out crude drawings, graffiti, scratched onto the rock.

"They are the gods," Khat explained. He didn't seem quite as much in awe of his companion as he had been. Listening to me snore and watching me sweat must have convinced him I was only human, Ramses thought wryly. The names Khat rattled off, indicating each figure in turn, were not the same as the ones the gods bore in Egypt, but Ramses recognized them: Isis with her crown of horns enclosing the disk; hawk-headed Horus; Khepri, the scarab beetle, guardian of the horizon, symbolizing the rising sun.

After the sun had dropped below the western cliff and the valley was bathed in a gentle light, Ramses took out the binoculars and showed Khat how to use them. The boy gasped in wonder.

"It is only a tool," Ramses said. "A thing of metal and glass, made by men. Show me where to find Tarek."

A spur of rock cut part of his view, but the air was clear

and he was able to make out the side wadi Khat described. The entrance had been fortified with cut masonry and what appeared to be a heavy gate. According to Khat, Tarek held the northern half of the oasis, with its villages and fields and springs, but he had not enough men to retake the city, and the usurper had not enough to overcome him.

Modern weapons would make the difference, Ramses thought. But even if they could get such weapons to Tarek, had they the right to bring the curse of modern warfare to this place? Did the end justify the means? There had to be another, better way—one that did not involve a band of peasants armed only with sticks and stones.

"I can find my way from here," he said. "Go back to your parents."

The boy let out a hiss of alarm. "I see them, through the—the tool. Climbing, searching. Lie flat and be still."

Ramses snatched the binoculars and focused them. The pursuers were some distance away and still far below, but they seemed to be following a path of some sort. Had someone in the village told them of the secret ways? The rekkit were loyal to Tarek, but there were potential traitors in any group, susceptible to threats or bribes.

He shoved the binoculars into his pack and slung it on his back. "We must move on," he said urgently. "Go back. Do you know another way?"

"Oh, yes," the boy said calmly. "But I will not go until one comes for you."

Ramses was about to reply when he heard the rattle of rock overhead. He turned, pushing the boy behind him, as a man dropped down onto the ledge. His head was bare, but he carried a soldier's weapons, bow and quiver and short sword.

He was as tall as Ramses, lean as a panther, and his dark face wore a broad grin of pleasure. Ramses drew his knife, knowing he had only a split second in which to prevent a cry of discovery. Then he saw what the man held in his outstretched hand. His arm fell.

∴

In the turmoil following Ramses's departure we made our way to the terrace in front of the palace, where we stood for several hours watching the proceedings. No one tried to make us retire to our rooms, though two of the guards, belatedly aware of their orders, took up positions at the head of the staircase that led down to the road. Daoud and Selim had remained to look after our possessions, though goodness knows there was not much left to interest our hosts. I had, of course, brought my parasol with me.

The search, I was pleased to observe, was somewhat disorganized. It took the guards quite a while to descend into the village. They remained there some time; when the torchlit march wended its way back up the stairs, I suggested to Emerson that we retire.

"Quite a busy night," I remarked when we reached our sleeping chamber.

"We certainly stirred things up," Emerson agreed, removing his garments and tossing them around the room in his usual fashion. "Do you suppose they believed us?"

"They know *they* were not responsible for Ramses's disappearance. That leaves only two possibilities: that he left of his own accord, or that Tarek somehow managed to get to him."

"I expect his illegitimate majesty is in quite a state of confusion," Emerson agreed. "Serves the bastard right."

He threw himself down on the bed. After assuming a night robe, I joined him.

"If Ramses should be caught," I began, unable to refrain from voicing my greatest fear.

"They have already searched the village." Emerson took me in his arms. "If they had discovered him, we would have heard, be sure of that. He must have finished his business there and got away before they came."

"I hope to heaven he was right about the woman—that

she was the one whose life you saved all those years ago
and that she indicated she was willing to help us."

"What other reason would she have for making that little
speech?" Emerson demanded. "Carefully composed in order to avoid offense, but including the key word: friend.
Try to rest, my love. The usurper will have a good deal to
say to us in the morning, and if you cannot spread a bit
more confusion and alarm you are not the woman I take
you for."

Needless to say, I did not sleep. It was a relief when
morning came to allow action. As we sipped our coffee,
Emerson said, "Hurry and finish your breakfast, Peabody.
We are going out."

"Where?" I asked.

"Hither and yon. It is time we paid courtesy calls on the
High Priests of Aminreh and Isis. They were rivals before,
and probably still are. Curse it, we are in the dark about a
number of things. This"—he raised his cup—"proves that
they have had contacts with the outside world. So do the
steel blades carried by the nobility and higher officers.
With whom are they trading? What other commodities
have they acquired? And why the devil would they bother
importing coffee? It certainly was not a delicate attention
on Tarek's part; he didn't expect us."

I dismissed this last question as unimportant—an error
on my part, as events were to prove. "We neither of us
speak the language fluently, Emerson."

"I believe I will be able to get my point across," said
Emerson.

The door was not barred. Emerson had got *that* point
across by wrenching the heavy wooden bar out of its sockets
and carrying it with him into our room. Looking neither
right nor left, he pushed the guards aside and proceeded on
his way, followed by me and Selim and Daoud. No one attempted to stop us until we reached the open salon that gave
onto the terrace, where we encountered the captain of our
guard. He informed us that the king wished to see us at once.

Emerson's eyes brightened. "Tell him, wait," he said. "Come, lady."

"Three imperatives in a row," I remarked, taking the hand he offered. "Can you explain to this agitated person, without imperatives, that we mean to call on the high priests?"

"I don't intend to explain anything, my dear. We will go to the Great Temple. One of the bastards is bound to be hanging about there."

When we reached the level of the road my eyes turned, not toward the temple but toward the rugged cliffs on the north. The newly risen sun illumined the western side, a pattern of dark shadows like the stitching of a crazy quilt. Was Ramses up there, making his slow and perilous way toward the mist-shielded northern part of the oasis? If his hopes of assistance from the villagers had failed, he might have sought refuge in the subterranean passages beneath our former habitation. I didn't know which to hope for. I didn't know which to fear more.

"Don't stare," said Emerson, steadying me as I stumbled.

Selim broke into a fit of the giggles when we passed between the great pylons that bore our images, but the sight of the courtyard beyond sobered him. Colonnades, supported by large pillars, lined all four sides, and huge bronze braziers flanked the doorway. The flames flickering in them were pale in the sunlight. The altar in the center reeked with the remains of the morning sacrifice. Priests were busy cutting up the carcass of the ox; the meat would be distributed to the temple servants after it had been presented to the god. It was a very practical arrangement, satisfying both the spiritual needs of the god and the alimentary needs of his priests. Our appearance brought all activity to a standstill; everybody stared, but we got as far as the inner colonnade before a priest summoned up nerve enough to stop us and ask what we wanted.

After a number of inappropriate imperatives we managed to recall a few appropriate nouns and were informed that the gentlemen we wanted were not at the temple, but at home. Apparently they left the daily rituals to subordinates except on special occasions. Relieved at seeing us go away, the priest took us back to the pylon and pointed out the high priests' dwellings.

"They don't shut the men up in stone cells," said Emerson, studying the columned facades and green gardens. "That is Murtek's former abode; it has passed on to his successor as High Priest of Isis."

Instead of mounting the steps toward the dwelling, he set off down the road at a brisk trot. We were all caught off guard, including our escort; I had to run to catch him up. "What are you up to now?" I panted.

"I am making use of the element of surprise," said Emerson. He caught me round the waist and swept me along with him, back the way we had come, past the palace, and then, without pausing, up a ramp toward a stately villa high on the hill. "Tarek's house." I managed to get the words out, though Emerson's arm was squeezing my ribs.

"He's certainly not there now," replied my spouse, not even winded. "But someone else is, and I think I know who. I want my guns back."

I made out several forms standing on the terrace, looking down at us. As Emerson pounded onward, one of them turned and vanished within. The others were quick to follow, and indeed, the sight of Emerson charging forward, with me under one arm like a cumbersome parcel, would have been enough to strike terror into the heart of the boldest.

"Barge straight ahead," shouted Emerson, doing so. "Are you with me, Daoud? Selim?"

I had never been in the house Tarek had occupied while crown prince, but the plan was similar to that of other noble dwellings: beyond the terrace was a series of anterooms and then a corridor that turned first to the right and then to the left. Emerson was moving at a dead run, and I could hear Daoud's ponderous footsteps behind us. The servants fled before us; Emerson herded them, as a dog herds sheep, into a handsome reception room, pillared and painted. Some huddled at the far end, crying out in alarm; others escaped through one or another of the curtained doorways along the walls of the room. Emerson set me on my feet.

"Try that one," he said, indicating one of the doorways and plunging through another.

The room I entered was a bedchamber, luxuriously appointed but unoccupied except for two servants who were trying to push through the far wall. A quick glance round told me there was nothing unusual about the furnishings; garments folded carefully over the footboard of the bed resembled those Merasen had worn the day before. Emerson had been right; this was his house. I was about to investigate further when a shout of triumph made me hasten back to the reception room. Emerson entered at the same moment, dragging a man who was struggling in a vain attempt to free himself from the hands that gripped him. He wore a linen robe and woven sandals, but I recognized him immediately, despite the distortion of his features.

It was Captain Moroney, the former veterinary surgeon's assistant.

Of course I had suspected him all along.

. .

# Ten

. .

"**Y**ou did not know!" Emerson bellowed. "Don't tell me you knew!"

"I had strong suspicions—"

"Of everybody!" Emerson transferred his inimical gaze from me to Moroney and dropped him unceremoniously onto the floor. "You are a disgrace to your uniform, a vile deceiver and a murderer. What have you to say for yourself?"

Moroney sat up, rubbing his shoulder. Having discovered that he was not in imminent danger of strangulation, he had regained his nerve, and his countenance was that of the pleasant young officer I had known.

"But not as a veterinarian's assistant," I exclaimed. "I remember now where I saw you—at the general's luncheon party, when Wallis Budge talked of the Lost Oasis."

"Aha," said Emerson. "Was that what set you on the track? You had better tell me everything. You murdered one of my men and tried to kill another. Only a full confession will save you."

Moroney sprang to his feet. "Sir, you must believe me! I am guilty of greed and deceit, but not of murder. It was Newbold who pitched your man into the jaws of the crocodile, and Merasen who cut the other young fellow's throat. He was dead before I arrived on the scene, or I assure you I would have prevented it."

"He lies," growled Daoud.

"Innocent until proven guilty," said Emerson regretfully. "Go on, Moroney, let's hear the rest of it. Be convincing," he added, putting out a hand to hold Daoud back.

Moroney made a clean breast of it. Budge's reference to the Lost Oasis at that long-ago luncheon party had been one of his ill-mannered jokes, but when Reggie Forthright told a similar story and announced his intention of going out into the desert to look for his missing uncle, it had stirred Moroney's imagination—which was, unfortunately for us, unusually well developed for that of a military person. Our subsequent disappearance into the wild and our eventual return with a mysterious young English girl were also, as he put it, suspicious. However, there was no way he could confirm his suspicions or pursue the matter. He had almost forgotten about it when, by one of those nasty coincidences Fate enjoys, the patrol he commanded had intercepted a caravan of slavers and found among the captives a young man whose appearance and manner were strikingly different from those of the cringing slaves.

"Arrogant," said Moroney, summing it up. "I wasn't accustomed to such behavior from natives. He demanded I return his property. I discovered the property consisted of rings of pure gold and several unusual weapons, and then I realized, with an astonishment which I can hardly find words to convey, that Forthright's story was true; that the boy had come from the Lost Oasis, where gold was as common as dirt."

"An honest man," I said, "would have reported this immediately to his superiors."

"I might point out," said Moroney, with some bitterness, "that I had served my country for twenty years with nothing to show for it except the prospect of a paltry pension, and that the lure of gold has seduced wealthier men than I. But I will not make excuses. I fell; and I found young Merasen a willing collaborator. He had been sent to bring you back to the Lost Oasis, and he candidly admitted that he had little hope of getting back there himself without you. I pointed out that he had no hope of getting anywhere without my help, so we entered into an agreement. I kept the gold; the young fool hadn't realized it was of no use to him, since an attempt to exchange it for currency would have got him scragged by a dishonest dealer or reported by an honest one. I was able to keep track of him through you; as soon as I learned you were on your way to the Sudan, I knew the first part of the scheme had succeeded. I resigned my commission and went to Aswan, where I found Merasen enjoying the dubious amenities of that place. He blandly informed me he hadn't yet succeeded in getting hold of a copy of Forth's map, but that he was sure he could after he met you in Wadi Halfa. So I shoved him onto the next steamer and waited for you. I had already instructed an old acquaintance in Kareima to begin getting a caravan together; I know the area well, having been stationed there for so many years."

"That is how you were able to get away two days before us," said Emerson, fingering the cleft in his chin.

Moroney nodded. "I didn't believe you meant to go on to Meroe, so I was ready when the train stopped at Abu Hamed. A robe and headcloth was sufficient disguise, so long as I was careful to keep my back turned."

He had enjoyed boasting of his cleverness, but a sound from without wiped the smile from his face. It took on a hunted look. "I don't know how you got past Merasen's guards, but it won't be long before he learns of your presence," he said in mounting agitation. "They don't intend to let us leave, you know. I haven't been allowed out of this house since I arrived, and I don't know what has become of my drivers. Merasen won't tell me. He lied to me. We are not the only—"

"Control yourself," I said sharply. "And do not attempt to deceive us. You have left this house at least once. You lost a button outside my chamber door."

I took it from my pocket and displayed it. Moroney gaped. "That isn't one of mine. I never—"

"It does not belong to my husband or my son," I interrupted. "You are the only other person here whose clothing is equipped with buttons."

"But—but that's what I started to tell you!" Moroney sputtered. "There is another white man here!"

Our skeptical expressions provoked him into frantic exposition. "It's true, you must believe me; he and Merasen are thick as thieves, he comes and goes undeterred. Merasen sends me away when he is here, but I have managed to catch glimpses of him—tallish, stoop-shouldered, long chin and large nose, ears that stick out like a bat's wings . . ."

He ran out of breath, since the entire speech had been unpunctuated. Emerson and I turned to stare at each other.

"It cannot be," I exclaimed.

"It must be." Emerson slammed his fist into his palm. "The description is too accurate. Curse it, I told you there was something suspicious about MacFerguson. But how the devil did he get here from Gebel Barkal? Good Gad! This isolated oasis is beginning to resemble Victoria Station!"

Moroney's premonitions had been correct. Running footsteps heralded the arrival of Merasen, accompanied by several soldiers. He was flushed with fury and haste. "Why did you come here?" he demanded. "The king has sent for you. You insult the king."

"No, no," Emerson said soothingly. "There was no insult intended. We came to consult you, Merasen, before we spoke with your father, so that we would know what to say if he asked us about you."

It was a fairly direct threat and Merasen recognized it as such. He bit his lip. "He will not ask. You will not tell him. I am the only one who will help you leave the Holy Mountain!"

"Well, well," said Emerson. "That is still open to negotiation, eh? You were not honest with us. You did not tell us our—er—friend was here."

Merasen glowered at Moroney, who was edging toward the door of his room. "He is no friend of yours. He forced me to steal from you. He killed your servant."

Moroney started to protest. Emerson waved him to silence. "Your word against his, Merasen. What about the other Englishman?"

Merasen's youthful countenance took on a look of innocent astonishment. "What other Englishman?"

"Never mind, Emerson," I said. "He never admits to anything unless he is caught red-handed. We may as well go and see the king."

"May as well," Emerson agreed. "Come along, Merasen."

"You will not tell the king what I said about the guns. It is to be a surprise for him. He would not believe you." Merasen was nothing if not resilient. He smiled. "Your word against mine."

"Hmph," said Emerson. "We shall see."

Emerson refused to be hurried. He strolled along, deep in thought, chewing on the stem of his pipe. After a time he said to me, "Merasen non parle français?"

I understood what he meant, even though his command of that language is exiguous. When his limited vocabulary fails him, he picks a word at random, and he has never bothered to learn the gender of nouns. "I don't suppose so," I replied.

"Très bien." Having got one phrase right, Emerson smirked complacently and went on, "We have placed him over a container—"

"A what? Oh."

"—and play him like a cat (m.) with a mouse (m.)."

"Yes, my dear, I see what you mean. But please don't speak French anymore, it makes my head ache."

Our audience that morning was private. The king was alone, and obviously put out, but the only signs of anger he allowed to escape him were a hard stare and a brusque order. "Sit."

"Thank you," said Emerson, helping me to a chair.

"Send them away" was the next order, indicating Selim and Daoud.

"Send him away," said Emerson, indicating Merasen.

The boy's jaw dropped. "No. The king does not understand—"

"Oh, I think we can make do without you," said Emerson. He went on in Meroitic, "Send him away, I send them away."

A spark of humor lit the king's eyes. He gestured at his son. Merasen dared not disobey; he left with dragging steps, looking over his shoulder. After Selim and Daoud had left the room, Emerson settled himself comfortably onto a chair.

"Good," he said. "We talk—you, I—a man to a man."

The king glanced at me. I smiled pleasantly.

"My son," said Emerson. "Where?"

"I do not know." He spoke slowly and in a very loud voice, as people do when they are trying to communicate with someone who does not understand their language. "Do you know?"

"If I did, I wouldn't tell you, you bastard," said Emerson in English.

"Just ignore the question," I advised.

"Hmmm, yes," said Emerson. "My daughter," he went on in Meroitic. "See, talk. Now."

The discussion continued for quite some time, slowed, as the Reader no doubt realizes, by the difficulty of communication. Emerson had to resort to sign language, and on two occasions, to drawings penciled on the stone dais. Somewhat to my surprise, the king patiently persevered. From time to time, when they hit an impassable language barrier, he looked at me, and I was able to supply the essential word. There was definitely a twinkle in the royal eyes when I did that. What a pity he was a traitor and usurper! A sense of humor is an attractive trait. But, I reminded myself, it is not always a sign of a virtuous nature.

It ended with our agreeing to appear at a formal ceremony in five days' time. It was longer than I had dared hope for. We ought to be able to think of a way out in five days! In exchange, I was to be taken to see and speak with Nefret.

"Today," I said firmly.

The king nodded. "Go to your house. One will come for you. Today," he added, and actually smiled.

"He is rather a pleasant chap," I remarked, as we joined Daoud and Selim and started back to our quarters.

"Pleasant villain," grunted Emerson. "I want to go with you, Peabody."

"Impossible, my dear. Let us settle for what we can get. The language barrier proved quite useful, didn't it? You were unable to agree to specific demands since you couldn't understand them, and he was unable to pursue his questions about a number of matters we might have found embarrassing."

"But I was unable to pursue *my* questions about a number of matters," Emerson said grumpily. "Does he know Merasen is harboring an outsider? Does he know about the other white man? Who is on whose side? Whom can we believe?"

"One thing at a time, Emerson. The first thing is to talk with Nefret and tell her . . . What?"

By the time "one" came to fetch me, we had settled that question. "One" turned out to be Count Amenislo. I rejected the litter he had brought and made him walk with me instead of getting into his.

"A little exercise will do you good," I informed him, setting a pace that made the count's jowls and lower back area wobble. "We aren't going far, are we?"

"The shrine of Isis," Amenislo panted. "But this is not . . . proper. People . . . are looking."

They were, and no wonder. I returned the stares of passersby with a wave of my parasol, while Amenislo covered his face with his sleeve in an attempt to avoid recognition. I trotted him all the way up to the courtyard of the temple, where he stopped and leaned against a column.

"I wait," he gasped. "Go on. There."

"You are not ritually pure?" I inquired. "Neither am I, you know."

"Uh," said Amenislo.

I felt rather ashamed of myself when I saw the perspiration streaming down his face. It was not worthy of me to torment such a hapless victim. I patted him on the arm.

"If it doesn't bother the priests, it doesn't bother me," I said cheerfully.

One of them was waiting for me in the shade of the arcade across the courtyard. Shaven head and spotless white robes proclaimed his status; bowing, he ushered me into the chamber where the goddess gleamed from her pedestal. He picked up one of the lamps that rested on shoulder-high stands and beckoned me to follow him through one of the curtained doorways.

The lamp was primitive, if gracefully shaped, of some translucent stone like alabaster. It gave little light; the end of the stone-cut corridor we had entered was shrouded in darkness until we were almost upon it. Here the passage turned, first to the right, and after a short distance, right again. We were heading back in the same direction. Then came another abrupt turn, to the left, and I saw light ahead—a faint glow shining through a linen curtain. My guide swept this aside and motioned me to enter.

Several lamps burned here, illumining a small chamber whose walls were covered with hangings. How many doorways behind them? I wondered. How many intersecting passages had we passed? The place was a confounded maze, deliberately designed to confuse an intruder. I could only pray that Ramses had abandoned his idea of reaching Nefret through the temple. If he attempted this route he would be caught or hopelessly lost. This room was obviously not part of the High Priestess's living quarters; it contained only a few stools and a small folding table.

The priest had gone. I was alone.

All to the good, I thought, squaring my shoulders. It will give me a chance to explore. Moving along the walls, I lifted one hanging after another, finding, as I had expected, other openings—black as pitch, all of them. I was about to pick up one of the lamps and pass through the nearest when one of the hangings on the far side of the room was pulled aside. Two of the handmaidens, swathed from head to foot in their white veiling, entered and took up positions on either side of the doorway. Behind them was Nefret.

It is unnecessary to describe the emotion that reduced my normally measured speech to broken exclamations. I had not realized until she ran into my arms and I was able to hold her close how worried I had been. At first she was just as incoherent, clinging tightly to me and repeating the same words of affection and relief over and over. Naturally I soon conquered my momentary weakness and encouraged her to do the same.

"We may not have much time," I said. "Let us not waste it. They haven't hurt you?"

"No." She wiped her eyes with the back of her hand and gave me a tremulous smile. She wore the High Priestess's robes, but she had thrown the veils back from her face. "The Professor—Ramses and Selim and Daoud—are they all right?"

"Yes, yes, don't worry about us. Do you know why they brought us here? Tarek has been overthrown by a usurper—"

"I know. They want me to bring the goddess back to her shrine."

"To prop up the throne of the usurper," I said, as cynically as Emerson would have done. "It seems to be somewhat shaky. Tarek is holding his own, in the northern section of the Holy Mountain, but neither he nor his successor can overcome the other. The new king is demanding that we support him, publicly and unequivocally, and that just might turn the tide in his favor."

One of the handmaidens turned her veiled face toward the doorway through which I had come. Someone outside coughed. I said quickly, "Naturally we will do no such thing, but it would be advisable for us to flee the city and make our way to Tarek. No, don't interrupt, just listen. The situation is not as desperate as it appears—"

"It never is, with you," said Nefret, trying to smile.

I gave her a reassuring smile in return and went on, "We have several schemes in mind. Daria is with you, I presume? How is she holding up?"

"Not as well as she was at first," Nefret said slowly. "They treat her like a servant, and some of the handmaidens delight in telling her dreadful stories of torture and human sacrifice. When I order them to leave her alone they obey for the moment, but I can't be with her all the time, they are preparing me for the ceremony, and . . . Oh, Aunt Amelia, I am beginning to forget! There are gaps in my memory, longer and more frequent."

My spine prickled, as I remembered the uncanny accuracy of her performance as High Priestess. I grasped her hands and held them tightly.

"You must hang on," I said urgently. "It won't be for long. Ramses has a plan . . . Oh curse it, here is that confounded priest come for me."

He stood in the doorway, the lamp in his hand. The handmaidens closed in on Nefret. I brandished my parasol and they backed away, squeaking in agitation. Nefret laughed aloud.

"You are a breath of fresh air, Aunt Amelia—a strong northern wind, in fact. What is Ramses's plan, and how can I help?"

"I presume the openings in the cliff above the temple roof lead to your rooms? Just nod. Yes. Can you leave a light burning in one of them tonight and hereafter? In a room that is, by preference, not occupied at night."

"I can try." Her eyes widened as the import of the question dawned on her. "Oh, no. He can't possibly—"

"It may not be necessary. I have a few ideas of my own. I had better go now, my dear, but you will hear from us soon again—tomorrow, if I can manage it. Pretend to be docile and compliant and leave the rest to me."

The priest was at my side, the handmaidens at hers. She nodded and smiled, but her hands clung to mine until I gently freed them. I followed the priest out of the chamber and I did not look back. I was afraid my resolution would fail if I did.

### From Manuscript H

"Harsetef!" Ramses exclaimed. "It is you?"

Harsetef reverently tucked the meerschaum pipe into his pouch and touched his fingers to Ramses's lips. "Softly. Lie flat on the ground."

"They are coming," Ramses whispered. "They will find this place."

"No. Look."

High on the cliffside to the south, a small figure had appeared. It stood upright, waving its arms and shouting—insults and challenges, Ramses deduced, for the pursuers turned to look in that direction. One of the soldiers nocked an arrow and loosed it. His quarry ducked, with insulting ease. A few seconds later a boulder rumbled down the cliffside, carrying a number of smaller stones, a rain of pebbles, and one soldier with it. The small figure screamed defiance and vanished into a cleft in the rock.

"So that is how you fight them," Ramses murmured, watching the decimated troop trying to find a way up the shattered cliff.

"One way." Flat on his belly, his chin resting on his folded arms, Harsetef added, "They will have to give up soon, the god's bark sails to the west. Then we will go on, you and I."

"You are still loyal to Tarek, then."

Harsetef turned his head and stared in surprise. "I belong to the Father of Curses, I am his man. The last words he said to me I have never forgotten. 'Serve King Tarek as faithfully as you would serve me.' He has returned, as we knew he would when he heard our prayers."

So now Father is a demigod, Ramses thought. The role would daunt most men, but Emerson would undoubtedly take it in stride. No wonder the usurper wanted his support.

Their pursuers were retreating, slowly and with difficulty, taking with them the body of their fallen comrade. Harsetef seemed to be in no hurry. Presumably he was waiting for darkness. Ramses tried not to think about the hair-raising climb ahead of him. "Tell me about Tarek," he said. "How did he lose his throne?"

"It is quickly told," Harsetef replied. "When you left the Holy Mountain, there were still a few who resisted the king. He was merciful. He offered forgiveness to those who would lay down their weapons and swear loyalty."

"Perhaps he was too forgiving."

"No." Harsetef shook his black head. "His brother was dead, there was no other king to fight for. The old High Priest of Aminreh died too—not by violence, for one does not raise one's hand against the chosen of the god, but after a year of imprisonment. He was an old man."

"And the white man—the redheaded Englishman who also supported Tarek's brother?"

"He was most certainly a follower of Set," Harsetef explained seriously. "The color of his hair was a sign of that evil god, and did he not fight against his sister, the Priestess of the divine Isis?"

Such, as Ramses's father might have said, are the uses of religion. The ancient myth telling of the murder of the good god Osiris by his envious brother Set had been neatly twisted to fit a specific political need. Isis, sister of both Set and Osiris, had also been the latter's wife, who had brought him back to life long enough to impregnate her with a son. Nefret had been Reggie's cousin, not his sister, but that was a minor point. Ramses thought he detected the fine Meroitic hand of old Murtek, the High Priest of Osiris, one of the cleverest politicians he had ever met.

"So the man of Set—er—died?" he asked.

"Struck down by the hand of Osiris."

Murtek's hand, rather. Ramses wondered how he had carried out the execution.

Murtek was dead too, of natural causes. The canny old man had kept the various power cliques in balance, playing off the priests of Amon against those of Osiris, and controlling Tarek's overly ambitious plans for reform. After he died, the trouble began. His successor was an elderly weakling who could not resist the ambitions of the priesthood of Amon. Tarek had made the fatal mistake of levying a toll on the wealthiest citizens, and on the temples, in order to carry out his reforms.

It was depressingly familiar. There was no standing army; like medieval knights, each nobleman had his own guard, and when open warfare broke out, these men followed their lord. The temple guardsmen rallied to the priests. The only soldiers who had remained loyal to Tarek were members of his own guard and a few others. Rather than see them slaughtered in a useless struggle, Tarek had retreated with them to the northern area. Since then, others had joined them, but their numbers were still small.

"So are those of the usurper," Harsetef said with a tight-lipped smile. "He has lost many men trying to force the pass. We hold the heights and defend them."

He rose. "On your way, young one," he said to Khat.

Ramses thanked the boy again and told him to be careful. After he had gone, Harsetef said hesitantly, "There is a thing that troubles me. I did not want to speak before the boy."

"What is it?" Ramses shouldered his pack.

"We were told," said Harsetef, "that the Father of Curses showed himself with the usurper at the Window of Appearance. That you and the Sitt Hakim were with him. That you spoke to the people, telling them to obey the usurper."

"It is true," Ramses said. Harsetef sucked in his breath, and Ramses went on, "We told the people to go home. They would have been slaughtered, men, women, and children alike. Surely you do not think we would betray Tarek? We are waiting and planning for the right time to act."

"I knew it was so," Harsetef said with a sigh of relief.

Politics be damned, Ramses thought. These people *believe,* in their gods and in us. We knew that, of course; we knew it intellectually, but we are too trapped in our rationality to comprehend fully how powerful that belief can be. Faith can move mountains? Maybe not mountains, but it has toppled kings and transformed societies.

Matters were more serious than he had realized, and his disappearance might have made them even worse. Zekare might try to push the ceremony forward, demanding public acknowledgment of his legitimacy. Emerson would never give it. It would be just like him to burst into a speech of fiery denunciation, which would inspire a bloody war and, very likely, get him and his wife killed. It would be a small war, only a few hundred men on either side; the population of the Holy Mountain had never been great, and if Ramses was any judge, it was slowly but inexorably decreasing. But people died in war, and one futile death was one too many.

Could they get his parents—and Daoud and Selim—out of the city right away? It would be hellishly difficult, if not impossible, and then what? The mental image of his mother trying to scramble over these cliffs in the dark was pure nightmare. Oh, she'd try it, all right. She would try anything. Or die in the attempt, which was the most likely scenario. Then there was Nefret. They couldn't leave her behind. If the rest of them escaped she would be guarded even more closely, and her value to the usurper was at least as great as theirs—even greater, if the priests were able to control her by means of drugs or threats. Threats to Daria, perhaps? Nefret would never let fear for herself guide her actions, but she'd buckle if an innocent person were at risk. And why in God's name was he thinking about Daria? She was only a pawn in the game. Nefret was the White Queen. But a pawn can become a queen if it moves all the way across the board . . .

Ramses's brain felt as if it were infested with mice, running frantically back and forth, trying to find a way out of the cage of his thoughts. He looked up. A sickle moon swung low above the cliffs, silvery pure and curved like the horns of the goddess's crown—Isis, divine wife and mother.

He turned to Harsetef. "I'm going back."

⋮

Emerson was waiting for me at the foot of the ramp when I left the shrine.

"Well?" he demanded.

I told him what had transpired. His brow furrowed. "I don't like the sound of it, Peabody. Do you think they are using drugs?"

"I fear it may be so, Emerson. She seemed brighter and more confident when I left her, but a reassessment of the situation is definitely called for. Where are Daoud and Selim?"

"Taking photographs of the temple pylons. And," Emerson added, "keeping their eyes open."

"For an Englishman with very large ears?"

We started back toward the Great Temple, accompanied by our escort. It was larger than before. Stamping along with his hands in his pockets, Emerson said irritably, "For anyone who isn't a native of the Holy Mountain. I expect the cursed missionaries and the German tourists will turn up at any moment. Everybody else is here. How many buttons do you suppose they possess among them? That famous clue isn't worth twopence."

I let him grumble on; his premise was absurd, but complaint relieved his feelings. In fact, I had had second thoughts about the button—not the object itself but the circumstances surrounding its loss. They did not fit the theory of attempted abduction. One man, not several, had stood outside my door and remained there long after Emerson's deep respirations had betrayed his presence beside me—long after his actual presence must have been seen by the burning eyes of the watcher. The deep sighs, the silent contemplation brought to mind . . . But I feel certain my intelligent Readers have anticipated me. I had not determined what steps to take, but there was no doubt in my mind that it would be a serious error to mention the idea to Emerson.

Selim was surrounded by a staring crowd. He always enjoys being the center of attention, and he made the most of it, taking exposure after exposure with the camera and barking orders at Daoud, who was assisting. Among the audience were several shaven-headed priests, half a dozen soldiers, and a miscellaneous collection of ordinary citizens, including a few children and a lady in a litter, whose black-wigged head protruded through the curtains.

"They told me to stop," Selim said, indicating the priests. "I did as you said, Sitt Hakim, and paid no attention. Did you see her?"

"Yes, and spoke with her. I will tell you about it later. Have you finished here?"

"One more," said Selim. With his most charming smile, he pointed the camera at the lady in the litter.

"I explained to them what it was for," Selim went on as the lady simpered and raised a ringed hand to adjust her wig.

"How?" I demanded, amused and bemused.

"With signs and pictures drawn in the dust. I have learned a few words . . ." He proceeded to use one of them, calling out, "Beautiful!" and smiling even more broadly at his subject.

"Astonishing, isn't it, how people respond to a camera?" Emerson remarked. The lady bared her teeth and tilted her head, her eyes fixed on Selim. Several spectators tried to crowd closer. "They are hypnotized by the confounded thing. No one is even looking at us. I wonder what other words Selim has learned?"

"Never mind," I said severely. "Come along now, we have a great many things to discuss."

"And to do," said Emerson. "What do you say we give a little soiree this evening, Peabody?"

"It is rather short notice, Emerson. Whom do you plan to invite?"

"Everybody, Peabody. The high priests, the captain of the guard, Merasen and his—er—guest, and His Majesty. He won't come, but it would be rude not to include him in the invitation. We will also invite the High Priestess of Isis and her attendants."

"She won't be allowed, Emerson."

"It can't do any harm to ask, Peabody. From now on we will proceed as if we had every right to do anything we choose. We have come to a friendly agreement with Zekare, haven't we? We are allies, aren't we?"

It took a while to convey our wishes to the servants, but once they got the idea they scattered to make the necessary preparations and to send messages to our intended guests. While I was giving my orders, Emerson wandered out into the garden. He returned to report that there was no message attached to the vine we had lowered from the wall and no sign that anyone had been near it.

"It is too soon to hear from him, I suppose," I said, attempting to conceal my disappointment. "But I do wish we could find a more reliable way of communicating with him. The situation is changing, almost hour by hour. We must . . . What is this?"

One of the women servants had entered carrying a large

tray. Daoud politely took it from her and put it down on the floor. "She asked if we wanted food"—he rubbed his stomach and pointed to his mouth—"and I said yes. It has been many hours since the morning meal, Sitt Hakim."

"Of course. It was a good thought, Daoud."

The young woman lingered, watching Daoud as he seated himself cross-legged before the tray. She was the same one who had followed us the day before, and I began to suspect it had not been Selim's charming smiles that had interested her. Attraction of that sort is absolutely unaccountable! Daoud was a fine figure of a man, but he was completely impervious to sidelong glances and fluttering lashes.

After the woman had reluctantly withdrawn, I told Selim and Daoud about Nefret.

"Then she is well," Daoud said between bites. "It is good."

"Not good," Selim growled. "She is afraid and alone. Sitt Hakim, we must get her away from there."

"I agree," I said. "And we have no time to lose. In less than five days' time we must commit ourselves publicly to the usurper or denounce him publicly. Nefret is in an even more invidious position. I see only one way out of this. We must, all of us, escape and join Tarek."

"Oh, quite," said Emerson, with excessive sarcasm. "As simple as that."

"It won't be at all simple, but it must be accomplished. The trouble with you, Emerson, is that you are spoiling for a fight. That is the last thing we want. Many innocent lives would be lost, including, perhaps, our own. If we come out in support of Tarek, it might be enough to tip the scales in his favor."

Emerson flung down the chunk of meat on which he had been gnawing, à la Henry the Eighth, and fixed me with a fishy stare. "I suppose you have a plan?"

"Several. The greatest difficulty, as I see it, is getting Nefret—and of course Daria—away. Once that is accomplished, we six can make a break for it."

"Make a break," Emerson repeated slowly.

"Overpower the guards, bind and gag them, and head straight along the Great Road to the northern pass. Audacity, speed, and those weapons Daoud so wisely retained should carry us through."

Emerson's eyes bulged. He let out a strange gurgling sound. His face turned red. His shoulders began to shake. I was about to administer a restorative slap when I realized he was not having a fit of spleen. He was laughing.

"I see nothing to laugh at," I said indignantly.

"No, you wouldn't." Emerson wiped tears of mirth away with the back of his hand.

Selim's eyes were bulging too, but not, I thought, with amusement. "Oh, Sitt," he began.

"It is a good plan," said Daoud.

"A very good plan," Emerson agreed. "Don't ask questions, Selim, they will only inspire her to wilder flights of fancy. She is at her best with a broad canvas. We will fill in the details as we go along."

We would have to do that, since it was impossible to anticipate every contingency that might arise.

The fact is that I had not thought the matter through. (I had no intention of admitting this to Emerson, who had not thought it through either.) What was, after all, our primary aim (aside from saving our own skins)? To overthrow the usurper and place Tarek back on his throne. Ramses had spoken glibly of starting and winning a revolution, but the memory of the trusting faces of the villagers had been haunting me. They would take up arms for us and for Tarek; and they would be slaughtered. There had to be a better way.

My most serious error had been my failure to anticipate the deadly peril that threatened Nefret. It was not peril of death, but of something worse—the annihilation of her personality and her will. Watching her flawlessly perform the Invocation to Isis should have prepared me, but not until I saw her haunted eyes and heard her faltering speech did I realize the seriousness of the matter. For once Ramses had had a clearer vision than I. He had argued vehemently in favor of his plan of trying to reach Nefret's apartments by scaling the cliff or finding a way through the temple, and had only yielded to my counterarguments after I agreed to ask Nefret to put a lamp in an appropriate window. He had promised he would not take that route unless he found a safe way of doing it, but I knew perfectly well that once he was out of my sight he would do precisely as he liked—and I had begun to wonder whether he hadn't had the right idea after all. Nefret had to be rescued before we made our attempt at escape—before the strong will of the girl I knew was completely overshadowed.

The preparations for our soiree were soon completed, and after we had freshened up, we sat down and waited to see who would come. There had been no answers to our invitations; I had been unable to explain the concept of "RSVP" to the messengers.

I had deemed it advisable for us to adopt the local dress, and the result, I must say, was very fine. Naturally I wore a linen shift under my delicately pleated garment. At my request the servants had produced additional jewelry: beaded collars, gold bracelets, and in my case heavy earrings. Emerson looked splendid, if somewhat self-conscious, and Selim swanked about like a peacock, flexing his muscles. Daoud had declined to appear in a kilt and collar, but he had assumed an elegant silken robe and imposing turban.

"We must have photographs," Selim declared.

"You can try, if you like," said Emerson, who obviously had no intention of allowing himself to be photographed. "But the light is fading, and we have no flash powder."

I suggested we wait until morning. Selim readily agreed, since what he really wanted was a photograph of himself to show to his wives.

The soft blue-gray light of evening had stolen into the room before the first guests arrived. Perhaps they felt there was safety in numbers, because there were half a dozen of them, all priests. Among them, I was pleased to note, were the High Priests of Isis and Aminreh. On their heels, almost literally, was Merasen. He greeted me in English. I replied in Meroitic. "Where is your guest? And the other stranger?"

My hope of catching him off guard failed. "Ask my father the king," he replied, smirking. I was beginning to hate that boyish smile.

"Is he joining us?"

"He is busy pleasing his women."

The arrival of additional guests saved me from the necessity of replying. They included Alarez, the captain of the guard, Count Amenislo, and several officials. Emerson advanced to meet them, an affable smile wreathing his features. "Come, sit," he invited, taking the count by the arm.

We had worked out the seating arrangements with some care. The small tables had room for only two or three persons each. Amase, the High Priest of Isis, was my quarry; I cut him out neatly from among the hovering priests and led him to a table. Emerson had Bakamani, the High Priest of Aminreh, with Amenislo to translate for him. The rest of them sorted themselves out, leaving Selim and Daoud alone at a separate table. Conversation was a trifle stilted—virtually nonexistent, in fact—until the wine began to take effect.

It was a pity we could not take photographs, for the scene was like the images of ancient Egypt produced by romantic painters: the flowing robes and curled wigs, the glitter of gold and glow of gemstones. The flames of the lamps swayed in a gentle breeze, bringing out the curve of a strong nose here and the sparkle of dark eyes there.

The Priest of Isis reminded me of my old friend Murtek, who had held the same position; he was a wizened, shriveled little person, but without Murtek's force of personality. It took me quite a while to get him to talk freely.

"The High Priestess did not come," I said. "I understand.

Why not the handmaidens? They came to us when we were here before this time."

"They come to the sick, lady."

"Hmmm," I said.

My attempts to induce further subjects of interest were interrupted by rising voices from the table where Emerson sat with the High Priest of Aminreh. How my spouse had managed to get into an argument about religion with his limited vocabulary I could not imagine; it seemed unlikely that the timid count would have translated his more provocative statements. He had managed it, though.

"Your god, their god"—he indicated Selim and Daoud and then pointed at me—"her god, many gods, all lies. No gods. Only men. Men use the gods."

He had found an adversary who was as fanatical as he and who had taken quite a bit to drink. Bakamani rose to his feet, swaying a little, but impressive, for he was a tall man with a face like a rectangular stone stela, with a long chin and jaw. "All gods are false save Aminreh. He is all gods in one, he is Re, he is Khepri the beetle who gave birth to himself, he is the one who judges the dead and places the crown on the head of the king."

"What did he say?" Emerson asked, poking Amenislo. The count started nervously and translated the speech.

"Ha!" said Emerson happily. He turned to me. "Peabody, did you catch the allusions? Bits and pieces of various hymns? I did this chap an injustice; he is not solely motivated by a desire for power, he actually believes this nonsense."

The High Priest poked Amenislo. "What did he say?" he barked.

There is no stopping Emerson when he receives encouragement of that sort, so I left them to it. As the evening wore on, everyone became quite animated; Emerson and the High Priest kept demanding translations from an increasingly flurried Count Amenislo, and as their voices got louder, the old Priest of Isis stopped looking nervously over his shoulder and became more forthcoming. He too was a believer; there were genuine tears in his eyes when he spoke of restoring the goddess to her shrine.

"We too will be happy to have the goddess come back," I said politely.

"Do you know her, in your country?"

"Some of us in our country honor the divine mother and her son."

"Is it so? She is kind and good," the old man murmured with a pointed glance at the debaters. "Not like other gods."

"It is true," I exclaimed, realizing I was in danger of getting into a theological debate of my own. "Can the High Priestess bring her back? She has been long away."

I gestured to one of the servants to refill the old gentleman's cup. We were now allies, if not coreligionists, and he saw no reason to guard his tongue. "The High Priestess remembers. More and more, day by day, she remembers. Every day we talk, she and I, alone together. And when the divine Isis returns, she will take her rightful place as queen of the gods of the Holy Mountain."

And her High Priest, Amase, would take precedence over his rival, the Priest of Aminreh. As Emerson would have been quick to point out, religion was often a guise for power.

Merasen went from table to table trying to overhear everyone's conversations. It was he who finally put an end to the proceedings; since he was of the highest rank among those present, everyone took their cue from him. Some were clearly reluctant to go, including the stalwart captain of the guard. Frustrated in his attempt to converse with Emerson, he had gone to sit with Selim and Daoud, and I did not doubt he had been regaled with a number of tall stories about Emerson. It is amazing how much one can convey with gestures and a few words. The only person who had not entered into the merriment was one of the officials, who seemed to be suffering from a severe cold. As the chill of the evening air increased, he wrapped himself more closely in his fine linen mantel, and he was the first to leave the room.

"You weren't of much help," I said to Emerson, as the servants began clearing away the remains of the food and mopping up puddles of spilled wine. "You were supposed to interrogate the High Priest, not argue religion with him."

"I realized early on," said Emerson loftily, "that there was no hope of corrupting the fellow or persuading him to turn against Zekare."

"How clever of you to accomplish that so quickly."

"Spare me the sarcasm, Peabody. Did you know Tarek had levied heavy taxes on the temples, especially that of Amon, and turned many of the priests out to earn an honest living? This chap felt his agitated prayers had been answered when Zekare took over the throne and restored Amon to even greater power."

"That is all very interesting, Emerson, but I cannot see that it helps us."

"Hmph," said Emerson. "What about you? No doubt you won the Priest of Isis over to our cause."

"I made considerable headway, in fact. He is an innocent old soul; he told me that as soon as the goddess has returned and Nefret has selected a successor, she can be with us."

"He lied," grunted Emerson.

"I don't think so. Someone else has lied to him. I learned something of much greater importance. I am only surprised I didn't think of it before."

Emerson was not going to give me the satisfaction of asking what it was. He turned to Selim. "Anything of interest to report, Selim?"

"The captain has much admiration for you, Emerson."

"Especially after the lies you and Daoud told him," said Emerson, who had apparently kept an eye on the proceedings.

Selim grinned. "Not lies, Emerson, and not told. Daoud

is as good a teller of stories without words as he is with them."

Daoud smiled modestly.

"I think," Selim went on, "that the captain would be your man if you asked him."

"It would take more than asking, Selim, I would have to do something that . . . Hmmm. I say, Peabody—"

"No, Emerson. I strictly forbid it."

Emerson's eyes narrowed.

"How did you know what I was going to say?"

"I know *you*. You were thinking of fighting the king—and, of course, winning. This isn't the Middle Ages, Emerson, and even at that time notions of chivalry were honored in theory more than in practice. Furthermore, he is probably a better sword fighter than you."

Fatigue had loosened my tongue, or I would have been more tactful. Emerson squared his mighty shoulders and glared at me. "It may come to that, Peabody, and if it does I will act as I see fit. Now come to bed, you have had more wine than is good for you."

"It isn't the wine," I murmured, passing my hand over my brow. "I have felt it coming on all evening. Dizziness, fever . . ."

I swayed slowly forward, giving Emerson plenty of time to catch hold of me. I felt a touch of shame when I saw his alarmed expression, but only a touch. It was his own fault for not listening to me.

## From Manuscript H

Ramses didn't believe in supernatural signs. Luckily, Harsetef did.

"If the goddess has spoken to you, you must obey," Harsetef agreed, after Ramses had explained what he meant to do. "It is a plan worthy of her, a clever plan."

"I thought so," Ramses said modestly.

"It will be dangerous. But with Her help you will succeed."

Inshallah, Ramses thought. God willing. And a tip of the hat to Saint Jude, patron of hopeless causes. He would need all the divine help he could get to pull this one off.

Ramses could not have explained, even to himself, why his tumbling thoughts had suddenly come into focus. Now that he had made the decision, he was able to justify it. The situation hadn't changed, but his understanding of it had. Their original plans had not taken all the facts into account. The facts of faith. If the High Priestess were to vanish without a trace from her rooms, and reappear in Tarek's camp, proclaiming her support for him, it would be a crushing blow to the usurper—and it might be enough to win without war.

It might also put his parents in greater danger. He told himself he couldn't worry about that. The girls were vulnerable, the intrepid foursome was not; his parents had always been able to talk or fight their way out of most situations, and they had Daoud and Selim with them.

"I may not be able to bring her away with me tonight," Ramses said.

"You must scout first," Harsetef agreed with an approving nod. "I will watch for you tonight and tomorrow and the next night, and I will warn the other scouts. You can find your way back to this place?"

"Yes," Ramses said with more confidence than he felt. "You will send word to Tarek? Tell him we are working for his cause and will join him soon. Tell him to do nothing until we come."

Harsetef went with him part of the way and left him wedged uncomfortably but safely in a crevice twenty feet or so above the Great Road. After he had gone, Ramses took careful note of his location. He could understand why the rekkit paths came this way—not many of the houses on the eastern side were inhabited—but it was confounded inconvenient for him, since the temple and palace area was on the other side of the valley. He would have to risk the

road or lose valuable time—and chance broken bones—
trying to find a path along the cliffs. He had to wait,
though; there were a good many lights showing across the
way: the braziers burning before the temple, the torches
carried by pedestrians, candle- and lamp-lit windows in
various buildings. He passed the time by inspecting the
scene through the binoculars and was intrigued to see that,
to judge by the number of torchbearers and litters leaving
the area, his parents had been entertaining that evening.
The departing visitors were too muffled in mantles and
cloaks to be recognizable, but for some not-so-obscure reason his spirits lifted. He ought to have known his mother
and father wouldn't sit with folded hands waiting to hear
from him. What on earth were they up to now?

The lights went out one by one. The leaping flames before the temple died into a red glow. Mist curdled in the
valley floor, but the sky above was clear and the stars were
bright. With a final glance at the horned moon, he descended to the road.

Resisting the temptation to skulk in the shadows, Ramses set out at a brisk walk, with the assurance of a man on
an important errand. The few others he encountered were
dressed as he was, with robes or mantles to protect them
from the cooling night air. The only positive aspect was
that he didn't have to pass the entrance to the palace. It was
heavily guarded and brightly lit. Until that moment he
hadn't dared think about what he intended to do or decided
how to go about it. Concealed behind one of the pylons, he
edged slowly forward until the little shrine of Isis came
into view; and some internal organ (his mother would have
said it was his heart) contracted when he saw a single
square of light high above the temple roof. They had managed to see her, then, and pass on his request. That settled
the question of how to go about it. He had never supposed
he had a prayer of getting to her rooms through the temple.

He had plotted a possible route the day they visited the
shrine. The first part wasn't difficult. There were other,

smaller shrines and a few dwellings, probably belonging to temple personnel, all on different levels, and he got onto the flat temple roof without difficulty. From there the climb was up a sheer rock face; but as he had told his father, the surface that looked smooth from a distance offered a number of hand- and footholds. He took off the robe and the clumsy sandals, put them in his pack, removed the rope, and paid it out between his hands. It was thin and strong and a good forty feet in length, longer than he had realized. Daoud had chosen well. He slung the newly coiled strands over one shoulder and under the other arm, knowing he might have to retreat in a hurry and clinging to the wild and improbable hope that he would find Nefret awake and alone. I must be out of my mind, he thought, gazing up at the lighted window. She won't be alone, the bloody damned handmaidens never leave the High Priestess unattended, and I'm not sure I could bring myself to knock out a bunch of defenseless girls, even supposing one of them didn't start screeching for help before I got round to her.

He started to climb.

The ascent wasn't much more difficult than many he had made in Egypt—except that this one was made in darkness and with the need for silence. Cautiously though he moved, he wasn't able to prevent an occasional bit of rock from snapping off and falling. The clatter of them on the temple roof sounded like a blast of dynamite to him, but there was no reaction from the guards in front of the temple. By the time he reached the level of the window he was sweating with nerves and his hands were bleeding. He grabbed hold of the flat sill, his toes wedged into a crack.

One look at the window told him the defenseless maidens were safe from him. The aperture was barred by two columns, part of the rock itself, carved into the shape of papyrus stems. He had seen this from below, but hadn't realized how narrow the spaces between the columns were. A child or a very slender woman might squeeze through. Not he.

He pulled himself up until he could get an arm round one of the columns. If he hadn't done so he might have lost his hold out of sheer astonishment when he saw, positioned between the pillars, bolt upright and motionless, a large brindled cat.

Ramses stared. The cat stared back at him, its large eyes lambent with reflected light.

Of course, Ramses thought, I ought to have expected something of the sort; my family attracts farcical situations the way sugar draws flies. This was one of the temple cats sacred to Isis, who had acquired the attributes of other goddesses, including Bastet. It wore a woven collar and an expression of polite disinterest. Or possibly, since reading a feline countenance is problematic, utter disinterest.

He knew better than to take hold of it. The sacred cats were large, strong animals, equipped with sharp claws and sharper teeth. "Are you standing guard, or just curious?" he whispered.

The cat's mouth opened. It was yawning, probably to indicate how completely he bored it, but for an incredulous moment he thought the answering whisper had come from its throat.

"You are mad to do this! Go quickly, before someone comes."

It wasn't Nefret—or the cat. "Daria?"

Her face appeared in the opening next to the one the cat filled. The lamp was on a low chest under the window; the flickering flame cast moving shadows across her features so that they seemed to grimace and twist. The effect should have been grotesque, witchlike, but it wasn't.

"Help me with this," he said softly. He handed her one end of the rope and swore under his breath as the cat turned and clawed at the dangling end. "Loop it around the column and pass it back to me," he ordered. "Ignore the cat."

Deeply offended at the removal of its toy, the cat gave Ramses a reproachful look and jumped down from the sill into the room. It stalked off, its tail twitching. Ramses adjusted the rope. As he had hoped, it was long enough to form a double strand that reached almost to the roof.

"Can you bring her to me?" he asked.

"Impossible. She lies in an inner room and the women sleep all around her, like kittens in a basket."

"But not you?"

"They don't care what I do so long as I am out of their sight. So I was able to light the lamp. I told them I was afraid to sleep alone in the dark. They laughed. What are you doing?"

"Sssh. I'm going to take you with me. You are small enough to slip through one of these openings."

"Me?" she gasped.

"Quiet! Do as I say, and quickly. Feet first. I'll catch you."

The cat had decided to investigate a basket on the opposite side of the room. Its scratching brought another of the animals into the room; both of them attacked the basket. Ramses sent out a silent apology; the cats were good luck, after all; the sleepers were accustomed to noises in the night.

Ramses guided the girl as best he could with one hand and with low-voiced instructions. She had to turn sideways to get her hips and shoulders through the opening. When she was sitting on the outer part of the ledge, with her feet dangling, she looked down and let out a soft cry.

"You can't go back now," Ramses whispered. "Put your arms round my neck and hold tight. I won't let you fall."

A shudder ran through her body. He had never been afraid of heights, but he could imagine the terror that gripped her and the courage it required to obey him. She had to lean forward, off balance, to get her arms over his shoulders. He caught her round the waist and lifted her off the ledge into a hard, one-armed embrace. She gripped him tightly, her nails digging into the back of his neck, and hid her face against his chest.

"It's all right, I've got you," he murmured. "Hang on, we'll be down straightaway."

The descent was a little faster than he would have liked, since he hadn't thought to tie knots in the rope. He hadn't really thought at all. He didn't dare think about what he was going to do next. But he was acutely conscious of the warm, pliant body pressed against his. She hadn't uttered a sound since that involuntary cry of fear.

The rope slid out from between his ankles and thighs before they reached the roof and he had to lower them the remaining distance using only one hand. The rough fibers burned his palm, but he managed to land on his feet.

She raised her head. "Is it over?"

He answered the childish question as he would have answered a frightened child. "Yes. You were very brave. You can let go now."

He set her down, pulled the rope free, and coiled it. She said softly, "Why?"

She stood motionless, her arms at her sides, and his heart failed him as the enormity of what he had done finally sank in. She wore a simple white robe; her head was uncovered and her slim brown feet were bare. They would be cut and bleeding before she had gone a mile, and as for scrambling up the cliffs . . .

There was no help for it, they had to go on; and there was only one place that might offer refuge long enough for him to think of a way out of the spot he had got her into. He shouldered his pack. "Come."

There was no one abroad at this late hour. After they had left the lighted areas around the palace and temple behind them they moved through the shadows, as quickly as they dared. She followed without a murmur of complaint or question until they reached the doorway of the abandoned villa. He didn't blame her for holding back; there was not a ray of light to be seen within, and the dry, rustling sound might have been that of rats or bats or something worse, and the tattered curtain blew in the wind like a bodiless spirit.

"It's all right," he said softly. "Take my hand."

He led her, feeling his way, around the turns of the corridor until they emerged into the desolate reception room he remembered so well. Starlight entered through the high windows and the opening that led to the garden. The room had been stripped of its furnishings except for a few cushions, full of holes and leaking feathers. He looked out on to the garden. The pool was dry and the plants withered.

"I'm sorry it's not very comfortable," he said. "But it should be safe, at least for the time being. Please sit down, you must be tired. It will have to be the floor, I'm afraid; I think the cushions are already occupied by mice."

She sank into a sitting position. Ramses rummaged in his pack. She accepted a sip of water but shook her head when he offered a handful of dates.

"I am not hungry."

"You're shivering. Here, put this around you."

He wrapped her in the cloak and sat down beside her.

Look on the bright side, his mother would have said. There was a bright side; he knew how to find Tarek, and he had got Daria out of the place without leaving any sign of how she had disappeared. That wouldn't do any good, though, unless he could get her clean away. Even if he succeeded, she was in for a hard time.

He glanced guiltily at the small huddled figure next to him. She had pulled the hood up over her head and looked like a miniature monk.

"Why?" she said again.

"I don't understand what you mean," Ramses said, sparring for time. He knew perfectly well what she meant.

She pushed the hood back. "Why did you do it? Why me? She is the one you hoped to rescue."

"I didn't suppose there was much hope of that, but I had to try. There was always a chance. You didn't suppose we would have left you there, did you? In fact," Ramses said slowly, "if I had had to make a choice, if I could have got only one of you away, it would have been you. Nefret would have been the first to realize that. She's in no more danger than she was before, but if she had disappeared into thin air, they might have . . ."

"Tortured me to make me tell where she had gone?" She finished the sentence he had left incomplete. She sounded quite matter-of-fact.

"Or threatened to harm you if she didn't give herself up. She would have done it too."

"Yes. I understand." She shivered and drew the cloak more closely around her. "What will happen now? We cannot stay here for long without food and water."

"That's right." Relieved at how coolly she was taking the situation, he gave her the bare facts: Tarek's loss of the crown, the usurper's demands for their support, and the steps they were taking to avoid that necessity. "So I must get you to Tarek," he finished. "It is a long, hard road, and we will need suitable clothing for you. I think I can manage that."

"How? You are a fugitive too."

He had thought of two possibilities: the woman in the rekkit village, and the arrangement he had made with his parents to leave a message in the ravine. His mother wasn't the woman he knew her to be if she couldn't figure out a way of lowering the necessary supplies down to him. He didn't relish either prospect; but one or the other had to be tried, and the sooner he got it over, the better. He pulled himself to his feet, wincing as bruises reminded him he hadn't got away scot-free either.

"Where are you going?" she asked.

"To get the things we need. I'll not be long." He opened the bundle he had carried. "There's some food and water left."

There were also a candle, matches, folded sheets of paper, and pencils—and a small flask of brandy. He scribbled a message on one of the papers and tucked it into his belt.

The huddled shape looked as if it had shrunk. "Please. Leave the candle."

So small a light couldn't be seen from without. "All

right. Just be careful it doesn't fall over and set the dried leaves ablaze."

"If you don't come back, I will die here."

"That should give me sufficient incentive," Ramses said caustically. "I'm sorry, Daria, I didn't mean to sound . . . If I don't come back, you may as well give yourself up."

He left everything with her except the rope, the matches, and his knife, which he had every intention of using if anyone got in his way. He wasn't sure why he was so angry. Uncertainty, for one thing, he supposed; he was making it up as he went along, and he was tired, tired of skulking in shadows, tired of his own indecisiveness.

The second of the two alternatives seemed safer, and he was anxious to communicate with his parents. They were so damned unpredictable, they might go looking for him if he didn't report.

Guided by a significant lighted window, the only one in that block of apartments, he made his way to the far side of the ravine, and blessed Daoud again for thinking of the rope as he lowered himself down. The uneven floor of the narrow canyon was littered with broken pottery and rotting food; the servants must be in the habit of pitching refuse over the wall. He was about to fumble among the trailing vines when he saw it—a pale, dangling shape like that of a hanged man.

It turned out to be one of his own shirts, tucked neatly into a pair of trousers and pinned in place, with boots tied by their laces to the legs of the trousers. After he had recovered from the sight, he realized there was writing on the back of the shirt. It was too dark for him to read the words. After replacing it with his own message, he stood for a moment, looking up at the lighted window and wishing he dared take the risk of calling to them. His self-confidence was as low as it had ever been; all he could think of were the innumerable mistakes he had made over the course of a misspent life. Was this another one? Had he done the right thing, or made matters even worse?

He ran into a slight snag on the way back; one of the men who guarded the entrance to the cemetery was awake, yawning and stretching. Ramses gripped his knife, but forced himself to wait, motionless in the shadow of the pylon. There was at least one other guard, his snores reverberated. A scuffle might waken him.

Finally the insomniac stretched out and after a while his regular breathing told Ramses he could go on. Once inside the deserted villa he lit a match and read the message. The firm handwriting was his mother's and he smiled a little when he saw she had used pencil instead of pen. No sense in ruining a perfectly good shirt.

"We have four more days. Must all escape and join Tarek. No war!" Then came an obvious afterthought: "Captain Moroney here. Says it is not his button. Suspect MacFerguson also here."

Ramses remembered Moroney, but who the hell was MacFerguson?

Four more days. No war. She was thinking along the same lines as he, which was all very well. But we "must all escape"? She might have been more specific.

The only light in the reception hall was the pale pearly nondarkness of predawn. At first he didn't see her, and his heart skipped several beats. Then she moved away from the column that had concealed her. "The candle went out," she said in a faint voice. "It was so dark, and there were noises . . . I was afraid they had caught you."

Then she was in his arms, clinging to him, her breathing hard and fast. She raised her head from his shoulder, and he saw the sparkle of tears on her lashes. "Why did you take me away? Was it only for the reasons you said?"

The words forced their way through the barriers he had raised in his mind. "I love you."

"You don't have to invent pretty words," she whispered, as her arms went round his neck. Her fingers slid through his hair, pulling his face down to hers. "You love *her*, I saw it. You want me. What is wrong with that? Take me."

He knew if he kissed her he wouldn't be able to stop. He held her away. "No, Daria, no. Not here, on this filthy floor, like an animal. Not now."

"When? How much time do we have? An hour, a day? I love you. I have loved you since the night I came to your room and you sent me away because of kindness and pity. Don't send me away now. We may both die tomorrow."

He kissed her.

⋮

## · ·
## Eleven
## · ·

After Emerson had placed me upon my couch he anxiously felt my brow and pressed his cheek against my breast, attempting, I presume, to listen to my heartbeat. He was off by several inches. I rather hated to stop him, but it would have been cruel to keep him in suspense.

"I am not ill, my dear," I whispered. "It is only a ruse."

Emerson sat up as if he had been stung by a scorpion. "Curse you, Peabody," he began.

"Sssh! You will spoil the whole thing if you don't play along."

"Rrrrr," said Emerson. It sounded like the amplified purr of a large cat but was, in fact, a growl. However, understanding had replaced resentment. He leaned closer and hissed at me.

"The handmaidens?"

"Yes. I would have told you earlier if you had been courteous enough to listen to me."

Emerson stroked his chin and studied me thoughtfully. "Let us abjure our habitual exchanges of reproach for the time being, Peabody. This may come to nothing, but it has—er—possibilities. I will tell the servants you are ailing and demand medical attention for you."

"You may express concern, but do not request a handmaiden until tomorrow morning. I don't want a lot of peo-

ple trotting in and out of here tonight. There is a chance
Ramses may try to communicate with us, and we must
leave a message for him."

Two of the ladies assisted me out of my elaborate costume and into a night robe. They had to roll me back and
forth, since I pretended to be so feeble I could not even
raise an arm. I heard Emerson shouting in the next room. It
was clever of him to express suspicion about the food and
the wine, though it was a little hard on the servants, who
were afraid they would be punished for negligence, if nothing worse. Eventually I declared I would try my own medicines and see how I felt in the morning. The ladies left in a
great hurry.

"That's settled," said Emerson, scrubbing vigorously at
my forehead with a damp cloth.

"Have they all gone away?"

"As fast as they could trot," said Emerson in a pleased
voice.

"Then stop doing that. You are rubbing the skin off my
forehead."

Emerson was somewhat surprised when I wrote the
message on one of Ramses's shirts, but I believe in killing
two birds with one stone whenever possible. An additional
garment might come in useful. After brief cogitation I
added trousers and a pair of boots. He hadn't wanted to
burden himself with their weight when he left, but he might
need them, and if he did not, there was no harm done.

At the first light of dawn I woke Emerson, holding my
hand firmly over his mouth until he had stopped thrashing
and cursing. "Go straightaway, before the servants turn up,
and see if there is any word from Ramses," I hissed. "I am
filled with the direst of forebodings about him. I know he
has done something of which I would not approve!"

"That is generally a safe assumption," Emerson mumbled, but he went at once to comply with my request. When
he came back he held a folded paper.

"What does he say?" I demanded.

Ramses had quite a lot to say, but it took us a while to puzzle it out. At the best of times Ramses's handwriting resembles the squiggles of Egyptian hieratic, and this letter looked as if he had used a rough block of stone for a table. I will reproduce the message as I remember it, without indicating the various points at which we interrupted its reading with exclamations of alarm and astonishment.

"Daria is with me, in the place you once knew well. Could not get Nefret away, handmaidens sleep in her room. Tarek's scouts patrol access to northern pass. One of them—remember Harsetef?—will meet me and take Daria on to Tarek's camp, but need shoes and clothing for her. Can you supply tonight, also food and water? Will return after dark."

"Need shoes and clothing?" I cried. "Good Gad, Emerson! Is she . . . She cannot be . . ."

"Stark-naked? Peabody, you have a positive gift for focusing on unessentials! Whatever she is wearing, and I feel certain she is wearing something, it must be unsuitable for a long, difficult trek."

"But why did he take her with him?"

"Because he was able to," Emerson said impatiently. "How the devil he pulled it off I don't know, but it means one fewer hostage to be released. And this tells us he is safe and still free. I would have thought that was the important point."

"Yes, of course. The place we once knew . . . Our former abode?"

"I should think so. He wasn't specific, in case this fell into the wrong hands."

"Good heavens, yes! We must destroy it at once."

"Groan," said Emerson.

"I beg your pardon?"

"I hear the servants. I presume you want to proceed with your scheme?"

"It is all the more imperative now," I said between groans. "If Ramses cannot reach Nefret, we must do the job."

"Damned if I know how," Emerson muttered, and went out.

The obvious possibilities had occurred to me. Holding a handmaiden prisoner and demanding Nefret's return in exchange for her freedom? Taking Nefret's place, swathed in veils, while Emerson and the others concealed her . . . where? Reluctantly I admitted the difficulties. At the moment I could see no way out of them. Ah, well, I thought, I will just have to think of something else.

While I waited, groaning whenever I remembered to do so, I considered Ramses's message again. I looked forward to hearing the full story of his adventures, which those terse, necessarily brief phrases could not begin to convey, but which maternal concern could easily visualize. He must have covered a great deal of ground during the previous two nights—much of it perpendicular. He had meant to go first to the village. We could assume, I believed, that this part of his plan had succeeded, for it was unlikely that he could have made his way to a rendezvous with Tarek's scouts without a guide. It was good to know that our old friend Harsetef was still alive and still loyal. Up to that point I could only commend Ramses. But instead of going on to join Tarek, he had come back and done what I had strictly forbidden him to do. Unless he had encountered Daria wandering about the street, which seemed unlikely, he must have got to her by climbing that sheer cliff.

I promised myself I would have a word with that boy. If he returned to the ravine that night I would be awake and ready for him, no matter how late the hour.

The curtain at the door parted and Emerson came in, followed by Selim and Daoud.

"They wanted to see for themselves that you were not really ill," Emerson explained. "You rather overdid the groans. Would you like coffee?"

"Why not?" I sat up and arranged the sheet modestly about my form before taking the cup from him. "I presume the handmaiden has been sent for?"

"Yes. What are you going to do with her once you've got her?" Emerson inquired. I looked meaningfully at the doorway, and he went on, "Don't concern yourself about the servants, they are afraid to come near you."

Selim wanted to know precisely what Ramses had said, so I obliged. He was a clever fellow, and I thought he might catch something I had missed. However, it was Daoud who came up with an idea that had not occurred to me.

"We know where he is. Why do we not take the clothing and food to him today?"

"Why, because . . . Because . . ."

"We don't want to lead anyone to his hiding place," Emerson said, frowning.

"The Sitt Hakim can think of a way," Daoud said comfortably.

"It would certainly save Ramses a great deal of time and effort and risk," I mused. "He could take her straight to the northern pass instead of coming all the way back here first."

Emerson went to the doorway and raised the curtain. "Here they come. Good Gad, it seems to be a delegation."

I handed Selim my cup and fell back onto the bed, while Emerson greeted the delegation. When he came back he was trying not to grin.

"They have just learned of Daria's disappearance," he announced. "Poor old Amenislo has been sent round to ask what we know about it, and the High Priest of Isis is here, in quite a state of agitation. Come along, Selim and Daoud, this should be amusing."

He stepped back and politely held the curtain aside to admit not one but two veiled forms.

It would have given a superstitious person quite a start to come upon them unawares. The wrappings covered their faces and reached to the floor, so that they seemed to glide rather than walk. As I believe I have mentioned, the priestesses of Isis were the medical practitioners of this society. They were trained in the methods their remote ancestors had employed, the knowledge having been passed down from generation to generation. Now as we all know, no scientific process can be truly scientific if it is weighted down by tradition and corrupted by superstition. The greatest achievement of ancient Egyptian physicians was the discovery that the pulse is "the voice of the heart" and that it may be a general indicator of health—no small achievement for an ancient culture, but somewhat limited in its applicability. I felt certain I would have no difficulty deceiving these girls; however, when one of them drew a small corked vial from under her garments and poured the contents into a cup, I realized I had better change my tactics. The liquid was dark and thick and smelled very peculiar.

I didn't bother asking what it was. Instead I shook my head and pushed the cup away. "I am well now," I said. "My medicines are good."

My attempts to engage them in conversation were not entirely successful at first, but I did manage to persuade them to unveil. One of the young women was quite beautiful, with well-cut, aristocratic features, but her narrowed black eyes studied me suspiciously. The other girl was younger, with rounded cheeks and a pretty smile. She responded innocently to my answering smiles and friendly questions. We were getting on quite nicely when Emerson burst into the room.

"Matters have become a trifle tense," he announced. "The king has sent a whole bloody troop to fetch us and they won't take no for an answer. Daoud is itching to fight them off, but—"

"No, no, that would be premature." I swung my feet onto the floor and stood up. "I am coming with you."

"I had intended to tell him you were ill. It may come in useful if we need to postpone the ceremony."

"I can always have a relapse." I nodded graciously at the handmaidens, who had retreated behind the bed and were desperately trying to adjust their veils. "Here is a little present, maidens, to show my gratitude."

The present was jewelry, which always goes over well with young ladies. Since I had not brought any jewels of importance, I had been forced to rob Daria. The earrings were large and gaudy. They were not a pair; one had long dangles of gold beads, the other sparkling red stones—probably crystal rather than rubies, but since the people of the Holy Mountain knew nothing of the art of cutting stones, they made a good impression. I handed one to each. The pretty child snatched hers with a murmur of thanks. The other girl inspected the ear-wire and said, "Where is the other one?"

As I had suspected, she was greedy and perhaps venal. Excellent, I thought. "I will give it when you come next," I said. "And more, much more, if you bring my daughter the High Priestess to visit me."

I had intended to work up to the suggestion more subtly, but Emerson hadn't given me time. The girls glided out without replying.

The king had sent Amenislo and a dozen guards, commanded by the rude young officer. I was beginning to feel quite sorry for the poor count. Wasn't there anyone else who could speak English well enough to interpret? A good many of the younger nobles, including Tarek, had learned the language from Nefret's father. Were they all dead, or exiled with their king?

The count was so relieved when I announced we would come at once he collapsed like a deflating balloon and with the same sort of dying whistle. I delayed only long enough to take Selim aside for a brief whispered conversation.

"What was that all about?" Emerson inquired as we were led along the corridors.

"I will tell you when we are not likely to be overheard." I glanced at Amenislo, who had edged up to me. He seemed to have something on his mind. "Yes?" I inquired politely.

"The woman disappeared," Amenislo whispered. "From

the guarded rooms of the High Priestess. How? Was it magic?"

I smiled enigmatically. "Guards do not impede us, Amenislo. Does His Majesty not know that?"

The count wiped the sweat from his face. "The king says do not speak of this. The people must not know."

"Not much chance of that," said Emerson, who had listened with interest. "A good many people already know, and they won't be able to resist spreading the story."

"And it will be embellished as it spreads," I agreed. "Did we, perhaps, render the girl invisible? Or supply her with wings?"

"Wings?" Amenislo gasped. He flapped his arms. "She flew to the sky, to the god?"

"Oh, do go away, Amenislo," I said impatiently.

The count fell back a few steps. I heard him whispering to one of the guards.

"Well done, Peabody," said Emerson.

"Matters are developing quite nicely," I agreed. "This is going to be a busy day, Emerson. I have just had another idea."

"My blood runs cold," said Emerson, grinning.

Once again we found ourselves alone with his illegitimate majesty, as Emerson termed him, and this time he had thoroughly lost his temper. He was stamping up and down the room, brandishing a sword, and he began shouting at us as soon as the entourage had been dismissed.

"What seems to be the trouble?" Emerson inquired interestedly.

"He is in such a temper I didn't understand everything," I replied. "But I believe he is demanding to know what we have done with the servant girl—I presume he means Daria—and Ramses. He appears to be threatening us with a number of unpleasant things if we don't tell him where they have got to."

"Tell him they flew away," Emerson suggested.

This reply only aroused Zekare to greater fury. "I didn't suppose he would believe it," I remarked, as the king advanced on Emerson. His weapon was like that of Merasen, of steel instead of iron, with a handsomely decorated hilt. It appeared to be very sharp. Emerson, of course, stood his ground, even when the naked blade was only an inch from his chest. I raised my parasol.

"Back off, Peabody," said Emerson out of the corner of his mouth. "I would as soon be run through as die of humiliation."

"Now, now, keep calm and don't move. Nobody is going to run anybody through."

As I had expected, Zekare had no intention of killing the goose that might still be persuaded to lay golden eggs. Slowly he lowered his blade. "You lie," he growled.

"Not lie," I said quickly. "We have not enough words. You have not enough words. Your son—Amenislo—they have the words. Bring them to talk for us."

The excuse obviously made sense to him, but after thinking it over, he shook his head. "Not Merasen. Not Amenislo."

Ha, I thought. He doesn't trust his son and he has doubts about the count. "Who?" I asked. "Who knows the words?"

I didn't want to propose the obvious candidate myself—men always prefer to believe they think of things themselves—so I waited with an expression of innocent curiosity while the king wrestled with the problem. Finally he shoved his sword back into the scabbard and turned to me.

"We will go to her. You and I."

"Now?" I had been holding my breath. The word came out in a gasp.

"At the fourth hour. Be ready."

He walked out of the room, leaving us standing there. Emerson said softly, "I must admit, Peabody, you are in top form today. That was bloody brilliant. He meant Nefret, didn't he?"

"Almost certainly. Unless," I added, "there is yet another European here. One of the ladies."

"Who speaks Meroitic?"

"It was just one of my little jokes, Emerson. Let us go back to our rooms. We have quite a lot to do today."

It was still early, but Daoud had persuaded his admirer to bring a tray of food. She stood watching with a look of idiotic adoration while he ate. Selim had been busy with the task I had set him. He brought the large camera case into my room and showed me. It had been specially designed to hold not only the camera but the folding tripod and a quantity of plates. He had managed to cram the entire bundle into it, even the little shoes. Like the other garments, they were clothes Daria had borrowed from Nefret.

"Well done," I said. "I see you have tied it securely. All we need do is get close enough to toss the bundle into the house without being observed. I have an idea about that . . ."

Selim grinned. "I thought you would, Sitt. When shall we go?"

"As soon as Daoud has finished eating. We may as well have a bite ourselves. Now that I think about it, I didn't have breakfast."

While we ate, I explained my strategy to the others. Selim would carry the camera and tripod and appear to be taking photographs, as he had done before. Daoud would accompany him, carrying the camera case. Emerson and I would point out objects of interest and appear to be giving instructions.

"People will follow us and watch," Selim objected. "Can we get close enough to act without being seen?"

"Emerson and I will provide a distraction," I explained.

Emerson gave me a very old-fashioned look but did not reply. He was in no position to be critical, and he knew it. So far he had not come up with a single useful idea.

## From Letter Collection C

I haven't been able to write much lately. They keep after me all the time. I spend hours with Amase the High Priest. He drones on about the glories of the goddess and her divine son Har, who is the same as Horus of the Egyptians, and coaches me in the words of the ritual, over and over and over till I fall into a sort of stupor. Sometimes there's another priest with him, who just sits and stares at me and never says a word. Poor old Amase is harmless enough, but I don't like that other man.

The handmaidens dress me and paint my face as if I were a doll and ask me questions. They are full of curiosity about the outside world. I can see they don't believe all I tell them. Machines that move faster than a camel can run, wires that carry words great distances, clothing spun by worms! They loved that story. They are like magpies, chattering and prying, pulling out the clothes from my cases (there were a few bits of silken underwear, which prompted the silkworm story) and playing with the cosmetics. Everything I could use as a tool or a weapon had already been taken away. There wasn't a scalpel or a probe left in my medical bag. Needless to say, my knife and the one I lent Daria are gone too.

And Daria is gone. It was Ramses who came for her, it must have been, she couldn't have got out any other way. I should have expected it, after Aunt Amelia asked me to put a light in the window, but when they told me this morning she had disappeared, I felt as if I had been stabbed to the heart. I thought that if he did risk that awful climb he would do it for me. She means nothing to him. She had no right to leave me alone.

I'm not being fair, am I, Lia? It's hard to be fair when you are afraid. I felt so much better yesterday, after I had seen Aunt Amelia. Until this morning.

I mustn't give up. She wouldn't. She'll find a way, she and the Professor and dear Daoud and Selim. And Ramses.

Why did he take Daria?

⁘

"**I** am becoming bloody tired of this bloody escort," said Emerson. "I keep stepping on their heels."

"Stop here," I ordered. "The gates of the cemetery are exceedingly picturesque, Selim, don't you think?"

"Yes, Sitt," said Selim, aiming the camera. I wondered if there was a plate in it.

"Just a minute. Emerson and I will pose between the pylons."

We repeated this same maneuver several times, going up staircases and onto private terraces, where we stood grinning and pointing as people do when they are being photographed. Emerson made a point of stopping and chatting—gesturing and smiling, rather—with all the guards we encountered.

"Merasen's house again?" Emerson inquired between his rows of teeth.

"Our little foray will distract the spectators, to say nothing of the guards, while Selim and Daoud carry out their instructions, and we will have another little chat with Captain Moroney. We ought to be able to make use of him some way or other."

"Hmph," said Emerson.

We strolled along the road, looking round like innocent sightseers and waving at passersby. Some of them flapped their arms back at us, and I heard the word "fly" repeated more than once. I deduced that the news of Daria's mysterious disappearance was already known. It is really astonishing that people prefer to believe the impossible and fabulous instead of employing common sense.

At a given signal Emerson and I whirled about, as smartly as soldiers, and trotted back the way we had come.

One would have supposed our guards would have got accustomed to this sort of thing by now, but they were very slovenly, uttering startled exclamations and jostling one another before they got themselves sorted out. I was pleased to observe that all of them followed us, leaving Selim and Daoud to stroll on with the camera.

"Discipline is very poor," I panted.

"Save your breath," Emerson advised. He caught me round the waist and broke into a run.

Since our first visit Merasen had increased the number of his guards. Emerson's cheery greetings had no effect on this lot; he had to push two of them out of the way. The reception room was unoccupied when we entered it. Emerson hastened at once to the doorway of the room I had identified as Merasen's bedchamber and pulled the hanging aside.

We had caught him, if not in flagrante, in a state close to it. He was on his feet when we entered, trying to wrap some sort of garment about him. The two young women could not decide whether to burrow into the tumbled bedclothes or make a run for it. They settled on screaming.

"My profound apologies," Emerson exclaimed. "We were looking for our friend Captain Moroney."

"He is not here." Merasen sounded as if he were choking. He managed to fasten the skirt round his waist.

"So I see," said Emerson. "Shall we retire to the reception room and allow the ladies to—er—in private?"

He bestowed his most winning smile upon those young persons, who immediately stopped screaming and studied his stalwart form with interest.

After taking in the scene in one quick comprehensive glance I had politely turned my back and was pretending to examine the pretty painted reliefs on the nearest column when Merasen followed Emerson out of his room.

"You go too far." Merasen's voice was a full octave higher than usual. "I could have you killed for this."

"I did apologize," Emerson said self-righteously.

We were wasting time, so I thought it best to intervene. "Your threats are idle, Merasen, and you know it. If you still want those weapons, you had better cooperate with us. Where is Captain Moroney?"

"In a place where you will never find him." The angry color began to fade from Merasen's face. "I treated him well, I offered him gold to bring me what I wanted, but he was too quick to agree. I did not trust him to come back, and I do not need him now. You will come back, with the guns, because she will stay with me until you do."

"Ah," said Emerson. "And afterward? Will she be free to go with us?"

"She must do as she likes. Perhaps—who knows?—she will want to stay—with me."

Emerson's hands clenched into fists. It was all I could do not to slap the smile off the boy's face, but I contained my wrath and stepped on Emerson's foot as a gentle reminder that he should do the same. It was useless trying to negotiate with Merasen. He had no intention of allowing Nefret to leave the Holy City. If he could not persuade her—and he was vain enough to harbor that delusion—he would employ other means.

"Let us talk about the weapons, then," I said. "How soon can we leave?"

"As soon as you have played your part in the ceremony. Your son must be there too. Send for him."

"How?" I asked.

Merasen made it clear that that was our problem and that it must be solved before the ceremony took place. On our way out Emerson looked into the sleeping chamber and said good-bye to the ladies. A duet of giggles answered him.

"That was unnecessary and rather rude," I said.

"I enjoy stirring the little weasel up," said Emerson. "A pretty proposition, was it not? Does he really suppose we are dim-witted enough to believe he will let us go after he's got his bloody guns?"

"Like most venal persons he believes what he wants to believe," I said thoughtfully. "Emerson—what if his talk about the weapons is only a blind? It would take us weeks to go and return with them. I think he means to act sooner, with or without his father's knowledge. He was very insistent that we all be present at the ceremony."

"Hmph." Emerson stroked his beautifully shaven chin. "Perhaps they mean to assassinate us after we have done the job for them."

"Goodness only knows. I will have to think about it. And about poor Captain Moroney. Merasen must have clapped him into a dungeon cell. I expect he is frightfully uncomfortable."

"Serves him right," snapped Emerson. "He is the least of my concerns at this moment. Why didn't you ask Merasen about the other white man?"

"Because he would have looked me straight in the eye and lied. Ah—there are Selim and Daoud. They look pleased with themselves."

We met at the foot of the staircase. "I have taken many excellent photographs," Selim announced. "Shall I put the camera in its box now?"

The box was empty. "No one saw you?" I spoke in a low voice to Daoud.

"No, Sitt. Those who did not go with you were having their pictures taken by Selim. He made them stand with their backs to the house."

It was hard to turn *my* back on the house, hard to think that Ramses was so close and yet so unreachable. I hoped—I sincerely hoped—that Daria was safe with him.

"We had better hurry," I said. "It is almost time for our meeting with the king."

"How do you know?"

"My watch, of course. I have kept it tucked away from dust and sand and remembered to wind it every day." I took it from my pocket. "Half past three."

"Yes, but you don't know that his fourth hour is the

same as four P.M." Emerson's face took on an abstracted expression. "I wonder how they do measure time. Most people without mechanical means count the hours from sunrise, and their hours are not sixty minutes long. The Egyptians—"

His steps had slowed as he lost himself in scholarly speculation. I tugged at him to keep him moving and gave him a little poke to get him back on track.

"Hurry, my dear. I am breathless with anticipation and suspense."

His Majesty's fourth hour was not four P.M. That hour came and went. The shadows lengthened and faded into the dusk. Anticipation had given way to doubt and then to despair before I heard at last the sounds I had been waiting for. I sprang to my feet as the curtain was swept aside by two of the inevitable, and in this case numerous, guards. They spread out across the chamber, peering into corners and looking into the adjoining rooms. Not until their commander had announced that the coast was clear (I translate idiomatically) did the king enter. Instead of sending for us, he had come in person—and he had brought her with him. She was veiled from head to foot and attended by two of the handmaidens, but I knew her, and so did Emerson. He sprang forward, shoving the king aside, and caught her in a bruising embrace.

"You will smother her, Emerson," I said, controlling my own emotion. "Nefret, my dear, will you unveil, if that is permitted?"

"Oh, sorry," muttered Emerson. He loosened his grasp and with his own hands put the veils aside—making quite a tangle of them, I might add. When he saw her face smiling up at him he embraced her again.

The king watched with folded arms. "She is dear to you," he said softly.

It was irrelevant and self-evident, so I did not waste time responding. "Nefret," I said urgently. "You have been brought here to translate for His Majesty. Try, if you can, to interpolate questions and answers to *my* questions without his noticing. Emerson, do stop squeezing the breath out of her."

"No, Professor, don't stop, I feel fully alive for the first time in . . . how many days has it been? I've lost track."

Zekare had listened with mounting suspicion to the exchange. He said something to Nefret that wiped the smile of happiness from her face. "He says we must not talk until he gives permission."

A brusque gesture dismissed the guards, and another indicated that Selim and Daoud should also leave the room. Nefret insisted upon embracing them both before they did. That left only the handmaidens, the king, and ourselves.

"We may as well sit down and be comfortable," I said. "Emerson, offer His Majesty a cup of wine."

His Majesty refused the wine. "Suspicious bastard, isn't he?" said Emerson, drinking the wine himself.

"He is taking something of a chance by letting us talk with Nefret." I accepted the cup he gave me and sipped it genteelly. "It is an indication, if one were needed, that there are few he can trust, including his own—"

The king interrupted with a long speech, to which Nefret listened attentively. She had settled onto a pile of cushions, with the handmaidens standing behind her like pillars of salt.

"He wants to know what happened to Daria, whether it was Ramses who got her away, how he accomplished it, and where he has taken her." Nefret added vehemently, "I too want to know. I couldn't believe it this morning when they told me she was not in her room."

"We took her away by means of our magic, of course," I replied. I used the Meroitic word for magic. The king snarled, and Nefret smiled faintly.

I was convinced the king understood more English than he had let on, so I had to choose my words with care. It made the ensuing conversation challenging, but if I may say so, I thrive on challenges. Naturally I denied any knowledge of Ramses's whereabouts or activities. He was, I explained, a venturesome lad who did not like being cooped up. This disingenuous statement made the king's eyes bulge with fury, so I went on, "It was against my wishes that he acted as he did, but alas, I have never been able to control him." I added, for Nefret's benefit, "A subsequent repetition would be inexpedient because of your sequestration, but 'my brain it teems with endless schemes.'"

I flatter myself that I got more out of His Majesty than he got out of me. We had decided not to raise the question of Merasen's underhanded dealings, since we were not certain what he had in mind and how it might be turned to our benefit. "When your enemies fight, they may leave one less enemy for you," as Emerson put it. (He claimed it was not an aphorism, since he had made it up.) My question about Captain Moroney elicited only a shrug of indifference. He was a person of no consequence and we could have him with us, to deal with as we liked—after the ceremony.

"What are we expected to do?" Emerson inquired. I had been about to ask that myself.

"She will tell you what to say." The king indicated Nefret. "After I have told her. You will stand at my side, at the Window of Appearance, before the people, and say that the gods have chosen me to be king and that any who fight against me will be visited by the wrath of the gods. I will honor you, with high office and collars of gold, as loyal officials are honored. Chosen ones will enter the shrine and see her bring the goddess back to her place. The goddess will speak through her. There will be feasting and food given to the people."

"It should be quite a show," remarked Emerson, after Nefret had translated. "A pity we will miss it."

"But, Professor," Nefret began.

"*All* of us will miss it," said Emerson.

The king had one more point to make. He did not mince

words. "I know what Tarek plans. I have spies in his camp, as he has in mine. I will know if your son has joined him. I will not harm you unless you defy me, but he is a dead man if he does not give himself up."

He rose, drawing his mantle around him, and beckoned to Nefret. She repeated the words in a faint, uneven voice.

"Don't lose heart, my dear," I said. "It isn't easy to kill Ramses. Is there a way to your rooms through the temple?"

"I don't want to go with him," she whispered.

Her voice was high and soft, like that of a frightened child. His face working, Emerson put his arms around her. "Why can't she stay with us?" he demanded furiously. "I will be damned if I will let you take her away."

"Emerson, no," I said. "Resistance would be futile and you are only making it harder for her. Nefret?"

Nefret drew a long, quivering breath and moved away from Emerson. "Yes, Aunt Amelia. I'm all right now." She went on, without a change of tone, "Negative, Aunt Amelia, my recollection is faulty and every step is guarded."

"Where there's a will, there's a way," I replied. "Keep that in your recollection, my dear. Oh, I almost forgot. Ask him about the other white man. We suspect him of being the archaeologist, Mr. MacFerguson."

"What?" Nefret stared in astonishment. "Mr. MacFerguson, here?"

"Ask him."

The royal reply required no translation. "You know him. He is your friend."


## From Manuscript H

The sun was high and bright when Ramses woke. His watch had stopped. He had forgotten to wind it last night.

He got carefully to his feet, so as not to disturb the sleeping girl, and tucked the robe that had been their only

covering back around her. He stayed longer than he needed
to in the dead garden, looking aimlessly for a possible
source of food or drink. There were birds' nests in the
withered vines. He didn't bother looking for eggs. They
weren't that desperate yet.

When he went back she was awake. Her eyes moved
slowly over him, from bare head to bare feet. She pushed
the covering aside and stretched like a cat, her muscles
moving smoothly under her pale skin. His response was instantaneous and uncontrollable; when she saw, she smiled
and held up her arms.

"Later," Ramses said. His throat was dry.

"With you it is always 'later.'"

"Not always."

"No." She drew the vowel out into a long sigh and
closed her eyes. "Was it pleasing to you? Do you still
want me?"

He sat down beside her and took her hands. "You know
the answer to that."

She opened her eyes. They were bright with laughter.
"Yes, I know."

He raised her hands to his lips, laughing with her, wondering what right he had to feel so happy. "You must have
something to drink, Daria. There is a little water left. And I
want to look at your feet."

He spared a few precious drops of water to wash the en-
crusted dirt and blood away. One of the cuts was deep. She
must have stepped on a sharp stone. "I should have carried
you," he said remorsefully, cradling the little feet in his
hands. "Or not bullied you into coming with me. I didn't
really give you a chance to refuse, did I?"

"I would rather be here than there."

"So would I rather you were. Now, none of that! Those
cuts need to be disinfected. I only hope I haven't left them
too long. Thank God for Mother and her brandy."

And the shirt. He tore it up to make bandages. They both
had a sip of water and a few dates, and then Ramses

reached for his trousers. "I want to have a look outside," he explained.

"And you feel powerless without clothes? It is quite otherwise."

"It's odd, but one does, you know," Ramses said, acknowledging the tribute with a self-conscious smile. "Except in certain circumstances. It's a civilized weakness, I suppose. I won't be long."

Carrying the binoculars, he felt his way along the turns of the dark passage, out into the open arcade, and came to a sudden stop, his heart hammering. The object lay on the floor, just inside the door. It looked like a dead animal, dark and huddled.

The slant of the rays of sunlight outside told him it was late afternoon. He had slept the whole day away. He couldn't believe his own carelessness. He ought to have been alert and listening, ready to retreat into the underground passages at the first sound of someone approaching. Someone had got this far, at any rate. The object hadn't been there the night before, they would have stumbled over it. And it wasn't an animal.

When he investigated the contents of the bundle he felt even guiltier. Everything he had asked for was there. How they had got the things to him so quickly, without being detected, he couldn't imagine. Standing behind one of the pillars, he moved the binoculars in a slow sweep of the valley, from one end of the road to the other. The only signs of unusual activity were around the small Isis temple, which was now surrounded by troops. Daria's absence must have been discovered early that morning, if not before, so why weren't they searching for her?

He tied the parcel again and carried it to Daria. They were finally able to drink their fill and eat hungrily of the bread and cheese. Ramses had a feeling he wouldn't relish dates for a long time to come. She was like a different woman, her eyes tender and her laughter gently teasing.

They did not speak of her past or their future, only of the moment. The light began to fade and the stars to come out, and they made love as if it were the first and the last time. When he woke her after a short sleep she reached for him and then drew away.

"We must go now?"

"Soon."

Silently she began to dress, pulling the trousers on under her sleeveless robe. He stopped her when she would have put on the heavy stockings and bathed her feet again before he bandaged the deepest cuts. Neither of them spoke until she stood up and stamped her feet into the shoes.

"Do they hurt still?" he asked. "Can you walk?"

"I can walk." Her voice was dry and hard. "Are you ready?"

"Almost." Carefully he gathered the scattered evidences of their presence and tied them into a single bundle. The mice would take care of the food crumbs. He put on the hooded robe and helped her into the lighter, long-sleeved mantle his mother had provided. His hands lingered on her shoulders, but when she moved away from him he knew she was right to do so. They had had their time, and it was over.

"Ready," he said. "Take my hand."

He made the climb as easy as he could for her, roping her up the steeper slopes and letting her rest as often as he could. Her mute, hard-breathing endurance reminded him (why?) of the time he had climbed up a cliff face to help Nefret down when she hit a bad stretch. She had cursed him royally for taking hold of her.

He let out a soft laugh and tightened his grasp on Daria's yielding waist. "You are thinking of her," she said.

"I am thinking of how to go from here. It's not far now," he added encouragingly.

When he lifted her onto the ledge her knees buckled and she would have fallen if he had not kept hold of her. "Sit down and rest. It's safe, there's plenty of room."

Not as much as he had thought. They were waiting for him, under the shelter of the low overhang.

"It's all right, they are friends," he said quickly. He had recognized Harsetef's tall, lithe form. The other man was even taller. He came toward Ramses, walking unconcernedly along the very rim of the ledge and gripped Ramses's arms in a soldier's greeting.

"Welcome," he said in a voice deepened by emotion. "Thrice welcome! You were a boy when you left me, and now you are a man."

He was dressed like a common soldier, with no sign of rank, but Ramses knew him. "Tarek! You shouldn't have come here, it's too risky."

"I do not ask my men to take risks I will not take. You have taken even greater risks to bring her to me." He dropped to one knee before Daria's crouching form. "My little sister, whom I loved. You have come back to me."

"It isn't Nefret," Ramses said, more loudly than he had intended. Tarek must be blind or bewitched to have mistaken the two, even in the semidarkness. And he was still talking like a character in one of the old-fashioned romantic novels to which he had become addicted.

Tarek put out a hand and lifted a strand of dark hair. "No," he said.

"I couldn't get to Nefret," Ramses said. The pain in that single word put him on the defensive. "It was impossible, she is too closely guarded. This is Daria. She—"

"I know." Tarek got to his feet. "I know all that has befallen you." He sighed heavily. "I should have been prepared. Only a god or a great magician could steal the High Priestess away. Let us go now, we can talk another time. It will be easier from here, lady, with three of us to help you." He raised Daria to her feet.

Gallant as ever, Ramses thought. "Two of you," he corrected.

Daria didn't look at him. She had expected this. Tarek wasn't surprised either. A gleam of white teeth broke the darkness of his face. "So, you would return to the city? What good could you do?"

"My mother and father are still prisoners, and so is Nefret. There is to be a ceremony in the Great Temple in four days. They want my father to proclaim his allegiance to the usurper."

"The Father of Curses will never do that," Tarek said calmly. "Have no fear, my young friend. We will free them. I have planned my attack to take place that night."

The faint starlight outlined Tarek's strong body and the proud tilt of his head. He had filled out in the last ten years, but he was still slim and fit.

"Listen to me," Ramses said urgently. "If you attack, many will die, including my mother and father. The usurper will kill them rather than let them be taken by you. There is another way, a better way."

Tarek held out his hand. He was still smiling. "We cannot talk here. Once we are over the pass and in my own country, we will plan together. Then, if you wish to return, I will not stop you."

The suggestion made excellent sense. He knew very little about the lay of the land and the strength of Tarek's forces, his defensive strategy, his methods of gathering information—a dozen other things that would prove useful. He couldn't imagine why he was hesitating.

"Come," Tarek said. "It will not take us long, I promise."

That's why I'm hesitating, Ramses thought. He's talking to me as if I were still ten years old. Maybe I deserve it. This is no time for childish sulks.

"You are right," he said. "Let's go."

This part of the ascent was even worse than the other—straight up the sheerest part of the cliffs, with only the faintest traces of what might be called a path. Harsetef had brought another rope, and in some places Ramses stamped on his pride and made use of it. He didn't argue when Tarek took charge of Daria, fastening Ramses's rope carefully round her slim waist, holding it taut as she climbed, murmuring words of encouragement and praise. The sun was rising when they reached the top of the ridge and were hailed by three of Tarek's scouts.

"Rest awhile," Tarek said. "The descent is easier."

Ramses would have liked nothing better than to collapse onto the rocky ground, but a combination of pride and curiosity kept him on his feet. The view was certainly spectacular. The spurs of rock that formed the pass were lower than the enclosing cliffs; the heights rose up ahead and on either side, shaped into fantastic towers. Other outcroppings jutted out around the circumference of the northern valley, like teeth in a gaping mouth. The air was clear that morning; in the distance, perched on the hillside, he saw several large structures that might have been temples or houses. Former country houses, perhaps? The floor of the valley was a pleasant, pastoral place, a green cup in the harsh grasp of the hills. He could even make out the heavy gate that blocked one of the side wadis—a fortress into which the defenders could retreat if necessary.

It was no wonder the usurper had been unable to get through the pass. Where it started to widen out, on Tarek's side, it was bounded by stone walls, machicolated like those of a medieval castle. Any attackers who managed to get over the boulders would be funneled into the space between the walls, helpless against the bows and spears of the defenders, and if they tried to scale the heights on either side they would be swept away by a rain of stones and arrows.

Tarek wasn't looking at the pass. Feet braced and shoulders thrown back, he watched the swollen red orb of the sun lift over the eastern mountain. "The god comes again," he said softly.

Which god? Ramses wondered. Khepri, the beetle, the rising sun, Atum, the setting son, Re, Harakhte of the Horizon?

As if he had read Ramses's thoughts, Tarek said, "He has many names but he is One."

Ramses knew his father would have leaped on this intriguing theological development. Was Tarek becoming a monotheist? At the moment he didn't give a damn.

By the time they reached the roughly built barracks that housed his garrison, Tarek was carrying Daria, and Ramses was wearily attempting to carry on a conversation with Harsetef. Did the Father of Curses remember him? Did he know that he, Harsetef, had been faithful to his trust? He had three sons now, the oldest ten years of age and already a good bowman. Had Ramses a wife? Children? He could see he went down in Harsetef's estimation when he admitted he wasn't even married and that—to the best of his knowledge—he was childless.

They were given the commander's room and left tactfully alone after they had been supplied with food and water, a change of clothing, and, at Ramses's request, a razor. The people of the Holy Mountain were clean-shaven, and his own beard was at its most unsightly. If, as he suspected, he was about to meet the leading citizens of Tarek's group, he had to make a good impression. Between the bronze razor and the bronze mirror he wasn't sure he had succeeded, but he did the best he could.

Daria had fallen asleep instantly. She didn't stir when Ramses took off her shoes and bathed her feet.

He forced himself to take the rest he needed, though it was hard to clear his mind of its multitude of worries. It was Tarek himself who wakened him, with courteous apologies. While he dressed in a fresh kilt and sandals, Tarek stood looking down at the sleeping girl.

"She is brave and very beautiful," he said softly. "You are fortunate to have her."

"I don't . . ." Ramses stopped himself. He did, didn't he? From Tarek's point of view, the arrangement was entirely reasonable. "How did you hear of her?"

"Two of the men in the troop who brought you from the first oasis are loyal to me." Tarek held the curtain aside and gestured him out. "There are others, who stayed at their posts to work from within."

"I must hear about them."

"And about other things."

The room they entered served as a sort of office, with several tables and chairs covered with papers. There were three other men present, whom Tarek introduced by name and title. The Keeper of the Secrets of His Majesty was a hard-faced man of late middle age, with deep-set eyes like dull pebbles. Whatever the title had implied in ancient Egypt, this fellow looked like a spy. The others were Tarek's vizier and the Commander of All the Armies of His Majesty. A resounding name for a force that probably didn't number over a thousand men.

"Tell me first," said Tarek, "of my friends. That the Father of Curses and the Sitt Hakim are well I know, for so it was reported to me. And you are still the only son."

"Yes," Ramses said, smiling a little as he remembered a candid statement of his mother's which he had happened to overhear. "One is quite enough." "But I have a friend who is close as a brother and dear as a son to them. He is an Egyptian, about to be married to my cousin."

Tarek wanted to know why Ramses's foster brother had not come with them. He seemed to be enjoying the news as much as any gossipy old lady, so Ramses obliged, describing their relationship with Selim and Daoud and others of the family. When he spoke of Abdullah's death, Tarek's eyes flashed.

"He placed himself in the path of death to save the lady! I did not know of it. He will be honored in the hereafter as a hero, he will sit in the bark of the god."

"He'd like that," Ramses said. "I hope so, Tarek."

"And my little sister? She is still a maiden?"

"She's not married," Ramses said after a somewhat confused pause.

"Why not?"

His voice was quick and hard, and the expression in his dark eyes made Ramses strangely uneasy. "In our world women do not marry unless they choose to. She has not chosen to."

Tarek's eyes fell. "She is as beautiful as ever, I am told," he said, as if to himself. "Many men must have wanted her. Perhaps she has set her heart on one she cannot have."

Ramses had no intention of going down that road. "She hasn't opened her heart to me," he said curtly. "Tell me of yourself, Tarek. Your wife—uh—wives. Your sons."

"I have no son. No true son. My queen—Mentarit—died giving birth to the last, stillborn like the others."

Ramses expressed sympathy, though the news did not surprise him. For generations the rulers of the Holy City, like the Egyptian pharaohs, had married sisters and half sisters. What the royal house needed was an infusion of new blood.

Tarek gave Ramses a quick, businesslike summary of his resources and their disposition, with occasional contributions from his staff. "Our plan is to come through the pass on the night of the ceremony, when all the people will be gathered together. The rekkit will rise and so will many others. They will attack from the rear and we will crush the usurper's troops like grain between two stones."

"It might succeed," Ramses said slowly. "But at the cost of how many lives?"

The hard-faced spymaster cleared his throat. "Men die in a war. Has the Brother of Demons a better plan?"

"No, but the Father of Curses will," Ramses said. "Let me go back to him and the Sitt Hakim with what I have learned from you. You must delay the attack until after the ceremony. They have thought of a plan."

Not just one—but he didn't want even to consider some of his mother's more imaginative ideas, much less explain them to his skeptical audience. The invocation of the dread Father of Curses kept them silent, but Ramses could see they were not convinced.

After a long pause, Tarek nodded and reached for a

piece of paper. "We will wait until tomorrow to learn the word of the Father of Curses. I will write the names of those who are loyal to me in the city and where to find them. Memorize them and destroy the paper."

Ramses stared. It *was* paper, ordinary writing paper—and Tarek held a pencil—an ordinary pencil. "Where did you get this?" he demanded.

"He brought it. He brought many useful things, medicines for fever and wounds, seeds of new kinds of grain, books and writing tools, swords harder than iron—"

"Who?"

Tarek's eyes widened in surprise. "Who else could it be? Your friend."

⁝

# Twelve

As soon as Zekare and his entourage left, Emerson charged out into the garden. He returned empty-handed. His failure to find a message from Ramses did not improve his temper, which was already explosive. He had been deeply distressed by our parting with Nefret. I too had found it difficult to let her go; she was acting very strangely, and the last look she gave me was one of pitiful appeal. What had they done to reduce a girl of her spirit to such a state?

"I will take a little stroll in the garden with you," I offered. "It must be lovely in the moonlight."

"Lovely, bah," said Emerson, sitting down with a thump. "The only thing about the garden that interests me is that which was not there. What's this?"

It was, self-evidently, a tray of food. Daoud's admirer had taken to producing one every hour or so. This one included fruit, bread, and a platter of some variety of small bird, plump and nicely browned. They looked quite tasty, but I can never bring myself to eat little birds.

Emerson also declined. Instead he fetched the bottle of whiskey.

"We will have to start rationing ourselves," I said, for the bottle was half empty.

"Perhaps our 'friend' will be able to supply us with

whiskey as well as coffee," said Emerson. "He seems to like his little comforts."

"It may have been Captain Moroney who brought the coffee, though I would not have supposed him to be such a sybarite. Never mind that now, Emerson, we must compose a message for Ramses. It is a pity we were unable to arrange a safer and more convenient method of communication. Bring the lamp, will you, please?"

I took out paper and pencil and wrote a lucid summary of recent events. "We need to tell him more than that, though," I said, frowning. "Confound it, this really is inconvenient, there is so much to discuss and so much we need to know. Hand me another sheet of paper, if you please."

"Don't tell me you are going to make one of your infernal little lists," Emerson said.

Daoud wiped his fingers daintily on a piece of cloth and sat down next to me. He was a great believer in my little lists.

"Not one of the usual sort," I replied with a forgiving smile at my spouse. "A plan of our campaign, rather. Let us first set down the difficulties we face, and suggestions for dealing with them."

"Hmph," said Emerson. "It will be a lengthy list, my dear."

"Not really," I said, writing busily, "the primary difficulty is of course Nefret. I don't like the way she is behaving. We must get her away from there, but the two most direct ways of reaching her, through the tunnels behind the temple or straight up the cliff to her window are, in my opinion, virtually impossible."

"I would eliminate the word virtually," Emerson muttered.

"In theory nothing is impossible," I explained. "But in this case, I am inclined to agree and I will inform Ramses of our opinion. Whether it will stop him from doing something foolhardy I do not know, but one can only hope for the best. I doubt the handmaidens will be of use. Even if I could corrupt one, there are too many of them."

"Why don't you leave off telling us what we cannot do?" Emerson grumbled. "Say something positive!"

"I put forth the alternatives in the hope that one of you might point out a possibility I had overlooked," I said patiently. "Since you cannot, I will proceed. Supposing I could persuade the king to bring her here again to interpret for him. Is there a chance we could substitute someone else for her?"

"Who, Daoud?" Emerson demanded. He was losing his temper again. Selim chuckled and Daoud looked puzzled.

"I do not think so, Sitt Hakim," he said, scratching his beard.

"I was thinking of myself."

"Oh, for God's sake, Peabody, control your rampageous imagination," Emerson shouted. "Aside from the fact that they wouldn't leave you two alone long enough to make the change of clothing, that would be trading one hostage for another. Is that the best you can do? And don't write it down! Ramses will think you have lost your mind."

"We can fight the guards and kill them all or tie them up and run away with Nur Misur," Daoud suggested.

"I thought of that too," I said. "There are four of us, all formidable fighters. But the odds would be heavily against us. In my opinion it should be our last, desperate recourse."

Emerson rolled his eyes heavenward but refrained from comment, and I went on. "Our best opportunity will come on the night of the ceremony. Nefret will then be in the sanctuary of the temple and I expect we will be among those invited to see her bring the goddess back to her shrine. Can't we think of some way of disrupting the performance, so that people are running around and perhaps falling down a great deal? In the confusion we could cut Nefret out of the crowd, disguise her by—er—in some way, and make our break for it."

"I could shoot the pistol," Daoud offered.

Emerson fingered the cleft in his chin. "It might work," he said thoughtfully, "if we were all armed. I wonder where Merasen stowed the weapons he took from us? Curse it, I ought to have searched his house when I had the chance."

"I didn't think of it either," I admitted. "Perhaps we should pay him another visit. One small problem with that scheme, however, is the order of the ceremony. If we are expected to make our public statement before Nefret summons the goddess, a great deal of damage will already have been done."

"Perhaps we can persuade his infernal majesty to change the order of the performance," Emerson said. "Or—here's an idea—we use the weapons when we stand beside the king at the Window of Appearance."

"Shoot him, you mean? We can't do that, Emerson, not in cold blood."

"I suppose not," Emerson admitted. "A pity. It would be a superb stroke. I denounce the bastard in ringing tones, and he drops dead at my feet, struck down by the god."

"Control your rampageous imagination, my dear," I said with a sympathetic smile. "If we can't come up with anything better, we will have to act during the ceremony, though not by means of assassination. That is not worthy of us. There. I have put down several of our schemes, and we can only hope to receive a response."

I gave Emerson the message. When he returned from the garden I inquired, "What time is it?"

"I have no idea," said Emerson. "What does that have to do with anything?"

"I am about to have another attack," I said, glancing at Daoud's lady friend, who was watching him shyly from behind a pillar. "A more severe attack."

Dropping the pencil, I toppled over and began twitching.

"The handmaidens?" Emerson inquired.

"Demonstrate a trifle more agitation, Emerson, if you

please." I let out a resounding shriek. "The handmaidens, the king, Merasen—I want the whole city to know, tonight, that I have been poisoned or possibly seized by divine frenzy."

"Very well," said Emerson. "Here, Peabody, don't overdo it, you will dislocate something if you throw yourself around in that melodramatic fashion. Daoud, pretend to hold her down, eh?"

The king did not make an appearance, but a good many other people did. Inspired by my growing audience, I screamed and spoke in tongues (French, German, and Latin) and put on a show of struggling against the big, gentle hands of Daoud. One of the handmaidens attempted to force a dose of medicine between my lips; I recognized it by the smell as some kind of opium derivative and knocked it out of her hand. It was rather fatiguing, and I was about to go into a restful coma when Merasen turned up.

"What is wrong with her?" he demanded with a conspicuous absence of concern.

"Poisoned," Emerson shouted. "Are you the one responsible, you young villain?"

"Why would I do that?" Merasen demanded, backing away from Emerson.

I resumed thrashing about and babbling while they discussed this admittedly reasonable question. Finally Emerson got out the whiskey, and I allowed him to administer a dose as my spasms began to subside.

"I trust only our own medicine," Emerson said with a generalized glare round the room. "Get out, all of you. All of you, I said."

As the handmaidens retreated, I bethought me of Nefret. Raising my head, I cried in Meroitic, "The goddess was with me! Divine Isis has blessed me!"

I rolled my eyes back into my head and went limp. Emerson picked me up and carried me into our sleeping chamber. "What was the point of that?" he inquired sotto voce.

"I didn't want Nefret worrying about me," I muttered.

"I meant the whole bloody performance," said Emerson, dumping me somewhat unceremoniously onto the bed.

"I am supposed to be unconscious, Emerson, I cannot continue conversing with you."

"You are simply trying to avoid answering my question. No one can see or hear us."

"What about another small sip of whiskey, Emerson?"

Emerson was back sooner than I expected. He caught me investigating the contents of my medical bag.

"I am going to put these bottles and vials on the chest by the bed," I explained, suiting the action to the words. "In order to add verisimilitude to the claim that I rely on my own medications."

"How soon do you expect to be fully recovered?" Emerson asked, handing me a cup.

"I haven't quite decided. But this episode sets a useful precedent, don't you agree? I can always fall down in a fit during the ceremony."

"Oh," said Emerson, accepting—as I had hoped he would—this excuse for my performance.

I put my cup on the chest. "I am a little tired from all that thrashing about. Would you help me off with my clothes, my dear, and hand me the night robe that is on the stool?"

It wasn't on the stool. While Emerson was searching for it, I put a few drops of veronal into his whiskey. I hated to do it, but if events transpired as I hoped I did not want to risk his interfering. The dear fellow dropped off almost at once. Affectionately I contemplated his supine form. It wouldn't do him any harm to have a good night's sleep.

I had no difficulty remaining awake, though it had been a busy day. I might be mistaken (though that was unlikely); my pretense of illness might not have deceived the individual for whom it was primarily intended. I didn't expect he would turn up before midnight, supposing he came at all, but I took up my position immediately, for I leave very little to chance, and he was, to say the least, unpredictable. I had been waiting for some time before I heard the sound of soft footsteps. They would have been inaudible to a sleeper, or even to one who reclined on the bed, a few feet away. He must be barefoot—as was I. I took a firmer grip on my parasol and moved closer to the doorway. I had left a single lamp burning. In its feeble light I saw a hand pull the curtain aside.

It was at this point that I made a slight tactical error. In my excitement at having been proved right I forgot the little speech I had prepared and caught hold of the hand. This provoked him into immediate flight. I went in pursuit, naturally. He was wearing local garb, a long pale robe that flapped wildly as he ran—not toward the main entrance, but toward the doorway that led to the rock-cut chambers behind our rooms. It was at this point that I made my second error. Fearing he would elude me, for he was running quite rapidly, I hooked him round the leg with the handle of my parasol. He fell with a thud and a cry. Having overbalanced, I also fell, flat on my stomach.

I had underestimated either the dosage of the veronal or the strength of my dear Emerson's attachment to me. A series of incoherent oaths announced his arousal and his discovery of the fact that I was no longer in the sleeping chamber.

It was at this point that Emerson made his own tactical error. Plunging wildly at the doorway, he got himself tangled up in the curtains. While he was attempting to extricate himself I seized the opportunity to speak to my quarry. He had rolled over onto his back, but his attempts to rise were feeble.

"Hush!" I hissed. "Remain silent and motionless."

"My leg is broken," muttered a voice—in English.

"No, it isn't." I stood up and nudged the member in question with my foot. A faint shriek was intended to suggest that my diagnosis might have been incorrect. It failed to convince me.

By that time Selim and Daoud had rushed in, and Emerson had unwound himself. All three converged on the tableau, which was dramatically lighted by moonbeams streaming through the high windows—myself, alert and erect, parasol raised, and the recumbent form at my feet, sprawled (rather gracefully) amid the spreading folds of his robe. My captive had wisely decided to accept defeat.

"What the devil!" exclaimed Emerson. "Who . . . By Gad, it's that bastard MacFerguson!"

"The ears are certainly distinctive," I agreed.

"What's wrong with him?"

"He appears to have fainted," I said. As always, I was strictly accurate. "Appears" was the key word.

"I beg you will leave this to me, Emerson," I went on. "Go away. You and Daoud too, Selim."

"But—" said Emerson.

"You may tie his feet if you like," I conceded. "But kindly leave the interrogation to me. He is, in my opinion, more likely to respond to kindness than to intimidation."

"You and your opinions be—er—" said Emerson. "Oh, very well, Peabody, arguing with you is a waste of time. I will give you ten minutes of kindness before I begin intimidating."

Daoud tied the fellow's feet while I put a cushion under his head. At my request Emerson fetched the whiskey before retreating into our sleeping chamber. I then lit one of the oil lamps and bent over the recumbent man. His eyes were open. I held the lamp closer and peered into them.

"An excellent disguise," I said. "Especially the ears. But you were not the man we met at Gebel Barkal, were you? His eyes were dark brown and he was several inches shorter."

"It is a classic technique," said Sethos. His breath came hard, but it would have taken more than discomfort to prevent Sethos from boasting. "You had determined I was not MacFerguson, so the next time MacFerguson turned up you would take him at face value."

"Not I."

"No, not you. That was a filthy trick, Amelia, luring me out of hiding because of my tender concern for you. Are you going to expose me to Emerson?"

"Not if I can help it. He would be bent on killing you, which would be a distraction."

"And not at all useful," Sethos muttered. "We are on the same side, Amelia. I am as anxious as you to restore Tarek to the throne."

"Such altruism is unlike you," I said skeptically.

"Altruism be damned. Tarek and I got on famously. We had quite a nice little arrangement, which worked to our mutual satisfaction. This new fellow is trying to cheat me."

His indignation was so genuine it brought a smile to my lips. "So you are willing to restore the rightful king in order to promote your business affairs? I am prepared to believe that. How long have you been dealing with Tarek?"

"It would take too long to explain. If you don't want Emerson to discover my identity, you had better let me go." He felt gingerly of his left ear. "It's coming loose."

"First we must come to an agreement."

"What do you want from me?"

"Nefret. Away from the shrine and safe with Tarek."

"Hmmm." Sethos went on fiddling with his ear. "I presume it was Ramses who carried Daria off? He must have climbed the cliff, there's no other way. Just like him to try such a fool stunt."

"You wouldn't?"

"Good God, no. I have no head for heights. Anyhow, Nefret is more closely guarded. What did he do with . . . the girl?"

"He said he intended to take her to Tarek. Why do you ask?"

"Idle curiosity. Very well, supposing I can remove Nefret, which will be no small feat even for me—"

"Oh, I feel certain your ingenuity will provide a way."

"I haven't entirely wasted my time," said Sethos—the implication being that I had! "Then what?"

"Then Emerson and I appear at the ceremony, denounce the usurper and take him prisoner, and Tarek marches triumphantly into a city won over to his cause by our eloquence and Emerson's prestige."

Sethos emitted a series of sputtering noises. "The plan is subject to revision as circumstances demand," I added.

"I should think so indeed," Sethos said in broken tones.

Emerson's head appeared between the curtains. "Time's up, Amelia."

"A few more minutes, Emerson, if you please. He is cracking."

Emerson growled and withdrew.

"How did you get in here?" I asked.

"You haven't found the entrance to the underground passages? I thought surely your ingenious son—"

"Don't *do* that," I said irritably but softly. "We have no time to waste. Just answer my questions. Er—Ramses did find the entrance, but was unable to open it."

"Not surprising, since it was bolted from the other side."

I thought of several bad names to call him, but stuck doggedly to the point. "How many of the tombs have you looted?"

"One or two."

"One or two hundred, you mean. So you know your way through the tunnels?"

"Fairly well," Sethos said cautiously. "What did you have in mind?"

Emerson thrust the curtains aside. "My patience is at an end," he announced. "Has the bastard confessed?"

"The—er—gentleman has agreed to help us," I corrected. "He is going to show me the entrance to the subterranean regions and assist us in delivering Nefret. Mr. MacFerguson, one of the tunnels leads to the rooms of the High Priestess. No doubt you are familiar with that route?"

Sethos grunted. I took it for agreement. "I will ask to see Nefret again tomorrow," I went on. "And tell her that if she can elude her attendants long enough to enter the tunnel, you will be waiting for her."

"Yes, ma'am," said Sethos meekly. "And then what shall I do with her?"

"Bring her here."

"What?" The word was a duet between Sethos and Emerson.

"Not *here,* into this room," I said impatiently. "Just lead her to the part of the passageway that adjoins our rooms—first explaining to her, of course, where you are going and why. I will then take charge. Don't argue, Mr. MacFerguson. You know what will happen if you don't obey me."

"What?" Emerson inquired.

Since I couldn't think of an answer, I ignored the question. "Untie his feet, Emerson. Now, Mr. MacFerguson, lead the way."

I made Sethos show me how the catch operated; it was the same arrangement as the one in the other house. As the heavy slab slowly rose, displaying a flight of narrow stone steps, I added, "You will of course leave the bolt on that side undone."

"Of course." Sethos climbed nimbly over the edge and relit the candle he had left on the topmost step. I have seldom seen a more grotesque sight than his face, distorted by shadows. The bulbous nose was a trifle squashed.

"I don't like this," Emerson announced loudly. "How do you know he—"

"Hush, Emerson. Mr. MacFerguson, we will meet you here tomorrow night at the same time. I am sure I can trust you to keep your word."

"Indeed, indeed," croaked Sethos, gazing soulfully up at me. "Mrs. Emerson, you are the kindest and most forgiving of women. You have convinced me of the evil of my ways. From now on I am a reformed character."

I might have known he wouldn't be able to resist a final

performance. I put an end to it by lowering the slab onto his head.

Emerson refused to retire until I had explained quite a number of things. This forced me to several flights of invention, though I combined fact with fiction as much as possible.

"There wasn't time for him to explain how he found out about the Lost Oasis," I said glibly. "But as you know, we realized a number of people might have done so in a number of different ways. On his first visit he won Tarek's confidence by representing himself as a friend of ours. This time he found the usurper in control and learned that his position was no longer secure. The usurper doesn't trust him, and with good reason. He is as anxious as we to return to civilization, and he knows that his best chance of that is through Tarek. That is why I know I can depend on him to assist us."

"Well, I don't depend on him," Emerson declared. "Why don't we go after Nefret ourselves, if there is a way to her rooms from the tunnels?"

"Do you remember the route we took before, when she came to meet us for the first time?"

"It was ten years ago," Emerson protested.

"I don't remember it either. Curse it, I wish we hadn't let Ramses go off like that. He spent several days exploring those passages and he has a memory like an elephant's."

"Nur Misur cannot stay long in that dark place," Daoud said. "She will be afraid."

"She'll never make it that far," Emerson said. "MacFerguson can't possibly pull this off."

## From Manuscript H

Tarek's description of their "friend" wasn't particularly helpful, though Tarek frankly admitted that "all foreigners" except them looked alike to him. However, a nasty suspicion took root and grew when Tarek went into greater detail about their encounters. The fellow was intimately acquainted with the appearance, activities, and history of the Emerson family. He had been fascinated by the culture of the Holy City, and when he returned after his first visit, bearing wonderful gifts, Tarek had not only allowed him access to every part of the city, including the old tunnels, but had bestowed gifts upon him.

"You let him loot—I mean, take funerary equipment from the tombs?" Ramses asked incredulously.

"Only the most ancient of the tombs, which had been forgotten and neglected," Tarek said. "Gold and jewels help the living, but they are of no value to the dead. It is a man's deeds that go with him into the next world, that ensure immortality."

"No doubt," Ramses murmured. "But still—"

"He said the objects were for the Father of Curses. I had seen that they were what the Father of Curses and his lady desired. And they bought food for my people."

The modus operandi was only too familiar. Suspicion turned to certainty when Ramses asked the man's name.

"Petrie," said Tarek. "He brought me one of his books."

Daria was awake when Ramses returned, drawing a comb through the long strands of her hair. Her worried frown turned to a smile. "It needs to be washed—and so do I!—but I did not think I should do that here."

"This is only a barracks for the guard," Ramses said. "Tarek will take you to his villa, where you will have all possible comforts. He means to leave almost at once."

He sat down beside her and took her feet in his hands. "They look better. But you won't have to walk, they are arranging a litter for you."

"For me?" Her eyes narrowed. "What about you?"

"I must go back." He stilled her incipient protest with a finger to her lips, stroked her cheek and temples. "Tarek and I have worked out a plan, and—"

"You are going back for her."

"That's part of the plan, yes, if it can be done." She turned her head away from his caressing hand, and he said in surprise, "What's the matter?"

"I don't want you to leave me. What if you don't ever come back?" She slid onto his lap and wound her arms round his neck, raising a pleading face to his.

"I'll come back, I promise." He kissed her parted lips. "But I must go, darling, I need to explain the plan to my parents so that they will know when and how to act, and fill them in on the situation here. I've just learned something that worries me a great deal."

"There is something I must tell you. About Newcomb, and why I—"

"You don't have to tell me anything. It's all right."

"You don't understand! Let me go with you. I can help."

The pretty, pleading look moved him, but he felt a faint touch of irritation. "I can't, you must know that. Tarek will take care of you."

A tactful shuffle of feet outside the door interrupted him. Tarek asked for his permission, and Daria's, before he entered.

"You see?" Ramses said. "He is a courteous, honorable man. You are as safe with him as you would be with me."

Her response convinced Ramses once again that he would never understand women. A faint smile curved the lips that only a moment before had been quivering pathetically, and the look she turned on Tarek was one of cool appraisal. He smiled back at her and inclined his head in salute. He was an impressive figure with his straight, muscular body and finely cut features and candid black eyes.

"You will be safe with me, lady," he assured her. It had the solemnity of an oath.

Ramses saw them off, along the well-traveled road that led to the villages and villas of the northern section. Perched regally on the litter carried by two of Tarek's men, Daria did not look back. Ramses wondered if he would ever see her again. If he had miscalculated, he would probably be dead before morning.

Tarek had bade him an emotional farewell, as if he fully expected that unfortunate event would occur. Ramses refused Harsetef's offer to accompany him, but agreed to wait until Tarek's scouts could be notified that he was coming over the pass. As he made his way up the inner slope, the declining sun cast a mellow glow across the rugged landscape.

He had had plenty of time to think about Tarek's news. It certainly hadn't been the distinguished and aging Flinders Petrie who had visited Tarek. Only one man would have had the imaginative effrontery to use that name. What name, Ramses wondered, was he using now? MacFerguson? Moroney? It had to be one of them, the idea that there were two other Englishman in addition to Sethos at large in the Holy City was ludicrous. He had remembered who MacFerguson was—or was not. The ears, Ramses thought, the goddamned ears! One of the basic rules of disguise, a feature so prominent that it drew the eyes away from the rest of the face. Sethos must be MacFerguson. That he was now comfortably in league with the usurper Ramses did not doubt. He would have dealt with Satan if it meant profit for him. If his parents didn't know about Sethos, they had to be warned before the bastard pulled some underhanded stunt.

Urgency prompted him to begin the descent at once, instead of waiting until twilight. The sun's rays struck the eastern ramparts with the intensity of a searchlight, but, he assured himself, his tanned body and the soldier's brown linen kilt were almost the same color as the stone, and it was a lot easier to find hand- and footholds in daylight. He was making excellent time when he sensed movement on the hillside below and paused to look down.

Like his own, the man's form was almost indistinguishable from the surrounding rock. Ramses didn't see him until he moved again, rising to his feet and raising the bow he held. Ramses acknowledged the salute with a wave before proceeding.

The arrow grazed his forearm. It was only a slight injury, but it was enough to make his left hand lose its grip and throw him off balance. His effort to break his fall only made the process more prolonged and unpleasant; it was a relief when his head hit the stone and the pain went away.

∴

"We need to think of a way of ridding ourselves of the servants," I said, sipping my coffee—and mentally thanking Sethos for the treat. It must have been he who had brought it. He was certainly a man who liked his little comforts.

"Why?" Daoud inquired. "They are friendly people."

"Hmmm," said Emerson, who thought he understood the reason for my suggestion. "Do you think you could bring yourself to be very friendly to the kind woman who keeps bringing you food?"

"I am friendly to her," said Daoud in surprise.

"Hmmm," said Emerson again. "Er—you see, Daoud, there is a chance—a far-out chance—that MacFerguson may be able to carry out his promise. If the servants are not here, Nefret won't have to stay in that dark place alone, we can have her with us."

"Ah," said Daoud.

"So . . . er . . . If we can convince Merasen and his father that there are spies among the servants—people friendly to us—very friendly—people who would help us escape . . ."

"I will ask her," Daoud said.

Emerson was trying to think of a way of explaining the idea of seduction to a man who had never in his life practiced that art, and Selim was chortling behind his hand when Merasen and his lot burst into the room. One look at Merasen's face told me we were in trouble. It positively glowed with triumph. He didn't even wait for his troop to search the room, but came straight to me.

"I have him," he exclaimed like a rooster crowing. "In my prison. Your brave, clever son."

## From Manuscript H

Ramses woke up with a vague memory of a dream that had involved rough hands and futile, painful struggle, and darkness. And laughter. Hearty, triumphant laughter that was worst of all.

It was still dark, but he knew he was awake because the pain was back. He must have hit every bloody rock on the way down to . . . where? He had no idea where he was. The air was close and hot, the darkness broken by a single ray of feeble light. As his eyes adjusted, he realized he was lying against a stone wall, with stone under him and more of the same overhead. The light came from a small opening in the ceiling.

It hadn't been a dream. Hands had pried him off the surface on which he landed, subdued his ineffectual attempts to fight them off, and brought him here. The location of the place was still a mystery, but there was no doubt about its nature, or about the identity of the man responsible. He'd heard that merry boyish laughter before.

"Goddamn it," he said, not loudly but with feeling.

"You speak English! Who are you?"

The voice startled him so that he made the mistake of sitting up. Once he'd got that far, there didn't seem to be any point in lying down again. He got his back against the wall and peered into the gloom. Not far away he made out a human form. The room—cell, to give it its proper name—was only eight feet square.

"More to the point, who are you?" he demanded. "MacFerguson?"

"Who the devil is MacFerguson?"

"Never mind. You must be Moroney, then. Unless you're Kevin O'Connell or the Reverend Mr. Campbell. Or Richard the Lionheart. I'm afraid there's no minstrel."

"If that's supposed to be funny, I am not amused," said the voice coldly.

"Sorry," Ramses said. "I guess I'm still a little light-headed. My name is Emerson—the younger. I met you on the boat from Halfa."

"Good Lord, are you really? I got a glimpse of you when they dumped you in here, but I didn't recognize you. Thought you were one of the local laddies." He came closer and hunkered down next to Ramses. "I guess you're entitled to ramble a bit. You look as if you've taken a beating."

"It wasn't a beating. At least," Ramses amended, "I don't think so. I fell off a cliff. With a little assistance from one of the local laddies."

"Is there anything I can do for you?"

"Water, if there is any."

"Oh, yes, we have all the customary amenities. Water, dry bread once a day, the most elegant of sanitary facilities." He indicated a clay pot in the far corner.

"So it was you who guided Merasen here," Ramses said, accepting a cup of water.

"You don't sound surprised."

"You were the most obvious suspect. I never believed Merasen's boasts of escaping the slavers. I suppose it was one of your patrols that freed him and the others."

"You seem to have figured it all out."

"Just as you figured out who Merasen was and where he came from. You'd heard about Willy Forth's lost civilization and you knew about our expedition ten years ago. Well done. In the best traditions of the service."

He sensed rather than saw the other man wince. "I don't blame you for despising me. But I swear to God I meant no harm to you and your family, or to anyone else. I've been in this hole for two days, long enough to realize that I am a miserable sinner and that I am about to pay the price."

"You've found religion, have you?" Ramses inquired skeptically.

"Sneer if you like. I don't expect to get out of here alive, but I'll do anything I can to help you."

Ramses stood up and moved around the perimeter of the cell, stiffly at first, then more easily. The room had been cut out of the mountainside. The only breaks in the solid stone were the square opening in the ceiling and a heavy wooden door.

"It's barred and chained," Moroney said, watching him push against the door.

"Naturally." Ramses looked up at the opening in the ceiling. It was less than four inches across. The beam of light was brighter now.

"What time of day do they bring you food and water?" he asked.

"Around midday, to judge by the light. There are always four of them. One replaces the water jar and the basket of bread while the others pen me in a corner with the points of their spears. Now that there are two of us—"

"We'll both be penned in a corner and held at spear-point. I don't think impalement is a sensible way out of here."

"Only one of us need risk that. If you get behind me—"

"Don't talk like a fool," Ramses said roughly.

"What other chance is there?"

"That isn't a chance, it's double suicide, even supposing I'd allow you to do it." He went back to his original corner and lowered himself to a sitting position. "If all else fails, we'll try the old 'Help, help, he's dying,' trick. Merasen won't want to lose me, not when he can hold me like a club over my parents' heads. And I have a feeling he won't wait until midday to pay us a visit."

It was not long until he was proved correct, but it seemed

long to Ramses, since he had plenty of time for bitter reflections on his own ineptitude. He had only made matters worse. The plan he and Tarek had worked out would fail if his parents weren't able to play their part, and if Tarek didn't hear from him before the night of the ceremony, Tarek's advisers, who obviously had serious reservations about the idea, might be able to persuade him to go back to the original plan. Carrying Daria off had been a mistake too. He had acted on impulse, and he knew what that impulse was. "Love clouds the brain and the organs of moral responsibility." Nefret would be guarded even more closely now. And if Tarek lost, Daria would end up as a prize for one of the victors.

Moroney sat with head bowed, wrapped in his own miserable thoughts. Another complication he didn't need—a repentant sinner wallowing in guilt and looking for martyrdom. Ramses had become convinced Moroney was sincere—people frequently repented when death stared them in the face—and his hair-raising offer to take multiple spears into his own body fit the pattern. He prayed—no, make that "hoped"—that Moroney was still capable of following orders. He'd explained in detail what he wanted Moroney to do and made him swear he wouldn't do anything else.

He thought a lot about Daria and felt even guiltier for finding delight in those memories.

Chains rattled. Moroney started violently, and Ramses dropped flat onto the floor. "Don't forget," he whispered.

They carried torches. The light sent crimson sparks flaring from the points of the spears. Ramses raised his hand to shield his eyes from the glare and could have crowed with satisfaction when he saw Merasen, prudently in the rear. The spearman surrounded Moroney and lined up along the floor where Ramses lay. The spears were sharp and pointed directly at his body.

Once his men were in position, Merasen edged into the room. He was decked out in the full regalia of a prince—

tight-sleeved tunic and long skirt, diadem, gold-hilted sword and dagger—but instead of the triumphant grin Ramses had expected, his face wore a frown. Ramses groaned and let his arm fall limply to his side.

"Stand up in the presence of your prince," Merasen ordered. "You were in the camp of Tarek. You will tell me what you did, what you said."

Ramses muttered something unintelligible and held his breath until—finally!—Moroney spoke his piece. "He's hurt badly, Merasen. He's been unconscious most of the time."

"Do something!" Merasen ordered. "Wake him!"

One of the spear points pricked Ramses's side, and he decided he had better respond. Merasen appeared to be in a bad mood.

"It was you," he said faintly. "You dirty little rat."

The word was the worst insult in the language of the Holy City. Merasen's upper lip lifted in a snarl. Reassured by Ramses's apparent helplessness, he pushed one of the spearmen aside and bent over him.

"Guard your tongue or you will suffer for it."

"You won't kill me," Ramses said, hoping he was right.

The spear dug deeper into his side; he flinched, and Merasen smiled. "Not quickly, no. The Father of Curses and his lady know you are my prisoner. They will now act as I order."

"They won't take your word, Merasen," Ramses said, knowing that this time he *was* right. "You're such a goddamn liar they wouldn't believe you if you told them camels can't fly. They will insist on seeing me."

Merasen's expression told him he had struck gold. He groaned again and said in a failing voice, "My mother has medicines . . ."

Merasen swung on Moroney. "You. Watch over him. If he dies, you will die."

He stalked out. The door slammed and the chains rattled appropriately.

"They forgot to feed us," Moroney said. "Maybe they've decided to let us die of starvation."

He seemed to have recovered from his attack of heroism. Ramses wondered how long this mood would last. He pulled himself to a sitting position and used the hem of his kilt to wipe away the blood that was running down his side. "You weren't listening. My life is as dear to Merasen as his own just now. I'll lay odds he's gone to get Mother. It should be an interesting encounter." He contemplated the stained edge of his garment and added, "Another kilt ruined."

⋮

Merasen was back sooner than I had expected, scowling so blackly that I felt a brief surge of hope that we had succeeded in calling his bluff—or that Ramses had got away. It was only too brief. "Come," he ordered, beckoning to me. "Bring your medicines. And bandages."

This time I knew he wasn't bluffing. I turned in mute appeal to Emerson, who had risen to his feet and was watching Merasen like a cat who is being prevented from getting at a particularly toothsome mouse.

"Don't lose your head, Peabody," he said. "He's still alive."

"Yes, and you will keep him alive," Merasen said. "You did not believe me when I said he was my prisoner? Now you will see. You, Sitt Hakim. Not the Father of Curses."

"Don't lose *your* head, Emerson," I implored. Emerson had begun growling and his fists were clenched. "I will be back before long. Won't I, Merasen?"

"Oh, yes, Sitt. The Father of Curses has called me a liar. I will prove I spoke truth. Get the things you need."

As I collected my supplies I heard Merasen holding forth in the next room. He must be very sure of himself, for the facade of boyish goodwill had been replaced by arrogance.

"You are the liars," he declared. "You told the king you would speak for him, but you did not mean what you said.

You sent your son to plot with Tarek. I am the defender of my father's throne, I am the one who sent spies into Tarek's camp, and now you will do as I say or your son will die."

"You can't have it both ways, you know," said Emerson. "If he dies you will have no hold over us."

Merasen smiled. "I did not say he would die quickly. Come, Sitt."

"We are going with her," said Emerson. "As far as your house, at any rate. That is not negotiable, so don't bother arguing with me."

Merasen snarled but gave in. I found this worrisome, and said so to Emerson as we walked behind him. "Ramses must be badly hurt, Emerson, or Merasen wouldn't be so anxious to have me tend to him."

"You forget our son's histrionic talents," said Emerson. "Good Gad, Peabody, Ramses has as many lives as a cat and an inventiveness equal to your own."

"That is true. Thank you, Emerson, for reassuring me."

"He was wrong to give Merasen the benefit of the doubt, anyhow," said Emerson. "Villains are not always villains, and heroes are not always heroic; it is a pleasure to find a villain who is exactly what we took him to be."

Merasen's men held Emerson and the other two back while Merasen marched me up the stairs without giving me time for fond farewells. Emerson's final words were not a fond farewell. "If you do not bring her back, Merasen, I will find you and tear you limb from limb."

I had never visited any of the Holy City's prisons, but I knew each nobleman had his own. It was quite a feudal system, really. Merasen's cells were at the back of the house and below it. Stygian darkness filled the narrow passages. Torches were lit and the escort proceeded along a tunnel lined with heavy barred doors. My sympathies went out to the other hapless prisoners who lay behind those doors. Moroney must be one of them.

I did not have to feign my cry of distress when I knelt

beside the still form of my son. He was covered with bruises, and patches of dried blood marked his body. His long lashes fluttered pathetically, and then one eye opened—and closed in an unmistakable wink.

"Meine geliebte Mutter," murmured Ramses, softly but, of course, with perfect articulation. "Wo bist du? Warum kommst du nicht?"

"What does he say?" Merasen demanded. "What language is that?"

"He always reverts to German when he is ill or delirious," I said, grateful for the hint and weak-limbed with relief. "Ich bin hier, mein Sohn. Any broken bones? Dizziness or clouded vision? Your father and I have not been harmed. What have you with the girl done?"

"Talk English!" Merasen shouted, jumping up and down with aggravation. His shout covered the gurgle of amusement that had escaped Ramses, and his murmur of "Straight to the point as always."

"I only asked about his injuries," I explained indignantly. "Someone give me a bowl of water. Thank you—oh, it is you, Captain Moroney. Forgive me, I neglected to wish you good morning. I was concerned about my son, you understand."

"With good reason, ma'am," said Moroney, blinking rapidly. "What can I do to help?"

"Keep quiet," I said. Ramses had started talking again. In broken but coherent phrases he brought me quickly up-to-date on the situation. It was useful information, especially his arrangement with Tarek.

"Yes," I exclaimed, forgetting myself for a moment. "That should—er—das ist ganz praktisch."

"What does he say?" Merasen shrieked. "Ask him what Tarek plans! When will he attack?"

"He is babbling about his childhood," I said, sponging the dried blood away and splashing the cuts with alcohol. "I can't get a sensible word out of him, Merasen, not while he is in this condition. You must bring him back to our house so that I can take care of him properly."

I didn't expect he would be fool enough to go along with that idea, but nothing ventured, nothing gained, as I always say. He refused, using several English bad words he must have picked up from Emerson, and I said in German, "I have this as much as possible prolonged, but he will soonest me remove. I have a plan to rescue her—you know of whom I speak. Then we will a way of delivering you discover."

"Stop," Merasen said. He caught me roughly by the arm. I saw Ramses's eyes flash before he closed them again. "Der andere Engländer," he muttered. "Vorsicht. Er ist—"

"I know," I replied in English. There wasn't time to ask how he had found out, though I was burning with curiosity. Merasen kept tugging at me. "Just give me time to pack my medical supplies," I said with a sob. "Dein Vater knows not," I added, stroking Ramses's cheek as if bidding him a loving farewell. "Tell him not."

"Ja, Mutter," said Ramses.

Between Emerson's relief at seeing me safely back and his concern for his son, he was somewhat less than coherent at first. Daoud and Selim kept peppering me with questions too. After I had got them all to be quiet I told them what had happened.

"Are you sure he is only pretending to be seriously injured?" Emerson asked anxiously.

"My dear, I have seen him in worse condition—worse and often! I don't doubt he was on his feet as soon as the door closed."

"We will go to that place and take him out of it," said Daoud fiercely.

Emerson snorted and rolled his eyes, but I said, "That is one of the possibilities. However, I have another idea."

"You have too damned many ideas," said my loving husband. "Good Gad, Peabody, you have come up with a dozen different schemes. Isn't it time we settled on one?"

"We must remain flexible, Emerson. What do you think of Ramses's arrangement with Tarek?"

"I am perfectly willing—in fact, I would be delighted— to cry havoc and let slip the dogs of war on old Zekare, and," Emerson went on modestly, "I might be able to carry it off. But I am not noble enough to risk Ramses's life for a noble cause. Merasen would murder him out of sheer spite if we won. And what about Nefret?"

"I have a few ideas," I began. "Now, Emerson, don't lose your temper. You are right, we need to settle on a plan. As a last resort, and in the—in my opinion—unlikely possibility that we are not able to free either or both beforehand, we will refuse to take part in the ceremony unless Ramses and Nefret are present. Merasen will have to produce Ramses, at least."

"With a knife at his throat," Emerson growled.

"We will have knives at people's throats ourselves, my dear. And Daoud's guns. Before that, we have a few details to attend to. Ramses promised Tarek he would bring back our answer within two days. Since he can't, we must do so. If Tarek doesn't hear from us, and if he learns of Ramses's capture, he may do something rash."

Emerson nodded grudgingly. "Right as usual, Peabody. The lady in the village?"

"If we can do it without endangering her. I will write a message. She will know who it's for and pass it on. The rekkit must also be warned of the change in plan. Under no circumstances are they to take up arms."

Emerson fingered the cleft in his chin. "I suppose you didn't get a chance to look for the guns while you were at Merasen's place."

"He hustled me in and out before I could. I'll try again later."

"What makes you suppose Merasen will let you come again?"

"He will have to let me if Ramses continues to fade away. Of course it is possible that Ramses will free himself and Captain Moroney before that."

"How, in God's name?" Emerson demanded. "He is locked up and unarmed."

"Not exactly, Emerson. I left him a weapon."

## Thirteen

**M**y optimism received a hard blow when we entered our sitting room and found a delegation waiting. It was headed by Amenislo, who informed us that in a few hours we must begin preparing for the ceremony.

"No, surely not!" I exclaimed. "Tomorrow is the day."

"You must have miscalculated, Peabody," said Emerson, fingering his chin. "I told you they don't reckon time as we do."

I don't believe my brain has ever worked as rapidly as it did then. This was an official and religious event, and there was no hope of demanding it be postponed, any more than there would have been to change the date of Christmas. We had only half a day in which to revise our plans or be forced to the last expedient, which in my opinion had never been very satisfactory.

"What of my son?" I demanded. "Does the king know he lies wounded and suffering in Merasen's cell?"

"He knows," Amenislo said. "After the ceremony—"

"Ha," exclaimed Emerson. "Not after the ceremony. Now."

"The king will not agree to that." The count wrung his hands. "The Brother of Demons cannot be with you. He must remain a prisoner."

"But not in that nasty dark cell," I exclaimed. "If he

could be moved to a more comfortable place, still under guard, but with someone to tend his injuries . . ."

A light—the light of hope, perhaps—shone in Amenislo's eyes. I said, "You can order this, Amenislo. You are high in the king's favor. If he questions your act, tell him you had to agree in order to win our cooperation."

Amenislo's expression indicated that he had no intention of being available to answer questions. "I will try," he muttered.

"I feel sure you will. It must be done soon," I added. "So that my mind will be at ease before the ceremony. I presume we will be supplied with proper garments and ornaments and instructed in what we are to do?"

"Attendants will come to you later."

"When? At what hour does the ceremony take place?"

"When the moon rises. They will come before that. Now I go."

Amenislo hurried out. "Confound it," said Emerson. "I thought we had more time. Tarek is probably gathering his men at this very moment. We must get word to the rekkit immediately. Give me a sheet of paper, I will write the note myself. Come with us, Daoud and Selim. From now on we stick together."

But we got no farther than the Great Temple. The guards had gathered round a shaven-headed priest who was waving his hands and shouting. Emerson stopped. "What's going on?"

"He keeps saying 'The king, the king must be told!' And . . . Good Gad!"

"What? What?" Emerson bellowed.

"'She is gone. She has vanished.'"

Emerson whirled round and pelted back toward the stairs to our rooms. None of the guards seemed anxious to break the news to the king; they gave way before Emerson, and the rest of us followed in his wake. Selim forged ahead, leaving me to Daoud, who assisted me with such zeal that my feet seldom touched the ground. Emerson and Selim were not in sight when Daoud and I dashed into the sitting room of our suite. Of course I knew where they had gone.

"Put me down, Daoud," I gasped. "Get the servants out of here, I don't care how, then close the door and don't let anyone in."

I stopped only long enough to snatch up a lamp before I ran toward the dark chamber at the rear of our quarters. I was pleased to discover that one of them had had sense enough to do the same—Selim, probably, since Emerson was in such a state he could not even find the concealed catch. He was tugging at the slab and swearing when I came in. I pushed him out of the way and pressed the indentation that released the spring. The slab lifted. Below, at the foot of the stairs, was a pale crumpled shape. It raised a white face.

As Nefret stumbled up the stairs Emerson reached down and pulled her up into his arms, narrowly avoiding braining her on the raised stone slab. I took the lamp from Selim's shaking hand; he was laughing and praying and, I think, crying, all at the same time.

"There, there," I said, patting him on the shoulder. "Emerson, take her into our sleeping chamber. I expect she could do with a restorative sip of whiskey. If there is any left."

Emerson picked her up. "Air," she gasped. "Air and light, that's all I need. I've been there for hours. In the dark."

"It can't have been hours," I said. "Your disappearance has just now been discovered. How on earth did . . . er . . . he manage it?"

"Don't badger her now, Peabody," said Emerson. "Nefret, my dear, are you all right? Did they hurt you? If anyone dared—"

"I'm all right now." She clung tightly to him. "Don't let them take me away again."

"No," said Emerson.

Daoud was standing by the door of the sitting room.

When he saw Nefret he ran to embrace her, and I had to remind him of his duty. "No one tried to come in," he reported after he had calmed down.

"They will," Emerson said. "They cannot accuse us of being responsible for her disappearance, since we were here the whole morning, but they will look everywhere."

"I can't go down there again," Nefret said faintly. "Please don't make me."

"Not under any circumstances," said Emerson.

"They will search the subterranean passages too," I said. "It will take them a while, though. I wonder what has become of . . . Put her down on the bed, Emerson, and get the whiskey."

The white robes and veils of the High Priestess were crumpled and dusty, and her pretty hair hung tangled over her shoulders. I found a comb and began gently working out the tangles. As every woman knows, this has a soothing effect. She began to relax, and after she had taken a sip of the whiskey the color came back to her face.

"Where is Ramses?" was her first question.

"At the moment he is in a cell under Merasen's villa," I replied. Nefret let out a gasp, and I went on, "But we have taken steps." At least I hoped we had; the news of Nefret's disappearance might make the king decide to keep Ramses in close confinement. I certainly would have done.

"How did you get away?" Selim asked. "We had given up hope."

"So had I. It was the most amazing thing. I told you—didn't I?—that Amase took me to a separate room every day in order to instruct me in the rituals?"

"No, you didn't," I replied. "It doesn't matter. Go on."

"Sometimes there was another priest with him, hollow-eyed and stony-faced. Even stonier than that look of Ramses's. Aunt Amelia, how are you going to get Ramses—"

"Have another sip of whiskey," I said. "And go on."

"It was the priest who took me away. He hit poor old Amase on the head and tied him up with his own robes. I was too astonished to move until he came toward me, and then I would have cried out if he hadn't put his hand over my mouth and spoken to me in English. In English! I asked him who he was, but he just shook his head and told me he would bring me to you. The priests know where the entrances to the subterranean passages are located; so did I, once, but I couldn't get to them. I was never alone.

"He led me along those awful dark passages for what seemed like hours. Some of it was familiar to me, but I couldn't have found my way here. He left me at the foot of the stairs while he went up and had a look round; but you weren't there, and the servants were, and when he came back he said I would have to wait while he went to find you and tell you, and I did, and the lamp went out . . ."

"It's all right," I said soothingly. My thoughts were in a whirl, but I managed to concentrate on the most important matter. "We must think of a way of hiding you. I have an idea—"

"So do I," said Emerson. "Yes, Peabody, I do occasionally have ideas of my own, and this time mine is the one we will follow."

## From Manuscript H

After the door had closed behind his mother, whose face was working and whose hair was coming undone, Ramses sprang to his feet. The blade of the object she had shoved under him had cut a gouge across his back. He picked it up and stared at it.

"A pair of scissors?" Moroney exclaimed in bemusement.

"The blades are pretty sharp," Ramses said, from personal experience. "And a good six inches long. Even if Merasen had sense enough to search her medical bag he wouldn't have recognized this as a weapon. It's a woman's tool."

He stooped and collected several other items from where

they had fallen. Hairpins. Another woman's weapon.

They also served to loosen the screw that held the scissor blades together. That left each of them with a dagger-like weapon and a hairpin apiece. Ramses had to explain about the hairpins. His mother's were specially made, stiffer and sharper than the usual kind. They could be concealed in one's hand, and they hurt like hell if they were jabbed into a man's body.

"Useful," Moroney admitted, gripping the scissors blade. "When they feed us tomorrow—"

"Tomorrow be damned. I've got to get out of here today or all hell will break loose. Led by my father," he added. "I know what Merasen's got in mind, and Father won't stand for it. He has a frightful temper."

"We can't cut through that door with a pair of scissors," Moroney exclaimed.

"So we'll have to get the guards to open it."

"How?"

"There are several possibilities—as my mother would say." Ramses stretched out on the floor, his hands under his head. "I expect she's started working on some of them. We'll give her an hour or two, and if nothing develops you can bang on the door and demand food. They haven't fed us yet."

"Then what?" Moroney demanded.

"You mean what do we do when they open the door? That depends on the circumstances, and I will make that determination. If you don't give me your word to wait for my orders before you act, I'll knock you over the head."

"You have my word. It's the least I can do to atone."

"Fine," Ramses said heartily. "Excellent. Keep that thought in mind."

He might have known it wouldn't take his mother as long as an hour. Not when she had help from other quarters. All the same, his breath went out in a long expiration of relief when he heard the voice he had hoped to hear—high-pitched, unnecessarily loud, and authoritative.

"Don't move," Ramses said urgently. "Cringe."

"What?"

"Cringe, dammit!"

The first man to enter the room was the answer to his prayers. He bent over Ramses, who groaned obligingly.

"Lift him," said Amenislo. "You two. Take him to a sleeping chamber. Put down your spears, fools, you cannot carry him one-handed. No, do not put them down, give them to one of the others."

Moroney sat hunched in the center of the small room, his head bowed. One of the guards made a token gesture, waving a spear at him, but the others were preoccupied with carrying out Amenislo's orders, which were, to say the least, confusing. "No, not like that! Put your weapons on the floor. Pick them up. Not you! You! Put the torches in the bracket."

He backed out into the corridor. Two of the men followed, carrying Ramses, who waited until he was outside the cell, with the remaining guards filling the doorway, before he moved, twisting free of the hands that held him and calling Moroney's name. He landed on his feet, stumbled forward as a stab of pain shot up his ankle, lowered his head, and slammed it into the face of the man who had held his legs. Five left. He turned on the man behind him, and then there were four. No—three. A body lay at his feet in a spreading pool of blood. Amenislo's face was a mask of terror, but his sword was red to the hilt. Ramses ran to the door of the cell. Moroney was grappling with one soldier; before Ramses could go to his aid the soldier fell, clutching at the scissor handle protruding from his side. Another of the soldiers was sprawled on the floor with a spear in his chest. The man who held the spear backed away from Ramses.

"Do not strike me, Great One, I am Tarek's man!"

"So I see. All right, Moroney?"

"Yes." The Englishman surveyed the fallen bodies and puddles of blood. His unshaven face was blank with disbelief. "How the hell did you do that?"

"Amenislo. His name was on the list of supporters Tarek made me memorize. I told Mother . . ."

"No time for talk," the count exclaimed. He was shaking violently and streaming with sweat, from his forehead to his round belly. "Hurry, hurry!"

They shoved the bodies, dead and alive, into the cell and replaced the bar. Ramses's inconvenient conscience protested at leaving the wounded, but urgency prevailed. His parents needed him.

"That went well," said Moroney. He looked like a new man, alert and confident.

"We aren't out of this yet. Have a spear and pray you won't need to use it. I'd feel better if we had something more effective, though. Amenislo, do you know where Merasen hid the weapons he stole from us?"

"No," Amenislo bleated, wringing his hands. "We cannot look for them. We must go, but I do not know where. The Sitt Hakim did not tell me what to do next!"

Ramses couldn't fault the man, though at that moment he was a perfect image of a dithering coward. He had risked himself every day spying for Tarek in the enemy's camp, and those fat perfumed hands had struck hard when they had to. Ramses gave him a slap on the back. "You've done brilliantly so far, Amenislo. What about the entrance to the underground passages? All the great houses have them. Do you know where this one is located?"

"Yes." Amenislo looked less despondent. "I was often a guest of my brother Tarek when he lived here. It is a good plan. If we can get to it. There are other guards."

They ran into two of these unfortunates at the top of the stairs that led up from the cells. Ramses wasn't able to prevent Amenislo from running one of them through while he stared in surprise at the count's raised sword. Moroney took care of the other one with a blow that would have done Emerson credit. It seemed to cheer him up quite a lot.

"This way," Amenislo panted. "Hurry, hurry."

Ramses rather hoped they would run into Merasen. In his present mood he would have been tempted to emulate the bloodthirsty count and run the little swine through.

However, the private part of the house was deserted.

"He is at the palace, preparing for the ceremony," Amenislo replied to Ramses's question. "Come, hurry!"

Ramses made him wait while he made a quick search of Merasen's rooms. There was no sign of the weapons. Either they were well hidden or Merasen had taken them with him to the palace. He wondered uneasily what Merasen planned to do with them. The boy couldn't hit the traditional barn door, and his men had had no chance to practice with the weapons. But if one fired straight into a mob of people, one was bound to hit something.

Amenislo snatched up a lamp and led the way into the back part of the villa. The chamber into which he took them was like the others, and the catch worked the same way.

"All right, Amenislo, so far so good, as we say. Is there a way from here to my parents' rooms?"

⋮

"**G**ive Ramses a little more time, Emerson," I urged.

"We haven't any more time." Emerson adjusted his wig and slipped his arms through the pleated sleeves of a robe. "In less than four hours Tarek will try to force the pass and the rekkit will rise to support him. With all due respect, my dear, your scheme of denouncing Zekare at the ceremony has one fatal flaw. It might win the day for Tarek, but at the cost of many lives."

"But Emerson, Ramses is—"

He came to me and took me by the shoulders. "I know, my dear. I know. But Ramses would be the first to urge this course of action. I only hesitated to propose it before because of Nefret. Now that we have our girl with us again, we must act, whatever the consequences."

"I am going with you," I said, reaching for my parasol.

"No, Peabody. If ever there was a one-man job, this is it. You will have to keep Nefret out of the way of the servants and conceal my absence as long as is possible."

We were all gathered in my sleeping chamber. Nefret, dressed in trousers and a coat, a black wig covering her hair, sat on the side of the bed. It wasn't much of a disguise, but it had served to deceive our attendants thus far. Only one of them had expressed surprise at encountering me in the garden when she had just seen me entering the servants' area. My only reply was a mysterious smile.

We wouldn't be able to put them off much longer, though. They had brought a variety of elegant garments—and several black wigs in various styles—and only their fear of our wrath had prevented them from entering the room and trying to get us into our costumes.

"I don't see how we can conceal your absence after you have marched out the front door," I said irritably. "You don't look like a priest or an official, Emerson. You won't deceive anyone."

"It would be a help if you could get rid of a few of the servants," Emerson admitted.

Nefret spoke for the first time in quite a while. "Tell them you don't like any of the clothes they brought. Send them to get others."

"Excellent idea," I said. "Are you all right, my dear?"

"Yes, Aunt Amelia. I am worried about Ramses."

"No need to worry, dear girl. I am sure my plan will succeed. Amenislo understood my hints perfectly." I spoke with more confidence than I felt. Ramses had told me Amenislo was a secret supporter of Tarek's, but I hadn't much faith in the count's physical courage. "Hang on a minute, Emerson. Nefret, go into the bath chamber."

I gathered up an armful of garments more or less at random, thrust the curtain aside, and shoved the clothing into the arms of one of the women who stood outside.

"Take them away, they are not good enough. Bring better."

"You must be ready," one of them began.

"We will be ready, if you hurry. Go at once."

That got rid of two of them. I stood with my back

against the curtain, effectively barring the door to my room, wondering if there was anything else I could do to minimize the risk. Emerson was right, curse him, he was the only one who might be able to avert a bloody battle—but at what cost to him? All the while my ears were pricked (figuratively speaking), hoping for some sign that my scheme with Amenislo had succeeded. Ramses's escape would certainly raise the alarm.

The sign was not the one I had expected. It was the sight of Ramses himself, emerging from the door that led to the back rooms. "Thank God!" I cried.

"Good afternoon, Mother," said Ramses. "Excuse me for a moment . . . Do not cry out," he went on in Meroitic, addressing the gaping servants. "Through that door, all of you. Go."

Ramses shoved a few of the ladies as politely as possible. The man who had followed Ramses, carrying a long spear in one hand and a scissor blade in the other, helped herd the bewildered attendants into their quarters.

"Good afternoon, Mrs. Emerson," said Captain Moroney.

He looked dreadful, unshaven, dirty, and rumpled. Ramses was not in much better case. His linen kilt was ripped and blood-stained, and the bits of bandages I had applied did not improve his appearance.

Emerson plunged through the curtain and ran into me. With his usual quickness he caught me round the waist before I fell.

"Good afternoon, Father," said Ramses. "I hope I have not kept you waiting."

"No," Emerson mumbled. "No. Er—all right, are you, my boy? Good Gad!"

Ramses's reunion with the others was warm, but necessarily brief. The sight of Nefret stopped him in his tracks for a moment. "How—" he began.

"We will explain later," said Emerson. "Now that you are here—and we will have to wait for an account of that too—we must act at once."

He proceeded to explain his scheme to Ramses.

"It is our best hope of averting bloodshed," Ramses said. "But the risk to you, Father—"

"It's no more of a risk than they will face here," said Emerson, with a betraying look at me and Nefret. "I beg you will not underestimate me, my boy. I am confident I can carry it off."

"Very well, sir," Ramses said. "I will accompany you."

"Yes, you had better. I was wondering whether I could get my point across without a translator," Emerson added. "The rest of you will stay here. No, confound it, Selim, no argument, I don't like this any better than you do, but the Sitt Hakim and I have talked it over, and she agrees that this is our only chance."

"Emerson's plan depends on speed and secrecy," I said, for Selim's expression was still mutinous. "We would only slow him down. He is the one who will be in greatest danger. It is a great relief to know you will be with him, Ramses."

"Yes, Mother. Don't glower at me, Selim, you and Daoud may have to fight after all. Some of the royal guards will remain loyal to Zekare. Merasen's private guard too. I hope to God you still have our weapons."

Daoud produced them. In silence we surveyed our pitiful arsenal: one pistol, one rifle, and a single box of shells for the latter. Mutely Daoud offered the weapons to Emerson, who shook his head. Emerson does not object to using firearms, but he is under the impression that he gets on just as well without them.

"I'll take the rifle," Ramses said in a voice that allowed no argument.

Emerson rubbed his chin. "I suppose it might come in useful. But I hate to leave them without some means of defense."

"A single rifle won't help much, and it may cause trouble," I remarked, frowning at Selim. "We'll keep the pistol—or rather, Daoud will, hidden as before."

"Don't let her have it," Emerson said, pointing at me. "And don't shoot anyone unless you must. We are trying to avoid bloodshed, not cause it. Peabody, you know what to do. If they come for you, don't resist unless they offer you bodily harm or try to separate you. Stall as long as you can. When they learn I have gone—"

"There is no need to repeat yourself, Emerson. You can depend on me, I believe, to come up with an appropriate strategy, whatever circumstances may arise. And may I add that your wholehearted confidence in me—"

"No, I beg you will not," said Emerson. His manly tones faltered, and he cleared his throat. "I . . . er . . ."

"Chin up, Emerson," I said. "In my opinion it is most unlikely that Zekare will allow us to be killed, and if he throws us in a dank, dark cell you will free us in due course."

"Quite," said Emerson. "Hmph. All right, Ramses, let us be off. There's no need for secrecy now. Straight ahead at full speed, that's our method. Er—à bientôt, Peabody. I know you still have that pistol of yours. Try not to shoot yourself in the foot."

"À bientôt, Emerson. Try not to get yourself shot."

"Be careful, Professor," Nefret whispered. "Ramses—"

"I'll look after him," Ramses said with a smile at his father.

Tears filled her eyes and overflowed. Ramses took a step toward her.

"Oh, curse it," said Emerson. "Come along, Ramses, I can't stand this sort of thing."

## From Manuscript H

"The tricky part will be getting past the guards and across the Great Road to the stairs," said Emerson, as they hurried along the turns in the corridor. "Are we adequately disguised, do you think?"

Ramses glanced at his father. He had never seen a less

convincing disguise. The robe was too short by at least a foot, and Emerson didn't know how to walk wearing skirts. The wig had been made for a man with a smaller head and less hair; it sat precariously on top of Emerson's head. "The rifle doesn't help," he said tactfully.

"True. Give it me."

Mine not to reason why, Ramses thought. He handed the weapon to his father, who clasped it to his breast and wrapped his voluminous sleeves around it.

"All right," Ramses said. "Wait a minute."

He began unwinding the bandages from hands and head and arms. His mother always overdid the bandages. "They're more conspicuous than a few cuts and bruises," he explained, meeting his father's eye.

"Hmmm, yes. Er—you sure you're fit, my boy?"

"Yes, sir."

"March straight ahead, at a good clip, and don't stop," Emerson advised, as they neared the portico.

"Yes, sir," said Ramses, who had intended to do so anyhow.

It was probably the sheer preposterousness of their appearance that got them through the guard—that, and the fact that people were slow to react to the unexpected. They made it all the way to the steps that descended into the village before somebody got his wits back and shouted for them to stop. Ramses headed straight down the stairs at breakneck speed, with his father close behind him. When they reached the bottom Emerson turned and got off a few warning shots. Stone splintered and sprayed, and someone screamed.

"That should hold them for a while," Emerson said. "What's the matter?"

"Goddammit, the rekkit have already taken out the sentries." Ramses had almost fallen over one of the limp bodies. "Get out of that wig and robe, Father, or they'll be after us next." He raised his voice in a shout. "Friends! The friends!"

It was the sight of Emerson, now unmistakably himself, that brought several little men out of hiding. Ramses bit back an oath when he saw what they carried.

"Looks as if they have beaten their plowshares into swords," said Emerson.

"Apparently there weren't many iron plowshares," Ramses muttered. "The rest of them have only clubs. Make it fast and forceful, Father; I'll translate when necessary."

Emerson was still being forceful when they reached the village square with their proud escort. The entire population poured out of their houses, the men and some of the women armed with those pitiful clubs or with stones.

Emerson, who was in a hurry, quelled the uproar of welcome with one of his loudest bellows.

"Talk to the women," Ramses urged. "Or to—Khat! Good, you made it home safely. Where is your mother?"

The boy was holding a stone he couldn't possibly have thrown farther than a foot. Inarticulate with excitement and with pride at being on such familiar terms with the Great Ones, he gaped at Emerson, whose stern face dissolved into a mask of sentimental tenderness.

"Got to stop this," he said to Ramses, patting the boy's head. "Where . . . Good Gad, what's that?"

"The village wisewoman," said Ramses, as the untidy bundle tottered toward them. "Tell her."

Emerson only got out a few sentences before her claw-like hands drew the wrappings away from her face.

"Yes, Father of Curses, I read your thoughts. They are good. Tell the people. They will obey."

Emerson was twitching with impatience, so he made it short, barking out sentence after sentence, which Ramses translated. If the soldiers came, the villagers were not to resist. The shedding of their blood would not be necessary. The battle was already as good as won. His magic, the magic of the Father of Curses, would conquer for Tarek.

"Have I got my point across?" Emerson inquired. "Some of the little chaps still look bellicose."

"They won't dare disobey you, sir. And if one of them is tempted to do so, his wife or his mother will stop him. The women agree with you wholeheartedly. Look at them."

"Your mother always says women have better sense than men. All right, let's go. Er—where?"

The fields beyond the village were lush and green with some variety of grain, high enough to provide cover when they encountered troops of soldiers heading toward the pass. Zekare must know what Tarek planned; he was mustering his men to resist an attack. Emerson kept mumbling to himself. He was rehearsing his speech; he kept asking Ramses to supply words he didn't know. Remembering the steep climb ahead of them, Ramses ventured a suggestion.

"Father, it will take quite some time to climb up and over the cliffs. Couldn't we reach the wall from this side?"

"No, no." Emerson spat out a mouthful of greenery. "That would be poor psychology—er—you know what I mean. We'll do it my way. I have it all worked out."

"At least let me go ahead. I've been this way before."

When Ramses raised a cautious head over the edge of the road he was pleasantly surprised to find no one in sight. The absence of hostile presences there and on the upper slope puzzled him until they reached the ledge and found a man waiting to help them up. He dropped to his knees before Emerson.

"Does the Father of Curses remember his servant?"

"Good to see you, Harsetef, old chap," said Emerson, too out of breath to remember his scanty Meroitic. "On we go, on we go. There's no time to waste."

With the help of two other scouts they got Emerson up the cliff at record speed. As they climbed, Harsetef explained why they had encountered no opposition. "We made sure the way was clear. I knew you would come today."

"Didn't you hear that Merasen's men had taken me prisoner?"

"Yes, but we knew you would escape. We did not expect the Father of Curses himself!" Harsetef's eyes shone with the fearful glow of belief. "With him to lead the assault we cannot lose!"

The sun hung low over the western cliffs when they reached the top of the cliff. Emerson looked up, looked down, said, "Hell and damnation!" and plunged down the slope, his arms waving like windmills to keep his balance. Before he reached the bottom he was engulfed by a mob of shouting, cheering men, who hoisted him onto their shoulders and carried him the rest of the way.

"Curse it," said Emerson. "Where is—ah, hullo, Tarek. What's going on?"

Tarek was dressed like a common soldier, with only the royal diadem to proclaim his rank. He had never looked more kingly or more handsome, a smile of welcome warming his features. "As you see, O Father of Curses. Now that you are here, we cannot be defeated. We will lead the charge side by side, you and I, as soon as the bark of the god sinks below the cliffs."

Ramses was only too accustomed to being overshadowed by his father, although it would have been nice to have Tarek acknowledge his presence. Tarek's troops were drawn up behind the wall, and one quick glance was enough to explain his strategy, if it could be dignified by that name. The ladders were ready, several dozen of them.

"Father," he said urgently.

"Yes, yes," said Emerson. "Get one of those ladders in place. No, just one."

"Make it two," Ramses said. "I'll cover you."

His father gave him a quick look and nodded reluctantly. "Two. You will await my orders, Tarek. The orders of the Father of Curses!"

Tarek and his entourage froze. "Ha," said Emerson in a pleased voice, and began to climb the ladder.

Ramses went up the second ladder. Standing on the top rung, he unslung the rifle and looked down at the opposing force. It was a mirror image of Tarek's, the same weapons, the same intent faces, even the ladders—a poignant reminder of the futile, fratricidal nature of this little war. All the faces were upturned, staring at the same spot.

The last rays of the setting sun framed Emerson in a halo of gold as he stood atop the wall, feet braced and arms raised. He looked larger than life-size, and the hero worship he would always feel for his father held Ramses as breathless and motionless as the soldiers below.

Not all were motionless, though. One man, in the last rank, had drawn his bow. Cursing his momentary lapse, Ramses got the fellow in his sights and fired, but not before the arrow was on its way. It struck Emerson square in the breast.

Emerson looked down. With a gesture of magnificent nonchalance he plucked the arrow out and tossed it away. A united gasp, like a strong wind, drowned out a quiet voice that said, "Er—what's that word again? 'Rightful'?"

Ramses managed to get it out, though he was painfully short of breath. Emerson's voice made the echoes roll.

"Friends! The Father of Curses speaks. Pull down the wall, embrace your brothers, and greet Tarek, the rightful king of the Holy Mountain!"

⁝

I couldn't get Nefret to stop crying. "We'll never see them again," she sobbed. "And it's all my fault. I was the one who insisted we come."

Obviously stern measures were called for. I took her by the shoulders. "Stop it this instant. This is not like you, Nefret. We have a job to do and I expect every English—er—woman to do her duty. And set your wig straight."

"Yes, Aunt Amelia." She wiped her eyes with her fingers.

"That is better. Now let us assess the situation."

Unbeknownst to Ramses and Emerson, Selim had followed them at a short distance. I am a woman of iron nerve, and I had accepted the risks they would face, but I wanted to know that they had carried out the first, most hazardous part of the plan successfully. When Selim came back he was smiling. "The guards did not try to stop them. They are safely on their way to the village. It is strange, Sitt Hakim, that there are no soldiers in the corridors. But there are many of them outside this house."

"Zekare is consolidating his forces, I expect," I said. "His spies will have reported that Tarek is about to mount an attack. I think . . . yes, I believe it would be advisable to send the servants away."

"But they'll tell the king," Nefret began.

"If he doesn't already know his schemes are in disarray, he soon will," I replied. "Step away from the door, Captain Moroney, and shoo the servants out of our suite."

The flight of the unhappy servants did rather resemble that of a flock of chickens before a fox, even to the noises they made.

"Now what?" Nefret inquired.

"Now we wait," I replied, taking a seat on one of the divans. "The rest of you may as well sit down and be comfortable."

"We could hide," Nefret said. "When they come for us. In the subterranean passages."

"I had of course considered that possibility," I replied. "But I do not think it would be a wise move."

In fact, I could not bear the thought of cowering in the dark, in ignorance of the fate of those I loved, while Emerson and Ramses were fighting for our lives. They might need me. Coups are never neat and clean, there are always pockets of resistance, and I felt certain that Zekare would make a last stand in the palace with the men who remained loyal to him.

We waited for some time. The delay did not sit well with Selim or with the captain; they paced restlessly up and down the room. I considered it a good omen, however, a sign that Zekare was too busy with other affairs, such as disaffection in the ranks of his men, to concern himself with us. Selim wanted to go out again, to see what was happening, but I would not let him. The longer we could delay, the better.

We had left the door open so we might have warning of persons approaching. When we heard the footsteps, Nefret let out a little cry. (What on earth was wrong with the girl?) Selim sprang to my side and Moroney clenched his fists. The only one who did not move was Daoud. He, sensible man, was waiting for my orders.

The delegation was headed by the High Priest of Aminreh himself. I looked in vain for Amenislo among the courtiers who accompanied him. That, I feared, was not a good omen. Had Zekare learned of his treachery?

Apparently the servants had had the good sense to go into hiding instead of reporting to the king. Bakamani's formidable countenance took on an extremely foolish look when he saw Nefret and me sitting side by side on the divan, dressed alike in trousers and coats.

"Why is this?" he demanded. "Why are you not ready for the ceremony? Where are the others? And who"—he leveled an accusing forefinger at Nefret, who drew back a little—"who is she?"

"My doppelgänger," I said. Nefret chuckled. It was a faint imitation of her melodious laugh, but I considered it was a good sign.

I had to admire the fellow. He was quick to comprehend a situation that would have baffled most people for much longer. His eyes narrowed. "The High Priestess," he said flatly. "So she is here. Good. She will come too. Assume your robes."

"No," I said without moving.

"Yes! Do as I say!"

"No," I repeated. "See here, Bakamani—er—curse it, Nefret, translate for me, will you please? Your Reverence, there is no need for a confrontation. Go back and tell the king we will come, but we will wear our own garments. The people will not know us if we are dressed differently.

Is that not so?" I waved my parasol in an unthreatening manner.

"You will come?"

"Yes, certainly. All of us."

"Where is the Father of Curses?"

"At the moment? I have no idea. No doubt he will join us in due course." He hesitated, and I went on, "You had better take what you can get, you know. If you try to bring us by force, someone will be injured, and I do not think the king would want that. Now run along and tell Zekare what I have said. We will await your return."

He swung round, the skirts of his long robe billowing around him, and stalked out, leaving several spearmen on guard.

"Good heavens," said Moroney, staring. "Mrs. Emerson, you really are the most—"

"Thank you," I said. "Conquer by confusion, I always say. I took Bakamani to be a man of sense rather than temper, and I was correct. I could not have dealt so easily with Merasen, who has no sense and a very bad temper. I wonder where the little wretch is?"

Nefret got to her feet and went into the garden. After a moment I followed. It was very still and peaceful there, the lilies on the surface of the water folding their petals and the vines rustling in the breeze. Nefret was looking up over the wall at the western sky. "It lacks less than an hour of sunset," she said. "How much time do we have, Aunt Amelia?"

Her nervous state had been succeeded by one of unnatural calm. I preferred it to the other, but I found it worrisome.

"Are you all right?" I asked.

"Oh, yes." She turned and held out her hands to me. "Now that I am with you. I only wish I could see the Professor and Ramses once more. And Tarek."

"You will see them, and before much longer," I said with a conviction I wished I felt. The attack was to begin at sunset. The western sky was streaked with gold. If Emerson could carry out his plan, there would be no fighting at the pass and he would hasten at once to my side. If he could not, a bloody, prolonged battle would ensue, with, I did not doubt, Emerson in the thick of it and Ramses at his father's side.

Win or lose, and I did not doubt he would win in the end, Emerson would find me and he would find me doing my part. I squared my shoulders and squeezed Nefret's hands.

"I depend on you, Nefret, to obey my orders instantly and precisely. Don't worry; I have it all worked out."

When Bakamani returned, the room was cool with shadows. He was in quite an unusual state of agitation, and we had a rather loud argument about the arrangements I proposed. Finally I turned to the men and said, "You will be allowed to accompany us, but you must agree to leave your weapons behind—your knife, Selim, and your scissors, Captain."

"But, ma'am, how can we defend you without weapons?" Moroney demanded fiercely. "I promised Ramses—"

"Never mind what you promised him, he has no business issuing orders on my behalf. Do as I say."

Daoud coughed politely. "Sitt Hakim," he began, his hand moving to the breast of his robe.

"No," I said quickly. "No, Daoud. Await my orders."

"Ah," said Daoud. "Yes."

This reminder, that Daoud was in possession of a concealed weapon, consoled Selim a little, but he was slow to release his grip on his knife. Ignoring Bakamani's demands that we hurry, I marshaled my troops and inspected them. I must say they did me credit. At my request Moroney had shaved, and he was wearing a tweed coat and trousers that belonged to Ramses. I had had to roll up the trousers and the coat was too wide across the shoulders, but the effect was not at all bad. Selim and Daoud wore nice clean galabeeyahs and their best turbans. The former had adorned himself with several pectorals and armlets, to which he had taken a fancy. I gave Nefret a little poke. "Step out strongly," I hissed. "And straighten your wig."

As we left the room I took one last look at the light—or rather, the lack thereof. It had faded quickly. The sun must have set, or be on the verge of setting. The next hour or two would determine our fate.

I assure you, Reader, that I had considered the possibility that Zekare might threaten to murder us should Tarek's victorious troops surround the palace. I didn't think he would, though. He must know that even if Tarek agreed to lay down his arms and surrender, a promise given under duress does not hold. Anyhow, I had no intention of submitting meekly to any such thing. I felt certain we could work things out. He had not struck me as a cruel or vindictive man.

The Reader will agree, I am sure, that my logic was impeccable. I could not possibly have anticipated the development that ensued.

When we were ushered into the reception room with the Window of Appearance, it was not Zekare who awaited us.

The room was crowded with people—courtiers, priests, soldiers of the royal guard. They had to squeeze back to make an aisle for us to approach the throne. Seated upon it, wearing the royal robes and the diadem, was Merasen.

"Where is your father?" I demanded.

"My father is dead. Where is the Father of Curses?"

Could nothing disturb the boy's monumental self-esteem? I wondered. The news that had staggered me had left no shadow of grief or anger on his handsome young face.

"I do not know," I stammered. "What do you mean, dead? How? When?"

"Killed," Merasen said coolly. "By my brothers. They too are dead, at my command, for their crime. I am king of the Holy City. And so you will proclaim me, lady, you and she who is now High Priestess of Isis, when the moon rises."

He gestured, and a priest stepped forward, carrying the gold-embroidered white robes of the High Priestess.

"Put them on, Nefret," Merasen said softly.

She shook her head. "I won't. I'll never wear them again."

"It will be the last time," Merasen said in his most caressing voice. "You will have another position tomorrow and finer garments."

Righteous wrath replaced my temporary confusion. Ramses had been right after all. The young villain wanted the throne, *and* Nefret. Love did not enter into it; I doubt he was capable of feeling it for anyone but himself. She was a symbol of that which is rare and precious, a trophy of victory over us and those who opposed him.

I do not believe Nefret fully comprehended his meaning. It was the garments themselves that frightened her, I did not know why. She turned to me in appeal, her face white.

"It will be all right, Nefret," I said. "Just drape the confounded veils over you. Here, let me do it. So, Merasen, you have decided you don't need the other Great Ones?"

Merasen's utterly charming smile broadened. "I was with you in England, lady. I saw how you lived. You are not rulers or even nobles of that kingdom. You are mortal, and you too can die. Like my father."

I heard a gasp and a muttered oath from Selim, close behind me. I murmured a word of caution, and Merasen went on cheerfully, "I know you do not have divine powers, but the people are fools, and they will yield to me if you command them."

"The Father of Curses has more authority than I."

"Then he will do as I say because you are in my hands. If he lives," Merasen added happily. "Do you think I was not told he had gone to Tarek? He will be foremost in the attack and I have offered the gold of honor to the one who slays the Father of Curses. I am only sorry that your son will die too. I would like to have killed him with my own hands."

There was another muttered remark from Selim. Roughly translated, it meant, "I'd like to see you try."

I removed the wig from Nefret's head and wrapped the veils round her, leaving her face uncovered. She stood still as a statue, and I made a leisurely survey of the audience, which I had not had the opportunity to do before. Amenislo was not there, nor the High Priest of Isis. Were any of the others secretly loyal to Tarek? Possibly; Ramses had not had time to give me any names save that of Amenislo. The tall commander of the guard met my gaze squarely but made no gesture of encouragement. When I turned toward the Window of Appearance I saw our missing rifles, held by six of Merasen's chosen guard. It was not an encouraging development. The young fools clutched them so awkwardly I doubted they knew how to aim them, but if they fired into the crowd they were bound to hit someone. That would never do.

I raised my parasol and waved it in intricate patterns, over my head and in front of me, and began chanting. "Arma virumque cano . . ." By the time I had finished the first two verses of *The Aeneid* I had everyone's full attention, including that of the rifle holders. Switching to Meroitic, I explained that I had put a spell on the rifles (I had to use the English word, but my pointing finger made the meaning clear). They would now shoot back instead of forward, killing the ones who held them.

"She lies!" Merasen shouted, shaking his fists. "Do not believe her!"

One of the men stooped and put the rifle carefully down on the floor. The others held them out at arm's length, jostling one another to avoid having either end aimed at them.

"Clever," Merasen said, breathing hard. "But not clever enough, lady. See."

The curtains behind the throne parted and two guards entered, dragging Sethos with them. He was wearing the false nose and preposterous ears, though one of the latter looked unstable.

"I have your 'friend,'" Merasen said. "He will be the

first to die if you do not obey me. Give me your word you
will do as I say."

Sethos gave me a doubtful look. "This is not up to your
usual standard of efficiency," I said.

"I was looking for you when they caught me."

It was a fairly pointed reminder of what we owed him.
He had obviously stopped to change from the priest's robes
to the MacFerguson disguise before going in search of us.
He would have to have done so, I supposed, since even
Sethos could not maintain the priestly role with anyone except Amase. He certainly had not wasted his time if he had
managed to suborn the aged High Priest of Isis. I wondered
what he had promised Amase in exchange.

"Er—ladies?" said Sethos. One of the guards had a
sword at his throat. "I believe the—er—new monarch is
waiting for your reply."

"Oh, very well," I said. "What do you want us to do,
Merasen?"

Merasen stood up and advanced toward us. "Come," he
said, and took Nefret by the wrist. I struck him smartly on
the arm with my parasol.

"We will follow," I said. "Lead on."

I had delayed as long as I could. The room was darkening, lighted by torches and braziers. We had gone only a
few steps when a man burst into the room and dropped to
his knees before Merasen. He wore the feathered helmet of
the royal guards and his chest heaved like that of a winded
horse.

"They are coming," he panted. "Save yourselves. The
battle is lost!"

"Huzzah!" I shouted, waving my parasol.

Merasen's royal foot knocked the legs out from under
the messenger. "You lie!" he screamed, his eyes bulging.

He was the only one in the room who clung to that fond
belief. There was a rush to the window. I hardly need say I
was in the forefront, pulling Nefret along with me.

At Merasen's orders the plaza had been packed with

spectators. Many of the rekkit were there; the village must have been emptied, at swordpoint, to behold Merasen's triumph. The word had already reached the audience, for they were swaying back and forth and crying out, but the spears of the soldiers flanking the staircase held them back. As yet there was no sight of Tarek's advancing army.

When I turned I saw that the room was emptying with a speed little short of miraculous. Some of the priests hoisted their robes to their knees in order to run faster. Merasen stood over the body of the messenger. He had met the fate oft meted out to bearers of bad news; Merasen's sword had cleaved his skull. A good third of the guards had also melted away, including the two who had held Sethos. His eyes met mine across the width of the room. For a moment he wavered, balanced on one foot as if about to spin round, and I fully expected he would beat a hasty retreat. Then he said, in a voice that carried clear across the room, "Goddamn it, Amelia, watch out!" and ducked efficiently as a spear whizzed over his head and clattered against the wall.

Not all the guards had retreated. There would be a last stand, with us in the middle of it. My shout of "Surrender! Lay down your weapons!" had not the slightest effect on any of them. Selim had acquired a spear, whence I did not inquire. Moroney took hold of me. "Get behind me, Mrs. Emerson," he cried.

"Nonsense," I replied. "Look after Nefret and get out of my way."

Merasen stood motionless, his bloody sword in his hand. He did not move until the commander of the guard touched him on the shoulder. "We await your orders, prince," he said. Then he looked at me. "Fear not, lady, none will harm you. But I have betrayed one king and I will not betray another."

"But he isn't the king!" I shrieked. "He killed his father and his brothers. If that isn't just like a man . . ." The commander looked bewildered, and I realized I had spoken

English. Before I could try again, I heard a commotion in the corridor. It heralded the arrival of Ramses, who pushed his way past two surprised guards and came to a stop, struggling to catch his breath. His black hair was wildly windblown and the linen kilt that was his only garment was in tatters. However, he did not seem to have acquired any new injuries.

"Your father?" I cried.

"Safe. I came on ahead." He didn't waste breath asking after the rest of us, he could see for himself. He looked round the room. His brows lifted at the sight of Sethos, but he was still saving his breath. I didn't doubt he would have a good deal to say to me later. When his cool black eyes came to rest on Merasen he frowned slightly and looked away, as if from an obscenity.

"Lay down your arms," he said. "All of you. Tarek is merciful."

Really, men do vex me at times. I had lectured the commandant (even though he hadn't understood) and ordered the rest of them to surrender, and no one had paid the least attention. Ramses's quiet voice produced a positive clatter of weaponry, and the commander of the guard bowed. I must admit Ramses looked the true son of his father, with the same air of authority and a form almost as imposing. The partially healed wounds made a visible impression; they assumed he had got them in battle, and men do admire a good fighter.

Unfortunately, Merasen did not react as the others did. His eyes narrowed. "You will not take me alive!" he shouted, and backed away, waving his sword so wildly that everyone got out of his way.

"That suits me," Ramses said.

"Ramses, don't be a fool!" I exclaimed. "Let him go. He won't get far."

"We may as well settle this now," Ramses said in the same remote voice. "Will someone be good enough to lend me a sword?"

It was the commander himself who drew his weapon and presented it, hilt first. Ramses swung the weapon a few times, trying to get the feel of it. He was a skilled fencer, but this was an entirely different kind of blade, shorter and heavier than a foil. I realized that no one was going to stop him. Selim and Daoud both believed Ramses could do anything, and Moroney was watching with the same open-mouthed fascination as all the others. They had fallen back, leaving an open space for the combatants, and I would not have been surprised to discover that some of them were already placing bets.

I did not know what rules, if any, governed duels in this country. Whatever they were, Merasen was not the man to follow them. He rushed at Ramses while the latter's blade was lowered, and only the agile twist of his body saved Ramses from a severe wound. He got his sword up in time to block the next blow, and lunged. Merasen beat the blade aside. Eyes intent and jaw set, Ramses seemed unable for several seconds to do more than parry Merasen's moves. I supposed it was taking him a while to get used to the weapon and the style of fighting, which seemed to be a combination of foil and saber, thrust and slash. He took a cut across the back of the hand and another on the hip before he got the hang of it and began to drive Merasen back with a series of quick movements that brought blood spurting from the boy's arms and chest. Selim was cheering and the spectators were shouting advice to both fighters indiscriminately when Ramses swung his arm back and brought it down in a hard blow that knocked the blade out of Merasen's hand. Merasen tripped over his own feet and fell flat on his back, with Ramses's sword at his throat.

The spectators let out a roar. They were united now, as the Roman audience had been when they turned thumbs down, ordering the victorious gladiator to administer the coup de grâce. Merasen was still conscious. He heard what they were saying, and he raised a trembling hand in appeal, too breathless or too afraid to speak.

Ramses stood looking down at him for several long seconds. Then his mouth twisted, and he tossed his sword aside. Turning to me, he said, "I couldn't do it, Mother. Were you afraid I would?"

"My dear boy," I began, and then let out a rather loud shriek. "Look out!"

Ramses whirled round. He was weaponless and off balance, and Merasen was on his knees, balancing his sword like a dagger, ready to throw. I didn't have time to move; the explosion was so loud and so close, it half deafened me. The bullet struck Merasen in the chest. He dropped the sword and toppled over, and I turned, very, very slowly, to confront Daoud.

"Did I do wrong, Sitt?" he asked anxiously. "I did not wait for your order."

## . .
# Fourteen
## . .

Cheers from the plaza below drew us all to the window. The Great Road was filled with marching men, all the way to its end. The torches they carried sent red sparks dancing from the tips of their spears and the gold of their ornaments, and as the head of the procession came into the light of the blazing cressets before the temple, I saw Emerson and Tarek. Tarek was a sight to draw any woman's gaze, his tall frame erect, his proud head lifted; but I had eyes only for the stalwart form at his side. I leaned forward, like a princess in her tower, holding out my arms to Emerson. He saw me; his eyes had sought me. He let out a bellow I heard even over the roar of the crowd.

"Get back or you will fall out, curse it!"

How could I do less than obey? I withdrew, for I wanted to make sure everything was in order before he joined me. Nefret seemed almost herself again; she had flung off the hated veils and was trying to persuade Ramses to let her bandage his cuts. Moroney was conversing with Daoud, and Selim was brandishing a sword which he had acquired from someone, "just in case." It would not be needed. All resistance had been overcome. The only casualty—aside from Merasen, whose body had been carried off by two of the soldiers—was Sethos. Someone had knocked him down, or he had knocked himself out falling to avoid the spear; I had seen him lying on the floor, but had not had time to attend to him, what with one thing and another. When I knelt beside him I saw that he was breathing steadily and that his ear had fallen off.

Snatching one of Nefret's discarded veils, I wound it round his face and head, hiding the disfigured member. There was no response from Sethos, even when the hastily wound cloth covered his mouth.

"Lie still and don't move," I whispered. "Emerson will be here momentarily."

I waited, my hands pressed to my pounding heart and my gaze fixed on the doorway, and the seconds seemed to drag. At last I heard him; there was no mistaking those footsteps. He charged through the opening and came directly to me.

"Everything under control?" he inquired.

"Oh, Emerson, can't you at least say . . ."

He could not; he never can, in public. But the glow in his sapphirine eyes was as eloquent as words, and his subsequent action was even more eloquent. Seizing me by the waist, he threw me up in the air, caught me, and gave me a bruising hug. "Another triumph, eh, Peabody? Er—all right, are you, my dear? Ramses, my boy, what the devil have you been up to? Selim—Daoud—well done, my friends! Nefret . . ."

She ran to him and he took her into the shelter of his strong arm. "All right, are you?" he asked.

Tarek's entrance was something of an anticlimax after our tender reunion. He embraced us all in turn, even Daoud, who did not like it very much but submitted after I had explained how his prompt action and skillful marksmanship had probably saved Ramses's life.

"Well, well," said Emerson. "It was nip and tuck for a while, but all's well that ends well, eh?" Realizing that he had uttered two aphorisms in a row, he went on hastily, "If you will excuse us, Tarek, we will . . . Who the devil is that?"

"Mr. MacFerguson fought bravely with us," I said, exaggerating a trifle. "I will see that he is cared for, Emerson, leave it to me."

"Hmph," said Emerson. "By Gad, there are our missing rifles! We didn't hear gunfire, though. Did Merasen have a change of heart?"

I explained my little ruse. Emerson let out a bellow of laughter. "Peabody, you really are the most . . ."

"Thank you, my dear. We should retire and leave Tarek to the duties of kingship, I believe; but first—shall we perform the ceremony?"

When Tarek showed himself at the Window of Appearance, the cheers were deafening—or so I thought, until Emerson appeared beside him holding the crown in his hands, and the voices rose to an even louder pitch. Emerson wanted to make a speech, but he could not get them to keep quiet, so after we had all waved and bowed, we carried out our intention of withdrawing. Goodness knows we were entitled to some rest, and I for one was ready for a stiff whiskey.

"What about him?" Emerson demanded, scowling at the recumbent form of Sethos.

"I will have him taken to your rooms," Tarek said. "Is he not your friend? How badly is he hurt?"

I was somewhat surprised to discover that this time Sethos did have a broken leg.

"That's the last of the whiskey," said Emerson, dispensing it with a lavish hand. "Drink up, my dear, you deserve it. Now tell me what happened after we left you."

The servants had returned; how many of them had been Tarek's adherents before I did not know or care, for they were all loyalists now. The lady who had favored Daoud was even more assiduous. Watching him do justice to an entire roast goose, she spoke, for I believe the first time, but so timorously no one heard her except Nefret and me. I asked Nefret to translate.

"She said she has never seen a man so strong and large who could eat so much," Nefret reported gravely. Daoud looked up, and Nefret went on in the same serious tone. "She wants to know if he is married."

Daoud choked on a mouthful of goose leg. I smacked him on the back.

"Tell the lady he is married, and that his wife is also large and strong and very jealous."

The lady went sadly away and we all laughed, except Daoud.

We talked until the lamps burned low, for each of us had a story to tell. Since I am a modest woman, I allowed Captain Moroney to narrate my activities. I will say he did me justice. When he described Ramses's fight with Merasen, Emerson shook his head.

"My boy, my boy, I am surprised at your taking such a foolish chance. In future I beg you will consider following my example."

"Ha!" I exclaimed. "Who was the one who climbed onto that wall unarmed and in full sight of the enemy?"

"There was no trouble at all," said Emerson complacently. "It was over the moment I made my speech."

"It was over the moment you pulled that arrow out of your body," said Ramses. "I still don't know how the hell you accomplished that."

"It was your mother's idea," Emerson explained. He began unbuttoning his unspeakably dirty shirt. "Deuced uncomfortable, but in view of the fact that I meant to expose myself—er—"

He unpeeled several strips of sticking plaster and removed the cover of the camera case, which was, as I have explained, specially made. The arrow had penetrated the outer layers of leather and wood and left a dent in the steel lining.

"You might have told me," Ramses said accusingly. "I didn't fire soon enough. I thought you were . . ."

"Sorry, my boy," said Emerson, rubbing his chest.

Before we retired I went to have a look at Sethos. I had splinted and bandaged his leg before we settled down. I found him plucking ineffectually at the cloth over his mouth, so I replaced the makeshift bandage with a smaller one that covered only the lumpy nose and one eye—and, of course, the missing ear.

"Now leave that alone," I ordered. "I have your ear and will return it later, but I don't want Emerson to see you without it. How do you feel?"

He muttered unintelligibly and turned his head away. I lifted it and tipped the rest of my whiskey down his throat.

"It is the last," I said. "You don't deserve it, but selfishness has never been one of my failings."

My shadow fled before me as I climbed, a long, gray caricature of myself. When I pulled myself up onto the plateau, Abdullah was waiting.

"Well, you were no help at all, I must say," I remarked. "You and your enigmatic hints! I suppose you were referring to Daria when you warned me against trusting the innocent, and you were completely wrong about her, she has done nothing to injure us."

"Not yet," said Abdullah, stroking his beard.

"What do you mean?"

"Remember, Sitt, that there are many different ways to harm someone. But it may not happen. The future is yet to be."

"You won't tell me anything more?"

He frowned and shook his head. "What would be the use? You never heed warnings. You tempt Fate and every god. One of them was with you this time, Sitt. Now go back to Luxor where you belong."

He stalked away. I had offended him, though I wasn't sure how. "Will you come to me again when I am in Luxor?" I called.

He stopped but did not turn round. "You did not say you were happy to see me."

"Oh, Abdullah, you know I was! We miss you very much. You will come again to comfort, if not inform me?"

He looked back at me over his shoulder, and I saw he was trying to repress a smile. "Is comfort enough?"

"In other words, that is all I can expect," I said, laughing. "Yes, Abdullah. It is enough."

We all slept late the following morning. I was the first to wake, and although recollection informed me that there was no longer any cause for worry, I felt the need to see with my own eyes that all those I loved (and one I did not love) were really safe and sound. I got out of bed without waking Emerson and tiptoed from room to room, finding Nefret slumbering sweetly, Daoud and Selim snoring in chorus, and Ramses, for once, where he was supposed to be. When I drew the curtain aside, he woke instantly and sat up.

"All is well," I said quickly. "Go back to sleep. I am sorry to have disturbed you."

He understood. One of his rare smiles warmed his tired face and he said, "Counting heads, were you? It's all right, I was about to get up anyhow."

I was unable to persuade him not to do so, or prevent him from following me when I looked in on Sethos. After I splinted his leg I had given him a dose of laudanum, so I was not surprised when he lay unresponsive as I checked his pulse and made sure his ear was covered.

Lounging in the doorway, Ramses said softly, "If you don't want Father to find out, you had better get him out of here."

"I had planned to do that this morning. How did *you* find out?"

"Logical deduction," said Ramses. "I don't quite understand, Mother, why you are being so tolerant of the—er—man. Here's our chance to lay him by the heels once and for all."

"We owe Nefret's deliverance to him, Ramses. And

frankly I don't want to take the responsibility of delivering
him to justice. I hate to think what he could and would do
during that long ride back to civilization."

"Hmmm," said Ramses. "Very well, Mother, it is your
decision, and I will abide by it."

Tarek was our first visitor, though he was courteous
enough to wait until he had been notified that we had
breakfasted and were ready to receive callers. With him
was Count Amenislo. The Reader may easily imagine our
pleasure at seeing them both, and the count smiled with
pardonable complacency when we expressed our admiration and thanks.

"You took me in completely," Emerson declared, wringing Amenislo's hand. "Well done! Where were you last
night? We were concerned about you."

"I was hiding in the underground places," said Amenislo.

"Very sensible," I declared. "And the poor old Priest of
Isis? Is he safe?"

Tarek, who was sitting with Nefret, interrupted their
low-voiced conversation long enough to reply. "Like
Amenislo, he was wise enough to stay out of the way until
my victory was known. He has done nothing to deserve
punishment."

We were extremely busy for a few days, what with ceremonies of honor for ourselves and everyone else who had
made the victory possible. Daoud finally balked at being
loaded down with collars of gold, and retreated into his
room, but Selim enjoyed every moment of it.

We had agreed to stay for a few more weeks, and Emerson took full advantage of the time, rushing from temple to
palace to tomb, photographing and copying as much as he
could. He kept the rest of us busy too, but we managed to
find time for the simple pleasures of life—chatting with
friends old and new, strolling through the fine gardens of
the city. Tarek and Nefret were often together. She seemed
almost her old self, but she had bad dreams now and then.
Hearing her cry out in her sleep, I had gone to her and

soothed her as one does with a child who suffers from nightmare; and like a child she slept again without remembering what had frightened her. After two of these episodes I decided it was time we made our farewells and started for home. Nefret's bad memories would surely fade once we were back in civilization, and there was no sense in prolonging our visit. I wanted to get back before my solicitor, Mr. Fletcher, sent my "farewell" letter to Evelyn. It would only alarm the poor woman unnecessarily, and I try to avoid doing that sort of thing.

## From Manuscript H

Ramses passed through the monumental gateway of the cemetery, carved with figures of the mortuary deities, and began to climb the stairs. Sacred places that had once been out of bounds were open to them now; the guards had saluted and let him pass. It was the first time he had come here, but he remembered what his parents had said: that the tombs here were more recent than the ancient rock-cut chambers in the cliff. The tomb of Willy Forth, Nefret's father, was among them. He was interested in seeing the place, but he couldn't help wondering why Tarek's message had asked him to come there, and why Tarek had been so insistent that he tell no one. He smiled a little as he remembered the inscription on the outside of the folded paper: Private. Confidential. Tarek must have got that from one of the English novels he read. The injunction had been repeated in the letter itself: Tell no one. Come alone.

Normally that was the sort of message that would have put him on his guard. However, there were only a few people in the Holy City whose English was that good, and he couldn't imagine MacFerguson/Sethos or Moroney laying a trap for him or being allowed within the sacred precincts.

He climbed slowly, enjoying the soft murmur of birdsong in the trees and the utter peacefulness. His own thoughts weren't so enjoyable. He ought to be helping his father, who was working furiously to record as many of the Holy City's monuments as he could in the few days remaining before their departure. He ought to be on his way to the northern valley, where Daria was still staying in Tarek's villa. When he'd asked Tarek why she had not come, Tarek had only smiled and said something about women. Perhaps she expected him to go for her in person.

He wanted to, and yet he didn't. He loved her. He intended to do what was right and what he desired (although he wasn't looking forward to telling his parents). So why did he delay? Nefret was a far-off mirage, a dream he would never possess. She'd been acting odd. It was as if she were two women: one the brave, laughing girl he knew, the other a remote stranger with haunted eyes.

When he reached the top of the staircase and the small shrine that crowned it, a sleepy-eyed priest came out to give him directions. He followed the pathway the man indicated, and as he went on, scholarly fascination overcame his morbid thoughts. It was as if he had been transported back in time, over two thousand years of it, to see the tombs of Meroe and Napata in their pristine beauty. The tombs were on the right-hand side; before each of them the cliff had been cut back to make room for a porchlike chapel, with a miniature pyramid perched on its roof. In front of the chapels, round-topped stelae gave the names and titles of the dignitaries who rested within and, in most cases, those of their wives and children. The colors of the painted reliefs were still bright, the outlines of the carvings still sharp.

He had gone quite a long way before he came to the tomb that must be that of Nefret's father. There was no sign of Tarek or of anyone else. He waited for a while, reading the curious inscriptions on Forth's stela, before he ventured into the little chapel. The light was cool and dim. The first thing he saw was a pair of life-sized statues standing against the facade of the tomb. The facade was not smooth and unbroken, closed for eternity after the burial. A square opening gaped between the statues. Someone had broken into the tomb.

The few seconds it took him to assimilate this cost him dearly. Hands gripped him and a rope closed round his neck, tight enough to cut off his breath, darkening his vision, weakening his efforts to free himself. He felt his knees strike the stone paving. His arms were pulled behind him and ropes wound round his wrists. The agonizing constriction loosened and he heard a voice, soft and rapid, urging him not to struggle, promising no harm would come to him, and—he wondered if he was hearing right—asking his forgiveness for their rough handling. He wasn't reassured but he was still short of breath, so he offered no resistance as the hands lifted him to his feet and propelled him forward, toward the open entrance and down a short flight of stone-cut steps. There was a light below, the flickering dim light of a lamp. His captors—there were four of them—lowered him gently to the floor.

A large granite sarcophagus occupied most of the space in the small chamber. It was covered by a rotting linen pall sewn with gold-sequined spangles that glittered in the light. The walls were painted with scenes of the funeral and the judgment of the soul, with gods and goddesses welcoming the dead man to eternal life. On the wall to Ramses's left was a carved doorway, with a small offering table in front of it. The door faced west; through it would come the ka of the deceased, to feast on the food supplied for it. The offerings were fresh: fruits and bread, a jug of what was probably beer or wine, a roast fowl.

Ramses was not superstitious about mummies, he had seen too many of them; but when a shrouded form appeared from behind the huge stone box where Forth's dry bandaged body lay, an involuntary shiver ran through him. Then he recognized the old wisewoman and realized she was leading another person by the hand. Nefret's hair glittered like the gold on the pall. She did not look at him, even when he spoke her name.

Ramses got his feet under him and tried to stand. The point of a spear pricked his chest.

"You are a fool," the old woman said. "Or a man in love. They are the same, yes? No harm will come to her unless you cause it. Do not move. Speak softly, if you must speak."

She led Nefret to the side of the sarcophagus and settled her on a pile of cushions. Nefret's face was calm, her body relaxed, her breathing deep and even. Ramses looked up at the man who held the spear. His expression was absolutely terrified. Not a comfortable position to be in, between the devilish old woman and the wrath of a brother of demons. He doubted the fellow would dare use the weapon, but it would have been foolish to take the chance. He forced himself to speak evenly. "What do you want then?"

"The past and the future. Her memories of the great Father Forth. Her foreseeing of what will come. For in this state all time is open to the sleeper. It is not a stream that flows in one direction only but a pool in which she may move at will."

In spite of his fear for Nefret, Ramses was fascinated. How had this illiterate, primitive old woman come upon a theory of time like that of certain advanced modern thinkers? He knew what was wrong with Nefret. It was the same trance state into which Tarek had once sent him—a technique practiced in many cultures and in many ages, called by many names. He had only the vaguest memories of what had happened during that bizarre episode, but he had waked as if from a dreamless sleep, without ill effects. Had his face worn the same expression—inhumanly calm, faintly smiling? He knew it would be worse than folly to attempt to rouse her. Only the hypnotist could do that safely.

The old woman settled Nefret more comfortably on the

pillows, her withered old hands as gentle as those of a nurse. She raised Nefret's bowed head and Ramses's skin prickled when Nefret held the pose into which she had been placed, like a jointed doll with blue glass eyes.

The old woman turned. "She is ready."

Though the height of the sarcophagus concealed the other side of the chamber, Ramses had deduced there must be other rooms behind this one, containing items of funerary equipment and offerings. The old woman had waited in one of them with Nefret, and so had someone else. He came out now, around the corner of the sarcophagus.

"I am sorry," he began.

"I trusted you, Tarek! So did she. Why have you done this?"

"It was necessary," Tarek said urgently but softly. "Forgive me for deceiving you and treating you roughly, but you would not have let me bring her here if I had told you the truth. It is for her good, and yours, and mine, that I do this. Listen and you will learn. And then, if you demand it, I will submit to whatever punishment you decree."

Ramses didn't doubt that he would. Tarek was still a bloody romantic, and the look of appeal on his handsome face seemed genuine.

"Do not wake the sleeper," the old woman droned. "The spell is cast. It cannot be broken now."

"Goddamn it," Ramses said helplessly. It was grisly, ghoulish, and horrible—Nefret's bright head resting against the hard stone coffin that held her father's bones, her eyes empty.

The worst was yet to come. The old woman began talking in a crooning mumble. And Nefret answered her. Nefret's face had changed; it looked rounder, softer. Her voice was a child's voice, high and sweet and quick. Tarek moved closer, his head bent as if listening. Nefret spoke in a mixture of English and Meroitic, interspersed with giggles. Her features altered from moment to moment, from laughter to solemnity to grief, from those of a very young child to those of a girl on the threshold of womanhood. Tears filled her eyes and overflowed, and then she was laughing again, a high childish giggle, while her cheeks were still wet. Ramses did not understand everything she said, but it became increasingly clear that she was responding, not to the old woman's voice, but to that of someone else—a voice only she could hear. She turned her head, pressing her cheek to the cold stone. In the recess of the false door, a shadow darkened.

"Stop it," Ramses gasped. He twisted his hands, trying to loosen the ropes. "Stop it!"

"It is almost done," the wisewoman said calmly. "Have you heard, my prince?"

Tarek nodded dumbly. The old woman took Nefret's face between her withered hands and looked directly into her eyes, whispering. In a flicker of time Nefret's face took on its former blank stare. Then her eyes closed and her head fell back, cradled in the old woman's hands.

"She sleeps now. Take her back to her own place before she wakes. She will remember nothing of this."

Ramses wrenched his hands free and sprang to his feet. "Don't touch her, Tarek. I'll carry her."

Tarek stepped back and Ramses lifted Nefret into his arms. She was asleep, breathing lightly, smiling a little.

"Did you understand what she said?" Tarek asked.

"Not all of it. What the hell were you trying to do? If she isn't perfectly normal when she wakes—"

"Then my life is at your disposal." Tarek followed him up the narrow stairs from darkness into daylight. "Ramses, my friend—"

"Don't call me that." He held Nefret closer, shifting her weight so that her head lay against his breast.

"You are my friend, my dear friend, even if I am not yours. Listen to me. She was speaking to her father, answering his words of love, promising to obey his commands. He knew many would seek her in marriage. She swore never to lose her maidenhood."

Ramses came to a dead stop. "That's insane."

"But it is true. We do not force women into marriage here. But she was warm and loving, and she . . . she cared for me. I could have won her, Ramses."

Not if Forth could help it, Ramses thought. Despite the Englishman's affection for the people of the Holy City, he had not overcome all the prejudices of his class and nation. It was unthinkable for his daughter to marry a "native." Forth hadn't meant to condition her against marriage with what he would have called "one of her own kind." Or had he? God only knew what had been in the man's tormented mind. In any case, the "spell" had succeeded only too well.

"But you didn't try," Ramses said. "You helped us to bring her back to England."

"I obeyed the orders of my father Forth," Tarek said simply. "I was young and I believed what he had taught me—that she was not for me, that I would win honor by giving her up."

"So he got at you too," Ramses murmured. "Am I to assume that you've had time to think it over and decide you made a mistake?"

"I would not have brought her back," Tarek said. "By force or trickery. But when she came, through no act of mine, I thought perhaps it was a sign. This—today—was a way of finding out. I know now she will never love me."

They had reached the top of the long staircase that led down to the road. Tarek took Ramses's arm, to guard against a stumble, and Ramses let it remain.

"There is one thing more I must tell you," Tarek said. "I put you under the spell ten years ago. The wisewoman had taught me how to do it. I meant to place a call in your mind that would bring you here. Do you know whose voice it was you heard?"

"Yes." Ramses hesitated. It was insane, but no more insane than the whole conversation. "Hers. Nefret's."

"I thought so." Tarek sighed. "I did not put her voice in your mind, Ramses. You heard what the god meant you to

hear. Though you were only a child, the god knew she was
the woman destined for you. And now you are a man, and it
has come about as the god intended."

"I wish you wouldn't talk that way, Tarek," Ramses said
sharply. "I don't believe in your god, or your destiny, and if
what you've said is true, I've a damned poor chance of
winning Nefret."

"Forth's spell is not easily broken," Tarek said. "It is
strong because it was forged of love. Only time can weaken
it. Do not abandon hope."

Talk about insane, Ramses thought. I'm listening to advice to the lovelorn from the Meroitic prince of a lost kingdom, who believes in magic.

"Thanks," he said sourly.

"You have forgiven me?" They descended the staircase.
Tarek's hand was still on his arm.

"I suppose so. Yes."

"Place her here." Tarek indicated a stone bench. "It was
here that she went to sleep."

Ramses sat down, holding her. She was beginning to stir.
Her lashes fluttered and she opened her eyes and looked up
into his face.

"What happened?" she demanded. "I was sitting here . . .
Did I fall?"

She sounded like the old Nefret, brisk and matter-of-
fact. "You—uh—hit your head," Ramses said. "Don't you
remember?"

"No." She rubbed her eyes. "It doesn't hurt . . . Where is
the wisewoman?"

"She had to go back to the village," Tarek said. "How do
you feel?"

"Fine." She smiled at Ramses. Her blue eyes were bright
and clear. "Thank you, my boy. You can put me down now."
She squirmed off his lap and sat beside him. "What a beautiful day. I'm glad you suggested we go for a walk."

\* \* \*

Daria did not come to the city until shortly before they were to leave for home. Ramses's offer to go and bring her back had been refused, but she sent for him as soon as she arrived. He followed the servant to a pretty little suite of rooms near theirs and found her sitting cross-legged on a heap of cushions, running a comb sensuously through her shining hair. When he bent over to kiss her, she turned her head.

"I'm sorry I didn't come to get you," Ramses said, thinking that was the cause of her vexation. "You told me not to. Are you angry with me?"

"No. I'm not angry."

"We are leaving the day after tomorrow. Can you be ready?"

She put the comb down, took a deep breath, and looked him straight in the eye. "I am not going with you."

"What?" He felt as if someone had hit him hard in the pit of the stomach. The sight of her had revived the memories of their night together, reminded him of how much he wanted her. "But, Daria . . . You must come with me. You don't understand, darling, I want—I want to marry you."

"I thought you would say that. Sit down."

He dropped onto the cushions beside her. She took his face in her hands. "What you have said is foolishness. No, don't speak." Her fingers brushed his lips. "There are many reasons why it is foolish; you know what I was and what I am. Shall I return to your England and be a good little Englishwoman and go out every year to Egypt with you to play at archaeology? You are a sweet boy and a wonderful lover, but I shall be a queen here. What woman could ask for more? I am sorry if I hurt you, but hearts mend quickly."

She patted his cheek, as she would have patted a child's. "I think we should not see each other again. Maassalameh."

Ramses got slowly to his feet. There was nothing he could say. She had anticipated every plea he might have made, countered every argument, and the kindly condescension in her description of him had cut like a whip. He was some distance down the hall outside her rooms before he realized he had forgotten to give her the flowers he had brought. He was still clutching them, bruising the stems. He turned and went back, meaning to throw them on the floor or onto her lap, or maybe in her face, if he could forget for a few seconds that he was supposed to be an English gentleman.

He was wearing the comfortable local clothing and his soft leather sandals made little sound. She wouldn't have heard him anyhow. When he entered the room she was lying facedown on the cushions, her body shaking with sobs.

Ramses fell on his knees and gathered her into his arms. She clung to him and raised her wet face. The salt taste of her tears only made her kisses sweeter, but after a while the little hands that lay on his breast stiffened, and she pushed him away.

"My heart is hurt too," she whispered. "I hurt you again, because I love you too much to hurt you even more. But what I said was true, my love. One day you will find a worthier mate, and I will learn to love Tarek, who is kind and good, and I will give him the sons he wants. Please go now. Please. Do not speak, do not look back."

⁝

I paid Sethos a final visit on the day of our departure, allowing myself plenty of time since I had a good deal to say. He was lying down when I entered—after, of course, announcing my presence before I did so—and his greeting was typically unorthodox. It consisted of a bottle, which he held in his hand. Offering it, he remarked, "Since you were good enough to administer your last drops to an invalid, the least I can do is provide you with whiskey enough for the trip home."

"I wouldn't want to leave you without," I said. But I took the bottle.

Sethos laughed aloud. "Nothing surprises you, does it? Say thank you, Amelia."

"Thank you. As you know, we are leaving shortly. I thought you and I might have a little chat."

Grimacing, Sethos pulled himself to a sitting position. I shoved a few cushions behind him, and he leaned back with a sigh. "If you can keep Emerson away from me, I'll tell you everything you want to know. It is a fascinating story," he added with the familiar twisted smile. He was obviously in pain still, so I opened the whiskey and joined him in a libation. Sethos had a number of maddening attributes, but he was never boring.

"I came here for the first time eight years ago, after you had confirmed the truth of Willy Forth's fantasy about a lost civilization. You were fairly discreet, even though you believed you were confiding in a dear old friend, but you gave me enough information to begin my inquiries, and to assure me that any effort I put forth would be worthwhile. I knew there was a map, and had a good idea where it was kept. Breaking into Emerson's strongbox presented no difficulty for my people; they took a copy and replaced it without leaving the slightest trace that they had been there."

The lines of pain in his face relaxed into a reminiscent smile. "That first journey was a unique experience, even for a jaded sybarite like myself. To see the city in all its fading glory, the shadow of what was once ancient Egypt, the temples and palaces . . ." He took a sip of whiskey and went on, with his old cynicism. "Your name was my password. It got me past the first oasis and into the presence of Tarek himself; and after I had described—in great detail and with my customary vivacity—your appearance, mannerisms, current activities, and affection for your dearest friend—me—Tarek came down from his throne and embraced me. He was particularly interested in how Nefret was getting on."

"But you didn't know that," I exclaimed, torn between fascination and fury.

"I knew quite a lot, as a matter of fact. You have never been far from my protective gaze, Amelia dear. Have a little more whiskey and don't shout. He's still in love with her, you know."

I recognized his maddening habit of dropping in provocative statements to get me off the track. "How many times have you come here?"

"This is my fourth trip. As I said, Tarek and I got on like a house afire. I was happy to supply the things he wanted, none of which was likely to cause me future trouble, and he was happy to pay for them with various trifles that had been confiscated from his defeated opponents. Since I know you are about to ask, I will explain that I sold them, at a considerable profit, to selected clients whose greed and discretion I could trust. If they ever do appear on the market, the world of archaeology will be set on its collective ear; but by that time there will be no way of tracing them back to me."

"This will have to stop, you know."

"I do know. In fact, when I set out this time I anticipated that it would be my last visit. I meant to get in and out before you arrived, even though it meant traveling at a deuced uncomfortable time of year. Don't you want to know how I learned of your plans?"

"You were spying on me, I suppose, disguised as one of the maids," I said with a sniff.

"No, no. I get around quite a lot, but even I am not omnipresent. I heard of it, and of the mysterious Merasen, through Wallis Budge. You had better not mention that to Emerson," he added with an infuriating grin.

"Curse it," I muttered. "Then MacFerguson—"

"Quick as ever, my dear. Yes, Hamish MacFerguson is a legitimate scholar, though, to be honest, he hasn't contributed a great deal to the field. He has been very useful. I've taken his place on a number of occasions. He was working at the museum when Budge happened to mention Emerson's visit, and of course he notified me immediately. So, as I was saying, I realized that my lucrative arrangement with Tarek was about to end. He was bound to tell you about your generous friend, and you would of course deny all knowledge of such a person. I didn't know he had been supplanted. When I found out, it was too late to head you off. Incidentally," he added, with a sidelong look at me, "I was not responsible for the accidents that befell your men. Newbold committed the first of them, in order to deprive you of a loyal aide, and Merasen cut the other fellow's throat. I'm not certain why; he enjoyed violence for its own sake. Ali may have got wind of his plans to leave that night."

"How do you know about those incidents?" I asked suspiciously.

Sethos grinned. "You have a mind like an awl, my dear. Sharp and straight to the point. I heard of them from one of my gang, who accompanied you from Shellal."

"Daria. How could you—even you—hand that girl over to a creature like Newbold?"

"Amelia, Amelia!" Sethos threw his head back, laughing. "You are incomparable. She was a criminal, my dear, and a prostitute—though a very select and expensive one. What do you care for a woman like that?"

"I do care."

"I know." Sethos sobered. "Take comfort in the fact that she did not have to submit to Newbold's—er—attentions. I am telling you this partly in the hope of getting back into your good graces . . ." He was quick to catch my change of expression and revised his statement. "Getting a little further out of your bad graces, then. This will give you a hold over the fellow. He's impotent."

"What?" I cried.

"An elephant got—er—got him," said Sethos, with an evil grin. "Ramses will enjoy hearing that. Newbold will do anything you ask to keep that information under wraps. He keeps a woman on hand solely to maintain his reputation."

"What will happen to her now?"

"That's up to her. I promised to set her up in her own establishment in return for her help in this little venture. She may have something else in mind."

"Daria's future plans interest me less than her past history. What precisely was she supposed to do to earn her reward?"

"Watch over you, of course. Newbold was my principal concern. I passed through Cairo a few weeks before you, and learned, from one of my many illicit sources, that he'd been asking questions of all and sundry about your plans. He'd heard about Merasen from a military gossip. If he got on your trail he could be dangerous; the man is obsessed with gold. Daria was supposed to keep his temper under control—she's good at insinuating ideas into male heads—and warn you if he meditated a direct attack. Pitching your man into the jaws of the crocodile was not premeditated, he acted on the spur of the moment, according to his nature, so there was no way she could have prevented it.

"That leaves us," he went on before I could respond, "with only one remaining topic for discussion. The survival of the Holy Mountain. I won't betray its location—why should I let anyone else in on it?—but by the time we all get back to civilization, too many people will know. How do you propose to keep all of them quiet?"

"I don't. I have another idea in mind."

"Not a bad idea, either," Sethos said smoothly.

"You cannot possibly know—"

"But I do. You see, I took the liberty of searching your luggage." Sethos's mouth twitched with suppressed laughter. "It filled my patriotic heart with pride to see the dear old Union Jack unfolded. I don't know how you concealed it from Emerson all that time—"

"Emerson respects my privacy," I said angrily.

"And you had it wrapped in a pair of ladies' underdrawers. Now, Amelia, I beg you will control your temper. As I said, it's an excellent idea. The Holy Mountain's location cannot be concealed forever. When the first invaders arrive, be they marauders or Egyptologists or treasure seekers, they will find the British flag floating bravely over the palace and a British agent in residence. That should give them pause."

"I am not an imperialist by conviction, but it was the only way I could think of," I admitted. "British agent? Not you!"

"Good Lord, no. I won't be ready to travel for a week or so, but I will leave as soon as I can. Moroney's the man. He has nothing to go back for, and he's become fascinated by the Holy City. He is also under the erroneous impression that God has demanded he make amends for his little slip by serving others. It's a perfect arrangement. Tarek would agree to fly the skull and crossbones if you asked him to, and Moroney has a number of talents that should be useful here."

"How do I know you will keep your promise to leave this place and not come back?"

"Because," said Sethos, "you will give Tarek a postdated letter exposing me and informing him that if I haven't gone by the time he reads it he has your permission to do a number of unpleasant things to me."

"Quite right." I finished my whiskey and slipped the bottle into one of my useful pockets. "Good-bye," I said.

Sethos lifted his glass in salute. "À bientôt, Amelia."

## From Manuscript H

The camels reached the crest of the first great dune. Walking beside the animal on which his mother and Nefret were riding, Ramses turned and looked back.

The ramparts of the Holy Mountain rose up against the sky in a fretted fringe of pinnacles. He wondered if he would ever see that fantastic sight again or learn what happened to Tarek and Daria. His mother would have said it had all worked out for the best. Daria and Tarek would get on well; her practical, somewhat cynical intelligence would help guide his idealism, and he was a man any woman could learn to love. Whatever love might be. He wasn't sure he knew, not anymore. He had loved Daria, though one part of him had known all along that he was thinking like a romantic idiot when he contemplated a marriage between them.

The camels passed in stately procession, and his father joined him. They stood in silence, taking their last look at the Holy City.

"Best move on," Emerson said gruffly. "All right, are you, my boy?"

"Yes, sir."

They went on together, beside the camel on which the women were riding. The curtains of the bassourab were open. His mother called to them to hurry, and Nefret smiled at him.

Perhaps it *had* all worked out for the best. "Hearts do not break . . ." How did it go, that favorite quotation of his mother's? "They sting and ache, for old love's sake . . ." But not forever.

⋮

NOTE TO THE READER: The Emersons' first visit to the Lost Oasis is described in an earlier volume of Mrs. Emerson's journals: *The Last Camel Died at Noon.*

*Now available in hardcover from William Morrow*

**The newest mystery featuring
the indomitable Amelia Peabody . . .
and the return of Sethos**

# The Serpent on the Crown

**by Elizabeth Peters**

"Between Amelia Peabody and Indiana Jones, it's
Amelia—in wit and daring—by a landslide."
*New York Times Book Review*

He woke from a feverish sleep to see something bending over him. It was a shape of black ice, a tall featureless outline that exuded freezing cold. He tried to move, to cry out. Every muscle was frozen. Cold air touched his face, sucking out breath, warmth, life.

We had gathered for tea on the veranda. It is a commodious apartment, stretching clear across the front of the house, and the screens covering the wide window apertures and outer door do not interfere with the splendid view. Looking out at the brilliant sunlight and golden sand, with the water of the Nile tinted by the sunset, it was hard to believe that elsewhere in the world snow covered the ground and icy winds blew. My state of mind was as benevolent as the gentle breeze. The delightful but exhausting Christmas festivities were over and a new year had begun—1922, which, I did not doubt, would bring additional success to our excavations and additional laurels to the brow of my distinguished spouse, the greatest Egyptologist of this or any age.

Affectionately I contemplated his impressive form—the sapphire blue eyes and ebon hair, the admirable musculature of chest and arms, half bared by his casual costume. Our son Ramses, who had acquired that nickname because he had the coloring of an Egyptian and, in his youth, the

dogmatism of a pharaoh, sat comfortably sprawled on the
settee, next to his beautiful wife, our adopted daughter Nefret. Faint cries of protest and distress drifted to our ears
from the house the dear little children and their parents occupied; but even Nefret, the most devoted of mothers, paid
them no heed. We were well accustomed to the complaints;
such sounds always accompanied the efforts of Fatima and
her assistants (it took several of them) to wash and change
the children. It would be some time before the little dears
joined us, and when a carriage drew up in front of the
house I could not repress a mild murmur of protest at the
disturbance of our peace.

Emerson protested more emphatically. "Damnation!
Who the devil is that?"

"Now, Emerson, don't swear," I said, watching a woman
descend from the carriage.

Asking Emerson not to use bad language is tantamount
to King Canute's ordering the tide not to surge in. His
Egyptian soubriquet of "Father of Curses" is well deserved.

"Do you know her?" Emerson demanded.

"No."

"Then tell her to go away."

"She appears to be in some distress," Nefret said. Her
physician's gaze had noted the uncertain movements and
hesitant steps. "Ramses, perhaps you had better see if she
requires assistance."

"Assist her back into her carriage," Emerson said loudly.

Ramses looked from his wife to his father to me, his
heavy black eyebrows tilting in inquiry. "Use your own
judgment," I said, knowing what the result would be. Ramses was too well-brought-up (by me) to be rude to a
woman, and this one appeared determined to proceed. As
soon as he reached her she caught hold of his arm with
both hands, swayed, and leaned against him. In a breathy,
accented voice she said, "You are Dr. Emerson, I believe? I
must see you and your parents at once."

Somewhat taken aback by the title, which he had earned

but never used, Ramses looked down at the face she had raised in entreaty. I could not make out her features, since she was heavily veiled. The veils were unrelieved black, as was her frock. It fit (in my opinion) rather too tightly to a voluptuously rounded figure. Short of prying her hands off his arm Ramses had no choice but to lead her to the veranda.

As soon as she was inside she adjusted the black chiffon veils, exposing a countenance whose semblance of youth owed more to art than to nature. Her eyes were framed with kohl and her full lips were skillfully tinted. Catching my eye, she lifted her chin in a practiced gesture that smoothed out the slight sagging of her throat. "I apologize for the intrusion. The matter is of some urgency. My name is Magda Petherick. I am the widow of Pringle Petherick. My life is threatened and only you can save me."

It was certainly the sort of introduction that captured one's attention. I invited Mrs. Petherick to take a chair and offered her a cup of tea. "Take your time," I said, for she was breathing quickly and her face was flushed. She carried a heavy reticule, which she placed at her feet before she accepted the cup from Ramses.

Leaning against the wall, his arms folded, Emerson studied her interestedly. Like myself, he had recognized the name.

"Your husband was Pringle Petherick, the well-known collector?" he inquired. "I believe he passed away recently."

"November of last year," she said. "A date that is engraved on my heart." She pressed her hand over that region of her person and launched, without further preamble, into the description I have already recorded. "He woke that morning from a feverish sleep. . . .

"This is what killed him," she finished. Reaching into the bag she withdrew a rectangular box painted with crude Egyptian symbols. "He had purchased it only a few weeks earlier, unaware that the curse of the long-dead owner yet clung to it."

A long pause ensued, while we all tried to think of an appropriate response. It had occurred to me, as I feel sure it has occurred to the Reader, that there was a certain literary air about her narrative, but even Emerson was not rude enough to inform a recently bereaved widow that she was either lying or demented.

"If I may ask," Ramses said, after a while, "how is it that you were able to describe his death so—er—in such vivid detail? He was—that is to say—he was dead, wasn't he?"

"He lingered for a while," said Mrs. Pringle Petherick composedly.

"Oh," said Ramses.

Nefret, who had been staring fixedly at Mrs. Petherick, said, "Forgive me, but your face is familiar. Aren't you Magda, Countess von Ormond, the novelist?"

Aha, I thought. That explains the accent. According to her publicity releases the Countess came from a noble Hungarian family. She had fled that country during the upheaval of the world war.

The lady's mouth opened in a wide, pleased smile. "You have read my books? I will be happy to sign the ones you have with you."

"I didn't bring any with me," said Nefret, her expression bland as cream. "I saw you several years ago at a literary luncheon in London. At that time, I believe, you were not married."

"My dear Pringle and I became one only a year before his dreadful death. And now," she continued, "the curse has fallen upon me. Twice I have beheld that grim black figure, and my intuition tells me that the third time will mean my death. Take it. I beg you!"

She thrust the box at Ramses. Eyeing it askance, he stepped back. I took it, and was about to lift the lid when Mrs. Petherick let out a ladylike shriek.

"Don't open it! I never want to see that evil little face again!"

"Am I to understand," I inquired, "that you are passing the—er—curse on to us?"

"But you are experienced in dealing with such things," Mrs. Petherick exclaimed, rolling her black-rimmed eyes. "You can do it safely. You have done it before. I have heard the stories."

The stories to which she referred were lurid newspaper articles, many of them written by our journalist friend Kevin O'Connell. Though in every case the purported curse had been proven false, and the evils attributed to it had been found to be caused by a human criminal, many readers remembered the sensational theories and ignored the rational explanations. If the woman actually believed we could cancel curses and defeat evil spirits, she had to be acquitted of deliberate malice.

The children would soon be joining us, and I did not want their juvenile imaginations stirred up by such nonsense. I was about to suggest to Mrs. Petherick that she tie a stone to the confounded thing and toss it in the Nile, when Emerson cleared his throat. His sapphirine eyes were bright and his handsomely tanned face bore an expression of amiable concern. Curse it, I thought.

"Very well," he said. "You may leave it with us, madam. I will perform—er—I will take care of the matter."

Mrs. Petherick leaned back in her chair, ignoring Emerson's hint. "What are you going to do? Return it to the tomb from which it was stolen?"

"That might prove a trifle difficult," Ramses said, with a critical look at his father. "If, as I assume, it was purchased on the antiquities market, there is little hope of tracing the original thief and finding out where he obtained it."

"Hmph," said Emerson, giving his son an equally critical look. "You know my methods, Ramses. Rest assured, madam, that you need not give the matter another thought. Good day to you."

This dismissal was too direct to ignore. Mrs. Petherick

rose to her feet, but made one more attempt to prolong the conversation. "It killed my dog, too," she offered. "My poor little Pug. He choked and twitched, and was gone, just like that."

Fatima, seeing that we had a guest, had managed to detain the children, but I could hear them expostulating in their high-pitched voices. Emerson heard them too; he got Mrs. Petherick to the door of the veranda, but not before she had told us where she was staying and had asked to be informed when the curse had been officially lifted. She added, with an air of complacency quite at variance from her initial distress, "Perhaps I should participate in the ceremony."

"That will not be necessary," said Emerson, shoving the lady into her carriage and motioning the driver to proceed.

"Really, Emerson," I said. "What ceremony? You made no promise, but your failure to deny her suggestion was a tacit—"

"Well, what else could I have done?" Emerson demanded. "The woman was in considerable distress. Her mind will now be at ease."

"Oh, bah," I said. "Are you familiar with the literary (I use the word loosely) works of Countess von Ormond?"

"Good Gad, no," said Emerson.

"I've read some of them," Nefret said. "*The Vampire's Kiss* was her first. All her novels are about vampires and curses and hauntings."

"Quite," I said. "I suspect that the vivacious account of her husband's death was the first paragraph of her next novel. She means to use us and our questionable reputation with the newspapers in order to get publicity. I understand that her sales have been falling off."

"The later books aren't nearly as entertaining as the first four or five," Nefret said critically. "They were really quite good. I had to leave the light on all night while I was reading *Sons of the Werewolf*."

"Good Gad," Emerson exclaimed. "I had no idea you indulged in such trash, Nefret. Peabody, why did you let her—"

"I do not believe in censoring the reading material of adult persons, Emerson."

"In fact it would be a question of the pot and the kettle," said Emerson. "Your penchant for sensational novels like those of Rider Haggard—"

"Which you also read on the sly," I retorted. "Hypocrisy does not become you, Emerson. To return to the point, I do not intend to allow the woman to make use of us. I will return that object to her tomorrow, unopened, with a stiff note."

"Not unopened," said Emerson. "Aren't you even a trifle curious about the accursed object?"

"It is only a crude wooden box, Emerson, not even ancient."

"Ah," said Emerson. "But what is inside the box? Your analysis of the lady's motives may be accurate, my dear, but it overlooks one interesting fact. Petherick was a wealthy, discriminating collector. She may have purchased the box in Cairo, but if the contents came from Petherick's collection it will be worth looking at."

He took the box from me and was about to lift the lid when I exclaimed, "No, Emerson. Not now. Put it away."

Seeing that our visitor had departed, Fatima opened the door to the house and the juvenile avalanche descended. There were only two of them, and they were only four years old, but they made enough noise for a dozen and moved so rapidly that they gave the impression of having been multiplied. As usual they dashed at their grandfather, who tried to hide the painted box behind his back. He was not quick enough.

"It is a present!" Carla shouted. Her black eyes, so like those of her father, shone with anticipation. "Is it for me?"

Her brother, David John, who had his mother's fair hair and blue eyes, shook his head. "The assumption is without foundation, Carla. Grandpapa would not have a present for only one of us."

"Quite right," said Emerson. "Er—this is a present for me."

"Did the lady give it to you?" Carla demanded.

"Yes," said Emerson.

"Why?"

"Because—er—because she is a kind person."

"Can we see what is inside?"

David John, whose methods were less direct than those of his sister, had already headed for the tea table, where Fatima had placed a plate of biscuits.

"Don't you want a biscuit?" Emerson asked Carla.

Carla hesitated only for a moment. Insatiable curiosity won over greed. "I want to see what is inside the box."

Emerson tried to look severe. He did not succeed. He dotes on his grandchildren, and they know it. "I told you, Carla, that it is not for you."

"But it might be something I would want," Carla explained coolly.

"It is something you may not have," said Ramses, drawing himself up to his full height of six feet and fixing his small daughter with a stern look. Not one whit intimidated, Carla stared back at him from her full height of three feet and a bit. She was comically like her father, with the same black curls and dark eyes and downy black brows that were now drawn into a miniature version of his frown.

I said, "David John is eating all the biscuits."

My understanding of juvenile psychology had the effect Ramses's attempt at discipline had not. Carla ran to get her share and Nefret informed her son he had had as many biscuits as he was allowed. A discussion ensued, for David John had inherited his father's Jesuitical skill at debate, and Nefret had to counter several arguments about the needs of growing children for sugarcoated biscuits. While they were thus engaged, I gestured to Emerson.

"Now you have aroused my curiosity," I admitted. "Open the box, Emerson."

The object inside the box was roughly cylindrical in

shape and approximately thirty centimeters long. That was all we could make out at first, since it was swathed in silken wrappings tied at intervals with tightly knotted gold cords.

"She was taking no chances, was she?" Ramses said, while his father picked at the knots and swore under his breath. "It could be a ushebti, it's the right shape."

"Surely nothing so ordinary," I objected. The little servant statues, placed in the tomb to serve the dead man in the afterlife, had been found in the thousands; most were of crude workmanship and cheap materials such as faience.

"Why not?" Ramses inquired. "The notion of a curse is pure superstition; it can be attached to any object, however humble."

"Petherick wouldn't have owned anything humble," said Emerson.

But his wife might have purchased something of the sort to add verisimilitude to her sensational account. I did not voice this sentiment, since Emerson would not have accepted it. Anyhow, I told myself, it would do no harm to have a look.

Since neither Emerson nor Ramses carried even a small penknife (David John was an accomplished pickpocket and particularly interested in sharp objects) Emerson had to go into the house to get a knife with which to cut the cords, the knots being beyond even my skill. By that time, I candidly admit, we were all agog with anticipation. Even Nefret abandoned her maternal duties and came to lean over my shoulder as Emerson removed the wrappings.

Sunset light set the small statue aglow, as if a fire burned within. This was no crude ushebti, of common material; it was the golden figure of a crowned king. His face was youthful, rounded and faintly smiling, his half-bared body gently curved. He wore an elaborately pleated kilt, the lines of which had been rendered with exquisite precision. The small sandalled feet and delicate hands were models of graceful beauty.

Nefret caught her breath and Emerson gave me a triumphant look. Even Ramses's normally enigmatic countenance betrayed astonishment verging on awe.

"How beautiful," I murmured. "There is nothing evil about this face."

"The devil with that," said Emerson, lifting it out of the box. "Where did it come from? Where did he get it? How could such a thing come onto the antiquities market without causing a sensation?"

"Is it genuine?" Nefret asked breathlessly.

Emerson weighed the statuette in his hand. "Forgers don't use solid gold."

We agreed to postpone further discussion until the children had been sent off to bed. Our friends Cyrus and Katherine Vandergelt were dining with us, and Cyrus was a knowledgeable and respected excavator. Conversation at dinner was entirely about the statuette.

Emerson pushed his soup plate away. "Frankly, Vandergelt, I don't give a curse who gets it. What I want to know is where it came from."

"A dealer, one presumes," I said.

"And before that?"

I shrugged. "Another dealer. A tomb robber or illicit digger. What are you getting at, Emerson?"

"Tell her, Ramses." Emerson picked up the little statue and handed it to his son.

"Yes, sir. We may or may not be able to trace the object back through its previous owners; but the statue itself offers certain clues as to where it was found." Holding the statuette up to the light, he ran an appreciative finger along the delicately modelled cheek and down the curves of the body. "It's one of the Amarna kings."

I nodded agreement. "The style is unmistakable—the soft outlines of the body, the delicate fingers and toes. Since this artistic technique was only employed during the reign of the so-called heretic king Akhenaton and his immediate successors, we can pin it down to a period of—oh,

I would say fewer than fifteen years, since it is of the later Amarna style rather than—"

"Amelia," said Emerson forcibly. "We know that."

"Katherine was looking a trifle confused," I explained.

"Thank you," Katherine said, with a smile.

"The term Amarna," I continued, before Emerson could stop me, "refers to the site in Middle Egypt where Akhenaton founded a city dedicated to the worship of his sole god, Aton."

"Can it be Akhenaton himself?" Cyrus asked. "There's no name on it, I looked."

Ramses turned the statuette upside down and inspected the soles of the little golden feet. "I think it stood on a pedestal, with perhaps a back column, which would have been inscribed with the name of the king."

"Maybe," Cyrus said doubtfully. "But that doesn't tell us where this came from, does it?"

"There are only a few possibilities," Ramses said. "Amarna itself is the most obvious. Mother and Father excavated there in the 1880's, and there have been archaeologists at work off and on ever since—not to mention local diggers. The site is huge. This might have come from a shrine in a courtier's house, or from a sculptor's workshop like the one the Germans found before the war."

Emerson shook his head. "Unlikely, my boy. Borchardt found plaster models, intrinsically valueless. Everything that could be reused was taken away when the city was abandoned. A statuette of solid gold certainly wouldn't have been overlooked."

"You can't be sure of that," Cyrus objected. "Maybe the owner buried it to keep it safe, and died before he could retrieve it."

"Anything is possible," Emerson retorted. "But don't pack up and head for Amarna just yet, Vandergelt. We know that Akhenaton's successors returned to Thebes. One of them was buried in KV55, the tomb Theodore Davis ripped apart back in '07."

"Unless the mummy in that tomb was Akhenaton," Cyrus said. "Weigall believes—"

"Weigall is wrong," Emerson said flatly. "The remains have to be those of Smenkhkare, Akhenaton's son-in-law. That's beside the point. This statue is precisely the sort of thing that might have been part of the tomb furnishings, which, as you recall, were a hodge-podge of objects belonging to different royals. You may also recall that Davis's workmen made off with some of them. And so did another individual. Isn't that right, Amelia?"

All heads turned, all eyes focused on me. Emerson's bright blue orbs were as hard as sapphires.

Bertie, chivalrous chap that he was, broke the silence with an indignant question. "Surely you aren't accusing your wife, Professor?"

"No," I said. "He is accusing his brother."